The Witness

By
Kevin Marsh

Author of:
The Belgae Torc

Dedication

To Joanne and Dean who once lived in Garmouth, a lovely little village in Morayshire. If it wasn't for the day we spent walking in Spey Bay, I would never had seen the artist painting a watercolour of the bridge and The Witness would never have been written.

Published by Paragon Publishing
© 2013 Kevin Marsh

ISBN 978-1-78222-068-8

Book design, layout and production management by Into Print
www.intoprint.net
+44 (0)1604 832149

Printed and bound in UK and USA by Lightning Source

Chapter
ONE

It was six thirty in the morning and Josie, sat on a folding stool beside a riverbank was painting. Her eyes hardly had time to focus as she glanced from landscape to paper, her brush dancing merrily as it conveyed colour and form to her work.

It never ceased to amaze her just how quickly time went once she became fully engrossed in her work, she had been sitting there for just over an hour but it seemed no time at all. She liked to paint in the early morning when the light was clear and the day was fresh and new.

Standing up she stretched out the stiffness in her shoulders then scrutinised her work carefully. Tilting her head to one side, she squinted through half closed eyes and chewed at the end of her paintbrush. It was a moment before she would admit that her work was done, and with a sigh of satisfaction, she smiled. Josie studied the iron bridge in the foreground of her picture, it was a true representation of the real thing, the bridge that spanned the river Spey. She had replicated the colours of the water perfectly. Sunlight dancing on the surface played mischievously with the multi-coloured stones until they shone like semi-precious jewels in the shallows, and where the water ran deep, delicate shades and movement made the river appear pleasingly realistic.

Josie was delighted with the results and she sighed contentedly. Her week had been a great success, not only was her sketchbook full but she had also completed three paintings. In the morning, she would be heading back to London but first she was looking forward to spending the rest of the day with Molly. Josie smiled again delighted at the prospect of shopping with her aunt. Later they would drive into Elgin, she wanted to photograph the cathedral ruins. Josie was planning a series of dramatic paintings based on the fire that had destroyed the beautiful cathedral generations ago.

Molly had left London the moment she retired, moving hundreds of miles north she went in search of a quieter life and found it in the small village of Garmouth. Situated close to the ancient city of Elgin in Morayshire, Molly loved this part of the world and wondered why she had not discovered it years earlier.

Josie had spent many summer holidays as a child in and around Elgin but she could not remember having come across the village before. She felt certain that Molly had not either. Josie often thought that her aunt had simply driven a pin at random into a map and moved to wherever it pointed. Whatever her motives, Molly had decided to uproot and move north. No once did she discuss her plans to retire to Scotland, but Josie was glad that she had. There was so much to see and she wanted to paint everything, she was also happy in the knowledge that her landscapes were very well received back in London. Josie felt certain that one day she would move from the city and settle in the village herself.

Before discovering Garmouth, she had been blissfully happy living in suburbia. Content with her city lifestyle, she loved the idea of being able to shop for groceries at any time, day or night and culturally she was spoilt, there was a variety of museums, galleries and theatres not far from where she lived. Having access to anything she wanted regardless of the time, was something that she treasured but coming to Garmouth for the first time had been a shock, everything here was done at a much slower pace. The village was set firmly in the past, the people who lived there were content to spend their time chatting over garden fences or meeting up at the post office or corner shop. There was no urgency and best of all there was no noise, it was very different from what she was used to and she just loved it.

Josie poured water from her bottle into a little pot and washed out her brushes before packing them away. Suddenly a scream shattered the silence and startled, she looked up. Scanning the riverbank she looked towards the iron bridge but could see nothing out of place, the sound must have come from a rabbit falling victim to a fox or an osprey. She stared up at the sky searching for the birds that operated along this stretch of the river. Usually they would be fishing for salmon, but would probably consider a rabbit a welcome change from their habitual diet.

Shaking her head, she smiled and cleared her mind of such thoughts.

Stuffing her brushes into her bag, she reached for her paint box and mixing palette then dried them off with an old cloth.

Without warning, another scream echoed along the valley and this time there was no mistaking the sound, her skin crawled as she sensed danger.

Josie looked up, there was movement near the bridge then she spotted a man dragging a woman along the ground roughly by her hair. Her cries carried clearly on the still morning air, and Josie watched in horror as the man slammed his fist into the woman's face knocking her down into the long grass. Standing over the spot where she had fallen he reached down and grabbed her, the sound of the woman crying as he hauled her to her feet spurred Josie into action. Moving quickly along the path she was determined to help. Perhaps she could distract him for long enough to allow the woman to escape but suddenly she felt vulnerable and very much alone. The nearest house was over a mile away and there was no one else in sight.

The man continued his assault and hearing the woman's terrified screams Josie realised that it would be a bad idea to draw attention to herself. Frozen to the spot she was filled with guilt and indecision and all she could do was look on helplessly. The man stepped back and forced the woman to her knees then very slowly reached into his pocket and pulled out a pistol. Thrusting the weapon into the woman's face, they stared silently at each other. Although defeated she remained defiant, it was the last thing she did. The force of the discharge threw her back into the grass like a broken toy.

Covering her mouth with her hands Josie stifled a scream and staggered backwards. Her vision blurred as her eyes filled with tears and she wanted to vomit. She could hardly believe what she had just seen, it had to be true because the sound of the blast was still rolling like thunder around the bay.

The man moved calmly, pocketing his pistol he glanced around searching for witnesses. Removing his cap, he dried his forehead with his sleeve and turning very slowly towards Josie, he grinned. She froze; it was as if he had known she was there all along. The evil that surrounded him seemed to reach out towards her and she shuddered. His grin turned into a sneer as he held her gaze then slowly he began to move towards the bridge. He didn't need to rush, his strides measured it was as if he had all the time in the world.

Josie brushed away her tears with the back of her hand, her mind was in turmoil but she knew she had to move quickly. Glancing towards the bridge, she wondered if she could get to in time. It was the only way to cross the river and the man had made his intentions clear enough but it was no good, he had almost reached the bridge.

Retracing her steps back along the path, there was no time to collect her things; she would have to abandon her painting in an effort to save herself. Emotions run wildly inside her head but despite this, she refused to succumb to panic. Running as quickly as she dared, she missed her footing on a clump of grass and fell heavily. Crying out in frustration and gasping for breath, she glancing back over her shoulder, he was closing in fast. Picking herself up she pushed on and managed to increase the distance between them and reaching the point where the path split she hesitated. To the right it followed the curve of the bay going towards a distant golf course. Turning her head the other way she could see the visitors centre standing beside an ancient icehouse. This had once been used to preserve salmon but it was now a museum. The place looked deserted, there were no visitors this early in the day and the staff who worked there would not arrive for at least another hour.

Heading that way Josie charged breathlessly into the yard and slipped on the loose gravel. Picking herself up, she pressed her back up against the wall of the nearest building and in an attempt to control her racing heart took some deep breaths. Pulling her mobile phone from her pocket, she flipped it open and with trembling fingers began to press out a number, holding it to her ear she waited, nothing happened. Glancing desperately at the tiny screen it was a few seconds before she realised that there was no signal. Groaning with frustration she pushed it back into her pocket. It was futile calling for the police, it would take ages for them to get to Spey Bay from Elgin.

He was very close now and she could hear him coming, so moving further around the building, she searched for a place to hide. The walls were curved, the bricks worn smooth by erosion and time, there were no recesses in which she could conceal herself and it soon became obvious that he would easily find her. There was nowhere else to run and as the man charged into the yard, he slipped on the gravel and fell heavily. The noise that he made sent a sea bird screeching overhead and Josie, looking up, heard the sound of waves breaking over the stony shore. Moving towards the pebble beach, she stumbled noisily over the loose gravel, and making her way awkwardly down the slope found the coastal path and started to run along it as fast as she could.

Sunlight flashed lemon yellow against the grey swell of the sea and as she went she managed to pull away from him, but she did not realise until it was too late that she was running into a trap. The path ended abruptly as it dropped down to meet the mouth of the river and stopping at the top of the steep bank, she could see it curving back the way she had come. Josie glanced around desperately searching for another way to go, she could see him moving slowly towards her, he seemed to be in no hurry and was obviously aware of her error.

She considered making her way back along the path but that would not work, as soon as he saw her moving in that direction he would head her off and there would be little chance of slipping past him. Turning her back to the water, she considered running straight at him, push past and maybe even knock him down but he looked much heavier and stronger than her so dismissing that idea she had to find another way.

She realised that he was not carrying his gun, if he meant to kill her that would surely be the most effective way. She had already seen him commit murder so he must be capable of doing it again. This time there would be no witness, no one to see where her body fell. The thought sent a shiver through her, forcing these unwelcome thoughts aside, she glanced towards the opposite bank willing someone to be near, a jogger maybe or somebody out walking their dog, anyone who might be able to help.

She could feel his eyes boring into her back and turning towards him was unable to see clearly, the sun was still low in the sky and he appeared like a shadow. The sight of him lumbering down the slope made her skin crawl and she cried out as the cold hand of fear ran its fingers along her spine.

Taking a few steps backwards, she stepped into the shallows and water seeped into her boots, it was cold against her skin but she hardly felt it. Glancing desperately at the opposite bank there was no one there to help and now she had nowhere left to run. An idea began to form in her mind, perhaps she could reason with him but then realisation took hold, he was not going to let her live, she had seen too much.

He was so close now that she could hear his ragged breathing and looking up he appeared black with evil intent. There was nothing left for her to do so plunging into the water she struck out for the opposite bank, it was not too far and she was a strong swimmer. Adrenaline coursed through her body as she propelled herself into midstream but the cold grey water was merciless, it pulled her down until she began to struggle. The current was too strong, she had underestimated its strength and as it took hold, it swept her away.

Gasping for breath, the cold was shocking and as her chest tightened

Josie did what she could to keep her head above the surface but to fight it was impossible. Her muscles were burning now and struggling to stay afloat was becoming painful, wave after wave poured over her head, and it became a relentless battle that was proving impossible to win. She was amazed at how quickly she had been defeated.

The man watching from the safety of the bank was keeping pace with the flow of the river. He was hardly surprised by her plunging into the water in fact he expected it, she had nowhere else to go and he didn't think she would give up easily.

Josie could feel her strength ebbing away, her limbs going numb with the cold it was all she could do to keep her face above the surface. The weight of her waterlogged clothing dragged her down and struggling only made it worse. Waves constantly washed over her head, the water so cold it was as if a thousand tiny needles were pricking at her skin. Here the water was tinged with salt, it was almost the point where the river met the sea. Gradually the waves were becoming larger and in the grip of the swell, she could feel the pull of the tide, it was attracting her body as effectively as a magnet draws iron. Josie began to panic, the North Sea was no place to be and struggling for breath was powerless against the flow. She would have to wait for the current to ease before attempting to swim back towards the shore, she realised that she would be swept further from the beach and the thought terrified her. She had to keep calm, and most of all she must remain conscious. She needed to keep moving, try to generate some heat into her muscles that was the only way to keep them from seizing up altogether.

The man standing on the shore watched as Josie was swept further away. He made no attempt to help or to alert the Coastguard and now she had almost disappeared from view. Licking his lips, his tongue flashed reptilian like from between his teeth and his mouth became a cruel thin line across his face.

He felt a stab of regret, distracted by a jumping dolphin, he took his eyes off her for a moment and now she was gone, lost from view in the vastness of the sea. He would never see her again and as the smile faded from his face, his eyes narrowed. He began to imagine the fun he could have had with her then his thoughts turned to the woman he'd left lying in the grass. He would have to be quick, tidy up the mess before others wandered along the path.

His pulse quickened, oh what fun he'd had with this one, she was the best so far, now it was like a drug and he craved for more. The voices in his head would soon return and their demands would become even more shocking, he would know no peace until he had done their bidding, but for now he was safe, their hunger satisfied.

Josie was slipping away, unconsciousness beckoned offering her a merciful release. This was nature's way of relieving pain and suffering, but she must resist the urge, to give up now would be the end of everything.

She managed to improvise a life jacket by trapping air under her shirt, it helped by keeping her head above the waves. This was a skill learned many years ago as a child at the local swimming pool, she had never imagined that one day she would have to employ the techniques for real.

Next, she attempted to remove her jeans but it was impossible, they were heavy and weighed her down, each time she moved she went under and choked. They would make a more effective float but it was not as easy as she remembered, practicing this in a heated swimming pool with help at hand was one thing, doing it for real was quite another. Frustrated and rapidly becoming exhausted she abandoned the idea and made do with her shirt.

The chill from the water continued to press in around her and her body, acting like a sponge, soaked up the cold until gradually her muscles began to shut down. She had very little feeling from her waist down and now her arms were beginning to feel heavy and tired. Her skin felt as if it was on fire even though she was freezing to death.

Josie was terrified; the thought of drowning filled her with dread. The current was gaining in strength and with her strength failing she would soon no longer be able to swim back to the beach.

At least now she was moderately buoyant, if she could just relax and go with the rhythm of the swell, precious air trapped beneath her shirt would not seep away so quickly. Often she had to refill it by lifting the hem above the water and scoop in more air, inflating it like a balloon. The effort of this process gave her something to focus on and moving her arms kept the blood flowing into her frozen fingers. This simple but vital act gave her hope, without it she would almost certainly drown.

The grey water was sapping her strength and she knew that she would have to do something quickly to help maintain her body temperature. The initial burning sensation of cramp from rapidly cooling muscles had now given way to a dull ache and the situation was becoming hopeless. She had tried to swim but the movement deflated her buoyancy aid and she no longer had the strength to stay afloat without it. Her eyes ached from the cold as waves slapped relentlessly against her face and it was as if a band of steel had been wound about her head, the pressure mounting by the second.

Gritting her teeth she moved her arms slowly, raising each in turn above her head but the effort was too much and she cried out in frustration, the pain was becoming too much to bear. Air escaped from beneath her shirt as she moved then she had to go through the inflating process all over again. It was a relentless battle but she had to ignore her nagging doubts, she was determined not to give up.

How long had she been in the water? The thought came from out of nowhere, it confused her and paying it no attention she focussed on more pleasant things. Going to her favourite place, she could feel the sun on her back. It was a delicious sensation, the warmth invading her mind soothed her body and she imagined herself dancing in a soft breeze. She could feel grass as soft as fur brushing gently against her bare legs and closing her eyes, the smell of freshly ground coffee invaded her thoughts, she could even hear the sound of breakfast sizzling in a pan.

How long had she been in the water? Faces appeared before her eyes, friends from long ago, colleagues from places she had worked and people with whom she socialised.

How long had she been in the water? Absurd thoughts burst into her head but were gone before she had a chance to grasp them. Was this what it was like to die, her life flashing before her eyes?

How long had she been in the water? Reluctantly she forced herself to open her eyes. She was crying with frustration, warm tears washed away by cold water, this was just another unwelcome emotion. Suddenly she was angry with herself, angry with the man who had put her in this situation but there was no time for self-pity, not now.

How long had she been in the water? There it was again that infuri-ating voice filling her head, always the same question over and over again. Like a tattoo drumming laboriously into her skull, she had no choice but to deal with it. With an effort she focussed on her wristwatch, she could hardly see the time the face was too small. It was then she decided to buy another watch, one with a larger face, she was always having to squint at this one. She almost laughed at the absurdity of it and concentrating on the task, recalled the last time she had checked her watch. It had been six thirty, just after she had finished her painting and now the time was six fifty five. Going over the events in her mind, she realised that everything had taken place during the last twenty five minutes. She estimated how long it had taken to run along the riverbank and evade capture by diving into the river. This must have taken fifteen minutes; that left ten. She was shocked, only ten minutes, it seemed as though she had been in the water for much longer. How long could someone survive in the North Sea at this time of the year? She started to think about seasonal water temperatures around the British Isles. She considered body mass and insulating layers of fat and for once in her life regretted being so slim, there was not an ounce of fat on her. She was in grave danger; there was insufficient insulation to protect her from the extreme cold.

Chapter
TWO

Molly was a neat sixty-something who kept herself fit by playing golf and walking in the bay. She could easily pass as a woman much younger than her years. Her hair was immaculate, coloured to perfection and she had a penchant for the latest fashion.

Fussing around the kitchen, she put the finishing touches to the breakfast table and clouds of freshly brewed coffee rose into the air, the bitter aroma competing with mouth watering scents of breakfast cooking in the pan. Classical music was playing softly in the background, the sounds as delicate as sunlight that filtered in through the windows.

Molly stood back to admire her work. The kitchen was a cosy, practical space with neat little windows overlooking the garden. This was her favourite place in the house and she spent a lot of her time here cooking all kinds of exotic foods and cakes. When she was younger, working and living in London, she had little time to for such pastimes but now she made the most of perfecting her culinary skills.

She was expecting Josie to appear at any moment, her niece would be ravenous from her painting expedition and pressing her face up against the window, she peered in the direction of the lane that led towards the bay. There was no sign of her yet but she could hear the sound of a distant helicopter. This was common enough hereabouts so she thought little of it.

Returning to her chores she hummed along with the tune from the radio then the telephone began to ring.

"Hello." Molly pressed the receiver against her ear.

"No, I'm afraid she's not here at the moment, she's out painting, expected back anytime soon though." Smiling as if the man on the other end of the line could see, she listened carefully to his dry, clipped tones.

"No not at all dear, we've been up for ages it's what we do in the country." Her smile widened as she gave him her full attention then, sticking out her hip, she shifted her weight onto one leg.

"Oh yes, of course she's by herself," she said. "It's quite safe you know no street violence here not since the English were thrown out." Probably thinks I'm a mad old bat, she thought.

"Her travelling arrangements, yes of course, she'll be arriving back in London tomorrow evening."

She studied her reflection in the mirror eyeing herself with interest. Raising her hand she touched her hair noting that it was in need of a trim, she would have to book an appointment at the hair salon. Distracted by her thoughts she frowned then focussed on what the young man was saying.

"Yes, Gatwick, no not sure of the time, perhaps you wouldn't mind calling back this evening," pausing she listened intently before going on. "Yes dear that will be fine."

Replacing the receiver she hurried back into the kitchen, it was then she realised that she had not asked the nice young man his name.

A fishing boat was heading out of the harbour at Lossiemouth. It was one of an armada of small vessels that were making their way towards the deep sea fishing grounds far off shore in the North Sea.

Her skipper, a hard man of forty three had fished here all his life and he was now instructing a young member of his crew to keep watch for floating obstacles. It was not unusual for large containers to be adrift having fallen off ships during rough weather. Sometimes these unseen threats would be lurking just below the surface, they could damage or even sink a small fishing vessel wrecking a man's livelihood and threatening the lives of his crew.

Logs and sometimes whole trees, washed down from the mountains, could be found floating in the bay. There was a whole number of hazards just waiting for the unwary.

Danny Corbett, the young man ordered to keep watch, was taking his job very seriously. He was a new recruit having joined the fishing boat just three weeks ago. He was looking forward to a long and fruitful career in deep-sea fishing but the tales he heard regarding the depletion of fish stocks and European quotas were not very encouraging.

Fifteen minutes out of harbour Danny Corbett's sharp, young eyes narrowed as he spotted a potential hazard. He alerted the skipper who immediately made steering adjustments to avoid a collision, then Danny saw something that caught his attention. Lifting his binoculars to his eyes, he focussed the lenses on a floating tree that was complete with branches. He could see something unusual caught up in its limbs. At first, he thought it was a ball or a float of some kind but as he studied the object, he realised that he was looking at a human head.

The throb of the engine was sufficient to make conversation impossible in the wheelhouse but by shouting and with some basic sign language he managed to persuade the skipper to take a closer look. Throttling back, he changed course. Not wanting to take his boat in too close a small inflatable was made ready and Danny was put over the side.

Carefully he manoeuvred the little craft towards the obstacle and after a few moments confirmed his suspicions, he had found a body. The skipper looked on anxiously as Danny hauled it from the water, then ducking back into the wheelhouse, he put out a call over the radio informing the Coastguard of their discovery.

"She's still breathing." Danny called out as he steered his little craft back towards the fishing boat.

Once he was alongside they lifted her carefully aboard before checking for vital signs then after a moment the skipper nodded encouragingly. She was alive but only just, so they set about making her more comfortable. Josie remained unconscious as Danny wrapped her in blankets, he did his best to rub some warmth back into her frozen limbs.

The skipper throttled the engines, he did not intend to return to harbour they were late enough as it was and he still had to fill his boat with fish. It was not only their schedule that was tight.

Twenty minutes later the helicopter located the vessel and a winch man was lowered to the deck. Josie was not aware of being winched into the helicopter that hovered overhead or that her chances of survival had now improved significantly.

An ambulance was waiting at the gate of a play park situated close to the harbour at Lossiemouth. The medics had already cleared the area and now a group of children were waiting excitedly for the helicopter to arrive.

Swooping in low over the warehouses that surrounded the park, it touched down gently in a storm of grass cuttings and the children squealed with delight. The medics waited as the rotor blades slowed before moving forward.

Josie had regained consciousness during the short flight but remained confused and unable to take in the events. Her body was frozen and her mind refused to work, she was suffering from exposure and shock. Her head was throbbing mercilessly and was not helped by the noise and vibrations of the helicopter.

The winch man had fussed over her, cleaning a nasty gash on her forehead and binding her arm tightly across her chest, this was to protect a suspected shoulder dislocation.

The medics now took over and lifting her carefully from the helicopter, shipped her expertly into the back of the ambulance before checking her over thoroughly. Josie was made comfortable before the ambulance moved away, and speaking for the first time she confirmed her name.

She was safe now but as her emotions welled up realisation began to sink in. The medic, holding onto her hand, soothed her gently with words of kindness but it was a while before she was able to relax. Sinking into the soft blankets, she bathed luxuriously in the warmth of the vehicle and as her tears soaked into the pillow, she could not stop thinking about the woman who had been murdered.

Her exhaustion was both physical and psychological but slowly she began the process of recovery. Her body temperature was dangerously low, it would have to be raised slowly and she would need to undergo a number of tests once they arrived at the hospital. She didn't have the strength to explain how she had come to be swept away into the Moray Firth, besides her story was quite unbelievable.

It was just after midday when Molly arrived. A doctor told her that her niece was stable after being plucked quite literally from the North Sea.

"You look awful dear," Molly said drily as she walked into the room. "How on earth did you manage to get yourself into such a state?"

Josie could hardly speak she was so relieved to see her Aunt. Molly hugged her carefully, avoiding her injured arm. She was shocked to see Josie in such a state but was determined to remain calm. Standing back to assess the damage, Molly scrutinised the ugly bruises that discoloured Josie's face. The gash on her forehead had been neatly stitched and her arm was still tightly strapped across her chest. Her skin felt chilled as Molly brushed her cheek but slowly Josie's colour was returning.

She was wrapped in what looked like kitchen foil and Molly, eyeing the equipment surrounding her, studied the drip that was feeding fluid through a cannula fixed into the back of Josie's hand.

"You're going to have a right old shiner," she said with a wry grin.

Josie tried to laugh but coughed painfully, spitting out foul tasting fluid into a bowl. Her chest was sore and she wheezed as the air rattled from her waterlogged lungs.

"They told me you had to be airlifted from a fishing boat."

"Apparently so," Josie coughed again with the effort of conversation.

She managed to tell her aunt what she could remember and Molly listened without interrupting. When Josie had finished Molly remained silent, the expression on her face inscrutable.

"Have you told anyone else?"

"Yes," she nodded, "not long after I arrived the police came in and took a statement. They appear to be very interested indeed when people are fished out of the North Sea."

"I dare say they are." Molly nodded as she considered the cost of a helicopter rescue mission. Diplomatically she kept her thoughts to herself.

They chatted quietly for a while mainly about changes to their domestic arrangements. Clearly Josie would be not be returning to London as soon as she had planned, and secretly Molly was pleased at the prospect of having her around for a few more days.

"You had a telephone call this morning." Molly said as she remembered the call she had taken.

"Oh yes, who was it?"

"I don't know I forgot to ask," she grinned ruefully. "Anyway, he sounded like a nice young man. He said he would call again this evening."

Josie coughed and gasping for breath, clutched at the cardboard kidney dish and holding it up to her face, spat out more foul tasting liquid. She was exhausted and collapsing weakly against the pillows it took a few moments for her to recover.

Molly hovered beside the bed and feeling utterly useless her heart went out to her niece. A nurse appeared, popping her head round the door.

"Everything alright in here?" she asked cheerfully, moving towards the bed. She felt Josie's pulse before pressing her hand against her forehead and after consulting her watch made some adjustments to her notes.

"I'll just take your temperature again." Popping a thermometer into Josie's mouth she paused long enough for the procedure to work, then, squinting at the thin glass tube, she plotted a line on a graph.

"Slowly on the up," she smiled. "It's going to take some time for you to recover your temperature." She checked the drip of saline solution that was sending rehydrating fluid into Josie's battered and bruised body.

"How do you feel?" she asked.

"Like I've been hit by a train."

The nurse grinned. "The doctor will probably want to keep you in tonight as you've got a wee bit of concussion. You've had a nasty bang to your head and swallowed a lot of sea water." She smiled then dashed away before Josie could ask any questions.

Josie closed her eyes and tried to relax. It felt heavenly resting her head back against the pillows safe in the knowledge that she was tucked up between soft, warm blankets. She could almost imagine that she were at home in her own bed, but her mind kept flashing back to events that had led up to this moment. So far, she had managed to block out the horror of the moment when she realised that all was lost and the cold, dark sea robbed her of her remaining strength. Giving up had not come easily and she would never forgive herself but what else could she do? Her tortured body had reached its limit even if her mind was willing to struggle on.

Molly thought that Josie was drifting off to sleep and studying her chalk white face, touched her hand softly.

"What did he say at the end of the phone call?" Josie whispered.

"What do you mean dear?" Molly frowned.

"Did he say goodbye?"

"Oh I see, no he said ciao."

"Ah," she made a face, "that would be Michael then. That's one of the many things I find so annoying about him."

"Oh dear, just one of the things," Molly chuckled. "He sounded like such a nice young man."

"He can be quite charming I assure you of that. Don't tell him what's happened when he phones back," she opened her eyes and fixed her aunt with a stare.

"What shall I tell him, your young man?"

"He's not my young man," Josie snapped. "Just tell him I've changed my plans. Tell him I'm staying on for a little longer, in fact, tell him I've gone off into the highlands to do some more painting and I definitely don't want to be disturbed."

"Oh dear," Molly stared at her.

Josie had never mentioned Michael before and full of curiosity Molly wondered what had happened between them to cause such a rift. She wisely decided not to take the subject any further, for the moment at least.

"I've got an interview for a job next week so I can't hang around for too long."

17

"Oh that's marvellous dear," Molly's face lit up. "What's that all about?"

"It's for a teaching job at a school in Kent, maternity cover for six months."

"I'm sure you will have recovered fully by the start of term if they ask you to join them." Molly said, trying to sound positive.

"Oh, I've just remembered," Josie bit her bottom lip.

"What's that dear?"

"I'm supposed to drop some paintings off at Tim's gallery at the weekend. My pictures have started to sell."

"Why that's splendid but I'm sure Tim will understand if you telephone him."

Josie closed her eyes as another wave of nausea swept over her. It was true, her body was thawing out and she could feel the warmth slowly returning to her bones but it was her muscles, complaining at the harsh treatment they had suffered that gave her the most pain. The intense ache behind her eyes was affecting her sight and occasionally it was difficult to focus her blurred vision. She was, however, thankful that her shoulder was not dislocated, just badly strained but every time she moved, she was reminded of the punishment that it had taken.

Chapter
THREE

Three days later Molly collected her niece from the hospital.

"I can't believe they kept me in there all weekend," Josie complained as soon as she was in the car.

"They were taking no chances," Molly said. "Besides, you had swallowed so much water that your lungs resembled wet sponges. You could have developed all sorts of nasty infections." Molly glanced sideways at her before going on. She could see that Josie was furious.

"Most of the doctors are off duty at the weekend so there was no-one left to discharge you."

"Wouldn't have happened in London," Josie sulked.

Molly was secretly relieved that the doctors had been so thorough, it had given Josie time to rest. She chose not to share her thoughts with her niece. Clearly, Josie was still sore and very depressed. The doctor had warned Molly about the nightmares and the melancholia that would continue for a while yet. It was not just her physical injuries that needed salving, time was what Josie needed and most of all some tender loving care.

Tentatively Josie touched the wound on her forehead, and pulling down the sun visor, studied herself in the little vanity mirror. The wound was healing nicely and she could feel the skin tightening around the bruised area. The doctor had reassured her that there would be minimal scarring and given time even that should completely disappear.

Glancing at her again, Molly knew that it was going to be difficult to tell her about the police report.

"The police didn't find anything on the river bank," she began, and holding her breath, waited for a response.

"How can that be?" Josie exclaimed after a moment's silence. Turning her head towards her aunt pain swept through her shoulder and she gasped, the colour draining from her face.

Molly felt dreadfully sorry for her.

"I know what I saw, I heard that poor woman scream and there was nothing I could do to help her."

The atmosphere in the car became charged but Molly did her best to sound positive.

"The constable was very nice dear. He collected your things from the riverbank. He liked your painting very much." She smiled weakly.

Josie remained silent, her throat tightened and an ache welled up from deep within her chest. She could hold back the tears no longer and all the frustration and shock that remained pent up within her poured out in a torrent of emotion.

Molly stopped the car and turning towards Josie took her in her arms. She comforted her as best she could. Molly was desperately worried, she knew it would be like this and realised that she would have to remain strong. She would be there for Josie, help her through this difficult time. It was going to take time for her to come to terms with what life had so cruelly thrown at her.

After a while, Josie recovered and delving into her bag searched for a clump of tissues.

"I know what I saw," she said softly. "Somebody somewhere is missing that poor woman."

Brushing a stray tear from her cheek, she dabbed at her nose with her tissues and pressing her head back against the headrest closed her eyes. The rumble of the tyres on the surface of the road was somehow comforting.

Molly stole sideways glances as she drove. Of course, she believed her story impossible though it seemed. Josie had no cause to make up such a horrid tale, besides she would never have put herself through such an ordeal. Something terrible must have happened to make her flee blindly into the North Sea. Molly was however, a practical woman who liked to deal in facts but currently there was just no evidence to back up Josie's story. The police found no signs that a murder had taken place on the riverbank, so for now there was no case to answer. The investigation had drawn a blank and she knew that the authorities would never believe her story, in fact everything was pointing towards Josie having experienced some kind of breakdown.

Molly was thankful that Josie could not read her thoughts and bringing the car to a stop outside a small shop she switched off the engine. She needed to pick up a pint of milk, there never seemed to be enough in her fridge these days and still she could not get used to the fact that there was no doorstep delivery in her village.

Climbing out of her car, she came face to face with an advertising board carrying the local newspaper's headlines. 'Pretty good catch in the Moray Firth.'

Molly bought milk and a copy of the newspaper and pushed the items into a plastic carrier bag before returning to her car. Throwing the bag onto the back seat she got in behind the wheel then, glancing quickly at Josie, she noticed with satisfaction that colour had returned to her cheeks. Starting the engine, she depressed the clutch and selecting first gear pulled smoothly away from the kerb.

"I saw the board outside the shop," Josie said calmly.

"Oh, I thought you were asleep dear."

Reaching carefully for the bag on the rear seat Josie pulled out the newspaper. She studied it in silence. 'English tourist chased into the North Sea by an early morning phantom.' Quickly she scanned the column. The story, covering the basic details told how the fishing boat had picked her up and of the Search and Air Rescue helicopter flying her into Lossiemouth. There was even a smudged photograph of the fishermen who had rescued her. The article went on to describe her injuries.

A police spokesperson was quoted as saying that because there was no evidence to support her story, they were unlikely to take the matter any further.

"At least they didn't publish my name," she whispered, and totally deflated by the article slumped miserably down into the seat.

By the end of the week Josie was much better, her injuries were healing and she was feeling more comfortable. Her appetite had returned and despite brief periods of despair, Molly was pleased with her progress. She was certain that Josie would make a full recovery.

Josie booked her return flight to London but was annoyed with Michael who telephoned more often than she would have liked. He insisted on driving up to Scotland to collect her but she resisted his offer vehemently. She was not up to being stuck in a car with him on such a long journey. She did however agree reluctantly to him collecting her from Gatwick.

She had concocted a story about sustaining her injuries from a nasty fall in the mountains. She hated the idea of lying but had no intention of telling him the truth. She had known Michael for eighteen months; their relationship had been explosive and just as destructive. She realised early on that they were not compatible but he would not let her go. He pursued her relentlessly even after all her efforts to distance herself from him. He became even more determined and producing a ring had begged her to marry him. The thought of marriage annoyed her enormously and as they rowed, his frustration turned to anger.

Josie thought him totally irresponsible, how dare he think she would consider such an arrangement. It was difficult for her to believe that he expected an acceptance to his proposal. That had been two months ago and now after much fighting they had agreed a truce, a cooling off period, time to reflect on their feelings for each other.

She sensed that he was just biding his time and would always be there like a shadow in the background waiting for an opportunity to get back in with her. She was feeling incredibly vulnerable at the moment and knew that he would take full advantage of her situation. She would have to be careful and find the strength to remain distant.

Chapter

FOUR

The newspaper article had been unfortunate, for her anyway, and he congratulated himself on covering his tracks so thoroughly. The whole affair could not have worked out better, not only had the police dismissed her story but the media had branded her a crank.

It had not been difficult to cover up his crime, but he decided to test the system, make it a little more interesting. He had left tiny traces of blood and scorch marks in the soil caused by firing the pistol, the grass had also been flattened where she had fallen. All of these clues would have been obvious if the police had believed her story about a murder. It satisfied him to know that he could fool the authorities. They were after all just ordinary local lads, overstretched by a system that relied too heavily on target figures and justification of resources. Their days were better spent imposing speeding fines on tourists, chasing shoplifters, targeting petty drug dealers and arresting teenage binge drinkers, this is what improved public opinion. These were crimes that corrupted the streets affecting honest, hardworking people and the establishment was better supported when seen to be dealing with such offences.

He frowned as he read about the gallant sea rescue. Maybe he should punish the fishermen for their part in the story, they looked so smug and self righteous as they smiled at him from the page.

He was surprised at first to hear that she had survived, he was certain that she would drown or die from the cold. Her witnessing him as he dispatched the bitch with the long hair had been unfortunate. Things had not gone to plan that morning, the woman had run much too far, she had almost escaped. Next time he would have to be more careful.

His pulse quickened as he remembered the things he had done to her, how she had screamed, cried out and pleaded unashamedly for mercy. He loved the power he had over people; he could make them do all kinds of things they would never consider doing and she had paid the ultimate price for all her whining. She had been a stuck up, plum in the mouth English bitch and as far as he was concerned, her suffering was justified.

He remembered the way she had looked at him when they passed in the street. It had been one of those simple instances when walking towards someone on the pavement, you get in each other's way. It was a moment of embarrassment when you both step the same way, split seconds like that can lead to all kinds of impulsive adventure and so it was that day. She had scorned him, thinking him no better than dirt on her shoe and the look she had given him was no more than a sneer. That had definitely been the wrong thing to do and he would make her pay. He hated everything about her, her fine clothes, her perfect hair and make-up, her refined accent, her rich husband. Nothing would save her and nothing could prepare her for the horrors that were to come. He chuckled at the memory; he had poisoned her body, stolen her mind and ultimately destroyed her. He grinned and licked his lips.

Clearing his mind of such thoughts, he began to formulate a new plan. His wanted to discover more about this woman, the artist who had plunged into the sea. He remembered the way she had looked, the stunned expression on her face the moment she realised that he knew she had seen the whole thing. He had enjoyed that part the most; she was an opportune witness, an unsuspecting audience.

In his mind's eye, he saw the way she had moved and he began to live through it all over again. Her hair rippling like silk around her shoulders as it was touched by the breeze had fascinated him. It was a shade of brown shining in the pale morning light. He frowned, was it brown or copper, or was it auburn? He did not care much he just remembered it dancing as she ran.

Oh yes how she had moved, he grinned, her young lean body tearing along the narrow pathway. He could still feel her terror, taste her panic, every moment of the chase had been a thrill. If she had turned right instead of going the other way then things may have ended very differently. Unfortunately for her she had chosen the path that took her past the visitors centre and on towards the mouth of the river. Fate had dealt him the winning hand that morning, recompense for the almost disastrous result of the earlier chase. He decided then that he would have to make her pay for witnessing him at work.

Finding out about her had been simple, all he had to do was ask a few well placed questions in a small community where excited locals were more than willing to point him in the right direction. Now he was sitting calmly at the wheel of his car overlooking the old woman's cottage in the sleepy little village of Garmouth. This was a quiet corner of the village and he was unlikely to be disturbed. Many of the houses here were unoccupied; they served as holiday homes for the wealthy. The remainder of the village was split between the elderly, the retired and the commuters, it seemed that only a small part of the population were in residence during the day. This suited him admirably.

Swinging round in his seat, he glanced towards the village shop. It was small but looked well stocked. Opposite the shop on the corner of a narrow street was an ancient building that housed a small hotel and bar, a sign high up on the wall boasted a restaurant. Visitors to the village at this time of day would be few so there he remained unnoticed but observing all.

The cottage was currently unoccupied, he had seen the owner drive away earlier and his plan did not include breaking and entering, not just yet at least so he waited.

When she returned she reversed her car onto the narrow driveway in front of the cottage and he watched as she jumped out to close the pair of wrought iron gates that marked the boundary of her garden. Her step was light as she moved towards the front door, then she stopped to rummage in her bag. This annoyed him immensely, why is it that women always did this? They would walk up to the front door before searching for the key, why can't they have it in their hand ready?

He waited fifteen minutes before making his move. Slipping out of his car, he checked over his shoulder before crossing the road, then pushing open the gate it moaned softly as it swung inwards on ancient hinges. Stepping up to the door, he rattled the knocker before smoothing down his hair.

"Good afternoon," he greeted her cheerfully, "so sorry to disturb you. My name is Mr Mac, I'm an independent journalist. I was just wondering, could I possibly have a word with Miss er...?"

He held up a copy of the local newspaper and indicated to the headlines on the front page.

"No, I'm afraid not, you're too late. She left this morning, gone home you see." Molly studied him suspiciously through narrowed eyes.

From the moment he heard her well clipped vowels he hated her. "You're probably wondering how I came to know where she was staying," he smiled as if addressing his own grandmother. "I have a friend, well a colleague really, who works on the local paper. He told me very discreetly where I might find her." He shrugged his shoulders apologetically and took a step backwards. "I will of course be very discreet myself if you'll just tell me where she lives."

His smile was innocent enough, if only she could read his mind.

"As I said, she's gone home to London." Molly folded her arms protectively across her chest. It was an instinctive movement; one that she felt compelled to make under his scrutiny.

There was something about him that didn't quite ring true. She considered herself a good observer of characters and this one she disliked.

"Oh dear," he tried a different approach. "I have such bad luck, typical of me," he made a face. "It's such a bizarre story." Shuffling his feet, he moved closer. "The local 'journo' nor the police seem to have taken her account very seriously but my editor is keen to put things right. He wants me to investigate her claims. We are willing to pay handsomely for an exclusive."

He was pleased at how convincing he sounded but hoped she wouldn't press him for the name of the organisation he was supposed to be representing. "Is there anything you could tell me perhaps?" He went on quickly in an attempt to take advantage of the situation.

"I couldn't possibly comment as I wasn't there you see. All I know is what I've read in the newspaper, I didn't press my niece for the details."

"You didn't discuss the details with Miss...?"

Again, she avoided his trap.

Probing for information, he looked over her shoulder, taking in the layout of her house. There were two doors leading off the narrow hallway, one to the left and one to the right, both were shut. At the far end, he could see another door. This one was slightly ajar; he guessed it led to a kitchen situated at the back of the house. Just over her left shoulder he could see a staircase leading to the upper floor.

"Och well," he said. "It's a pity. I won't take up any more of your time." Once again, he smiled charmingly. "Can I give you my telephone number, perhaps you could pass it on so she could contact me if she has a mind to."

He was beginning to sweat, a sheen had appeared on his brow and he could feel it cooling against his skin. This was proving to be much harder than he anticipated. The old woman was shrewd, he had under-estimated her and it was all he could do to control the urge to force his way into her home and torture the information out of her.

He made a show of searching his pockets. "Oh dear, I seem to have left my business cards in my car."

Pulling a mobile phone from his pocket he flashed his own number up on the screen then copied it down on a scrap of paper.

"How unprofessional," he confessed. "Mobile phones, I've no idea what my number is, never have to dial it myself."

Shrugging his shoulders, he made light of the moment before handing her the scrap of paper. She avoided touching his fingers.

Thanking her most graciously for her time, he made his way back towards his car muttering obscenities under his breath. He was furious; the whole fiasco had revealed nothing, not one scrap of useful information.

Molly watched him suspiciously from her front window, she was old enough and wise enough to listen to her instincts and the message that she was hearing was full of misgivings. Although he appeared pleasant enough there was something about him that unnerved her. Glancing at the piece of paper he had given her, she read his name. Mr Mac, what kind of a name was that. Turning away from the window she shuddered then, letting the curtain fall back into place, she dropped the scrap of paper onto the small table next to the telephone.

Chapter
FIVE

Tim Granger was the proprietor of an art gallery and framers situated just off Piccadilly in London. He sold paintings to the rich and famous and he was a good friend of Josie's.

He had been tempted to telephone her the moment she arrived home but he knew that Mike would be there with her. Michael Cowper-Smith was one of his clients, he had made no secret that he would be collecting Josie from the airport. It was Mike who had introduced her to him in the first place and it wasn't long before he realised her potential as an artist. He had managed to convince her to display some of her paintings in his gallery and within a few days had sold a few of her watercolours, now he was eager to see what she had been working on in Scotland. This was not his only reason for wanting to see Josie. Tim hoped that she could be more than just a friend, he felt sure that given time she could become someone very special in his life.

Eventually he found the opportunity to phone her, it was late on Monday morning but she was not at home, so he left a message on her answer phone. He considered trying her mobile phone but decided against the idea.

Later that day she returned his call and he was elated when she agreed to meet him for a drink.

"So, what will it be tea, coffee or something stronger?" Tim smiled.

"Coffee would be great; it's still too early for a proper drink, besides I'm still taking these damn pain killers."

At times her shoulder and neck would stiffen causing her discomfort.

Ugly bruises had spread across her shoulders and she felt a little self-conscious about the marks left on her face, luckily, she was able to conceal the worst of it with make-up.

She studied him carefully as he spoke to the waitress and could not help but notice the effect he was having on the poor girl.

"Do you know her?" she asked as soon as he returned to their table.

"No not at all."

"Well I'm certain she would like to know you." Josie grinned as Tim stared back at her blankly.

"Didn't you notice?" Josie continued.

"Notice what?" he asked, shrugging his shoulders innocently.

"She fancies you something rotten!"

Tim made a face then glanced to where the waitress was working, after a moment he changed the subject. "How's your aunt?"

"Molly, oh she's great, the highland air does her very well."

"Auntie Molly," he corrected her with a grin.

"I forgot that you know her or rather your mother does. I'm afraid I didn't ask her about your mother when we were chatting on the phone the other day. I would very much like to know what she remembers about you as a child. Would she have any photographs?" She giggled mischievously. "It's such a coincidence them knowing each other."

"Small world I suppose." Tim shuffled uncomfortably in his seat. "So, you enjoyed your trip then apart from the obvious of course."

"Not the so obvious I hope." She replied, touching her forehead carefully with her fingertips.

Tim could feel the atmosphere around them beginning to change as shadows swept across her face.

"The painting was good if that's what you mean, the clean air flushed out the London smog and it was great to get away." She told him a little too quickly.

"Sorry," he glanced at her. "Tell me to mind my own business if you like."

His mobile phone began to ring and he looked up apologetically before turning away. He kept the call short then putting his phone down on the table between them was relieved to find that she seemed a little less tense.

"After our coffee we should go back to my studio, I'll show you what I've done."

"Excellent idea," he smiled.

The waitress almost fell into his lap in her eagerness to deliver their

29

drinks and she fussed around them for longer than was necessary. As she worked, Josie studied Tim who remained silent then her emotions begin to stir. She had never thought of him as a potential suitor before, she had enough trouble fending off Mike's advances. She liked Tim very much, he didn't seem to have any hidden agendas, he was uncomplicated. With Mike she never knew where she stood, he could be so domineering and stubborn at times; he wanted everything his own way.

She realised of course that Tim thought highly of her artistic abilities, he wanted her to fit neatly into his business plans. He did seem dependable though and she liked him for that.

"Penny for them," he startled her.

The waitress had gone and the table was laid out beautifully, their cups standing in tiny saucers and a regency style coffee pot steaming from its spout.

"Oh you wouldn't want to know," she smiled, thankful that her thoughts would remain her own. "How is business anyway?" She was feeling uncomfortable and that was all she could think of to say.

"Doing very well," he nodded.

Reaching for the pot, he poured coffee into her cup; she added a spoonful of sugar then offered a spoonful to him. He nodded adding a dash of cream to hers. They worked harmoniously together, it was as if their movements had been choreographed. She would never have achieved that with Mike.

"I've just discovered a ceramicist," he told her. "I'm planning an exhibition of his work."

She could hear the excitement in his voice and was charmed by the way he nodded occasionally, emphasising some point or other. The tone of his voice and his use of language pleased her enormously. It made him sound even more interesting. Would it always be like this, she wondered, if they were to spend the rest of their lives together. Pushing the thought from her mind she blushed, and reaching for her cup, hid behind it sipping at the steaming liquid.

The coffee was deliciously smoky against her tongue and very slightly bitter, just how she liked it. She looked at him again, he was definitely a romantic, she thought, and when he spoke about the things he enjoyed his back would straighten and his eyes flashed.

Leaving nothing out, he told her about his business plans and the people he admired. He hoped to have the opportunity to work with them all.

His sandy coloured hair fell across his forehead and unconsciously he pushed it away. She loved his mannerisms and letting her mind wander, she found herself thinking about what their children would look like. Almost choking on her coffee she returned the cup quickly to its saucer, then crossing her legs held her hands to her throat.

"Are you okay?" he asked, leaning across the table his face full of concern.

"Yes of course, just went down the wrong way," she smiled sweetly at him.

He settled back into his chair and was silent for a moment and she thanked her lucky stars that he couldn't read her thoughts. It was then she made up her mind; she really would like to get to know him better.

They finished their coffee then strolled back to her little house where she laid out her paintings of Scotland. He studied them in silence, and lost in his own thoughts he stood back. Josie, giving him space, was thankful that he remained unaware of her scrutiny.

"You have been busy," he said at last. "I'm impressed."

She smiled delighted by his initial reaction.

"I can see you had good weather and the light must have been just perfect."

"I know you asked me for landscapes but I just couldn't resist painting some of those lovely old buildings."

"You have a perfect mix," he nodded approvingly. "I love this one of the old distillery and the ruins next door."

"They are some old buildings that were destroyed by fire over 150 years ago." She repeated the story an old man had told her. He had spent his life living and working at the distillery.

"I recognise this," Tim picked up one of the paintings. "I went to Elgin years ago with my mother and fell in love with the place."

He spent the next few minutes scrutinising the scene, imagining her work in mounts bordered by frames and Josie was more than happy to have him comment on her paintings. He loved her work and all his criticisms were positive.

"I'll display them all." He said suddenly making up his mind.

"Are you sure Tim?" She wasn't expecting that. "What about space, don't you have others waiting to exhibit?"

"I'm pretty sure I have a buyer for this one. You have a great talent you know, I'm certain they won't be in my gallery for long." His enthusiasm was infectious.

"You know Josie, we would make a great team you and I."

Her heart agreed with him.

"You producing such fine works of art and me marketing them," he continued.

These were not quite the words she wanted to hear.

"So Mr. Granger, is that all you think of me, a business prospect?" Crossing the room, she jabbed at him playfully and they laughed together.

Tim felt an almost overwhelming urge to wrap her up in his arms; he wanted to tell her what he really felt but a second later the moment had passed.

"So," he broke the awkward silence that followed. "What have you got in your sketch book?"

"There are enough ideas here for a dozen more 'masterpieces.'" She assured him and picking up the book began to thumb through the thick pages.

Tim was drawn towards her and his senses flared as he caught her scent then his heart began to beat faster.

Suddenly she threw her sketchbook down and jumped back.

"What's the matter?" Catching her in his arms, he held her steady.

Her mind was reeling and she felt faint, she had to make up a plausible excuse.

"I caught a nerve in my arm." She lied convincingly and gently pulling away from him, massaged her shoulder.

He was concerned, suddenly she looked very drawn and tired. "Would you like a glass of water or something?" he asked.

"I'm fine Tim really, you don't need to fuss."

She sat down leaving her sketchbook where it had fallen on the floor. Her heart was racing and she couldn't stop her hands from shaking. Clutching them tightly together in her lap, she took a deep breath and managed to compose herself.

"So, are you sure you want all my pictures?" she asked striving to sound normal even though inside she was in turmoil.

"Do you mind?" He settled in a chair opposite her. "Are there any you would rather keep?"

"No," she smiled weakly. "Sentimentality doesn't pay the rent."

She allowed him to gather up her pictures and watched as he placed them carefully between stiff cardboard wrappings. Once he was satisfied, he moved towards the door.

"Thanks for the coffee Tim it was great to see you." She smiled and he was pleased to see the colour returning to her cheeks.

She stood facing him in the open doorway, then reaching up kissed him lightly on his cheek, breathing in his aftershave she lingered close to him.

"See you later then," he whispered into her ear. "And don't forget to look after yourself."

She watched him from her window as he headed off along the street. He glanced back once then was gone.

She sighed, then folding her arms protectively across her breasts turned to face her sketchbook. It lay on the floor where it had fallen but she just stared at it. Shaking her head she told herself that it was only a book, then scooping it up threw herself into a chair. Her hands were trembling as she fumbled with the pages and finding what she was looking for she studied it. Someone had scribbled a crudely drawn sketch of a seascape; it was clear enough to make out a figure foundering in the water. Struggling to face up to her fears, she managed to control her fragile nerves before seeing it more clearly. The shadowy figure of a man was standing on the shore, he seemed to be staring out of the page and she could clearly make out an expression on his crude face. Grotesquely his tongue was protruding from his lips and he was smiling.

Snapping the covers together, she pushed it away then leaning forward cradled her head in her hands. She thought about the murdered woman and tears dropped silently onto the carpet as she wept. Filled with sorrow for a woman she had never known, Josie realised that she would never forget her or the way she had died.

Swallowing hard she pushed her feelings to one side then reaching for her sketchbook tore the page out. Standing up she went into her studio and stuffed it into the bottom drawer of her desk before slamming it shut. She felt easier now it was out of sight.

The killer must have done the drawing and she wondered if the police officer who had recovered her things from the riverbank had seen it. Sniffing loudly she brushed her tears away with the back of her hand.

Chapter
SIX

When he returned to his shop Tim unwrapped Josie's paintings carefully and studied them before beginning work. He knew exactly how he was going to frame them and clearing a space in his workroom he set about the task.

An hour later they were done then, hanging them in his gallery, he stood back to admire them. He was pleased with the results, with a nod of satisfaction he went into his office where he picked up the phone. In no time at all he had arranged a private viewing with one of his clients then he made another call.

"Josie, would you like to come out for a meal?" Tim asked.

"Why are you insinuating that I'm too thin?" she joked.

"No of course not."

"I would love to Tim that would be really nice."

"Good." He sounded relieved. "How does Thursday sound, around eight?"

"I have a job interview on Thursday but I should be back in time, so Thursday would be perfect."

"Are you sure? I can make it Friday or another time, the weekend perhaps?"

"Tim, Thursday will be fine, honestly, I'm looking forward to it already."

He told her that her paintings had been mounted and framed and as he dropped the receiver into its cradle, he realised that he had not mentioned the private viewing.

Josie was standing by her desk gripping the telephone firmly in her hand, she was smiling as warmth permeated throughout her body. It felt so good it chased away the despair that just a few moments earlier had upset her so badly. Her physical wounds were healing quickly but the mental scars were going to take a while longer to fade away.

Suddenly the phone rang and she almost dropped it. Struggling to overcome her shock, she was breathing heavily when finally she answered.

"Have you been running dear?"

Josie almost cried with joy at the sound of Molly's cheerful voice.

"How are you? I would have rung yesterday but I thought you would probably need to recover from your journey."

"I'm not jet lagged you know." Josie laughed.

They chatted for a few moments, their conversation a roller coaster of topics. Josie was amazed at the diversity of her aunt's mind and she had to have her wits about her just to keep up.

She told her about her paintings and Tim's gallery.

"You haven't told me much about this Tim." Molly accused.

"He's just a friend. Incidentally, he told me he knows you."

"Does he really dear, what's his surname?"

"Granger, he tells me you know his mother."

Molly thought for a few moments. "I used to know a Mavis Granger but that was years ago. I haven't spoken to her in a long while."

"Yes that would be her he told me his mother's name is Mavis."

"Of course I remember little Timmy Granger, though I guess he's not so small these days," she chuckled. "Nice family from what I can remember, you'd do well to keep in with him."

"You're doing it again." Josie accused.

"Can't think what you mean dear." Molly laughed.

"You're incorrigible."

"By the way," she began, her tone becoming serious. "There's something I have to tell you." She paused for effect. "When I returned home the other day from dropping you off at the airport, there was someone waiting here to see you. He told me he was a journalist."

"Did he say which newspaper he represented?"

"No dear, said he was an independent. He said something about wanting to investigate your story and that someone from the local paper told him where to find you." She stopped to take a breath before going on. "He didn't know your name of course and I didn't give him any of your details. He left his telephone number though and asked me to pass it on to you. He wants you to contact him." She read out the number and Josie scribbled it down on her blotter.

"Called himself Mr Mac," Molly continued. "I didn't like him much."

"Why do you say that?"

"There was something about him that I didn't care for."

"Well perhaps you are suffering from 'journo phobia,'" Josie smiled.
"You never know what they might print about you."

"How many skeletons have you in your cupboard?" she mused.

An hour and forty minutes later their conversation came to an end and Josie was exhausted but happy at hearing her aunt's voice.

Leaning against her desk she stared at the number Molly had given her. She thought about it for a moment as she held onto the telephone but then with a shake of her head she placed it down in its cradle and walked out of the room.

By the middle of the week, Mr Mac was becoming impatient. He had expected a call from her by now but his phone remained silent. Maybe the old woman had not bothered to pass on his number. Worrying and cursing he paced the floor and glancing out of the window he saw nothing. Images flashed inside his head and allowing is imagination free rein he wondered what it would be like to kill the old woman. He could work on her until she told him what he wanted to know. She would beg him for mercy; he would torture her until she pleaded for release.

He grinned and licked his lips, then steadying his shaking hands he turned away from the window. Perhaps not he thought, her time had not yet come, he would have to think of another way.

Back and forth he paced, almost wearing a line in the carpet then after a while he shook his head and pulled a face before heading in defeat towards a cabinet. Throwing open the flimsy glass doors he reached for a bottle of single malt and pouring a generous measure, he moved back towards the window. Unconsciously raising the glass to his lips, he took some of the amber liquid into his mouth. The malty flavour burned against his tongue and flooded his sinuses; it was a satisfying sensation as the liquid slipped luxuriously down into his stomach. Smiling at his reflection in the window, he raised the glass to himself then drained it.

He thought about the girl and the picture he had scribbled in her sketchbook. He also thought about the places she had visited. He knew where she had been from the sketches she had made; she was obviously an artist.

He should have taken something, a sketch from her book or even the painting she had just finished. It was then an idea struck him, he would have to find some of her work. She was good; the portraits of the old woman were a perfect likeness. He should have searched through her bag he would almost certainly have found details of her address or some other personal reference.

He did not expect her to survive the North Sea; she should have perished. She was the second mistake he had made that day and the thought enraged him. Re-visiting the drinks cabinet, he tossed another measure of malt into his glass and his eyes narrowed as he remembered the initials inscribed into the cover of the sketchbook. J.E.Mac.D. J, he thought, Jenny, Jane, Joanne, he couldn't think of any more girls names beginning with J. His glass was empty again and he frowned.

She came from London that much he knew. She looked like the city type, how he hated the English. He could feel his head beginning to pulse so turning towards the cabinet he poured another generous measure of scotch.

He must remain calm, he could not afford to let the voices in, it wasn't their time, he must remain in control.

Turning his thoughts to the sketch he had made, he began to regret doing it. He wondered if she had found it yet and worried that she would have something on him, part of himself foolishly left at the scene of a crime. Forensics could maybe read something into it, doctors could come up with his psychological profile, that would be unfortunate.

Tossing the contents of his glass down his throat, the strong taste made him choke and brought him back to reality. He hated being out of control, drawing in the sketchbook was like leaving a clue. He would have to be more careful in future, leaving clues could spiral out of control and it would not be long before it would all be over.

He continued pacing and sometime later jerked to a stop. Slowly a grin began to spread across his face and suddenly he knew what he must do. It was like divine intervention, a higher authority was showing him the way. He would break into the old woman's home and discover what the initials J.E.Mac.D stood for. He felt certain that all the information he needed could be found in that cottage.

He was pleased with himself; he was back in control. The voices in his head remained on the fringes of his mind for the moment at least. Once again, he stepped up to his drinks cabinet.

Later he drove to the old woman's cottage in Garmouth. Her car was parked on the drive so muttering a curse he drove on past. A little way along the road he pulled onto the grass verge, stopped his car and switched off the engine. He would have to bide his time but an hour later he was still there.

He was fuming, things were not going his way so turning his head he studied the cottage. It was all so infuriatingly perfect with its neat little garden and picture windows. He growled in frustration.

He considered walking to the shop to buy a paper but decided against the idea he did not want to draw unnecessary attention to himself. He could of course just break into the cottage, murder the old woman then search the place at his leisure, but that idea was flawed. She could prove to be useful, he could always torture the information out of her.

His mind was in a whirl and his heart was racing madly. Voices whispered in his head again so pushing them away he focussed on remaining calm. He knew they were coming and would soon be raging, urging him on, taunting him with their vile demands but for now, he was still in control.

He glanced at his mobile phone willing it to ring. If only she would contact him, then this waiting would be over but it remained frustratingly silent. Starting the engine, he engaged first gear then drove away.

Josie left her house early on Thursday morning; she had a busy day ahead of her and she was looking forward to going out with Tim later that evening. Swinging her bag onto her shoulder, she headed off towards the underground station.

Her job interview was at a school in Maidstone where there was an opportunity for six months maternity leave cover. As a relief teacher Josie taught two subjects, History and English. She was happy that this job was going to cover her favourite period in history.

Taking the train into Kent had been an easy decision, she hated driving, she was not a natural behind the wheel of a car and navigating her way around London was her worst nightmare, consequently she found public transport a boon. She intended to take a taxi directly from the train station in Maidstone to the school; this was a stress free solution to a potentially nerve-racking day.

"Good morning," she smiled brightly at the man in the ticket kiosk.

He nodded and said something that was lost as a train rumbled into the station. With a squeal of brakes, the train came to a stop then doors began to open noisily as commuters poured out of the carriages.

Josie settled into her seat between a couple of elderly ladies. Smiling at each other they exchanged the customary words that strangers always did when travelling, then once the train was moving Josie found the rhythm of the carriage soothing and letting her mind wander she thought about Michael. He had been particularly difficult lately; he was becoming even more insistent and demanding. She thought she had made it clear to him that their relationship was over, but annoyingly he would not accept the fact and continued to pester her.

The train maintained its rhythm and her thoughts did the same. Once the journey through the subterranean passageways had ended, she changed trains and made her way into Kent. The scenery beyond the window began to change and soon she had a view of the countryside. It lifted her mood considerably to see fields and trees and occasionally she caught site of farm animals. The day was bright and the sun was busy chasing away early morning mist that was reluctant to move from the low-lying land. It was going to be a beautiful day and her spirits soared.

Josie left her nagging thoughts of Michael buried beneath the streets of London and smiling back at her reflection in the window, she rummaged in her bag for a compact mirror. Thumbing it open she studied her face, she was conscious of the bruises that were slowly fading along with the scar on her forehead. She did not want to turn up looking like she had been in a street brawl, that would hardly make a good impression so, with careful application of make-up, the marks all but disappeared. Satisfied with her appearance she snapped the mirror shut and dropped it back into her bag.

At that moment in Scotland Molly eased herself into her car. She backed it off the drive and headed out of the village taking the road towards Elgin. The sun was master of the sky and it made her grin, she would never grow tired of living here and she knew how lucky she was. The air was clean and the light extraordinarily clear, this was the kind of day that could only be found in the highlands. Molly's admiration for the view meant that she would never take it for granted. She had never been so happy or content and having her niece to stay and share it all with her, albeit for just a little while, was pure magic, she could think of nothing better.

On such a beautiful morning, she chose not to think of the unfortunate events that had taken place in Spey Bay. She was looking forward to meeting up with her friends, spoil herself with shopping and gossip. 'Retail Therapy' she had called it when living in London. It sounded so 'chic' there but up here in the highlands, it hardly seemed the right phrase to use.

It had been easy for Molly to settle in Scotland. She made friends easily and once she had moved from the city, it did not take her long to cultivate a wide circle of companions. She found it hard to believe it had taken her so long to make the move. Of course, her career at the Home Office had been her life and, looking back she had no regrets. She had been young then and life was full of excitement. Her work was extremely enjoyable and had consumed her, she found it challenging and best of all there had been no shortage of gentlemen friends, her dance list was always full. Cocktail parties and luncheons had been the norm and she rubbed along with some very influential people. Her motto had been 'never say no to an invitation'.

She had given no thought to marriage, children never an option, but she had no regrets. Her work had been her life and men married or otherwise were always in abundance and more than willing to help her out one way or another. She smiled wondering why she was mulling over such thoughts.

She hardly noticed the car that pulled to the side of the narrow lane. It left enough room for her to pass and she waved absentmindedly, not seeing the face that was grinning back at her from behind the wheel.

Mr Mac recognised her immediately and easing his car from the side of the road could hardly believe his luck, her cottage would be empty and that suited his plans perfectly.

A few moments later he parked his car by the playing field on the edge of the village, then walking back along the lane he met nobody along the way. It was going to be much easier than he thought and nipping in through the gate, made his way around the side of the cottage where he found the back door.

The rear garden was secluded, it backed neatly onto the playing field and the nearest house was far enough away not to overlook the garden so quite casually Mr Mac went to work.

Placing his canvas tool bag down on the ground, he snapped on a pair of surgical gloves before pulling out a roll of sticky backed plastic. Cutting a length from the roll he peeled off the backing and pressed it carefully over the glass in the window frame then, with a small hammer he struck the glass. It broke soundlessly but did not shatter, the plastic sheet holding it in place. Carefully he eased the panel out of the frame and in one piece laid it on the ground next to his bag. He teased the few remaining shards from the wooden surround then placing them onto the plastic sheet, he glanced over his shoulder. There was no one in sight so easing through the hole he entered the house.

Once inside he paused, listening for the tiniest of sounds. He knew the place was deserted but all his senses heightened and his hearing became acute. Satisfied that no one was at home, he made his way along the hallway. There were two doors leading from the narrow hallway, ignoring the first he continued to the front of the house where he turned to face the door that he guessed led to the living room and gripping the handle eased it open.

The room beyond was surprisingly spacious, a huge picture window looked out onto the small front garden and warm sunlight flooded in filling it with a soft golden hue. He found the place annoyingly neat and tidy.

Keeping away from the window he made his way around the furniture. He had already spotted the telephone table and guessed that was where he would find the information he wanted. Picking up a leather bound address book he shuffled through the pages until he found what he was looking for.

Josie MacDonald, the name matched the initials that he had found printed on the painting equipment. In his excitement he almost ripped the page out but that would not be a good idea, searching around he spotted a pen and some paper and with shaking hands copied down her details before slipping the piece of paper into his pocket. He congratulated himself his morning was going very well after all.

Looking around the room, he spotted a photograph of Josie and recognised her immediately. Picking it up, he moved towards the window for a closer look. Her rich brown hair matched the colour of her smiling eyes, he grinned and licked his lips.

After a moment he returned it to its place on the little side table. He would have liked to take it with him but he had what he came for so retracing his steps he made his way back towards the kitchen.

Josie MacDonald he mused, an English woman with a Scottish name. Hating her even more, he would make her pay for that insult to his country.

His eyes narrowed and he grinned, licking his lips again he was completely unaware of his little habit.

Easing himself out through the hole in the glass panel, he began to peel the broken glass from the sticky backed plastic sheet. Piece by piece he tossed the shards through the hole, the glass bouncing over the kitchen floor shattered into smaller pieces.

Once the job was done he rolled the plastic sheet into a ball and pushed it into his bag, then pulling a golf ball from his pocket he toyed with it, rolling it through his fingers. He had considered bringing a cricket ball but the idea appalled him, cricket was far too English. Tossing it in through the broken window, it bounced around the kitchen before settling in the middle of the floor amongst the shards of glass.

Glancing at his watch he slipped off his rubber gloves then swinging his bag up over his shoulder he strode away. The whole operation had taken less than fifteen minutes.

Chapter
SEVEN

Tim picked Josie up at eight o'clock sharp; she guessed that he would be punctual so was ready even though she had only been home for a short time.

"You look wonderful." He told her the moment she opened the door. Stepping back to admire her he missed the opportunity for a kiss. She smiled then moving forward stepped out into the street, closing the door firmly behind her.

"So, where are we going?"

Linking arms, they strode towards his car.

"I've a friend, well associate really who's just opened a French restaurant. I thought we might go there, support his new venture."

"Sounds great." She nodded, hoping that he would not pick up on her lack of enthusiasm. Generally, she liked most foods but detested garlic, hopefully the food tonight would be light on garlic.

It was only a short drive into town and fifteen minutes later they were searching for a somewhere to leave the car. Like everywhere in the city parking was a problem but they soon found a place not far from the restaurant.

"Bonsoir mes ami." A tall dark haired man greeted them at the door and Tim shook his hand enthusiastically.

"I would like you to meet my friend Josie," Tim beamed. "Josie, this is Raymond Duval, proprietor of this splendid establishment."

"Enchantez Mademoiselle." Brushing the back of her hand lightly with his lips, not once did his eyes leave hers.

She was indeed enchanted and found him very handsome. His continental good looks were dark and mysterious. He was not as tall as Tim but Raymond looked fit and in proportion.

"I'm glad to meet you Monsieur," she replied and her legs turned to jelly.

"Non, non, you must call me Raymond if you please. All my friends call me Raymond," he smiled and gave back her hand.

Turning his attention to Tim, he continued. "It is good to see that you find time to visit us again and so soon."

Ushering them to their table he fussed around Josie ensuring that she was comfortable.

She fell in love with the place immediately. Charmed by the atmosphere she began to relax the moment they arrived. The air was full of wonderful aromas and soft music was playing in the background. She smiled as Tim admired her from across the table.

They were delighted to find their table decorated with cleverly folded napkins.

"This is a very special place," she said, "I'm impressed."

"Raymond is a perfectionist he strives to create the perfect atmosphere."

"An ambience for lovers," Raymond said helping him out.

"Oh I think you've achieved that." Josie agreed.

He was overjoyed and clapped his hands together like an excited child before excusing himself as more people arrived.

"This is definitely a place for couples." Josie said as she watched Raymond fussing over his guests. All the tables around them were set for two.

A waiter approached with menus then another stopped by with warm bread rolls and two glasses of champagne.

"Compliments of Monsieur," he smiled setting them down carefully.

Subtle light from the candles cast shadows over their faces and Josie, reaching for her fine cut glass champagne flute, found enchantment in the tiny lights that danced like fairies around her glass as hundreds of tiny bubbles rose to the surface. It was a magical moment that she would cherish forever.

"His bank manager advised Raymond against setting up a French restaurant." Tim began as he sipped his ice cold champagne.

"Why ever was that?"

"Apparently London cannot support another restaurant like this," he raised his eyebrows. "French restaurants are rather passé." He did a poor imitation of a bank manager.

"That's not fair of him," she said making a face. "I fell in love with it the moment we arrived. It's so chic and typically French and wouldn't be out of place in a trendy quarter of Paris."

"Quite," Tim agreed. "Raymond certainly creates an impression."

"I'm sure that given time he'll prove his bank manager wrong."

"He didn't get an invitation to the launch party," Tim laughed.

"Were you invited?"

"Of course, I was here."

"So why didn't you invite me?" she grinned, wondering who had accompanied him.

"Well, you were away in Scotland."

Her face darkened and her fingers tightened around the stem of her glass. She put it down quickly before spilling its contents.

"I came here on my own," he continued, "I was asked to bring a friend but as you were away..."

"You should have invited that waitress from the coffee shop," she said forcing a smile.

When her hands had stopped shaking, she picked up her glass again and studied him over the rim. He caught her looking and when she smiled, he noticed that this time it did not reach her eyes.

"Well you know me, I'm always far too busy to be spending time with the fairer sex."

"That's probably going to be your undoing Timothy Granger. You spend far too much time in that gallery of yours. You should get out more often."

"Must be the entrepreneur in me," he grinned boyishly.

His mentioning Scotland brought it all back. Thoughts that she struggled to subdue threatened to resurface and suddenly her evening was in danger of being spoiled. Nightmares haunted her relentlessly, memories of the murdered woman chilled her to the bone and she would never forget the terror of being swept out to sea. She was vulnerable and far more unsettled than she was keen to admit. Tonight, however, she was not going to allow her demons to haunt her, she was determined to have a good time.

They chatted easily during the course of the evening covering a multitude of topics. Each time his conversation swung towards work she cleverly steered him away onto another subject. They toasted each other with a fine French wine and the food was perfect, much to her relief there was very little garlic.

"I sold two of your paintings today," he told her, unable to keep the news to himself any longer.

"Oh that's wonderful news," she exclaimed, "which ones?"

"The Cairngorm landscape and the view of the distillery."

She nodded, picturing them both in her head. She knew all of her paintings intimately, they were like children to her and occasionally she found it difficult to let them go. Tim laughed when she had told him this.

"Penny for them!" he said when she became quiet and reflective.

"I was just remembering how cold it was perched up on that mountain."

"You should have taken a photograph and worked in the comfort of your studio"

"Philistine," she smiled and the light in her eyes matched the sparkle from her glass.

He found her enchanting and could hardly believe his luck, especially when she agreed to come out to supper with him.

"Well, it was worth it because I managed to get a very good price for them both," he continued.

She was amazed when he told her how much she would receive from the sale, it was much more than she had anticipated.

"Well, I did warn you. As you become more popular the value of your paintings will soar."

"And I'm very grateful to you Tim," she smiled.

"I had better watch out because once other galleries get in on it they'll all be after your work."

"Don't be ridiculous." Her face flushed with colour and as she moved pain shot through her shoulder.

"Are you okay?" he was almost up on his feet.

"Yes, I'm fine, just caught a nerve," she rubbed her arm. "I'm a bit sore and it's been a long day. Excuse me Tim, I won't be long." She needed a few moments by herself.

He watched as she made her way elegantly between the tables. He had no idea what had happened in Scotland. Michael had said something about her falling in the mountains but did not tell him much and not wanting to pry into her business, he let the matter drop even though he suspected there was more to it than that.

Mr Mac was on his way. He crossed the Humber Bridge like a cold, unpleasant whirlwind heading towards the capital city of England.

The thought of London filled him with dread and his anger was difficult to contain. The only thing driving him on was the thought of Josie MacDonald and the things he was going to do when he arrived. He grinned, he was not thinking about seeing the sights.

Their evening was coming to an end and the restaurant was beginning to empty. Raymond joined them at their table; he was carrying a bottle of Calvados. He was a splendid host, doing his rounds he visited each table in turn and by the end of the evening had shared a 'digestif' with all of his guests, most of whom were friends anyway. This was an old custom he had brought with him from France and he was determined that it should continue.

When he spoke, Josie was enchanted by his accent and as he moved she breathed in his scent detecting the musk of his cologne. Strangely, it was a perfect blend, the tang of calvados and other aromas of his work made her smile, it was not an unpleasant experience.

Turning towards Tim, she could feel the effects of the wine, and sipping the calvados the sharp edges of her life were fettled even more. Tim was lovely she thought, and with a wicked grin wondered what he would be like in bed. Shocked by the sudden and brazen notion she realised that she must have had too much to drink.

The men were looking at her expectantly and she was relieved they could not read her thoughts.

"Sorry," her cheeks coloured. "I was miles away."

"I was just saying how much I admire you and your work," Raymond smooth talked. "You have a rare talent I think, a gift from God."

"Thank you," she whispered blushing even more, "you are so kind. I enjoy painting very much."

"It shows in your work. You are so fortunate to be able to express your passion so creatively."

Tim was beaming he was so pleased for her.

"You, mon ami are blessed," he said turning towards Tim. "You have such a beautiful and accomplished companion."

"I'll drink to that." Tim said raising his glass.

"Come, I have something to show you both." Raymond eased back her chair carefully before taking her arm. "Please permit me." Leading her across the floor, Tim followed in their wake.

In a small alcove, where an intimate table was hidden he proudly displayed one of her paintings. The first thing she noticed was the frame, Tim had done a wonderful job. Raymond was now the owner of her Cairngorms painting.

"C'est magnifique non?" he whispered before continuing in English. "I was born in a small village in the French Alps and this reminds me very much of my home."

"I had no idea," Josie whispered, "I'm glad you like it so much."

"I am your greatest fan."

"Where did you hang the other one?" Tim asked, interrupting their personal moment.

"The distillery, it hangs in my office. It too has great sentimental values; it reminds me of another of life's little pleasures." They laughed, sharing a private joke that Josie did not understand.

"Raymond is a great fan of single malts," Tim explained as they crowded into his small office.

"I always go to this place whenever I visit Scotland. So you see, your paintings are very special to me also."

He checked his watch. "Alors! The hour, it is very late and we have much to do." His expression became grave and very animated and Josie couldn't help but giggle behind her hand.

Raymond escorted them to the door where he showered Josie in continental kisses before making them promise to visit him again very soon.

Chapter

EIGHT

The telephone rang just as she was preparing a canvas.

"So, where were you last night?" he sounded angry. "Out with Tim bloody Granger I suppose!"

"Oh hi Mike and how are you?" she asked cordially before placing a hand on her hip.

"So, where were you?" he demanded.

"That's really none of your business."

He took a deep breath before going on. "I called round last night but of course you were out."

"I'm sorry Mike but there's no crime in that, besides, I don't have to ask your permission every time I want to go out." She carried the telephone into the living room and stopped by the window.

"So when can I see you?" He sounded like a spoilt child. This was something he did whenever he wanted his own way.

"I don't know, I've got quite a lot on at the moment," she said, knowing that was the wrong thing to say.

"You're not working so we could go out for lunch."

"I am working," she replied defensively, "I'm busy in my studio."

"That's not work," he sneered. "I don't call doodling with your paint box work, you can do that anytime. I want to see you for lunch."

Swallowing down her rage she stared out of the window and focussed on the cars parked along the street.

"Now just listen to me," she began sharply. "I'm busy today and you must respect that. I simply can't drop everything to go out with you."

"Can't or won't?" he was angry now. "You find time to go out with Granger."

Her heart began to beat faster and her grip tightened around the telephone. How did he know she was out with Tim? Then she realised it was probably guesswork on his part, he was just trying to annoy her. Well he was succeeding in that but what did it matter anyway. Frowning, she looked out at a man who was walking along the street. When he drew level with her he stopped and glanced up, they made eye contact and he grinned. Holding his stare, she was unable to look away but after a moment, he lowered his head and went on his way. She shuddered then continued with her argument.

Mike was still ranting but she was hardly listening. Unable to follow the logic of his argument she had heard enough.

"I'll live my life as I please," she told him firmly, interrupting his flow.

It was pointless arguing with him, all she wanted to do was get on with her work but now because of his abrasive remarks, she had lost her creative impulse. Arguing with Mike left her drained she hated confrontation of any kind.

He managed to invite himself round later that evening and she was furious with herself for allowing him to manipulate her in such a way. Sometimes it was easier just to give in, besides he possessed an amazing power of persuasion. Early in their relationship she had found this endearing. It amazed her how he always managed to get what he wanted, he made it seem so easy but now it was just annoying.

She had lost sight of the man in the street but he was still there watching her. He stood hidden, out of view behind a car and from his vantage point, he could see into her room. With much amusement, he saw her stamp her feet in anger then she threw the telephone down in frustration. She excited him, such fire such passion and he could hardly wait. After a while, she seemed to regain control of her emotions and crouching down picked the phone up from the floor. Finally, she moved away from the window and he was left thinking about the first time he had set eyes on her; that had been in Spey Bay. He grinned and licked his lips. Mr Mac had arrived.

Several hours later, he was still there waiting for her to emerge. Eventually she appeared hesitating on the doorstep and pushing her hand into her pocket, checked to see that she had her keys before closing the door firmly behind her.

Waving to a neighbour, she began to walk quickly along the footpath.

At the end of the street she turned the corner and disappeared from view, only then did he leave his car.

She was a little way ahead when he reached the corner so settling easily into her stride he matched her pace. He studied her as she walked, the way her hair lifted in the breeze, the swing of her hips, the angle at which she held her chin and especially how she moved, all of these things pleased him.

His plan had seemed simple; pop down to London, locate Josie MacDonald, abduct her then return to Scotland. There he would have his fun until he grew bored then kill her. He liked that plan but soon realised it would not be that simple. He would have to observe her movements, learn her schedule. There was no point in blundering straight in especially as he was having such fun simply watching her.

She stopped in front of him and glanced back. She didn't acknowledge him, her gaze passing straight through him he might as well be invisible. This both pleased and annoyed him in equal measure but no matter, of one thing he was certain, she would acknowledge him long before he was finished.

Hunching his shoulders, he thrust his hands into his pockets and walked on by. She stepped back on the pavement to wait for a bus and as he passed he breathed in her scent then his imagination ran riot. He had to be careful he didn't want to enrage the voices in his head, not yet anyway.

Peering back along the road he could see the bus coming and was seized by indecision, he had to decide what to do next. Should he leg it to the next stop or follow her onto the bus? He decided to wait.

The bus stopped and the doors hissed open as if carried on a cushion of air. Josie got on and told the driver where she wanted to go. This was the first time Mr Mac had heard her voice and it thrilled him even more. Following her onto the bus, he repeated her destination. Most of the seats were empty so making his way to the back he settled where he had a clear view.

The sound of her voice kept running through his mind, he closed his eyes and grinned. He must remain calm so pushing his fantasies to one side he reached into his pocket and pulled out a book of maps. Opening the pages, he soon found their destination. It appeared to be a built up area, shops he guessed, typical of the city. Following the coloured line with his finger, he discovered that it ran beside what appeared to be a park. Memorising the street names and the layout of the area he looked up, their stop was only a short distance away.

The bus pulled up at the Memorial Park and he waited calmly as Josie got off, then he continued to follow. Remaining hidden amongst the crowd, he moved with the tide across the park and not once did he take his eyes off her. Suddenly she waved her hand above her head and quickened her pace. She met up with a fair-haired girl who laughed joyously at something Josie said. He was too far away to hear what they were saying so putting his head down he pushed through the crowd and managed to get ahead.

Their voices rose cheerily above the din of the city and slowing his pace, he allowed them to regain the lead and, as they passed, he caught their scent. His mind began to work feverishly, ideas turning over in his brain at an alarming rate left his head in a spin.

Suddenly he realised what he was going to do and with the shock of it, he failed to spot the obstacle in his path. A beggar was sitting on the ground with his back against the railings and Mr Mac, not watching where he was going, tripped over the man's legs kicking a hat full of coins all over the path. The beggar shouted, swearing expertly, and Mr Mac not wanting to draw attention recovered quickly and blended back into the crowd.

Panic almost overwhelmed him, he had lost sight of them, they were no longer in the crowd and glancing desperately above the sea of heads, he realised that none of them belonged to Josie MacDonald. Scanning further ahead, he managed to locate them moments before they disappeared into a brightly coloured shop called 'The Art Workshop'.

"Tim's going to arrange an exhibition and he wants me to complete as many paintings as I can."

"Wow, that's fantastic," Sarah replied enthusiastically, cupping her mug with both hands. "So when is this all going to happen?"

Mr Mac was surprised when he entered the shop, he expected it to be full of artist's supplies, what he did not expect to find was a café. Slipping in unnoticed, he ordered a strong black coffee before settling at a table close to where they were sitting.

"What does Mike think about you spending so much time with Tim?"

Josie rolled her eyes and tossed her head. "He keeps pestering me, he simply refuses to accept the fact that we're finished. I can't imagine how I became so involved with him in the first place."

"Something to do with him being tall, rich and handsome," Sarah remarked dryly.

Josie told her about their argument on the telephone and Mr Mac listened but allowed most of their conversation to drift over his head.

He did however, make mental notes of names and places as they came up.

From time to time he glanced up from the leaflet that he was pretending to read. He was attracted to Josie's friend, there was something about her that fascinated him and he found the sound of her laughter appealing.

Another plan was beginning to take shape in his head, a plan that was even more audacious than the one before. Why had he not thought of this before? He was certainly going to have some fun if he could pull it off. Gradually, as he thought it through, it all began to click into place then he knew exactly what he was going to do. Josie MacDonald was going to regret ever having met him; he was determined to make her life hell before he even got his hands on her.

Smiling into his coffee mug, he took a deep breath and savoured the bitter aroma. Oh yes, he promised himself, he was going to have some fun and it was going to start with this one, the girl whose name was Sarah.

Their laughter brought him back to reality.

"We're all meeting up tonight then, has it been arranged?"

"Yes, both Lizzie and Lindsay are up for it, we're meeting at Paul's Place."

Josie frowned, looking blankly at her friend.

"You know, Abingdon Hall."

"Oh yes how silly of me, I know where you mean."

"Are you staying at mine after?"

"I'm not sure, maybe. I've loads of work to do so I might go straight home. I'll pop some things in an overnight bag and drop it round though just in case."

Their conversation went on for a while longer as they discussed their domestic arrangements and Mr Mac could hardly contain his excitement. Finally, they drained their mugs and headed for the door then, paying for their drinks at the counter they left the shop.

Consulting his book of maps, he studied the index and after a while he gazed vacantly across the room. He was satisfied that his plan was going to work, at least for now it all seemed clear. Pleased with himself, he ordered another mug of coffee.

Chapter

NINE

Abingdon Hall was an old red-bricked mansion that had been built in a grander time, and whoever had commissioned it was rich enough to afford the best. Standing alone in the middle of the city it was now an up market nightclub. A wide gravel driveway, that could have once been a moat, swept majestically between rhododendrons and ornamental trees, the shrubs carefully planted to act as screens blocked out most of the surrounding noise.

Mr Mac, hidden from view, watched as a line of vehicles circumnavigated the building, each one offloading its cargo of young people in front of the grand main entrance. Thick necked, smartly dressed door attendants went about their business checking bags and occasionally asking for identification.

He began to wonder if he would actually see Josie MacDonald and her friends. There were scores of young people milling about, all converging on the same spot. He checked his watch, it was later than he thought, he had been there for over two hours before realising that he must have missed them. They would already be inside by now so he decided to head back to his car; they would not emerge until after midnight.

Much later the line of vehicles began to return, this time he would have to be more careful. Standing in the same spot as before, it was not long before he spotted them, the sound of their laughter giving them away. They were moving slowly away from the nightclub entrance with a group of others, and scanning them carefully he caught a glimpse of

Josie. They were too far away for him to hear what they were saying but, as they drew closer, he watched as she climbed into the back of the taxi with her friend Sarah.

Dashing back to his car he just had enough time to start the engine and pull out as the cab drove past. Following it through the streets, he was careful not to get too close or lose sight of it in the traffic. Eventually it swung off the main road and stopped in a quiet, well lit street.

He pulled up beside the curb just in time to see Sarah climb out. She strolled unsteadily towards her front door and Mr Mac watched as she turned to wave at Josie. The cab driver waited for a few moments longer and only when she was safely inside did he pull away.

Mr Mac was left alone to hunt and as he watched the house where Sarah lived, lights on the ground floor came on. After a while a light appeared in an upstairs window and he saw her draw the curtains across the glass. Fifteen minutes later the light went and the house was plunged into darkness, then his heart began to beat faster. Checking his watch the illuminated hands indicated 01-45; he would wait thirty minutes before making his move.

The street was silent, nothing stirred, not even a cat prowled in the shadows so, leaving his car, Mr Mac slipped along the narrow pathway that took him past the front door. Turning to his right his rubber soled shoes made no sound as he slipped along a passageway that ran between the house and a high brick wall, and using a thin pencil light to guide his way he melted into the shadows.

Not far along the alley he located a side door and surveying the wooden frame he checked the brickwork surrounding it. The door itself was made up of a simple construction, a large single thickness glass sheet held in place by a thick wooden frame. This would be his point of entry.

Shining his light through the glass he could make out a compact kitchen and grunting with satisfaction dumped his bag down and snapped on a pair of latex gloves. From his bag he pulled out a sharp knife and a roll of sticky backed plastic then expertly cut a piece to suit the size of the panel. Peeling off the plastic backing, he stuck it carefully to the glass and with a small hammer shattered the window. This was his preferred method of breaking into a property, forcing a lock or smashing down the door was crude and left the police in no doubt of an unauthorised entry. This way the broken window could be explained away providing he was careful not to leave any clues. Tonight however, he was going to leave the police a mystery to solve.

He wanted them to suspect that someone had kidnapped the young woman that lived here.

Working in silence, he pulled the plastic sheet and shattered glass away from the door before lowering it carefully to the ground then he picked out a few sharp edges that remained in the frame. Wriggling through the gap he stood silently in the kitchen listening to the noises of the house and using his torch, he played his thin light around searching for clues. He wanted to know if she lived alone or with someone else, he found no evidence to support a partner.

Making his way along the short passageway that separated the front of the house from the kitchen he began to climb. Two stairs creaked as he ascended and on the landing at the top he found three doors. The first he guessed correctly opened into a bathroom, the second led to the front of the house where she was sleeping and pressing his ear up against the door, he could hear the muffled sound of her breathing. He checked out the final room but did not expect to find it occupied. Flashing his light around he found a small overnight bag belonging to Josie MacDonald. Picking it up he pulled back the zip and slipped his hand inside. The fabric of her nightdress was soft against his fingers and he considered taking it with him but he decided to leave it so, returning it to the bag, he made his way back towards the master bedroom. Pushing lightly against the door it slipped open and as silently as a ghost, he went into Sarah's room.

The air inside was heavy with fumes, a sweet combination of alcohol and perfume that was not unpleasant. Moving towards the bed he found her curled up under a duvet and silently pulling back the cover let it slide to the floor. Yellow light from the streetlamp outside the window cast an eerie glow around the room but it was sufficient for him to see.

She was lying on her side with her long bare legs curled up to her chin. Her hair, fanned out like silk over the pillow partially framed her face and as she slept and she resembled an innocent child. Leaning closer he breathed in her scent. She smelt good, sweet and warm and he could detect the pleasant coconut fragrance of her hair.

She didn't feel the sting of the needle as it passed through her skin. She was going to have a headache when she woke up he thought, then carefully returning the syringe to its case he pushed it back into his pocket. Frowning, he wondered if he had given her too much. He had no way of telling how much alcohol she had consumed. Shrugging off the thought, he gripped his pencil light between his teeth and lifted her from her bed.

She was lighter than he anticipated and her head lolled against his shoulder as he moved. Going from the room he quickly descended the stairs and at the bottom dumped her on the carpet, propping her up against the wall whilst he unlocked the door. Easing it open, he checked the way ahead before dashing out to his car. He unlocked the door and opened the boot lid before returning for the girl.

Lowering her into the luggage compartment he closed the lid before going back to the house to pick up his bag. He made a final check overlooking nothing then, slipping the deadlock he closed the door behind him before making his way calmly to his car. Thirty seconds later he left the street and pulled out onto the main road. There was no traffic at this early hour, no one to witness him leaving.

Chapter

TEN

When Josie finally woke it was mid morning, her head was jabbering like a troop of monkeys and her throat was as dry as gin. Her shoulder aggravated her mercilessly, she must have been lying awkwardly and with a groan, rolled out of bed asking herself if it had been worth it. Her recollections of the night before were a little vague but she was certain they must have had a good time. It would take several cups of coffee before she would be able to face the world.

Later that morning she telephoned Sarah and after several rings, her answer phone clicked in.

"Still in bed?" Josie said, talking to the machine. "I'll be calling round later so get the coffee pot going." Glancing up at the clock on the wall she was appalled, most of the morning was gone already. 'May as well have stayed over,' she thought.

Suddenly she was startled as the doorbell rang, so making her way into the hall she stopped to check herself in the mirror before opening the door.

"Hi Mike," she said, smiling sweetly at him.

"Thought I'd just turn up as you're clearly avoiding me," he glared at her. "I was under the impression that we'd arranged to meet up last night. I called round but you weren't in."

"Ah, I'm so sorry about that." Her mind working overtime was searching for a plausible excuse. "Girl problems, you understand?"

Pushing past her he forced his way into her home leaving Josie standing on the step fuming, she counted to ten before closing the door.

"I'm sorry Mike. Sarah had a problem so I went round to help her out."

She hated herself for the lie and realised that her excuse sounded a bit lame. Bracing herself, she was desperate to avoid another confrontation.

"We're going out for Sunday lunch." He told her throwing himself down on the sofa.

"I'll go and get changed then." She was annoyed but there was no point in arguing. Clearly he was in one of his moods and she could hardly blame him.

"Don't keep me waiting long," he growled.

"Damn, damn, damn, damn!" She stamped up the stairs.

After a while, he became restless and heaving himself up off the sofa went into her studio. He was shocked by what he saw, the place was a mess it was in total contrast to the rest of the house which she kept immaculate.

"How the hell can she work in here?" he asked himself turning his nose up.

Stepping over canvasses that were piled high on the floor he headed towards the window where an easel had been set up in the bay. Clearly, a painting was in progress. He stared at it and moving backwards tilted his head to one side. Screwing his eyes up as she had told him to do when studying paintings, he could not decide if it was a landscape or seascape. A river flowed across the canvas from left to right, the water looking convincingly cold. Coarse grassland swept from centre to top and away into perspective, the colours merging cleverly into the distant mountains. The foreground was yet to be completed and it took him a while to work out what it was that she was trying to achieve. The painting seemed to be from a seaward perspective with a view inland towards the mouth of a river. The picture gave the impression of a view from the surface of the water. It was certainly unusual and he could see the shape of a fallen tree being swept along by some unseen current. It had no colour at all and was depicted in simple shades of grey with finger-like branches all pointing towards the sky.

He did not think much of it at all, in his opinion this was not one of her better paintings. She was using thickly applied oils, usually she worked in watercolour preferring gentle colours and techniques. It was so unlike her, this was completely out of character, she was known for her delicate brushwork.

Moving in closer for a better look, he could make out the ghostly outline of a figure standing on the riverbank but he couldn't tell if it were male or female, the details were not yet complete.

"There you are." The sound of her voice startled him. "So where are we going?"

"I thought a traditional Sunday lunch at a good old country pub."

"Bit of a journey then," she was not feeling up to a long trip.

"Not far, it won't take long." Annoyingly, he rattled the car keys in his pocket and he glared at her. "You really must clean this place up it looks as if you've been burgled."

Standing her ground, she resisted the urge to make a comment, what was the point it would only start another argument.

Mr Mac stopped once to re-fuel. There had been no movement from the boot of his car but as a precaution he parked well away from the other vehicles in the car park, then he went in search of strong coffee.

By the middle of the afternoon he finally arrived at his destination, a remote part of Scotland overlooking Spey Bay. His was an old and imposing house nestling comfortably amongst acres of fields, forest and glen. This was his legacy, the spoils of many generations of successful ancestry. He was the last of the line and unfortunately did not inherit the gene that had made his forebears wealthy.

Steering his car along the wide gravel driveway he stopped at the foot of a sweeping stone staircase and turned off the engine. He was exhausted, and rubbing his face with the palm of his hand, he groaned loudly. The stress of the long distance drive and the abduction of the girl had taken more out of him than he would have guessed. After a moment of reflective silence, he dragged himself from the car and breathed in deeply. The sweet highland air filling his lungs made him smile, this more than compensated for the foul air he had been forced to endure in London.

Strolling to the rear of the car he released the boot lid and a cloud of stale air tinged with the sharp stench of urine and vomit rose up to greet him. Growling with disgust, he poked her sharply with his fingertips.

Her legs were still folded knees to chin and she was hugging herself tightly with both arms. She groaned and stirred as the cool air flooded into the cramped space then, raising her head, blinked rapidly as the bright light assaulted her eyes.

Reaching in he grabbed hold of her and hoisting her violently from the car dumped her unceremoniously onto the gravel. She cried out in agony as the muscles in her legs cramped, and stretching her limbs in an attempt to ease her pain shards of gravel ground into her hip. After a few moments, the cramp began to ease and she was able to move into a more comfortable position. Sitting up she leaned back against the car and tried to work out where she was but it was no good, the throbbing inside her head was relentless and lights flashed each time she closed her eyes. This was aggravated by the brilliance of the day.

She was aware of the man standing just a short distance away and could feel him watching her. She could not see him clearly, the light behind him made him appear like a silhouette. It was then she realised that she was wearing nothing more than a flimsy nightdress, this only added to her confusion and discomfort.

"Where am I?" she asked shading her eyes with her hand. Her mouth was dry and her words rasped at the back of her throat. "What am I doing here?"

He ignored her questions and she wondered if he had actually heard.

"Who are you?" she tried again, louder this time.

Remaining silent, he moved slowly casting a shadow over her then suddenly without warning he reached out and hauled her to her feet. The flimsy fabric of her nightdress ripped revealing her shoulder and crying out she staggered back against the car.

"What do you think you are doing, why are you doing this to me?"

He continued to ignore her and she groaned with the effort of standing.

The knot forming in the pit of her stomach became stronger until it overwhelmed her then her legs gave out and she collapsed to the floor. This did nothing to ease her nerves and she dry retched into the gravel. She was close to fainting and the hammering inside her head refused to stop. Fear and confusion swept over her in waves, and troubled by so many unanswered questions it all too much. All she wanted to do was lay down and rest but forcing herself to look up she discovered that she was alone. It took a huge effort to remain calm, so breathing deeply she concentrated on clearing her head. She had to discover what was happening.

He soon returned and her stress levels began to soar as he moved towards her. He dumped the bucket that he was carrying down on the ground and water slopped over the rim then he pulled her to her feet. It was all she could do to remain upright as he pushed her along the side of the car, and drawing level with the rear door, he forced her head into the luggage compartment.

"You can clean up that bloody mess," he shouted.

She had no idea what he meant and his heavy Scottish accent was confusing.

Forcing her head even lower, he almost wiped the carpet with her face and as stale acrid fumes filled her nose, she gagged.

"Clean it up," he hissed menacingly into her ear.

Her world turned black and she collapsed against him.

Much later, the darkness surrounding her began to clear and the first thing she became aware of was the ache in her arms. Moving to ease her pain, she lurched from one nightmare to another.

Her arms, stretched out above her head, were taking her weight and cold metal bands attached to her wrists cut cruelly into her skin. She opened her eyes and as they became accustomed to the light, she could make out lengths of chain secured to rings sunk into the walls and each time she moved the links made dull metallic sounds. Her ankles had been secured in the same way and looking around she groaned. She was in some kind of a cellar or cell like dungeon. The brick walls had been white washed and there was a single light bulb strung from the ceiling, it was barely sufficient to illuminate the corners of the room but it was enough to reveal the horrors of her surroundings. She counted three more sets of chains hanging menacingly from the walls then she groaned again.

She had no idea where she was or why this was happening and it was all she could do to remain calm. Her heart was beating madly against her ribs and she considered screaming very loudly, but then she remembered the man who had done this to her. Fears that she had experienced earlier threatened to return and as she struggled, the rough steel manacles pinched the skin from her wrists. Tears of frustration spilled from the corners of her eyes and rolled unchecked over her cheeks, she was alone and terrified.

Suddenly he was there. Moving confidently into the centre of the room he stopped and stared at her.

"Who are you?" she sobbed. "Why are you doing this to me?"

Folding his arms across his chest, he studied her then he grinned and licked his lips.

"Where am I?" she tried again. "What's going on here?"

Very slowly, he began to move towards her and she could feel her panic begin to rise. Pushing back against the wall all she wanted to do was run but the chains held her firmly in place. The pain in her wrists was unbearable and now she could hardly feel her fingers.

Stopping in front of her he reached out and traced a line over her face with his fingertips and all the while he remained silent, his face almost expressionless. She was convinced that he was a mad man and tears spilling from the corners of her eyes ran freely over her cheeks.

He continued to stare, the effect that he was having on her pleased him immensely and as he studied her pale, drawn face, he could almost taste her fear.

Squealing loudly, she turned her head away and the chains rattled, she had to move in order to relieve the pain in her wrists. Without warning he grabbed her chin and forced her head round so she was facing him, then he moved his fingers over her cheeks again drawing a pattern over her lips. This time she didn't move, holding herself rigid as he moved his hands down over her throat. She could hardly believe that this was happening, maybe if she refused to look at him he would disappear and she would wake up from this nightmare.

The touch of his fingers against her skin appalled her and she could not stop trembling. He was standing so close now that she could feel his breath hot against her skin and she shuddered, then without warning he grabbed the torn neck of her nightdress and in a single movement ripped it from her.

Crying out her legs gave way and she almost blacked out. The pain in her wrists was unbearable and willing her legs to respond, she found it quite impossible to hold herself up by her arms alone. Her breaths were coming in short gasps and she moaned with the effort and the shock, she could hardly believe that this was happening. The humiliation of standing there naked in front of him sent her mind into turmoil and she imagined all kinds of horrors. In her state of panic it was a while before she realised that she was alone, he had left the room.

Gradually her heart rate began to return to normal and she could breathe more easily. She remained as still as possible even the smallest of movements sent shock waves through her body. She soon discovered that by distributing her weight evenly between her legs she could stand in relative comfort. It was, however, difficult to remain in this position for long because her legs were spread so wide apart.

Cold from the concrete floor seeped into the soles of her feet turning them to blocks of ice and she could feel the blood draining from her arms. In an effort to keep the circulation going in her hands she wriggled her fingers constantly. Her head was still aching but was not as intense as it had been before and now she was able to go over the events leading up to this moment. The last thing she could remember was going out with Josie, the taxi had dropped her off at home and she could vaguely remember climbing into bed. The rest was a blank, she had no idea how she had ended up here. He was on his way back, she could hear him coming and her stomach lurched again.

He entered the room and casually placed a bucket of water in the middle of the floor, and remaining where he stood he stared at her. After what seemed and age he suddenly lifted the bucket and in a single movement threw the contents over her. Water hit her like a solid wall of ice, it threw her back against the wall and pain like bolts of lightning shot through her body, her legs buckled and mercifully, she passed out.

Chapter

ELEVEN

After lunch Josie persuaded Mike to drive her to Sarah's house. She was worried, she had telephoned her friend three times from the pub but still there was no answer.

"Stop fussing," he moaned, "she's probably gone out." His patience was wearing thin as he failed to gain her undivided attention.

Mike stopped the car outside the house and immediately Josie noticed that curtains were still drawn across the windows.

"It's not like her to be in bed at this time of day."

"Some party," he sneered. "Just how much did she have to drink last night or did she bring some bloke home?"

Ignoring his comments, Josie pulled off her seat belt and climbed from the car. Rushing across the road she made her way along the little pathway leading to the front door but when she rang the bell there was no reply. Peering through the letterbox, she called out her name but still there was no answer.

Josie was becoming increasingly worried and as she made her way round to the side of the house she glanced back towards Mike. He was standing by his car looking bored, obviously in no mood to help and irritated by his attitude she hurried off along the passageway.

Broken pieces of glass stuck to some kind of plastic sheeting were on the ground beside the backdoor. At first, she had no idea where it had come from but then she noticed the door. The whole glass panel was missing and her sense of unease turned to dread. Clearly someone had broken into Sarah's house.

"Mike," she called out, "Mike, come here quickly."

"What now?" He appeared at the end of the passageway. "What the..." He saw the broken panel.

Without waiting Josie reached in and unfastened the door.

"Josie don't go in there," he called out but it was too late. Swearing under his breath, he ran along the passageway as she disappeared into the house.

Following her into the kitchen he could hear her going up the stairs so, rushing after her he took them two at a time and reaching the top turned towards the open bedroom door.

"She's not here," Josie appeared in front of him. "Her bed looks like it's been slept in though."

"Then she must have gone out earlier."

"How do you explain the glass in the back door? Besides her purse and mobile phone are still here," she indicated to where Sarah had dumped her bag, the contents spilled all over the floor.

"She wouldn't have gone out without her phone. I'm calling the police." Pulling her phone from her pocket, she moved away from him.

"What?" he glared at her, "you must be mad. Call her friends first, there has to be an explanation."

"Something horrible has happened, can't you see?" she screamed at him in frustration. "How can you be so insensitive?"

The look she gave him made him feel like a villain.

"You can do what you like, I'm out of here." Pushing past her, he thundered down the stairs.

She could hardly believe it, how could he leave at a moment like this. With trembling fingers she called the emergency services.

Sarah was shivering, her body temperature had dropped, she was exhausted and sick with shock. She realised that she must have been drugged that would explain her dry mouth and dehydration and why her head was pounding mercilessly. Moving carefully she distributed her weight more evenly, bending her knees a little in an attempt to work some warmth into her limbs, then suddenly the door swung open and Mr Mac entered.

He was carrying a small folding table, a bottle of spring water and a digital camera. His movements were deliberate and businesslike and he ignored her, it was as if she was not there at all.

Setting up his table, he placed the objects on top before clasping his hands behind his back then he turned to look at her. He studied her for a few moments and she could feel his eyes feasting on her. She would not allow him the satisfaction of seeing her humiliated, so concentrating her efforts on breathing she did her best to remain calm.

"Hello my bonnie one," he said cheerfully as if he were passing the time of day.

She remained silent.

Picking up the bottle of water he unscrewed the top and tossing it across the floor he moved towards her.

"Look at me," he commanded. The tone of his voice made her do as she was told.

"Refreshments first I think."

Forcing her head back, he upended the bottle and poured cool spring water into her mouth, he did not let up until she began to choke. Water ran out of her mouth and over her chin, her throat working as she struggled to keep up with the flow. She knew she had to drink as much as possible.

When the bottle was empty, he stood back leaving her gasping for air. Unconcerned he returned to the table where he carefully placed the empty bottle down.

"Now," he began, turning to face her. "Some questions."

"Who are you and why are you doing this to me?" she gasped.

"I don't think you quite understand," he said calmly. "I will ask the questions and you will answer."

She stared at him incredulously.

"Let's start with some easy ones. What's your name?"

"Sarah."

Of course, he knew that, he was just testing her. "Sarah what?" he growled.

"Hamilton."

"So Sarah Hamilton it's nice to see you," he grinned. "In fact it's very nice to see all of you." He chuckled at his own little joke and she looked away, hiding her shame.

"My name," he paused. "Would you like to know my name Sarah Hamilton?"

She did not reply.

"Well for your information my name is Mr Mac," he paused again as if expecting her to say something.

Tears began to run freely over her pale cheeks.

"I take it you're not keen to make my acquaintance?" He feigned hurt.

Slowly he began to pace back and forth across the room, talking as easily as if they were enjoying tea in his parlour then suddenly his questioning changed tack.

"You know Josie MacDonald?" he sneered accusingly. It was as if her name was something foul on his tongue.

Sarah frowned.

"What does Josie MacDonald do?" he stepped up beside her and pushed his face into hers.

His dull eyes terrified her and she knew then what it was like to look into the face of a mad man.

"Well?" he demanded.

"I don't understand."

He glared at her menacingly and she almost cried out.

"For a living, what does she do for a living?"

"She's a teacher," Sarah whispered.

"Not an artist then?" his eyes narrowed and he stood back.

"An artist?" she frowned. "No, painting is her hobby." She failed to tell him that her friend was accomplished enough to earn a meagre living from her hobby.

"I see," he said quietly before moving away.

Distracted by his own thoughts he turned back towards her and reaching out traced his finger over her cheek, drawing it down over her shoulder. He hardly noticed her discomfort or the way she trembled as his hand continued to move over her breast.

Rigid with shock she hardly dared move but after a short time, he seemed to lose interest and backed away. Breathing a sigh of relief more tears spilled over her cheeks. She could hardly believe that this was happening and as she stared at him, she hated him even more. Why was he so interested in Josie, her mind began to work, what was her connection with this mad man?

"Give me a name," he shouted and she was startled.

He moved towards her again with astonishing speed and she closed her eyes expecting the worst.

"A name," he hissed.

Sarah hesitated and suddenly she realised the consequence of his demands.

"Well," he glared, his face inches from hers.

"Michael Cowper-Smith." Was the first name that came into her head.

"Your girl-friends," he growled his breath hot against her face.

She was trembling and feeling nauseous, the implications were unimaginable. Whom could she betray? One of her friends would probably end up suffering the same or worse.

The voices in his head were just distant whispers but they were there all the same. Moving his head to one side he could not make out what it was they were saying, he didn't want to know anyway because for now he was in control. He wanted to enjoy this young woman, have her all to himself. He could play his games and live out his fantasies. He knew that when the voices finally arrived he would have to do their bidding and he shuddered.

The blow took her completely by surprise, driving the breath from her body it left her in agony. The ground tilted beneath her feet and the chains around her wrists gnawed relentlessly at her flesh but this was secondary to the fire that raged within her belly. Gradually her head began to clear and she was left gasping, her heart thundering wildly inside her chest, and slowly her eyesight began to return.

Thrusting himself up against her his tongue flashed from between his lips and he licked the tears from her face. He could taste their saltiness then he took her earlobe between his teeth and nibbled softly.

Sarah hardly dared to move for fear of reprisal, she was shocked and filled with disgust. He was a devil and she was helpless to his demands.

"My mother always told me never to hit a girl in the stomach." He whispered, caressing her neck and shoulder.

She wanted to vomit, the sensation growing even more intense as he worked his way lower nibbling at her skin. She could do nothing to stop him, he was leaving bite marks on her neck and she wanted to scream.

He began to fondle her breast roughly, it was more than she could endure and as she cried out he suddenly stopped.

"Later," he promised his face a mask that was full of lust.

His mood changed abruptly and reaching for the camera that was standing on the small table, he turned to face her.

"Watch the birdie," he chuckled as he began to take pictures.

Josie was standing alone at the gate and she was fuming. Mike's behaviour was unforgivable, clearly he was not concerned about Sarah and the more she thought about it the more frustrated she became. He had never shown any interest in her friends, it was always his circle that she was expected to move in. Taking a deep breath, she struggled with her emotions.

It was not long before the police arrived and immediately she began to feel better. At least now something would be done to help find Sarah and solve the riddle that she was facing.

A woman police officer took Josie into the house leaving her colleague to investigate the broken glass by the back door.

"When did you last see Miss Hamilton?" she began.

Josie told her about the previous evening at the nightclub.

"So you returned here in the early hours?"

"Yes," Josie confirmed, "it must have been about 1 o'clock. The taxi dropped Sarah off first before taking me home."

"You saw her enter the house?"

"Oh yes, the driver was very good, he waited until she was safely inside before driving away."

"Did you notice anything unusual, was there anyone acting suspiciously or waiting nearby for example?"

Josie told her that she had not seen anything out of the ordinary.

"Okay." The police officer scribbled in her notebook. "Can you show me Sarah's bedroom."

The room was a mess, this was typical of Sarah but through the chaos Josie was able to confirm that nothing seemed amiss. At first, the police officer did not enter the room she simply remained standing in the doorway taking in the scene.

Sarah's bag was on the floor with some of its contents spilled out around it then she noticed a mobile phone on the table beside the bed.

"Was her phone on the dressing table or on the floor?"

"It was by her bag. I'm afraid I picked it up."

"Did you check it for messages?"

"No I didn't look. I picked it up on impulse I guess."

The police officer nodded then began to examine it. She checked the inbox for texts and looked at the incoming and outgoing calls. The messages had come from friends during the previous couple of days and Josie was able to confirm their identities.

They went methodically around the room looking in drawers and cupboards and all the time chatting about Sarah. The police officer had an easy way about her and Josie was happy to give an accurate description of her friend including examples of her habits.

It was looking less likely to be a burglary nothing seemed to be missing. Josie provided a list of their friends and Sarah's phone confirmed their telephone numbers.

"We will naturally check with her family and friends first but I'll get a Scenes of Crime Officer down here to check out the back door."

Josie pointed out what she had touched, she also told them that the door was locked when she arrived, she had opened it herself.

"We will also arrange to have the property secured, it will be done by a local glazier who will probably replace the panel in the door or at least board it up."

Josie agreed to remain at the house until the other officers arrived and the door repaired. At least she would be there if Sarah returned.

Resisting the urge to scream and keep on screaming Sarah felt as if she was drowning in some kind of terrifying nightmare. She had never experienced anything like this before and desperately wanted to wake up.

He had finished taking his pictures and she was left feeling even more violated. She tried desperately to make sense of it all, she needed to understand what was going on and why this was happening. He had asked so many questions and his interest in Josie was confusing. What did she have to do with this?

The mad man had spoken with a Scottish accent so perhaps the connection with Josie lay in her recent trip to Scotland. She had said very little on her return and even less about her accident. Her injuries were still something of a mystery, explained vaguely away. She had mentioned having a fall when in the highlands but had been very reluctant to elaborate. The more she thought about it the more bizarre it became.

Suddenly she realised that she must be in Scotland, the thought stunned her and she wondered if it could be true. Focussing her mind, she began to piece together the events. It was obvious that she was no longer in the city because outside she had been aware of a chill in the air. It was refreshing and clear, sweeter than the air in London.

Perhaps it was a coincidence that he spoke with a Scottish accent. How could she possibly be in Scotland, hundreds of miles from London? She had no idea how long she had been in the boot of his car but she realised it would have taken hours to drive up. Thoughts raged around inside her head until she thought it might explode.

She had obviously been drugged, time was just a hazy period of semi-consciousness spent cramped in the darkened luggage space of his car. She had no way of telling what time of the day it was, and groaning loudly she moved in an effort to find a more comfortable position. She thought about Mr Mac and shuddered, he was a monster who seemed so unpredictable.

Sarah was sure that he was going to rape her, it was only a matter of time. She closed her eyes and tried to push the thought from her mind, then thinking about Josie, her eyes flew open as she imagined all kinds of scenarios. Maybe that is how Josie came by her injuries. Sarah shuddered at the thought and could not believe it was true, Josie would have confided in her. A host of horrors entered her head but she refused to believe any of it. Why was he so interested in Josie?

A noise startled her; he was back.

"Now," he began as if addressing a group of work colleagues. "Give me the name of one of your girlfriends." He moved towards her aggressively.

"No," she screamed. "Please don't hurt me again." She sounded pathetic and it irritated her enormously. How could she be so weak?

"Lizzie Baines," she blurted out devastated by her vulnerability. She hated herself and loathed her inability to endure more discomfort.

"Lizzie Baines." He said rolling the name off his tongue. "A pretty wee thing is she?" He stopped pacing and stared at her. "Does Josie MacDonald know this Lizzie Baines?"

Sarah nodded but remained tight lipped.

"Good," he smiled. "Describe her."

"Red hair, green eyes, quite tall..."

"Enough," he snapped. He recognised the girl from her description, he had seen her before in London.

"Address," he demanded.

She told him through clenched teeth and when he left Sarah was devastated. Her imagination went wild as she considered the consequences of her weakness.

After a while, her tears evaporated and emotionally drained, she changed position again. She was in agony, even the smallest movements sent jarring bolts of discomfort through her spine, so arranging her legs she tipped her hips forward and managed to relieve her suffering for a while at least. Such was her depression it was as if she deserved the pain, justification for betraying her friend.

Later when he returned his mood was buoyant and he smiled pleasantly. He brought with him a bucket of steaming hot water and Sarah eyed him suspiciously.

"I've checked the information you gave me. It seems you've been a good girl." He paused to stroke her cheek with the back of his hand.

Absentmindedly he drew his fingers through her hair and she held her breath hardly daring to move. Closing her eyes in an effort to remain calm the urge to scream was almost overpowering and she could not stop her body from trembling. The touch of his hand against her skin disgusted her and it seemed an age before finally he moved away.

"As you've been so co-operative I've decided to be nice to you." He turned back towards her again and she let out a gasp.

For the first time he noticed her eyes, they were red rimmed and wild, hardly windows to her soul. She was just like the others he thought, they were all the same. Her face was as pale as alabaster, her exhaustion plain. The satisfaction of feeling her squirm every time he touched her excited him and he grinned. Josie MacDonald will suffer through this girl.

"I'm going away for a wee while," he confided and reaching into his pocket he produced a key. Moving up close he unlocked the shackles that held her wrists.

She cried out in agony as her arms fell like dead weights to her sides. Kneeling down in front of her, he unfastened her left ankle but ignored the other, leaving her tethered to a length of chain.

Sarah collapsed onto the cold concrete floor and curled up into a protective ball. Life returned to her fingers as blood rushed into her hands and her muscles cramped violently. Gritting her teeth as the discomfort took hold she sobbed and waited for the sensation to pass.

"Clean yourself up," he said, indicating to the bucket of hot water then he left her alone.

When he was gone she moved slowly, relieved to be stretching her muscles. Easing the cramp as best she could it wasn't long before she could move her fingers again.

The bucket of warm water was heavenly it helped to renew her strength and its warmth cleansed away some of her physical discomfort, silently she wept.

Sometime later he returned with a blanket which he draped carefully over her shoulders. He left bottles of spring water and a bag of apples.

He didn't utter a word or even look at her he simply left banging the door shut, the sound echoing around the room like a prison cell. At least he left the light on.

Chapter
TWELVE

Josie answered the phone on the third ring.

"Oh hi, Auntie Molly."

"Were you expecting someone else dear?" Molly asked with a chuckle.

"Oh I'm sorry. It's just been such an awful day." Josie told her aunt about Sarah.

There was no news about her friend and she was becoming increasingly concerned. She chose not to dwell on Mike's unforgivable behaviour.

"I just wish I'd stayed with her last night," Josie groaned.

"Hindsight my dear, life's riddled with it. The fact is you didn't and given the circumstances I'd say that was rather fortunate."

"That may be true," Josie sighed, "but I can't help thinking I might have been able to have done something. At least I would know where she is."

"You said the glass panel had been removed from the back door."

Josie described in detail how she had found the glass on the pathway.

"I didn't tell you did I? Molly began. "Well how could I we haven't spoken since it happened."

"What are you talking about, didn't tell me what?"

Molly chuckled. "Well, I came home from a shopping trip the other day to find broken glass all over my kitchen floor. The window by the back door had been broken in."

Josie sat down, her legs unable to support her.

"It's nothing to worry about dear," Molly went on quickly, sensing her concern. "In my case it was nothing to do with an intruder, well apart from a golf ball that is." She went on to explain how she had found a golf ball amongst the glass on the kitchen floor.

"But your garden doesn't back onto a golf course." Josie reminded her.

"You're right of course but it does sit at the boundary of the playing field. Obviously someone was practicing their swing and a stray ball came in through my window."

"Are you sure nothing was taken?" Josie was still sceptical.

"Quite sure dear, there's nothing to worry about. In fact, the insurance company is taking care of everything. So you see no harm done."

"Did you call the police?"

"No need to dear, as I told you before, nothing to worry about."

They talked animatedly for some time, mostly about the circumstances surrounding Sarah's disappearance.

By the middle of the following morning, Mr Mac had arrived on the outskirts of the London. He was exhausted, but having made good time he decided to check into a motel before continuing his journey through the congested city. He slept soundly through the afternoon and by early evening was ready to go so grabbing a sandwich and a cup of coffee he consulted his book of maps. As soon as he was confident that he knew the way, he climbed into his car and navigated to the street where Lizzie Baines lived.

Cruising the neighbourhood it wasn't long before he located the house and parking his car close by he settled down to wait.

The property was a neat 1930's semi set in a smart suburb. Every house had a neat little front garden and some were surrounded by picket fences, but it was the individually painted front doors that made them stand out. Each one painted a different colour, their designs remained the same and the house that he was interested in had a royal blue door. Every door had a coloured glass fan light over the porch, a retro design that harked back to an earlier time. He wondered if these were original or modern replacements. The house belonged to the girl's parents, he had confirmed this earlier during a brief telephone conversation with directory enquiries.

After a while he lost interest, so starting the engine he pulled out into the road. At the end of the street he turned right and headed in the direction of Curzon Grove.

Josie wiped her brush on a rag and stepped back to admire her work. She critically examined the canvas chewing at the end of the paintbrush and half closing her eyes in order to study the colours. After a few moments she relaxed, satisfied that her work was done. She was certain that Tim would be pleased and as she smiled, the telephone began to ring.

"Hi Lindsay," she said tucking the receiver under her chin and using the rag wiped paint from under her fingernails. "No I haven't heard anything yet," she paused. "No nothing from the police either."

"No news is good news I suppose." Lindsay did not sound convinced.

Josie, listening to her friend, carried the phone into the living room and stopped in her favourite place to glance out of the window. It was evening, she had been so engrossed in her work that time had passed without her noticing and she was grateful for that, at least she had not spent the afternoon worrying.

Lindsay went on to remind her of their plans to go out the following evening.

"I really don't feel up to it," Josie told her. "You go out with Lizzie, besides I wouldn't be much fun anyway."

"Are you sure you're okay? I could come round later and we could talk it through."

"There's really no need, I'm going to soak in a hot bath and have an early night."

"Well if you are sure you're okay, I know how close you are to Sarah."

"You two enjoy yourselves and don't worry about me."

"Call me tomorrow if you change your mind, no promise you'll call me anyway."

A lump formed in the back of her throat as she said goodbye to her friend. She hated letting her down but she was desperately worried, she couldn't help thinking that something terrible had happened to Sarah. Hauling herself up the stairs, she went into the bathroom and began to run a bath.

The hot perfumed water was sublime as she relaxed and it wasn't long before her eyelids became heavy, resting her head back against a folded towel she closed her eyes and began to doze. She did not hear the click of the letterbox flap as an envelope dropped onto her doormat.

Mr Mac returned to the home of Lizzie Baines. The light was fading steadily, the afternoon turning to dusk. He would soon have to decide what he was going to do, remain with his car for the night or go and find somewhere to stay. He did not yet have a plan but he was determined to discover a little more about the girl before making his move. He licked his lips in anticipation, oh what fun he was going to have. He began to

76

think about Sarah Hamilton, he should have had some fun with her. The thought of her chained up in his cellar thrilled him and he congratulated himself on his self-restraint. Of course the temptation had been quite overwhelming but she was a useful source of information, her time would come he assured himself of that.

Suddenly a light showed through the fan light above the royal blue door. It cast a warm yellow glow out over the garden as a woman appeared in the doorway and he watched as she placed a little crate of empty milk bottles onto the step. She looked up briefly and as the light played over her face, he saw with disappointment that it was not Lizzie Baines. The door closed firmly behind her then she was gone.

The following morning he was still there waiting in his car. He had managed to avoid suspicion as the milkman and other early morning risers went about their business, then promptly at eight am Lizzie Baines appeared. He watched eagerly as she left her parent's house and with a swing of her narrow hips she turned right by the little picket gate and made her way past his car.

With an iron will, he controlled the urge to jump out and follow her immediately. He waited until she had gained some distance before casually leaving his car and strolling towards the end of the street.

She was just a short distance ahead and this was his first opportunity to study her up close. Her thick red hair was light enough to bounce as she moved, the style fashionably cut, he thought it suited the shape of her face. She was dressed in a navy blue suit, a jacket over a white blouse with a pencil skirt, which stopped just above the knee. He admired her well-shaped calves and long legs. She was tall, above average height, at least a head above him and he frowned, she was not as attractive as he had first thought, not to his taste at all. Her hips were too narrow and her shoulders a little too wide but she was pretty enough and the scent of her perfume was pleasantly sweet.

Although she moved gracefully, her gait was not natural and as he watched, he was unable work out what it was that seemed so different about her. Walking elegantly was obviously not easy for Lizzie Baines perhaps it was her shoes. Putting his thoughts to one side, he closed the gap between them.

Suddenly she looked back, and glancing over her shoulder made eye contact with him briefly before looking away, her concentration focussed on the traffic she crossed the road. Stopping at the edge of the pavement he waited for his chance, then weaving amongst the cars he crossed.

Her mobile phone began to ring and swinging her bag from her shoulder she rummaged around until she found it.

"Hello."

Increasing his pace and closing the distance between them he listened to her conversation.

"Hiya Lindsay," she paused to listen to her friend's voice. "That sounds good but it's a pity about Josie, I hope she's okay. So where do you fancy going this evening?"

He listened very carefully.

"Toni's Italian sounds perfect. Do you think she'll change her mind and come with us?" The pause was longer this time and occasionally she nodded. "Okay I'll order a taxi and see you around 8 then."

Terminating the call, she dropped the phone back into her bag and Mr Mac stopped. He continued to study her as she walked away and a plan began to formulate in his head.

Josie woke later that morning and was horrified by the time. Flying out of bed, she dragged on a tee shirt and a pair of jeans. Tim was calling round at lunchtime and she had intended to have another painting finished before he arrived. Hurrying down the stairs, she spotted a white envelope on the doormat, scooping it up she flew into the kitchen and dropped it on the table before turning her attention towards a cafetiere. Spooning fresh coffee into the pot, she added hot water and savoured the rich aroma that rose up into the air, then rushing into the living room she threw back the curtains and allowed light to flood in.

Back in the kitchen she poured herself a mug of much needed coffee and, breathing a sigh of relief, sat down at the breakfast table. Pushing her hair back behind her ears she remembered the plain white envelope and reaching for it frowned as she turned it over. There was no name or address label so it must have been delivered by hand. She wondered who could have sent it and running her thumb under the seal withdrew a folded sheet of A4 paper. Leaping up, her chair tumbled backwards and coffee spilled over the tabletop. The paper fluttered to the floor landing face up and her hand flew to her mouth. Moments later she scrambled over the fallen chair and rushing towards the sink, her legs hardly able to support her, she splashed cold water over her face.

After a while, she managed to regain her composure and returning to where the paper had fallen she reached down with trembling fingers to pick it up. Her eyes focussed on the computer-generated photograph and she could hardly believe what she saw. Sarah was chained to a wall, she was naked and the look of terror on her friend's face sent a chill down her spine. Josie was numb with shock and when at last able to move she stumbled into the living room where she collapsed onto the sofa. She had to calm her nerves so counting to ten she breathed deeply before reaching for the telephone.

When the police arrived Josie was comforted by a WPC who was sympathetic and understanding and while they were talking, her colleague studied the picture. He handled it carefully with a tiny pair of tweezers before slipping it into a plastic envelope.

Gently the WPC probed asking questions about Sarah and the picture but Josie had no idea who had put the envelope through her door. Her immediate neighbours were consulted but no one had seen a thing.

When they were gone Josie paced nervously around the room. She could not get the image of Sarah out of her head; she was upset and confused, so many questions remained unanswered. Unwelcome thoughts haunted her mercilessly but she could think of no one who would want to harm Sarah. She had no one special in her life, no current boyfriend or any other distractions, the only time she went out was with their circle of close friends. She had not mentioned any problems at work either, but someone must have been stalking her, or perhaps an opportunist had kidnapped her.

Josie knew that Sarah would not just disappear without telling her where she was going. Holding her face in her hands, she threw herself down onto the sofa and sobbed. She would go mad with worry if she didn't stop, so drawing in a deep breath she counted to ten for the second time that morning.

The police had warned her to be vigilant, the abductor knew where she lived and she could be his next target. There were no CCTV cameras operating in the area so she would have to be very careful. They also told her not to discuss this with anyone especially her friend's mother. They promised to inform her of any developments as soon as they had examined the photograph in more detail. The WPC suggested that she spend the night with a friend or at least have someone stay with her for a while. She did not think it wise for her to remain on her own.

Josie sat alone in her living room staring into space. Hugging herself, she fought back her tears then suddenly the doorbell chimed.

"Hi Tim, come in." She closed the door quickly behind him.

"Are you okay?" he eyed her suspiciously. "You look awful."

"That's no way to greet a lady," she attempted a smile but failed miserably. "Just out of sorts today, nothing to worry about. Women's problems, you don't want to know." She spoke a little too quickly and looked away in embarrassment.

"So," he shrugged. "What have you got for me?"

She took him into her studio.

Mr Mac decided to follow Lizzie Baines. He had overheard her telephone conversation so knew her plans for that evening. He was tempted to let her go on her way, but it would do no harm to find out where she was going. Maybe he would discover where she worked and what her life consisted of, besides a contingency plan might prove to be useful.

Lizzie took the bus into the city centre where she made her way towards a massive glass building and passing through giant revolving doors, she was greeted by a uniformed security officer. Mr Mac stood discreetly on the other side of the street and watched, he memorised the name over the door before continuing on his way.

Josie was on her third pot of coffee and the caffeine was making her light headed. Her hands were still shaking but at least the phantoms haunting her were gone, for the moment at least.

Tim was worried, he was not used to seeing her like this, she was pale and drawn and had been acting strangely ever since he arrived.

"Penny for them!" she said, aware that he was watching her.

"Oh it's nothing," he smiled, "nothing to worry about, just men's problems."

"Touché," she said, smiling for the first time.

"So, would you mind if I took your paintings away with me later today?"

Cleverly, he steered the conversation away from her personal problems.

"I'm thinking about setting up an exhibition of sorts from next weekend. We are running something at the moment but when it's finished yours could begin," he studied her closely. "How does that sound?"

"It sounds great but are you sure? Back to back exhibitions sounds awfully like hard work. Wouldn't you like some time to get things straightened out before starting something else?

"You don't have to worry about me," he smiled. "Just concentrate on yourself."

"It's so good of you to take such an interest in my work. I really don't deserve your efforts."

"I disagree, you are very good and I have every confidence in you."

"I should have some more ready for you by the end of the week."

"You're not overdoing things?" he asked. "You haven't stopped since returning from Scotland."

She knew to what he was referring. She had told him nothing about her ordeal and felt uneasy inventing un-truths to explain away her bruises. Fortunately, the story that the local paper ran in Elgin had not reached London and she was thankful for that.

"Sorry," he said misinterpreting her expression. "I shouldn't criticise your decision."

"Oh Tim," realising his error she reached out and touching his arm treated him to one of her most endearing smiles.

He loved it when she smiled.

"Look Josie," he said checking his watch. "I really must be getting back." Placing his mug on the table, he stood up. "I'd love to stay and play all afternoon." He winked and his remark brought colour to her cheeks.

"I wish you could too." She whispered softly to his back as he made his way towards the door.

They stood together on the step and reaching up she kissed his cheek and held onto him briefly.

"I'll wrap the pictures for you," she whispered. "Would you like to collect them later?"

"Yes please," he nodded, grasping at her invitation. "I'll call in after work at about six thirty."

Mr Mac hated everything about the city but most of all he loathed the noise. He was intimidated by so many people, they clogged the pavements, invaded his personal space with their stinking bodies and he was choked by the pollution and the fumes.

Eventually he located the building that he was looking for. Older than its neighbours, it had been built sometime during the previous century. Its architecture belonged to an era when red bricks were laid in patterns and from the quality of its construction he knew that it would be standing long after the others around it had gone. Once inside however any connection with its past had vanished, now modern materials ruled, plastic and glass, strip lighting and computer terminals.

Shrugging off his disappointment Mr Mac sat down at a computer terminal and pulled a storage device from his pocket. Connecting it to the machine, he accessed his personal files and once he found what he was looking for, he printed off a number of colour photographs and some address labels. When he was finished, he purchased some plain white envelopes and a book of first class stamps from a nearby shop. He grinned, another stage of his plan was about to begin. Slipping a photograph into one of the envelopes, he attached a label and a stamp then dropped it into a post box. No one noticed that he was wearing surgical gloves.

Chapter

THIRTEEN

Tim arrived at Josie's house a little after six thirty, he was sure that he was going to be late. He was often delayed at the gallery but this time had managed to slip away on time.

"Would you like a glass of wine?" she asked the moment he had settled.

"That would be very welcome."

"You look tired," she called over her shoulder.

"And you look much better."

Smiling to herself, she filled two glasses with red wine. She felt good in his company and had been looking forward to seeing him all afternoon. Handing him his wine, she settled down beside him on the sofa and curled her legs up beneath her. They were conscious of each other but remained lost in their own thoughts.

"Penny for them," he whispered and as they made eye contact she held her breath.

Reaching out he took her hand and squeezed her fingers gently. He was delighted to discover that they shared so much in common.

"So," she broke the spell. "What have you got planned for this evening?"

"Home alone I suppose, watch a bit of TV maybe, shower then bed."

"What an exciting life you lead," she wrinkled her nose. "Look I'm supposed to be going out with Lizzie and Lindsay but I really don't feel like it." She paused, toying with the stem of her glass. "I told Lindsay yesterday that I probably wouldn't go," she glanced at him. "Would you like to stay for supper?"

"I'd love to," he smiled, "but won't your friends think you rather boorish if you let them down?"

"I'm sure they won't mind."

"I really could do with freshening up." He rubbed his fingers over his chin. "I've been hard at it all day."

"Tim," she laughed, "you're fine, believe me, you're okay."

Mr Mac returned to his car and drove out into the suburbs. Having consulted his book of maps, he'd already chosen a location out of town. The map suggested that it was a rural area and he hoped it would prove to be remote. On the way, he stopped to fill his car with petrol and purchased a fuel can that he also filled before storing it away in his car.

Eventually he arrived at his destination but was disappointed, there were not as many trees as he had hoped. The area was made up of parkland surrounded by large houses, many of which were hidden from view behind huge thick hedges and neat wooden gates. He frowned and bringing his car to a standstill was uncertain, he considered searching for a more suitable place but letting out the clutch crawled slowly along the road. He almost missed a gap in the hedge and stopping suddenly peered back over his shoulder. Reversing his car, he found a large wooden farm gate that was closed across the entrance of a secluded yard. This was exactly what he was looking for so swinging his car round, he parked nose in against the gate before getting out.

The air was still and he could smell the dampness clinging to the hedges and trees, this lifted his spirits. He was satisfied that no one could see his car from the road so locking the doors he went in search of a bus.

Josie and Tim busied themselves in her galley-like kitchen. They worked in harmony raiding her fridge and cupboards and managed put a meal together before another bottle of wine appeared. They had agreed earlier not to talk about work. Tim thought he would be at a disadvantage as his whole life revolved around his business, but as Josie chatted about herself, her friends and her hopes for the future, he knew they had made the right decision. She had telephoned Lizzie and Lindsay to let them know that she was okay and told them to have a great time without her. Lizzie suggested she wrap up warm especially if she was feeling under the weather. Josie chose not to mention that Tim was there with her.

Mr Mac caught a bus back into town and as it slowed, he jumped off onto the pavement, then checking his watch he swung his bag over his shoulder before walking quickly along the path. His schedule was tight and if his plans were to succeed he would have to get a move on. He must also have a contingency plan just in case he was unable to pull this one off.

Earlier he had located Toni's Italian restaurant, then having consulted his book of maps, was now familiar with the area. The route back to his car was lodged firmly in his brain and he felt certain that nothing could go wrong, only then would he allow himself to think about Lizzie Baines. He grinned and licked his lips.

The telephone rang and Josie left Tim to cope alone in the kitchen.

"Mike, how nice to hear from you," she lied.

"Josie, I'm free tonight so I thought we could go out for supper."

"I'm sorry Mike but I can't. I've already made plans to go out with Lizzie and Lindsay." Chewing at her bottom lip, she was uncomfortable at having lied twice in the last two sentences.

"Can't you put them off?" he growled.

"No Mike I can't, they are my friends."

"And we are supposed to be a couple," he retorted sharply, "you know, a couple that's two people doing things together."

Offended by his remark, his sarcasm annoyed her and she was forced to hold the phone away from her ear, he was shouting so loudly that she was convinced Tim could hear every word.

"If you hadn't noticed Mike I'm a single woman, free to do as I please. If I choose to see my friends then it's of no concern of yours."

"I see," he hissed. "So the last eighteen months mean nothing to you then?"

She wanted to tell him that she was tired of being treated like his plaything, that he was insulting, domineering and his threatening behaviour was beginning to get her down. How could they hope to build a secure and happy relationship when he wanted everything his own way? She knew that she would have to tell him but the time was not right. She could not bear a fully blown argument not at the moment, not in her present state of mind besides she had Tim to consider.

"Of course they do Mike," she told him sweetly. "We've had some great times together, but now I just need a bit of space. I want to spend some time with my friends."

Tim popped his head around the door and looked at her enquiringly. She pulled a face so he retreated back into the kitchen.

Eventually she joined him and it was obvious that she was troubled.

"You okay?" He shot her a sideways glance.

Throwing herself down into a chair she wound her hair nervously around her fingers, then picking up her wine glass, she drained it.

"That was Mike," she began, "being bloody minded as usual."

Reaching for the bottle, she re-filled her glass. "It's been one of those days."

Mr Mac wandered through the centre of London until he found what he was looking for. A pub at the end of a cobblestoned alley suited his purpose admirably. Heading towards it, he pushed his way into the crowded bar where he ordered himself a scotch.

After a while he slipped unnoticed into the gent's toilets where he found a collection of business cards pushed into the cracks between the brickwork. They were advertising all kinds of services so selecting one he slipped it into his pocket before returning to the bar. Using the public phone on the wall by the door, he dialled the number on the card and ordered a taxi.

The driver backed his cab carefully between the buildings, the tyres rumbling over the worn cobbles.

"Where to mate?" leaning out of the side window he called out to the man standing in the shadows.

"I've got a heavy box here." Mr Mac indicated towards the door. "Can I put it in the boot?"

The cabbie nodded but swore under his breath as he levered himself out of his comfortable seat. Squeezing past the man in the alley he unfastened the boot lid and swung it down, it was the last thing he did.

Mr Mac stepped forward and slipped a long bladed knife between the driver's ribs until the razor sharp point pierced his heart. With his other hand clamped tightly over the man's jaw, he held him rigid until the life went out of him, then heaving the driver into the storage space he discovered that it was not as spacious as he had expected. It was almost impossible to close the lid and grunting with the effort he managed to force it shut.

Fortunately, no one came out of the pub and wiping blood from the paintwork, Mr Mac slipped in behind the wheel. He switched off the radio cutting the controller off in mid sentence, then, engaging first gear bumped slowly towards the end of the alley. Steering the black cab onto the main road he accelerated smoothly away.

Josie and Tim settled down to enjoy their meal. He was surprised by the variety of food that she kept in her cupboards, she was a healthy eater and it put him to shame.

"We could watch a film later," Tim suggested. "I haven't sat down to watch TV for ages."

Josie nodded chewing thoughtfully on her food. "There's not much on TV I'm afraid but I do have a pretty good DVD collection."

"Not all 'chick flick' I hope," he grinned.

Josie made a face, she was happy with the comfortable atmosphere that had settled around them. After such a terrible day she thought she would never be able to relax again. She was overjoyed at having him there all to herself, he was easy to be with and he made her feel safe, she enjoyed his company immensely. Unlike Mike, he did not appear to have any hidden agendas, Tim was honest and open and she was thankful for that. It was then that she made her decision; she wanted him to stay the night.

It did not surprise her to think this way, in fact it seemed a natural conclusion to a perfect evening so, hiding her grin, she sipped her wine thankful that he could not read her thoughts.

Mr Mac manoeuvred the taxi into the road where Lizzie Baines lived and cursed. Slapping the steering wheel with his hand, he pulled up sharply at the side of the road. He was just a few moments too late, Lizzie Baines was climbing into a taxi and there was nothing he could do but watch as she turned to wave to her mother who was standing by the royal blue front door.

Controlling his rage was an effort and shoving the gearstick forward he followed at a discreet distance.

After their meal, Josie and Tim worked together clearing away the mess they had made in the kitchen. They giggled like children over some joke and as they talked, they touched each other's hearts.

Once their task was completed, she re-filled their glasses.

"If I drink anymore wine I'll have to call a cab." Tim exclaimed.

"Why don't you stay," swaying towards him she looked up into his face and smiled seductively, "besides, I have a spare bedroom." She toyed with one of the buttons on his shirt.

Moving into the living room they curled up together on the sofa before settling down to watch a film. Tim was left in no doubt that things were moving far quicker than he could have dared to hope for.

Realistically there was little chance of him sleeping in the spare room and he wondered how they would both feel when sober in the morning, pushing away his doubts he was determined to enjoy the moment. It was clear to him that she was happy with the way the evening was going and, sipping his wine, he smiled finding it difficult to keep his mind on the film.

The black cab pulled sharply to the kerb and came to a stop outside the restaurant. Lizzie Baines appeared first tossing red hair from her face and her friend climbed out behind her. Smoothing down her skirt, they linked arms and walked towards the door attendant who was standing discreetly in the shadows. As they approached, he moved to open the door and Lizzie greeted him with a nod of her head.

Mr Mac drove on, there was no point in hanging around, he would have to implement his contingency plan. Things were not going his way and he was not pleased.

Crowds of people were milling about on the pavements looking for places to eat or just enjoying the warm evening and as he drove further into the city people began to hail him. It was then he realised the light on top of his cab was on. He made a rude gesture to the group standing on the pavement then flicked the 'for hire' sign off.

The film was coming to an end as was their bottle of wine. Tears began to slip silently over Josie's cheeks; she always reacted this way when this particular film ended. Tim hugged her tenderly and planted a kiss on top of her head, she responded by reaching up to kiss his cheek and he brushed the back of his hand over the spot.

"Hey, you're not supposed to wipe it off," she slapped him playfully.

"You're face is all wet," he grinned.

Suddenly he became serious. "Would you mind if I use your shower?"

"Of course you can." She replied easing herself up off the sofa. "I'll find you some clean towels." She was a little unsteady on her feet.

Following her into the hallway Tim watched closely as she locked the front door and turned out the lights then, leading the way, she took him upstairs and pointed towards the bathroom. Going in he turned on the shower allowing it to run for a few minutes as the water warmed up.

Kicking off his shoes he ran his fingers over his chin and studied himself in the mirror. No chance of a shave tonight he thought, then Josie appeared with an enormous pink towel and some of her less perfumed shower gel.

"A little pink and fluffy I'm afraid," she giggled.

Going into her bedroom, she perched restlessly on the end of her bed. She was painfully aware of him and could hear the water splashing into the shower tray around his feet. She ached for him and could feel her body beginning to respond. She longed to feel the warmth of his arms wrapped tightly around her and could taste his lips against her own.

Slipping out of her clothes, she stood naked in the open doorway and hesitating for a moment grinned before making up her mind. Moving towards the bathroom, she pushed gently against the door and as it swung open clouds of perfumed steam escaped and curled away into the stairwell. Parting the shower curtain, she stepped in beside him.

Mr Mac emerged from his hiding place and consulted his watch for the hundredth time, it was almost time to go. Opening his bag he checked the contents and removing the pistol made sure it was fully loaded. Fingering the safety catch, he locked it into position before laying it down beside him. Next, he filled a syringe with clear liquid, drawing it expertly from a glass phial, he removed the bubbles from the needle before sliding it into a protective sheath then he slipped it into his pocket. Reaching for the pistol again, he weighed it in his hand, it felt good then pocketing the weapon he started the engine and drove off in the direction of town.

There were still plenty of people milling around outside Toni's Italian restaurant and on the first pass, he failed to pick out Lizzie Baines. Slowing the taxi to a crawl he passed for a second time before realising it was hopeless, so swinging the cab round in a tight U turn, he pulled into the kerb and stopped. He didn't have to wait long, standing out in the crowd she towered above most of the others, her magnificent red hair glowing like a beacon. She stopped to check her mobile phone and waited for her friend who was speaking to a uniformed door attendant. The man touched the peak of his cap, laughing at some private joke that passed between them before moving across the pavement.

Mr Mac watched intently as the man gestured towards a line of parked taxis and rolling down his window he called out.

"Taxi for Miss Baines."

The door attendant walked them the short distance to the cab and opened the door. Mr Mac waited patiently as they climbed in. He could hardly contain his excitement as the dark haired girl leaned forward and spoke through the glass partition that separated them.

"Blackberry Grove please," she said, her voice light and cheery.

He watched through the rear view mirror as they made themselves comfortable, and almost immediately, they began to talk, their heads turned towards each other. He couldn't hear what they were saying but he caught the occasional word amongst the general babble.

His mind was racing as he engaged first gear and pulling out into the traffic had no idea where he was going, he wondered how long it would be before the girls realised. This was not part of his plan he was only expecting one passenger. Perhaps he should ask her the way, drop her off then deal with Lizzie Baines, but he soon forgot that idea. As he drove, he began to work it out.

Checking his mirrors, he turned off the main road and the girls, still deep in conversation remained unaware of the direction he had taken. He wondered what they had to say to each other, he assumed they had been talking all evening. One of them laughed and as he glanced back he could see that it was Lizzie Baines. The sound of her merriment made him grin, she would never make that sound again he would make sure of that.

Slipping the pistol from his pocket, he gripped it between his knees and slowly, his fingers working at the syringe, he flicked off the plastic cover. Once that was done he checked the rear view mirror again then he grinned and licked his lips.

The road ahead was dark and they had not passed another car for a while, he was ready. Pulling sharply to the side of the road he jumped out and heaved open the passenger door.

The girls froze, wide eyed with terror they had no idea what was going on and as he pointed the pistol at Lizzie Baines, she stared at him in disbelief. Suddenly she felt a scratch on her arm and crying out in alarm she tried to fight him off but it was too late. Her head struck the side window as she slumped down in her seat. At the same moment, he turned the pistol towards the other girl. She was huddled in the corner of the seat her face twisted with dread.

"Get out," he hissed.

She was too terrified to move so he pushed her from the cab and she stumbled heavily onto the road. Climbing over Lizzie Baines, he leapt out and grabbing a handful of hair hauled her to her feet, she cried out.

"One more noise like that and its curtains for you." He said, pushing her up against the side of the cab.

Holding onto the open door her legs turned to jelly.

"Reach in there and get my bag." He indicated to the space beside the driver's seat.

Slowly she did as she was told and with the gun pressed firmly against her head, he made her kneel in the road and re-fill the syringe.

"Now get back into the cab." He moved in close behind her.

"Inject yourself." He ordered.

She stared at him in disbelief even with a gun pointed at her head she was unable to do it. Grunting with frustration, he grabbed the syringe and jabbed the needle into her arm, moments later she slumped lifeless onto the floor of the cab.

Mr Mac grinned and licked his lips. Rocking back on his heels and with his heart beating crazily, he could hardly believe his luck. He studied his prize. Lizzie Baines looked as if she was sleeping and turning towards the other girl he reached out and ran his fingers through her dark hair. This must be Lindsay, he thought, Lizzie had been talking to her on the phone earlier. He would have some fun with this one.

Climbing back into the driver's seat he engaged first gear and the cab roared away leaving behind a black cloud of diesel fumes.

Josie led Tim to her bedroom where they dried each other with warm towels. The excitement of his touch made her tremble and as her body responded, she kissed him passionately. The stubble on his chin burned her skin but she didn't mind, then slipping under the duvet they explored and worshipped each other until exhausted they fell to sleep.

Mr Mac drove to where he had left his car and parking the taxi climbed out. Going to the rear of his car, he released the boot lid and reaching for the fuel can he had bought earlier, returned to the taxi where he opened the side door.

First, he grabbed Lizzie Baines. Lifting her from the seat, he carried her to his car and dropped her into the boot. He had to fold her long legs in order to squeeze her into the tight space. Once that was done, he dragged the other girl from the cab and heaving her in on top of Lizzie, arranged them as best he could. He knew they would be out for most of the journey.

One of the girl's shoes was missing, he would have to find it. He could not afford to leave too many clues behind. It had rolled under the cab so retrieving it he tossed it into the boot before slamming the lid shut. He paused to take a breath before climbing into the taxi, starting the engine he moved it well away from his own car before reaching for the fuel can. Going to the rear of the cab, he opened the boot lid and splashed petrol over the corpse before pouring the rest over the interior of the vehicle.

91

Once the can was empty, he tossed it onto the driver's seat before striking a match. Fire took hold immediately.

Running to his car he started the engine and roared away, a few moments later the cab blazed up furiously sending a dirty yellow flame into the night sky.

Chapter
FOURTEEN

The first thing Josie heard when she woke was the sound of birdsong coming in through the open window. She smiled, the memory of their lovemaking was still fresh in her mind and she wanted every morning to begin like this.

Turning her head, she studied Tim as he slept. She could hardly believe her luck, and reaching out she touched him gently with her fingertips just to confirm that he was real. He looked so childlike, just how she imagined him as a boy and she dared not move for fear of spoiling the moment. Hugging herself she felt safe and warm curled up beside him and wished the moment would last forever. If she wished hard enough then maybe it would come true.

She knew she had to move, break the spell that bound them together, so sliding carefully from beneath the duvet she wrapped herself in her gown, then crept silently out of the room. At the bottom of the stairs, she stooped to pick up her mail before dashing into the kitchen. Her first job was to fill the kettle, so holding it under the tap until it was full, she turned it on to boil and giggled as her heart quickened with joy. This morning was different; today she was making coffee for two.

Reaching into the cupboard, she pulled out two mugs and placed them onto a small tray. Whilst waiting for the kettle she turned towards the table and began sorting through her mail, separating the circulars from the letters. Hidden in the pile was a plain white envelope, turning it over in her hands she noticed that it was stamped with a London postmark and dated the previous day. She frowned and tracing her finger lightly over the address label ran her nail under the seal. Her stomach tightened as she tore open the flap and sliding her fingers in, pulled out the folded papers. Suddenly all the warmth and happiness that she was feeling evaporated leaving her chilled to the bone.

On the table in front of her lay a computer generated image of what appeared to be a section of Spey Bay in Scotland. Someone had produced a crude drawing that resembled the sketch she had found in her sketchbook. Rushing into her studio, she pulled open the desk drawer and snatching up the page, compared it with the drawing on the table. The only person who could have done this was the man she had seen in the bay. Her hands began to shake and her mind raced as she realised the implications. She did not understand where Sarah fitted in with all this, it was impossible to see a link. Dropping heavily into the chair she cradled her head in her arms and went through all the possibilities. She had seen him commit a crime but had escaped his clutches. She had no idea who he was so could not even identify him, all of these things were true so why had he traced her to London?

The more she thought about it the more confused she became. Of one thing she was certain, the picture of Sarah in chains had been delivered in a large white envelope just like this one.

"Oh no!" she cried. "It has to be the man from Spey Bay."

She was convinced, there was only one logical explanation, he must have discovered where Sarah lived then found her own address. Perhaps he had forced the information out of her. The implications were startling but it all began to make sense. Her mind raced on. The glass door at Sarah's house had been broken just like her Aunt Molly's. She covered her mouth with her hand and her blood ran cold. There had to be a connection, it must have been done by the same man.

Josie realised that he had broken into her aunt's house with the sole purpose of finding her details. That would explain it, how else would he know where to find her? He must have been following her ever since. She shuddered at the thought and her mind raced on even faster. If it were true then she was to blame, she was the cause of Sarah's situation. Josie stared miserably at the papers in front of her. She hated the sight of them and suddenly began to feel cold and very much alone.

Tim woke suddenly and knew that he was not in his own bed. It took a few moments for the events of the previous evening to come flooding back but when they did, he grinned with pleasure. Rolling over he buried his face into her pillow and breathing in her scent his heart missed a beat. Last night had been amazing and Josie was wonderful. Her presence filled the room and thinking about her, he became aroused. He had to go and find her, so hauling himself out of bed, he dressed quickly before descending the stairs two at a time.

She was standing in the kitchen lost in her own thoughts, and with her back to him, didn't hear as he came up behind her.

"Penny for them," he whispered as he slipped his arms around her waist.

Turning she buried her face into his chest and he could feel how tense she was.

"What on earth's the matter?"

"It's all my fault." She said in a tiny voice.

Holding onto him, she sobbed and was grateful that he was there. She realised then that she was not alone after all, Tim would support her, she was certain of it. The bonds they had forged through their lovemaking were powerful and she was comforted knowing that the love they shared was genuine.

Gently guiding her into the living room, he eased her down onto the sofa, and without a word returned to the kitchen where he poured two cups of strong coffee from the pot. He was desperate to know why she was so upset but it was clear to him that she needed a few moments by herself.

Leaning in towards him, she told him everything beginning with the moment she had witnessed the murder in Scotland and the horrors of being swept out to sea. Leaving nothing out, she spoke of her fears regarding Sarah.

He listened without comment and when she was finished, he sat quietly sipping his coffee. He needed a few moments to take it all in, and studying the picture that came in the post that morning, he compared it with the page torn from her sketchbook. He was amazed that she was able to function whilst carrying around such burdens.

Biting at her bottom lip she begged him for forgiveness, she should have confided in him earlier.

"The police warned me not to tell anyone about the picture of Sarah." She described it to him and fresh tears appeared on her cheeks.

"Was the postmark on the envelope the same as this one?"

"No, the first one was delivered by hand."

"So he's been here before." Alarm sounded in his voice.

"I guess so. The police told me to be vigilant."

"How did he manage to track you down?" Standing up he began to pace the room.

Josie stared into her mug and told him about the damage to her aunt's kitchen door.

"A few days ago my Auntie Molly told me that a journalist wanted to make contact with me. He asked her for my details."

He stopped pacing and sat down again.

Josie rummaged in her bag. "Here," she held out a slip of paper. "I made a note of his number."

"Mr Mac," he read her small, neat handwriting. "So you think he's the man you saw on the riverbank in Scotland?"

"Yes, I'm sure of it."

He thought for a moment before agreeing that she could be right.

"So he's hell bent on getting back at you," Tim said looking at her. "He's killed at least once already and now through your friend he's making you pay for having witnessed his crime."

Her blood ran cold as he confirmed her own thoughts. Looking up at him she was hardly able to believe that they were thinking the same thing.

"He's a mad man, there's no sense in trying to understand why he's doing these things." He said reading her mind perfectly.

"Will the police take any of this seriously?" She asked miserably.

"They have the picture of Sarah."

"Well yes but it's hardly proof that she's in the clutches of a mad man. That picture could have been taken anywhere it could even have been altered by a computer program."

He had to agree but the fact remained Sarah was missing, her house had been broken into and the police would have to respond to that.

"The police in Scotland found no evidence to back up my story," she told him miserably. "In fact I was very lucky not to be charged for the cost of the helicopter that rescued me. The police here won't be so quick to react once they contact their colleagues north of the border."

"It does sound a bit unlikely," he agreed, then wished that he had kept his comment to himself.

Mr Mac arrived home. Bringing his car to a stop, he slumped forward in his seat and rested his head against the steering wheel. The noises from the rear of the car had finally stopped. Earlier there had been screams of anger and shouting, then more recently sobs of frustration but now there was only silence.

The muscles in his neck and across his shoulders were tense, but as he relaxed, his mind became alert and he began to anticipate the prospects that lay ahead. Chaining the girls to the wall in his cellar was something he was looking forward to greatly, he was going to take pleasure from every moment.

Climbing stiffly from his car, he stretched his arms above his head and arching his back glanced up at his house. His ancestors had been very good to him and he never grew tired of marvelling at the legacy they had left. Shrugging his thoughts aside, he went to the back of his car and opened the luggage compartment. Stale air rose up forcing him to take a step backwards.

Lizzie Baines was conscious. She blinked, squeezing her eyes shut as the light assaulted her senses. Her head was thick from the effects of the drug and from being cooped up in such a small space. Her red hair was damp, plastered against her skull and her complexion was sickly pale.

"Miss Baines I presume?"

Reaching in, he grabbed a fistful of Lindsay's blouse and hauling her unceremoniously from the space, dumped her onto the gravel. She cried out although barely conscious.

With Lizzie he was not as rough. Taking hold of her elbow, he helped her up and she groaned as she straightened her legs. He allowed her to lean against him as she climbed stiffly from the car and lowering her carefully to the ground, he left her beside Lindsay.

Her legs had not yet regained sufficient strength to support her and she needed some time to recover. A wave of nausea swept over her as cool fresh air filled her lungs but slowly she regained her strength and her eyes grew accustomed to her surroundings. Struggling to her feet, she leaned against the car for support and began working the feeling back into her legs.

She wanted to vomit, there was a hollow feeling in her stomach and it was making her head spin. Catching her reflection in the car window she groaned with disbelief and running her fingers through her hair she hardly recognised herself.

"Don't try anything big girl," he growled.

She was confused and disorientated, but slowly events leading up to this moment became more apparent. Things had happened so quickly once the taxi swerved suddenly and stopped. She thought it was to miss another car or an obstacle in the road, but then she remembered the gun.

Massaging the side of her head with her fingertips, she fought against another wave of nausea. Her throat was dry and her muscles cramped again as another spasm shot through her legs.

"Come on missy," he nudged Lindsay with the toe of his boot.

Ignoring her own discomfort Lizzie helped Lindsay to sit up, and smoothing her friend's skirt around her legs, whispered encouragement into her ear.

Lindsay retched and vomited into the gravel; this made Mr Mac very angry and he kicked out viciously. Lizzie glanced up at him stunned by his behaviour and cradling her friend protectively in her arms, she did her best to protect her from further blows.

"Where are we, what's happening?" Lindsay croaked, her throat as dry as dead leaves.

"I wish I knew," Lizzie replied softly.

Miserably they surveyed their surroundings. Lizzie felt certain they were in Scotland but she had no way of knowing for sure, it was merely a feeling.

Mr Mac returned carrying a bucket of water and a broom.

"Clear up that mess!" he shouted.

Lindsay took hold of Lizzie, and hauling her to her feet, groaned with the effort. They did as they were told and after a while, Lindsay began to feel stronger. She had recovered sufficiently to confront him when he returned.

"Who are you?" she demanded. "Where are we?"

Ignoring her, he pushed them roughly towards the house.

"Don't you dare touch me," Lindsay turned and glared at him.

Lizzie had a very bad feeling about this, she hated confrontation and she knew he had a gun. It would be far easier for them to do as they were told, at least for now.

"You had better watch your tongue lassie." He pushed her even harder this time and she fell to the ground.

"How dare you push me," she screamed, and scrambling to her feet, turned to face him.

"So what exactly do you think you're going to do about it?"

Lindsay snapped. After hours of being imprisoned in the boot of his car she had reached her limit, flinging herself at him with nails extended, she hissed like an angry cat.

Raising his arm against her onslaught he held her off and she slipped on the gravel. Seconds later, she was up and recovering her balance, attacked again.

Lizzie stood rooted to the spot horrified by the violence. Clearly,

Lindsay was no match for him, he was much stronger and was just toying with her.

Lindsay's anger was as hot as boiling lava and bending into her attack went at him head on. He was enjoying every moment of it and wrapping his arms around her, he lifted her off her feet. Screaming out in frustration she kicked and struggled but he simply squeezed even harder forcing the air from her lungs. Lindsay felt her ribs flex and pain shot through her chest. He tightened his grip knowing that she would not be able to breathe. Her eyes were bulging and she could feel her strength beginning to fail. Panic seized her and she became light headed as her lips turned blue.

"Please," Lizzie stepped forward.

She had to do something, unable to take any more of this violence she put her hand gently on his shoulder and begged him to stop. As she looked into his cold dark eyes, her stomach lurched. Seeing into the depth of his madness, she was convinced that he would not release his grip, but then without warning he cast her away like a broken toy. Lindsay collapsed to the ground gasping for breath and Lizzie, going to her, gently rubbing her back until her friend began to recover.

"Now get moving," he snarled.

Lindsay wept silently as like animals they were herded towards the steps leading up to a heavy wooden door. Once inside, he forced them into a richly furnished room and, slamming the door behind them, turned the heavy lock before going off along the corridor.

Lindsay stood trembling with shock, her body covered in bruises she was stunned by the force he had used to overpower her. She felt certain that he would have killed her if it had not been for Lizzie. Sinking carefully into a chair she folded her arms protectively across her breasts and stared miserably around her.

Lizzie also took in their surroundings. The room was lit by shafts of sunlight coming through cracks in the heavy wooden shutters that were drawn across the windows. Moving towards them, she reached out and touched them gently with her fingertips. They were locked and had not been opened for years. Peering through the gaps, she could see a thick layer of dust that had built up on the ledge between the huge sash windows and the shutters. The walls looked substantial enough and she was reminded of a castle or a prison, it was then she realised that they would never escape from here and her spirit sank even lower.

Mr Mac shot the bolts on the door leading to the cellar and the moment he stepped into the room, he could see Sarah. She was huddled on the cold concrete floor covered by the blanket that he had given her.

He was looking forward to seeing her again, so striding over to where she lay he grabbed a corner of the blanket and snatched it away.

"It's very nice to see you again," he leered. "Now get up."

He pushed her roughly up against the wall and she did nothing to resist as he locked her in chains, the links making hateful noises as they rubbed together. Old wounds were opened by the roughness of the shackles and she pulled a face but did not cry out. She had just lost her little bit of freedom and the humiliation was about to begin again. She had never felt so miserable.

He stared at her, doing nothing to disguise his lust and his eyes flashed as he gloated then, suddenly his mood seemed to change and he moved away.

"Very nice indeed," he hissed, admiring her from a distance.

It pleased him that she was so obedient, she did everything that was asked of her and did it without complaint. He thought about the fight he had just had with the other girl and it filled him with excitement. She displayed such spirit, he would have to watch that one.

Sarah watched him wearily as he glared at her. She had no idea what was going on in his mind but was convinced that he was about to attack then, suddenly he turned and left.

Mr Mac returned to where he had left Lizzie and Lindsay. Unlocking the door, he pushed his way into the room and they both looked up at him wide eyed. Their body language displayed fear and uncertainty, they had no idea what was about to happen and this pleased him, he was looking forward to settling them in.

Striding across the room, he grabbed a handful of Lindsay's hair and hauling her to her feet, forced her head back violently.

"Any funny business and she gets it," he nodded towards Lizzie, his eyes flashing alarmingly as he stared at her. "Now get moving."

Lizzie, slipping her hand into Lindsay's glanced at her fearfully, then they followed him out of the room.

At the end of a gloomy corridor they stopped at the top of a short flight of stairs, then they were pushed down into the darkness. At the bottom they came up against a solid wooden door, and reaching past them, Mr Mac turned the latch and the door swung inwards.

Lizzie was the first to see Sarah and gasping with horror she came to a halt in the middle of the room.

"Sarah," she cried, "what has he done to you?"

Without a sound, he moved in. Taller than him, she was not as aggressive as her friend but he reckoned she posed the greater threat and he would feel happier once she was chained to the wall. There was something about her that he found strange, she seemed different to the other women he had encountered and it bothered him. Maybe he just needed time to get to know her better.

The force of his attack drove her against the wall. Lights flashed inside her skull and she was stunned as her head smashed against a metal ring that was jutting out. She was powerless to resist as he attached the chains to her wrists.

Working quickly he pulled on the loose ends hoisting her arms up above her head and she cried out at the agony. Stretching upwards in an effort to relieve her pain she stood on tiptoe.

Next, he forced her legs apart, and snapping manacles around her ankles it was over and she was hopelessly trapped.

Lindsay, seeing her chance, dashed up the stairs and made her way back along the corridor. She had no idea where she was going, her fight or flight reflexes drove her blindly on through the house.

Mr Mac was unconcerned, enjoying every moment of it he took his time in settling Lizzie in. He checked the shackles carefully and made some final adjustments before stepping back to admire his work.

Lizzie's head was spinning and she was finding it hard to focus. She was however fully aware of what was going on, the heavy metal bracelets ground painfully into her delicate wrists and every time she moved the pain became even more intense. Images of Sarah chained naked to the wall were still fresh in her mind and she was confused and sickened by the violence of it all. Never before had she felt so vulnerable and the enormity of her situation was beginning to take hold. Closing her eyes, she tried to ignore the wave of nausea that swept over her.

He could hardly believe his luck, there were two women in his cellar at the same time, this had never happened before. He grinned and licked his lips.

Lizzie seemed taller now that she was stretched out against the wall and turning towards her, he contemplated ripping her clothes off right there and then. He could make her ordeal even more unpleasant but he decided to leave that until later, there was unfinished business to take care of first. He must go and find the other one.

"Lizzie," Sarah whispered the moment he had gone. "Are you okay?"

Lizzie swallowed back her tears. That was typical of Sarah, she always thought of others before herself.

"Yes I think so, how about you?"

Sarah recalled briefly the events of her ordeal and with an overwhelming sense of guilt, cursed herself for allowing her friends to become involved.

"Lizzie I'm so sorry," she sobbed. "It's because of me you are here."

"It seems you had no other option, besides, he was torturing you."

"How come Lindsay's here too?"

Lizzie told her about how they had been abducted in the taxi.

"Poor Lindsay," she gasped. "I guess it's my fault that she's here too."

They were silent for a while both caught up in their thoughts of guilt and despair.

"Has he touched you?" Lizzie asked, unable to hold back any longer.

"No, not yet," Sarah said, her expression grim.

Lizzie looked pale and drawn, her skin tight and transparent. Naturally, her complexion was pale, it went with her red hair, but in the dim light she looked terribly ill. Her head was throbbing mercilessly and an ugly bruise was beginning to appear on the side of her face.

Closing her eyes tightly she was unable to hold back her tears any longer and squeezing through her lashes, they tumbled unchecked over her cheeks. A sense of doom overwhelmed her, their situation was hopeless and she felt sure they would never escape. She also knew that she would not be able to endure the horrors that she imagined were coming their way. A dull ache was beginning to form in the pit of her stomach, already her stress levels were soaring and the blow to her head did not help. She could not bear the thought of being touched, she had never been with a man before and this she kept strictly to herself. She made up boyfriends, dreams created to make her friends believe that she enjoyed normal relationships, but she despised herself for having to hide behind a lie even if it was necessary to prevent them from asking too many difficult questions.

The chains holding her chattered as she wept, she knew that she had to regain control, calm her tattered nerves, but the horrors continued to whirl mercilessly around inside her head. The thought of being stripped naked like Sarah tortured her mercilessly. She could not bear it, she would break down and die of shame, it was all too monstrous to imagine.

Noises were coming from along the corridor. They could hear Lindsay screaming obscenities, then suddenly the door burst open and she was thrown into a heap in the middle the floor. She was a mess, her blouse was torn and there were streaks of mud along her legs and skirt.

Standing over her and looking for an excuse to beat her again he was wild and menacing, his chest was heaving, his face ruddy from the chase. Grabbing the collar of her blouse it ripped as he hauled her to her feet and buttons went skittering across the floor, then holding her in a vice like grip he pushed her against the wall and attached a shackle to her wrist.

Lindsay struggled violently and kicking out she attempted to wriggle free, but he aimed a sharp blow to her kidneys and her legs turned to jelly.

Mr Mac went to work and in a few seconds, she was helpless. Her arms felt as if they were being pulled from their sockets, and as he hoisted her into the air, her toes came off the floor. The pressure from the shackles around her wrists was unbearable and she cried out, her breaths coming in huge sobs. She could hardly believe how easily she had been overcome and was angry with herself. Her back was painful where he had hit her and she hated him even more for it.

Mr Mac slackened the chains until her feet rested on the ground. At least now, she could support her body weight with her legs and the pressure on her wrists was relieved. Once she had recovered her breath, she tested the chains by pulling on them but it was no use, they were immovable, fixed solidly into the wall.

Despite all this, Lindsay was determined not to have her spirit broken, ignoring her discomfort she stared back at him her eyes blazing defiantly. Mr Mac was delighted, he loved a girl with determination she was different from the rest, he was going to enjoy this one.

Slowly reaching for the collar of her blouse, he gripped the soft material between his fingertips and shuffled closer until he caught a faint smell of her perfume; she was a mixture of delights. Beneath the scent he could detect her natural fragrance and it drove him wild with desire, his heart was racing madly inside his chest and not once did he break eye contact with her. Suddenly he moved, ripping her blouse from her shoulders he tossed it away.

Lindsay, gasping with shock, closed her eyes tightly and braced herself for the onslaught.

Lizzie was terrified, she fully expected him to continue his attack but as she watched, he simply stood back to admire his work.

He was shaking with excitement. The girl was humiliated, he had done away with her bravado and he was pleased with that, it was enough for the moment. He studied her for a while longer before turning away then he left.

Lindsay gasped. "He's a maniac," she said shaking her head in disbelief. "Why are we here, why is this happening to us?"

Sarah remained silent, her heart racing, she was sick with shock. She had not yet worked out where Josie fitted in with all this but she knew nothing good would come of it. She chose to keep her thoughts to herself.

Chapter

FIFTEEN

Josie and Tim spent most of the morning at the police station. The station sergeant was helpful enough, taking out the files relating to the break in at Sarah's house he passed them along the chain of command.

Inspector Lacey had studied the paperwork earlier that morning and standing up from behind his desk, welcomed them into his office.

"I agree that someone appears to be playing tricks on you and a very unpleasant experience it must be," he began once they were seated.

"I think the man in Scotland is doing this."

"And why would you think that?" he asked glancing at Josie.

"I saw him shoot that poor woman and he obviously wanted me dead too but I was lucky enough to get away." She could see that he was unconvinced so she continued. "I feel certain he's using Sarah to get back at me."

"Quite frankly Miss MacDonald, I don't think these incidents are connected. Why would someone want to get at you through a third party?"

"Maybe he took her in order to intimidate me," she said. "He's probably getting a huge kick out of sending me these pictures."

"I think you have blown this out of all proportion. You are obviously a young woman with a very active imagination."

That was not what Josie wanted to hear.

Tim, sensing her frustration, slipped his hand over hers as he realised that nothing she could say would change the Inspector's mind.

"I will however make some enquiries with my colleagues in Elgin." He promised and sitting back in his chair regarded her carefully.

"I'm not happy about this Inspector Lacey, there is a lunatic out there who's kidnapped my friend. At this very moment she could be going through the most dreadful ordeal and you're quite prepared to do nothing about it."

"I didn't say that, I can assure you that everything possible is being done to locate your friend. We are taking her disappearance very seriously indeed."

His attempt at reassuring her with a cliché like that infuriated her so they left the police station and headed into town. Tim had to lengthen his stride in order to keep up with her.

"We had better grab a coffee, you need to calm down. Did you honestly expect him to take you seriously?"

"I'm sorry Tim." She slowed her pace allowing him to fall in beside her. "I just can't believe it, they don't seem to be listening to me at all."

"Your story does sound a little thin," he said glancing sideways at her. "Don't get me wrong I believe you, but it just doesn't make sense."

Slipping his hand into hers, they walked on in silence and she allowed him to guide her through the crowds. He took her into the first coffee shop he found.

"Listen Josie, you have to let go a little. I know it's easy for me to say but what else can you do? The police know what they are doing so let's just be patient and let them do their job."

"I know you're right Tim, but seeing Sarah chained up like that." Her voice trailed off.

He knew how badly affected she was by her friend's sudden disappearance and he understood what she was going through.

Later that day she tried to paint but found it impossible. She couldn't stop thinking about events that had taken place over the last couple of weeks and now her whole routine had been turned on its head. It was true that her relationship with Tim was blossoming and she was very happy with that, she realised how lucky she was to have him around at such a bleak time in her life. Her smile faded and she began to feel guilty. How could she feel this happy when Sarah was going through who knows what?

Her thoughts continued to whirl around inside her head, her emotions a rollercoaster. Her appalling experience in Scotland still haunted her but now the nightmare had just got worse and frustratingly there was nothing that she could do about it. Folding her arms across her chest, she hugged herself and biting at her bottom lip turned away from the window. Throwing herself down onto the sofa, she reached for the phone. She had an overwhelming urge to talk to her Aunt Molly.

The following morning she was up early. Talking to her aunt the previous day had lifted her mood and now after a good night's sleep was working in her studio. After a couple of hours she stood back from the canvas to appraise the emerging scene.

The letterbox clattered as the post arrived and, cleaning her brush carefully, she made her way towards the kitchen but then the telephone began to ring.

"Hi Mrs Baines," she greeted her friend's mother.

"I'm sorry to bother you Josie but is Lizzie there with you?"

She could hear the strain in the woman's voice obviously, something was wrong. "No, she's not here."

"She hasn't been home for two nights now and we're so worried. Didn't she meet up with you and Lindsay the other evening?"

Josie felt her stomach lurch. "I'm afraid I didn't see them after all, I cried off at the last moment."

"Oh I see. I didn't realise."

"Why, what's happened?" The image of Sarah flashed into her head.

"As I said earlier she hasn't been home. Usually when staying out she lets us know but this time we haven't heard a thing. It's so unlike her to go off without telling us first. She hasn't been seen at work either."

"Have you tried her mobile phone?"

"Yes of course, it seems to be switched off."

"What about Lindsay have you spoken to her?"

"I've tried but there's no answer from her phone either. I've even been to her flat but there's no-one there."

The woman's mood was infectious and Josie began to fear the worst. Mrs Baines was clearly not aware that Sarah was missing.

She had to remain positive so responding calmly she said. "Look Mrs Baines I'm sure there must be a simple explanation. I'll phone around our friends, find out where Lizzie is then I'll call you back."

Josie was no longer able to ignore her sense of growing unease. She said goodbye to her friend's mother and steadying her hands, made some phone calls but none of her friends had seen either Lizzie or Lindsay. Some of them were beginning to ask after Sarah who had not been seen for a few days and Josie didn't know what to tell them.

Once she had made her last call she could not bear the thought of talking to anyone else. She knew that she would have to speak with Mrs

Baines but that would have to wait. Putting it off for a little while longer she needed time to think so going into the hall she collected her mail.

There was just one item on the mat, a plain white envelope. The moment she saw it Josie froze and held her breath, she knew it would contain more bad news. Summoning up her strength, she snatched it from the mat and tearing it open her fears were confirmed. Inside were four colour prints; individual A4 pictures of Sarah, Lizzie and Lindsay. The fourth was of the three of them together and they were all chained to a white washed wall. It was like something out of a medieval dungeon or an antiquated prison. This was the evidence that she needed, proof that Sarah had indeed been abducted and now he had two more of her friends. Throwing the prints down she flew into the kitchen and holding her head over the sink retched until there was nothing left inside her.

It was a long while before she had the strength to reach for a cloth and wetting it under the tap, held it against her face. It was refreshing and cool, just what she needed, it helped to calm her nerves. She could not tell Lizzie's mother that would have to be done by the police.

Moving unsteadily towards a chair she threw herself down before reaching for the pictures again. She had to find some kind of clue, perhaps by studying them she might discover where they were being held. Turning one of the pictures over she discovered a message.

'To have been where you have been, to have seen what you have seen, clearly in the wrong place at the wrong time.

Now these who are your friends will dance to my tune and before long you too will be mine.'

Mr Mac, making his way through his house, noticed that in places the corridor was a little dark and oppressive. The faces of his ancestors peering down at him from the cold walls seemed strangely intimidating. In the spaces between these sombre portraits hung rich tapestries, some of which were hundreds of years old. Most of these treasures bore the scars of time and were in need of restoration. The cold, damp winter months and years of neglect was responsible for their poor condition but he did not care about such trivia.

Arriving in the main hall he paused, then lifting his head he admired an imposing painting of Robert the Bruce, King of Scotland. It was huge, covering most of the wall above the fireplace. Robert the Bruce stared impassively down at him, his countenance majestic and heavy with contemplation.

On the wall facing this potentate was the likeness of William Wallace, he was equally resplendent. Mr Mac stared in wonder at the fire burning in his eyes. Wallace exuded self-confidence. This was Scotland's brave governor and protector. He idolised both these men, they fuelled his hatred for the English, the persecutors of the Scottish clans.

The English Lords angered him and the suffering of his kinsmen at the hands of these invaders haunted him mercilessly. Their misconduct and wrongdoing over the years had unbalanced his mind. History weighed heavily on his conscience, it was as if he had been there himself, borne witness to the evil deeds that had consumed his country. Voices from the past plagued him, begged him to do their will, urged him to exact vengeance against the perpetrators of evil. His ancestors wanted retribution for all those who had suffered, the women who were raped, the children who were murdered, they demanded justice for their bloodline.

"Today," he began, his voice rising high into the beams blackened by time, "you will receive the blood of an English whore."

His passion, corrupted by the rage of his nation stirred him and in this maddened state, he turned and made his way towards the cellar.

Standing in the middle of the floor he stared at their faces, each one pale under the dim light. The voices in his head were becoming louder, they were stronger now and would soon impose their will. Like parasites he could sense them feeding off the women's fear.

Mr Mac was dressed in a costume befitting the occasion, a kilt in the colours of his clan once outlawed by the English King so long ago. His chest was covered in tattoos, body art etched into his skin, complex swirls and spiritual designs reserved for warriors and he looked fearsome. He was a man from another era, an ancient warrior about to do battle.

Sarah was horrified and as he moved towards her, she could see the madness etched in the lines of his face.

Eyeing her greedily, he grinned and licked his lips. "Today," he began, his voice booming off the walls. "One of you will run free." He looked at each of them in turn. "Who will it be?" He began pacing back and forth. "Who will it be?"

They watched as he struggled with his emotions. It was as if someone was there beside him, urging him on but the choice had to be his alone.

"Not you my pretty one," he moved away from Sarah and she was able to breathe again.

Slowly he went towards Lizzie and she shuddered at his manic expression. It was hellish, whirls and loops painted across his cheeks was the embodiment of the devil.

Closing her eyes tightly she attempted to block out the image and drawing back, flattened herself against the wall. She cried out as his hot breath brushed her cheek then he crushed her lips with his own. Very slowly he began to open the buttons of her blouse, his hands cold against her skin and she thought she was about to die.

Her fiery red hair contrasting dramatically with her cool pale skin fascinated him. Her body was soft and pure and she smelt like meadow grass. His tongue probed her mouth making her retch.

"Will it be you my Celtic lass?" his voice rasped dryly. Drawing back, he left her trembling.

Her skin was crawling and she felt unclean, she looked away and fixed her eyes on Sarah. Panic threatened to overcome her and she could feel her sanity beginning to slip away.

Sarah, holding her gaze, reached out to her in silence.

"No lass, not you, not just yet."

She wept with relief.

Lindsay's muscles tightened and her chains rattled as he made his way menacingly towards her. She had already decided to do nothing to provoke him, she simply had to control her temper.

Like a creature stalking its prey, he stopped beside her and she could feel his eyes boring relentlessly into her soul, she almost screamed.

"How about you my high spirited one?" he whispered intimately into her ear. "You're not supposed to be here at all, do you know that?" His breath burned like a furnace against her skin.

"Let's just say you're my little bonus." He grinned and licked his lips. "Unfortunately for you, you were in the wrong place at the wrong time. Ironic don't you think?" He closed his eyes and breathed in her scent.

"Strawberries and cream," he whispered then he began licking her neck.

His tongue flashed reptilian like as he worked down below her ear. Holding her head in an iron grip he kissed her lips then her face and along the curve of her neck.

"Who is it to be?" He ran his hands over her body, his fingers toying with her bra strap.

She closed her eyes, willing him to leave her alone.

"Who is it to be?" he shouted.

Startling them with his rage, he turned on the spot, struggling with indecision. He was becoming frustrated and his anger began to rise, then pulling a dagger from his stocking he held it high above his head, its razor edge flashing as it caught the light.

Sarah gasped. The sound caught his attention and turning, he moved towards her slowly bringing the tip of his blade down until it touched the skin between her breasts. With her chest rising and falling rapidly her heart hammered against her ribs and closing her eyes she began to pray.

Slowly he drew the blade down leaving a mark on her skin but the pressure was not sufficient to draw blood. She felt the point of the blade stop level with her navel.

"No!" Lizzie cried out startling them all.

Turning his head, he moved away from Sarah and held his blade out towards Lizzie. He was enjoying himself, the effect that he was having on the girls excited him immensely. Pressing the blade flat against her cheek he grinned.

Lizzie could feel herself losing control, her breath coming in ragged gasps. His attention was drawn to her small breasts heaving against the fabric of her clothing.

"Shall we let them out?" he hissed.

Slipping the edge of his blade against the exposed strap, she felt it part, then forcing open her blouse he ran his hands against her breasts pinching her skin roughly.

Crying out she was devastated and tears squeezed from between her lashes. How dare he violate her like this, she was mortified and could hardly bear the horror of the moment.

Leaving her distraught, he laughed and moved away. Lindsay whimpered softly as he focused his attention on her once again. She looked into his face and was hypnotised. His eyes were yellow pools of hatred and she could see the poison that fuelled his rage. With an enormous effort she managed to turn away.

Lashing out he grasped her chin and forced her head round.

"Look at me," he growled.

She looked at him and it was clear that he had made his choice. Pushing the cold blade of his knife up against the hollow of her throat, he felt her body go rigid then she closed her eyes.

"Look at me girl," he shouted, "open your eyes."

Through tears that blurred her vision she stared at him. He grinned and licked his lips. The tension in his face distorted his features and he appeared even more like a demon. Suddenly he stepped back and lifting his kilt exposed himself to her.

"Here's a proud cock don't ya think?" he shouted, "a cock all the better for the crowing."

He lunged forward and she screamed as his knife slashed away at her clothing and within seconds she was naked. Howling like a demented beast, Mr Mac stood triumphantly over his victim.

Then he raped her.

Chapter
SIXTEEN

The police took her more seriously this time. Josie presented Detective Inspector Lacey with the pictures and he became increasingly more concerned. Lizzie Baines' mother was contacted and officers sent out in search of Lindsay Murray's family.

When she was finished Josie was exhausted. Tim arrived to collect her and was appalled to see her in such a state. The events of the last few hours had been particularly distressing and finally her frustration had turned to tears of anger. Without comment, he drove her straight home.

The house was cold and silent when Josie pushed open the door and going into the living room she threw herself down onto the sofa.

"I'll put the kettle on." Tim said allowing her time to herself.

Josie was numb, she could hardly keep up with the terrible things that were happening and her mind was running wild with all kinds of distressing images. She could not put the thought of Mrs Baines out of her mind, the poor woman had collapsed when she saw the picture of Lizzie chained against a wall. It was enough to drive her over the edge and a doctor had to be called to administer sedatives.

Josie could hardly believe that just a few days ago they had all been out together enjoying an evening of fun. Everything had been so normal then, they had talked about work, discussed their holiday plans, she had even told them about Tim and they were all looking forward to her forth-coming exhibition.

"We have to decide what to do next." Tim said his voice slicing through her thoughts.

"Why Tim, why?" she whispered.

"Because we have to ensure your safety."

"No not that. Why Lindsay, why Lizzie, why Sarah?"

"We've been through this before." He reminded her as he placed a mug of coffee on the table.

It was obvious to Tim that she was struggling to control her emotions. Sitting down beside her he slipped his arm comfortingly around her shoulders and she rested her head against his chest.

His heart was beating steadily, it was a comforting sound and closing her eyes, she let herself drown in his warm embrace.

"Don't you see he's making your life hell and I'm sure it's only time before he makes his move on you." He held her tighter. "We must be prepared."

Her tears soaked into his shirt as the pressure of the last few days was finally released.

"Please tell me this is not happening," she sobbed.

Tim feared for her safety, he could not get the image of Sarah out of his mind. He dared not dwell on the unimaginable indignities that she was suffering and he was determined that this was not going to happen to Josie. He would do whatever it took to keep her safe. His immediate concern was for her sanity and he wondered if she was strong enough to get through this. He felt certain that things were about to become a lot worse but, keeping his thoughts to himself, he dropped a kiss on top of her head.

Mr Mac returned to the cellar, he was still bare chested and dressed in nothing but his kilt. Both Lizzie and Sarah reacted when he appeared, fearful that he was looking for more.

Lindsay was beside herself with grief and sobbing inconsolably there was no more fight left in her. He had destroyed her spirit and the horror of his actions left her shattered.

Lizzie and Sarah were both horrified by what he had done. They had expected as much but when it finally happened were left shocked and sickened. There was no longer any doubt in their minds, they knew exactly what to expect, he was capable of anything.

They had attempted to reach out to Lindsay but it was no good, she was unreachable and had withdrawn into a world of her own. She had not yet responded to their words of sympathy or taken comfort from their support.

Mr Mac stood eyeing them, re-living the fun he had just enjoyed.

"Not so lively now I see," he jeered. Reaching into his sporran, he produced a key.

Lindsay backed away as he approached and her panic flared up as she strained frantically against her chains. Her mouth twisted pitifully and as she cried out a chilling sound filled the air.

Ignoring her terror, he reached up and unlocked the shackles holding her arms, laughing out loud as Lindsay collapsed to the ground. Her legs, unable to support her, were cold and lifeless and along with her courage, her strength had gone.

Shaking his head, he continued to laugh and stepping over her was unable to comprehend the depth of her despair. To him she was merely a plaything and the game had just begun.

Glancing at Lizzie and Sarah, he studied them and found their shocked expressions gratifying but he did not stay, suddenly he turned and was gone.

Lindsay curled up into a tight ball on the cold concrete floor and her shoulders shook as she wept. Lizzie, sharing her desolation, felt hopelessly inadequate and ached with grief. She was unable to comfort her friend or help with her misery and silently tears flowed unchecked over her cheeks.

Eventually he returned carrying a bundle of clothing under his arm.

"Get dressed, you are free to go." He tossed the clothes down beside Lindsay then, without another word, was gone again.

Sarah stared in disbelief, she was convinced that he was about to attack them too, his irrational behaviour made no sense and unanswered questions nagged at her brain. She had no idea what was going to happen next because he was so unpredictable. In an effort to remain calm, she tried to comfort Lindsay using words of encouragement. Lizzie was far too distraught to help.

Sarah knew she must motivate her friend but it was impossible, Lindsay was in too much distress. She needed more time to come to terms with what had happened, only then would she be able to make any sensible plans. Lindsay was their only hope, she would have to raise the alarm. It was important that she understood what had to be done their lives depended on it.

"Lindsay, get up, get dressed quickly before he comes back."

Lindsay slowly raised her head and stared blankly around the room. She looked totally defeated and Sarah began to think that she would be unable to respond but she was wrong. Pulling herself up into a sitting position Lindsay began to rub life back into her legs. The skin on her ankles had been chafed raw and her wrists were bruised but thankfully nothing was broken. Waves of nausea robbed her of her strength but slowly as her limbs began to respond she managed to pull on some clothes.

Wrapped in the bundle she discovered a bottle of water and forcing her fingers to work she unscrewed the top. It was a relief to flush the foul taste from her mouth, the water was cool and heavenly, it soothed her burning throat.

After a while she began to feel stronger and less vulnerable now that she was dressed, albeit in a collection of ill fitting garments that were years out of fashion. Slowly she limped across the floor and in turn helped her friends to drink from the water bottle then, they began to make their plans.

"You must get to a phone," Lizzie told her.

"Or another house, raise the alarm," Sarah added.

"But I've no idea where we are."

"Someone is bound to be out driving or walking, just find a road and flag them down." Sarah did her best using only words of encouragement and slowly she began to get through her friend.

Lizzie realised that Mr Mac was not just going to let her go but she kept her thoughts to herself. There must be a catch and she felt certain that Sarah was thinking the same.

"Well my wee beauties," he startled them when he returned.

Lindsay cried out, she was terrified and backed away into a corner.

"I see my choice in vogue suits you," he laughed. "Not too big I hope, don't want you tripping over when you try to run. Now Lindsay Murray," suddenly he became serious. "This is what we do."

Pausing for effect, he paced the floor. "Have you heard of a wee game called Logan's run?"

None of them answered.

"No? Then let me tell you how it goes. You run and after five minutes I follow and when I catch you..." He lifted his finger to his temple, "bang!" Drawing a pistol from his waistband he waved it at them.

They stared at him incredulously, hardly daring to believe what he had just implied and Lindsay, whimpering with fright, was unable to move. She felt faint and was about to collapse.

"You never know," he hissed, "you might even get away."

Tucking his pistol away he moved in and grabbed Lindsay roughly. She cried out as he dragged her across the floor and pushing her up the short flight of steps she was gone.

Sarah and Lizzie stared after their friend in utter disbelief. They were experiencing the same emotions and their inability to help Lindsay left them both devastated.

At the end of the long corridor Lindsay was pushed out of the house and her mind began to function. This is how a condemned prisoner must have felt when being led to the hangman's gallows, she thought grimly.

It was the first time she had been out of doors in days, time had stood still during her imprisonment and she had no way of knowing how long she had been in the cellar. Pushing these thoughts from her mind, she had to focus.

It was a beautiful morning, the sun had just risen above the treetops and a light breeze kissed her cheeks and ruffled her hair. She was standing on a gravel driveway that swept around the house and glancing in both directions wondered which way to go. Turning slowly she looked up at the house searching for a number or a name, some kind of reference with which to identify her whereabouts but there was nothing, the house remained anonymous. The windows on the ground floor were shuttered, this only added to air of abandonment that surrounded the building but that is where it ended. The lawns and gardens were immaculately kept and flower borders, blooming with colour, were pleasing to look at. She had no time to stand and stare, she had to get moving. He had given her five minutes and time was rapidly running out. Spurred into action by a sound which came from somewhere over her shoulder she started forward. Her body was a mass of hurts and sobbing with every step, she fought to catch her breath.

Willing herself on, she made her way across the lawn. Here the ground sloped gently down towards the garden boundary and beyond she could see across the valley. In the distance, she could just make out the sea, the horizon an almost invisible line separating sea from sky.

She stopped in the middle of the lawn, and filled with indecision turned a full circle following the curve of the driveway with her eyes. Maybe she should follow it, try to find the road. There was plenty of cover from huge shrubs that were growing along the way, these would surely hide her progress, this had to be her best option. Racked with indecision she glanced nervously back towards the house.

After some thought she decided that way was far too obvious, he would be expecting her to head towards the road. Cursing her inability to make up her mind she continued to cross the lawn and struggling with the excess fabric hitched the skirt up to her knees. When she arrived at the boundary fence, she searched for a way through. Savage barbed wire stretched between thick wooden posts formed a barrier that was designed to stop wild animals from wandering into the garden. There were no gaps along the fence and no other way to go but over the top. It was not very high but encumbered by her skirts it was difficult to overcome.

Carefully she used the wire as steps and clutching at a wooden post pulled herself up. Shaking unsteadily at the top, she eased her legs over the sharp barbs then the hem of her skirt caught and ripped as she lost her balance. Falling forward, Lindsay put her arm out to protect her face and pain shot through her shoulder as she landed awkwardly. She was winded but fortunately no bones were broken. It took her a few moments to catch her breath, then heaving herself up she pushed her way into the undergrowth.

Hidden by the trees her spirit began to lift as she followed the path through the forest. She was determined to get away, she had to find someone to help Sarah and Lizzie but soon realised that if he discovered the way she had come he would use the same path, so picking up her pace she had to put some distance between herself and the house.

Here where the trees grew close together there was less light, but as she pushed her way through the foliage, the going became easier. Where the light was reduced the undergrowth was not as dense and she was able to make better progress. Branches were more of a concern, reaching out they snagged at her clothing and tangled her hair, they also whipped her skin mercilessly. On more than one occasion she had to stop and pull herself free from entanglement, it was strenuous work and she had not gone far before she had to stop altogether. Her breath was rattling in her chest and she had a sharp pain in her side. Cocking her head to one side she listened but could hear nothing, the silence around her as impenetrable as her surroundings, not even a bird was singing. The only sounds were her heart beating rapidly inside her chest and her own laboured breathing.

The canopy above her head was filled with a variety of broad leaves but as she moved further down into the valley, the cover became less dense.

Here the trees had been arranged in rows, a legacy of the ship building industry that had once flourished in the bay. The way ahead opened up a little more but, after a while, she had to stop again. Unused to such physical punishment she clutched at her side and held her breath.

Once she had recovered, she moved on and where the trees thinned, shafts of sunlight penetrated the thick canopy overhead to form rich golden pools on the forest floor. Underfoot a thick carpet of moss made the going soft and occasionally she found secret circles of mushrooms and toadstools growing at the base of trees. With a smile, she remembered childhood stories of fairies dancing beneath the moonlight in sacred groves just like this one. This was truly a magical place and she had stumbled upon it quite by chance. Ordinarily she would never have discovered a place like this and the beauty of her surroundings filled her with pleasure.

Soft pine needles that had fallen on the moss released the most wonderful scent as she moved. She would have loved more time to appreciate the beauty of the forest, here she could forget all her troubles but she had to keep moving, he would not be far behind.

Mr Mac moved silently through the forest every bit the hunter. He was certain that she had come this way; human nature dictated that running down a slope was far easier than running up one. There was evidence that she had passed this way, fabric from her skirt was snagged on the fence, this told him where she had crossed the garden boundary and he even managed to find the spot where she had left the path. It had crossed his mind that she might have scaled a tree in order to wait until darkness, but none of the others had had tried that before, besides who would want to lose themselves amongst the trees after dark. He knew exactly where she was going so there was no rush. In his mind he saw the place where she would emerge from the forest. They all came this way they were so predictable. He grinned and licked his lips.

Lindsay stopped, she was certain that she could hear the sound of running water so holding her head up high she hardly made a sound. Straining her ears, she listened to the wind. The trees had thinned out considerably now and she could make out a clearing not far ahead so creeping silently to the edge of the woods she stopped. As nervous as a deer she stepped out onto the meadow. The grass was rich beneath her feet and the scent of wild flowers perfumed the air as she brushed against them. It tickled her legs and she could feel the sun on her back. Under different circumstances, she would have enjoyed these sensations but the occasion denied her these small pleasures. Turning towards the riverbank, she wondered what she might find on the opposite side and in her mind's eye imagined a house full of people who would be willing to help. They would offer her sanctuary from the horror that was in pursuit and would make everything right.

Mr Mac saw her the moment she stepped out of the forest and he watched as she danced through the long meadow grass. Keeping out of sight, he moved along the riverbank. She would have to pass this way if she followed the path across the meadow and he grinned, she had no way of knowing that he was there.

Cresting the raised bank, she sank to her knees and brushing hair from her face peered out across the river. Unfortunately there was no house, no sanctuary and no one to help. Letting out a small cry of despair she glanced in both directions but all she could see was water. Here the river was wide and swollen; it snaked its way around the bay nearing the final part of its journey. She had never been here before but Josie had described Spey Bay to her often enough and in the distance she could see the iron bridge that her friend had painted so beautifully.

This was such a tranquil place it was little wonder that Josie loved it so much and Lindsay would have liked to stay longer. The thought of going any further dismayed her, she was exhausted both physically and mentally and her body ached from the torture that she had endured.

A lump formed at the back of her throat and she struggled to hold back her tears. Thoughts of her friends chained in the cellar drove her on; she had to get moving, she owed it to them. Lizzie was aware that he would not be far behind but the effort was too great, she just had to rest for a little while longer.

Suddenly, startled by a hand that touched her shoulder she swung round and her eyes widened with shock as she stared into the barrel of a gun. She did not hear the sound as it fired.

Mr Mac carried her lifeless body back to his house where he took great delight in photographing her; she was after all another prized trophy to be added to his collection.

Later, he printed off the pictures that had been loaded onto his computer, and selecting one, pushed it into a plain white envelope. Sealing it he added a printed address label before going off in the direction of the village.

Chapter
SEVENTEEN

Josie spent the morning in her studio laying down the foundations to what would become one of her greatest paintings and as she worked, she allowed her mind to wander. She thought about her friends and gradually realised that Tim was right. His theories began to make sense, but what troubled her most was being unable to convince the police that the events were linked to the murder in Spey Bay. She was convinced of it but had no tangible evidence to give her story credence. There were of course the pictures, proof that her friends were being held against their will but there was nothing to say they were in Scotland.

Glancing up at the clock on the wall she was surprised to see that the morning was almost gone. It was often like that, when engrossed in her work time would pass her by without her noticing.

Laying down her brush she smiled and using a rag to wipe paint from her fingers she moved away from the canvas. Thoughts were still going round inside her head, she had no idea who Mr Mac was or where he could be found then suddenly she remembered the telephone number her aunt had given her. How could she have been so stupid?

Throwing down the rag, she rushed into the living room and rummaged around in her bag for the scrap of paper, reaching for the phone she threw herself down into a chair. She hesitated, and chewing at her bottom lip wound the strip of paper round her fingers whilst thinking carefully about what to say, then she began to dial the number.

After a few moments, she heard the ringtone but there was no answer and the phone went to voice mail. Stabbing the re-dial button, she was surprised when he answered immediately.

"Hello," he said disguising his voice with an English accent.

"Oh hi," she began nervously. "Can I speak to Mr Mac please?"

He could hardly believe his luck; he recognised her voice the moment she began to speak.

"This is Mr Mac speaking."

"Oh hi," she said again, "I'm Josie MacDonald. You gave this number to my aunt. Apparently you wanted to speak with me regarding my story in the local paper."

"Ah yes, I did didn't I." Working hard at his accent, he continued. "But don't you see that was then and this is now, a day may as well be a lifetime as far as the media is concerned. Yesterday's news is old news. People forget you see especially when there's no body to be found. Now how can that be?"

"I see." She did not see at all, in fact she had no idea what he was talking about.

"Maybe you have a greater story to tell," he continued in syllables of silk.

"It's you isn't it?" Suddenly things became a little clearer. "I think I know what's going on."

"And what might that be do you think?" he asked arrogantly.

"Where are my friends?"

"Ah yes, your friends, I wondered how long it would take for you to ask," he chuckled quietly into the phone. "Well, as you asked so nicely let me tell you about your friends."

The sound of his voice made her skin crawl and she shuffled forward onto the edge of her seat.

"Sarah Hamilton, such a deliciously lovely young woman," he paused. In his mind could see her hanging naked in his cellar. "I like Sarah." He continued. "I like to see her often; in fact I see all of her every day."

Her stomach lurched as the evil sound of his laughter insulted her ear. Tim was right, this man is mad.

"Then of course there's Lizzie Baines," he chuckled. "Tall thin Lizzie, my red haired beauty, oh what fun we shall have. Can you tell me," he paused, "is she a true red head?" He laughed some more. "I think it's time I found out don't you Josie MacDonald?"

Closing her eyes, she fought against the urge to vomit. She could not understand how he managed to remain so calm, he was obviously enjoying every moment and she hated him for it.

"Do you know," he continued suddenly. "I have something very special in mind for Lizzie Baines."

She gasped as he described in minute detail the despicable things that he was going to do to her friend and clamping a hand over her mouth, she managed to stifle her revulsion. She wanted to throw down the phone, smash it against the wall and disconnect the call. She could bear it no longer but she knew that she must, she had to find out where he was hiding them.

"You are sick, do you know that?" she screamed, unable to hold back.

"Oh yes, I think I do," he laughed softly, "but that's no concern of yours. You asked me about your friends did you not, well now I'm telling you, it wouldn't do to lie would it?"

She remained silent hardly daring to speak. She had to remain calm.

"You women, you exist in your own little worlds, your lives of pure fantasy. You dress up and paint your faces in a most provocative way, you wear perfume to make you smell irresistible and you tease and taunt your way around in high heels. Well, this is the real world, as real as Stirling and Bannockburn," he paused for breath, his face flushing with excitement. "Your English Lords had no regard for the women of our clans, they were mere play things, raped and murdered indiscriminately and left to rot on the fields with the bodies of their men. Did you know that Josie MacDonald?"

"On their wedding night our women were forced to sleep with your English Lords, that was an attempt to breed us out and if they didn't comply they were murdered." He paused again waiting for her to react.

Josie was speechless she had no idea what he was talking about.

"Oh and by the way, your friend Lindsay Murray has gone." His laugh was a snort of evil.

"What do you mean, where has she gone?"

"Oh what fun we had before I let her go." His voice dropped to a whisper then suddenly he was gone, the connection had failed.

Josie stared at the phone in disbelief, her hands were shaking and thoughts whirled around inside her head. She was at a loss, paralysed by fear she didn't know what to think. He had said that Lindsay was gone but he failed to tell her where she had gone. What state was she in and where was she now? He had said such terrible things; would he really carry out his threats?

She could not imagine anyone being so heartless, and covering her mouth with her hand, rocked backwards and forwards sobbing in shocked disbelief. She could hardly believe the things he had said and she was frightened for Lindsay. She was still no closer to discovering where they were.

Snatching up the phone, she re-dialled, this time she would ask him outright but it was no use, the number was no longer available.

Mr Mac tossed the phone onto the table, the battery had finally expired, he had no more use for it anyway. Sitting for a moment deep in thought he rubbed his fingers over his chin. His conversation with Josie MacDonald had been quite unexpected, it came as a complete surprise and left him feeling exhilarated. He had enjoyed talking to her especially the part about what he had in mind for her friends. He would continue sending her pictures and he might even enclose the occasional subtle clue. If he played her right, she would be drawn into his trap. He grinned and licked his lips. Oh what fun he was going to have with Josie MacDonald.

Eventually she managed to reach Tim; she had been calling him on his phone for the last thirty minutes. His assistant had told her that he was busy with a client and promised that Tim would phone her back at the first opportunity.

When eventually he returned her call, she was beside herself with grief.

"Oh Tim, I'm so sorry to bother you but I really need to talk."

"Are you okay?" He could hear the distress in her voice.

In a tidal wave of words charged with emotion, she told him about her telephone conversation with Mr Mac.

"I'm so worried," she said. "He told me he'd let Lindsay go but we would have heard from her by now. She would have contacted me I'm sure of it."

Tim wondered what Mr Mac meant when he told her that Lindsay was gone, he frowned but kept his suspicions to himself.

"The connection was broken before I had chance to find out where he was. I tried to phone back but the line was dead," she sobbed with frustration. "He's mad and totally unpredictable."

She paused and took a deep breath before continuing. "It seems to me the only way we are going to discover where they are, is for him to take me too."

"What!" Tim shouted into the phone, "I don't think so." He lowered his voice as people in the gallery glanced his way.

"That's not one of your better ideas," he told her. "You're not thinking straight, besides you're far too upset to be making those kinds of decisions."

"Sorry Tim but I feel so helpless."

"That's exactly what he wants; he's happy knowing that you're suffering. I know the authorities seem to be dragging their feet but it's much better to let them deal with it. Of course we'll help in any way we can." He paused and glanced up at the people who were admiring the paintings on the wall.

"Look Josie, I have to go. Let's discuss this later. I'll call round as soon as I've finished here."

Placing the telephone down he walked towards the smiling couple, they had made up their minds.

"We would like this one please," the man said indicating towards a Josie MacDonald.

Mr Mac strolled into the cellar as if he were on a Sunday afternoon outing. Glancing sideways, he admired Sarah before positioning himself in the centre of the floor where he studied them both thoughtfully.

"A wee bit of housekeeping is required here I think," he kicked an empty water bottle across the floor. "Before we clear up this mess I want some information. I know you girls are good at gossiping so let's have some." He paused and glared at them.

"In return for this information, I will give you food, water and some freedom. How does that sound?" He smiled and waited for an answer.

"Josie MacDonald sells her paintings?" he continued. "Well, does she not sell her paintings?"

"Yes." Lizzie nodded.

"So where does she sell them?"

"On the internet."

"Ah yes, the internet," he said thoughtfully as a number of ideas entered his head, "anywhere else?"

They remained silent.

"Oh come on girls." Thrusting his hands into his pockets, he began to pace the floor. "I've seen her paintings she's very good so they must sell elsewhere, in a gallery perhaps?"

Sarah shot Lizzie a glance, she could not forgive herself for giving him her name and she was certainly not about to tell him anything more.

"I see," he said as he saw the look that passed between them.

"What have you done with Lindsay?" Lizzie asked.

He stopped pacing and stared her.

"Ah yes Lindsay Murray," he said softly. "She's gone."

His words struck terror into their hearts.

"I explained the rules of the game," he shrugged. "I gave her a sporting chance. Isn't that what you English say, a sporting chance?"

He paused before going on. "Well, that's more than the women of the clans could expect."

He produced a key from his pocket and released Lizzie first. She collapsed into a heap on the floor and as soon as her fingers re-gained some feeling, she fastened the buttons of her blouse.

"Now clean up this mess." He snapped before going off to find a plastic bag for the rubbish.

Tim arrived at Josie's house later that evening and when she opened the door she had the telephone clamped between her chin and shoulder. It was clear that she was having a heated discussion and feeling self-conscious, he hurried into the living room, leaving her to continue her call in private.

A little while later he heard her cry out in frustration then she slammed the receiver down.

Her face was flushed when she appeared and he could see that she was angry. He remained sitting on the sofa as she came into the room.

"Sorry about that," she said.

Crouching down beside him, she brushed her lips against his cheek.

"I hope you don't mind," he grinned raising a glass of white wine.

"No of course not." Turning away, she stood up and went to the side table where she poured herself a glass.

"Have you had a busy day?" he asked, thinking she looked exhausted.

"I was painting when he phoned," she began working dried paint from her fingers.

"I guess that was Mike," he shot her a lopsided grin.

Nodding she slipped in beside him on the sofa. She was in no mood to continue with that line of conversation and it was not yet the right time to bring up their earlier discussion.

"Are you okay about the exhibition?"

He realised that she was probably in no mood to be entertaining people from the world of art and media.

"I can't back out now, besides you've worked so hard, you have arranged everything."

Shifting in his seat, he pulled a sheet of paper from his pocket. "Here's the invitation list."

Scanning the list of names she said, "Wow, how do you know these people? This represents my celebrity wish list."

"Networking," he shrugged, "besides I don't really know them as such." He took a sip of wine and winked at her over the rim of the glass.

"But all the same it's a mighty impressive catalogue of names."

Leaning forward she kissed him and his heart missed a beat and he realised how lucky he was.

"A national newspaper is keen to do something in one of their colour supplements."

"Really, I can't keep up with it all." Clapping her hands together with excitement, she almost spilled her wine. "Why would a national newspaper be interested in me?"

"Because you're the new kid on the block, take it whilst you can and don't waste a second because tomorrow it will be someone else."

She almost drowned in his enthusiasm, it washed over her in waves as they chatted and he answered all her questions.

"Oh, by the way, my sister has designed a new website for you."

She looked at him in astonishment.

"You haven't met Kate yet," he grinned, "but she's looking forward to meeting you."

"I didn't even know you had a sister, why haven't you told me about her before?"

"Never thought about it," he shrugged, "besides, a chap doesn't like to mention his sister when he's trying to impress a lady."

She punched his shoulder lightly and he grinned. "Well you've certainly impressed me Timothy Granger." She kissed him again.

"Tell me about Kate, does she design websites for a living?"

"No, she's a micro-electronics engineer."

"That's a mouthful, what does that mean, what does she do?"

"Kate designs specialist equipment that's used in many fields, for example, key hole surgery, engineering, space and underwater exploration, military equipment, that sort of thing. Her latest wizardry was something to do with head up display systems used by fast jet fighter pilots."

"My goodness!" she exclaimed, "and she wants to meet me."

He laughed and hauling himself to his feet went to re-fill their glasses.

"You weren't serious about what you said earlier were you?" he asked as he reached for the bottle.

"What do you mean?"

"Allowing him to kidnap you in order to discover where he's holding your friends."

Her comment had clearly unsettled him.

"Well, it had crossed my mind."

"I won't let you do it," he said firmly. "Not on your own."

He turned towards her and she could see that he was determined.

"We'll think of something together," she reassured him.

"Let's just get the exhibition out of the way first," he said softly and moved to where she was sitting. "Besides, you might not realise it yet but after tomorrow evening you might have to make some drastic lifestyle changes."

Mr Mac was once again in his car speeding south. He had considered flying this time but in the end had decided against the idea. He would need his 'bag of tools' and he would never have got them onto the plane. He hated the thought of using the train so there was no other option, he would have to drive.

He had managed to extract the information he wanted from Lizzie Baines, some of which he found very interesting indeed. She told him that Josie was about to host a celebrity exhibition at the Timothy Granger gallery, so checking it out on the internet he discovered that some of her work was already displayed there. It also revealed that the exhibition was going to take place the following evening and a plan had immediately lodged itself into his brain. The event would be an ideal opportunity for him to get up close. This time he would be able to study her without her realising it. The prospect thrilled him and he began to have all kinds of ideas. Suddenly the long drive into England became less of a hardship.

Chapter
EIGHTEEN

Tim's gallery was buzzing, the noise reminding him of chickens cackling in a barn. The volume ebbed and flowed like the tide and occasionally one voice would rise up above the rest. Laughter could be heard from all around the room and as the champagne flowed a party atmosphere replaced the formal opening.

Andrew Wilkes, a respected author, painter and socialite had declared the exhibition open with a speech that would further his own career then the party began.

Cars were still delivering minor celebrities eager to be seen arriving fashionably late and upstage each other in front of the cameras.

Tim's networking scheme was proving to be a great success and looking around the room there were more heads than there had been invitations. Secretly he congratulated himself for over ordering the champagne, at least his wine merchant would be pleased.

Josie looked wonderful. She was wearing a long peacock blue evening gown that shimmered gloriously in the light every time moved and her hair was piled stylishly on top of her head. A carefully arranged smile adorned her face and she did her best to hide her brittle nerves.

She was in much demand, mostly from people who had bought her paintings, many of them wanting to pose with her in front of the cameras. This made her feel as popular as a celebrity at an award ceremony.

"You look fantastic." Tim whispered in her ear the moment he got the chance.

She smiled and grabbed a glass of champagne from a tray that was floating past.

"You've done a wonderful job Tim and I'm so grateful."

"I couldn't have done it without you, you're the star here." He smiled again and touched her shoulder affectionately. "Most of them are here for the booze." He looked around the room.

"Why you're such a cynic," she laughed. "Here am I convinced that they're here to celebrate my work."

"And so they are," he reassured her. "Seriously though, they are mostly social climbing parasites but they also have very deep pockets. They are all in it to outdo each other and as long as we're in favour then I see no harm in exploiting them."

"I'll drink to that." She raised her glass.

"Ah," Tim waved his hand in the air. "There's someone I'd like you to meet." Guiding her by her elbow, he negotiated his way across the room almost losing her on more than one occasion.

She didn't notice the barrel chested man with wild hair who was studying her painting of Spey Bay. He was turned out splendidly in traditional Scottish tartan his jacket and kilt immaculate. Not only did he admire her work he was studying her every move.

"Josie, I'd like you to meet my sister Kate."

Kate Granger stood barely five feet tall, her petite frame was perfectly formed and she was elegantly dressed. She was not at all what Josie had imagined. Her long black dress matched the colour of her hair and her heels added at least four inches to her height. Josie noticed immediately that whenever she smiled there were traces of Tim in her face.

"Hiya," she grinned, reaching out for Josie's hand. "He's told me all about you."

"You've stolen my opening lines," Josie laughed. "He's told me all about you too."

Hitting it off at once they soon had their heads together and were deep in conversation. Tim feeling like an intruder wandered off leaving them to get to know each other.

"I must congratulate you on your work," Kate said. "I simply must have one of your paintings whilst I can still afford one."

"Tim has told me about your fascinating work."

"Oh, he's such a bore," Kate made a face. "Tell me about your painting, how do you manage to come by your inspiration?"

They talked easily about her work, Josie telling her about her recent trip to Scotland and as she studied Kate, Josie was amazed by how much she resembled Tim. It was not obvious at first, but as time went on she was struck by their similarities. Kate possessed a calming nature, she reminded Josie of someone at ease with the world and she found it easy to relax in her company. Her skin seemed to tingle with tiny electrical currents as she stood beside her, it was a pleasantly warming sensation. It was as if Kate could see into the depths of her mind, she seemed to know what she was thinking before she had chance to say it. She was an extraordinary woman quite unlike her brother who was much more down to earth.

"No I haven't had any formal training," Josie was saying. "In fact my degree is in History and English."

"Then what we have displayed here this evening is the result of raw talent." Kate marvelled.

'Beware of the man with the wild hair!' A voice sounded inside Josie's head.

"Well you know what they say, practice makes perfect if you don't mind my saying." A deep voice heavily laced with a Scottish accent invaded their space. "Forgive me for butting in but I overheard your conversation and couldn't help but wonder why most of your paintings are scenes of my own bonny Scotland."

Josie was startled and turning to face the man with wild hair she managed to compose herself before replying.

"My connection with Scotland should be quite obvious I would have thought."

"Of course," he said, inclining his head slightly before smiling. He was aware of her discomfort. "With a name such as yours Miss MacDonald, I should imagine you have links there."

"I do have a passion for Scotland," she agreed. "I simply love the landscape, the scenery is of course a pure joy to paint and I find the people who live there pleasant enough."

"I can understand that," he inclined his head.

"And what do you think of Miss MacDonald's work Mr...?" Kate eyed him suspiciously.

"You can call me Greg," he informed her cordially. "I much prefer that to Gregory." Turning back to Josie, he continued. "You do us proud Miss MacDonald, I have an eye for one or two pieces myself."

Josie noticed that his smile never reached his eyes, they remained distant and hard like dark stones set into his face.

"And where do you call home Greg?" Kate interrupted again.

"Well," he hesitated, peering coldly down at her. "These are scenes of my own back yard you might say."

"So you come from Morayshire then?" Josie said with a nervous laugh.

"Aye, that's correct," he nodded.

"And what brings you here tonight?" Kate cut in sharply.

Josie could feel the tension rising between them and she had no idea why Kate was behaving so callously towards this man. Perhaps she was simply annoyed by his intrusion but Josie did not believe that, there seemed to be something else.

"It is because of Miss MacDonald herself," he stared at Kate with disdain. "She was involved in a wee incident shall we say, when visiting my country."

"Oh," Josie exclaimed, the colour draining from her face. "So you've heard about that then?" she murmured. "The story in the local paper."

"I'm not in the habit of believing everything I read in the newspaper but I must admit you are the subject of my curiosity."

They were silent for moment as the atmosphere between them thickened.

"I see the cathedral at Elgin inspired you," he said going off on a tangent.

"Yes," she nodded. "I like Elgin very much."

"Did you know that the present clan chief of the Bruce's is The Right Honourable Earl of Elgin?"

Josie frowned, her knowledge of Scottish history was limited but she remembered reading a leaflet that she had picked up during her visit to the cathedral.

"Yes I do, he's the 11th Earl of Elgin and also the 15th Earl of Kincardine."

"Aye lass you're right." He was impressed. "The Earl is the 37th chief of the name of Bruce and Robert the Bruce is something of a hero of mine."

"I love all that romantic stuff. I'm quite a fan of William Wallace." Josie confided in him.

"William Wallace eh," he said eyeing her with suspicion.

"The English chronicles regard him as a bit of an outlaw, a murderer, the perpetrator of atrocities and a traitor." Kate said butting in on their conversation.

Josie was appalled by her comments.

"Is that so?" Greg stiffened and regarded her with another hostile stare. "William Wallace, young lady, was in fact an exemplar of unbending commitment to Scotland's independence who died a martyr for the cause."

"Well," Josie said sliding between them, desperate to defuse the situation before it got out of hand but before she got the chance Tim arrived.

"Josie, excuse me," he smiled. "I want you to meet some people over here."

Taking her by the hand he led her away before she could offer her apologies.

Anger and hatred bubbled up inside him as hot as lava from a volcano but from the outside he looked calm enough. He could not afford to do anything rash, give himself away or jeopardise his plan and as her friend turned to move away there were no words to describe what he was feeling towards her. All he wanted to do was grab her by the throat and throttle the life out of her but that would have to wait. Of one thing he was certain, he was going to teach her a lesson that she would never forget.

"What was that all about?" Tim snarled when he finally caught his sister alone.

"Not sure, bad vibes," she said brushing him off. "Who is he anyway?"

"He signed in as Gregory MacLaren. He turned up out of the blue claiming to be a fan of Josie's work."

"I don't like him," she shuddered. "He leaves me with a very bad feeling."

"Women's intuition?" he shot her a patronising grin.

She ignored him.

Tim had grown accustomed to his sister's strange ways but he would never understand how an academic mind such as hers could entertain such archaic beliefs. His sister was far too spiritual for his liking. In earlier times she would have been condemned as a witch and burnt at the stake. He had no time for her 'mumbo jumbo', he never had. Throughout their childhood he had teased her calling her strange predictions 'women's intuition', this had infuriated her.

Josie was disturbed by Kate's behaviour, she had no idea why she had been so mean to Greg MacLaren and searching the room, she discovered that he had gone. Going over their strange conversation in her head something stirred in the back of her mind, an incomplete thought that got away before it had chance to fully develop.

Kate touched her arm unexpectedly and whispered. "I'm off to the little girl's room."

"Wait for me, let me grab my bag first then I'll come with you." Josie led the way to Tim's office where she had left her things.

"I'll just take the opportunity to use his phone." Kate said moving towards his desk that stood in the middle of the room. Glancing quickly at Josie, she took the telephone handset from its stand and slipped it into a drawer.

"Would you believe it!" she exclaimed.

"What?" Josie looked up in surprise.

"Well look," she indicated to the telephone stand and Josie could see that the handset was missing.

"I had to leave my mobile at home because the battery needs charging."

"Here, use mine." Josie rummaged in her bag. "He's probably got it in his pocket." She smiled, handing over her phone.

The car that Tim had organised to take Josie home arrived and as she settled onto the back seat, he leaned in through the open door and kissed her. He promised to call round later even although the hour was late.

Kate, standing on the pavement beside him smiled warmly at Josie as the car pulled away.

"Did you manage to do it?" Tim asked without taking his eyes off the receding car.

"Yes eventually." His sister replied. "She was a very busy lady this evening."

"Where did you put the device?"

"I attached it to her mobile phone, give me yours and I'll show you how it works."

Handing her his phone he watched as she flipped it open and entered a code on the keypad. The LCD screen came to life and booted through a series of readouts before settling on a display of program icons.

"How did you do that?" He asked amazed by what she had just done.

"I've modified this so all you need do is go into the program menu and select this icon." Touching the screen, she activated the symbol labelled 'tracking', and it went into GPS mode. Tim watched as a tiny red light began to flash and move steadily across the screen.

"There she goes." Kate was satisfied that the device was working. "As the indicator moves it will update itself using GPS signals. In theory she should never fall off the edge of the screen."

Looking up at him she grinned and handing it over said. "If she leaves the boundary of the city your phone will alert you."

"Blimey, how on earth did you do that?"

"Don't ask." She dug him in the ribs with her elbow before becoming serious. "Look I know you don't think much of my 'intuition', but I really think you should go to her, she's about to receive some very bad news."

Mr Mac was waiting in the street when Josie returned home. He watched as the driver handed her from the car and walked her to the door. Once it was open, she stooped to pick up her mail from the mat and the man returned to the car. He waited long enough for her to close the door before pulling away from the kerb.

Squirming with excitement Mr Mac watched as lights went on tracking Josie's progress through the house. The curtains were not yet drawn so he had a clear view as she stopped by the living room window. She began sorting through her mail and he could not help but notice how different she looked. Even from this distance he could see the way the light played magnificently against the fabric of her dress. She was elegant and attractive and he could still smell the fragrance of her perfume. Moving in his seat, he tried hard to shake these thoughts from his mind.

She was studying a white envelope, his white envelope, and as she turned it over in her hands, his heart began to race. She seemed to hesitate then tearing it open pulled out the single sheet of paper. He could not see the expression on her face but her body language told him everything. He grinned and licked his lips.

Josie cried out in shock as her eyes filled with tears, and as she stared at the computer-generated picture, her mind refused to believe what she saw. It was just like the previous pictures but this time the victim was Lindsay. Staggering blindly away from the window she collapsed into a chair and was transported back to the riverbank at Spey Bay. She had watched him commit murder but this time it was not a stranger who had been shot, it was Lindsay. Surely this cannot be happening, she sobbed, struggling for breath. How could it possibly be Lindsay?

Her mind in turmoil, she refused to believe the evidence that was laid out before her. Tears flowed unchecked over her face blurring the image on the page. It must be a clever hoax, she thought in an attempt to convince herself that it was not real. It had to be another computer-manipulated photograph, a picture designed to torture her mind. Her hand was trembling badly as she brushed away her tears, and taking in a deep breath, she tried to remain calm. She took another look forcing herself to see it objectively but there were no mistake, it was definitely Lindsay. Her eyes were staring sightlessly out from the picture and her skin was pale. Josie was looking at a death mask and gasping at the enormity of it she realised that one of her friends may have died because of her.

Mr Mac was laughing, the evil sound filling his car. This was a perfect end to his day and he congratulated himself, not only had he managed to stand beside her without her realising his identity but he had also engaged her in conversation. Now he was outside her house at the very moment she opened his envelope. He had not bargained on that little bonus, fate had intervened dealing him a winning hand; he could never have planned this.

He realised how lucky he was, if she had seen it earlier the reception at the gallery would have been very different, perhaps it would not have gone ahead. He was overjoyed with his front seat view she was performing flawlessly. He was shaking with excitement, oh how he was going to enjoy having fun with her; she had surpassed his every expectation.

The voices in his head were beginning to stir but he knew they were satisfied. He was also aware that before long their whispering would become louder and more insistent, they would not stop until they were shouting.

A car turned into the street and stopped outside her house and Mr Mac became alert. He watched as Timothy Granger and the little black haired bitch got out then they hurried towards the house where Josie MacDonald lived.

Josie collapsed against Tim the moment she opened the door and holding onto him tightly she sobbed uncontrollably. All of his attempts to soothe her failed.

Kate, pushing past them both, went into the living room. She could see the sheet of paper lying on the floor, and stooping to pick it up, was horrified by the image but it was not long before her logical mind took over and she began to see it for what it was. Studying it carefully she was satisfied that it was genuine and not just some made up graphics churned out by a computer program.

Moving into the centre of the room she shuddered, negative vibrations hung thickly on the air but there was something else. Glancing around, she drew her shawl closer around her shoulders. Someone was watching, she was sure of it so turning towards the window she peered out. The curtains had not yet been drawn and pressing her face up against the glass she watched as a car pulled away. She was unable see who was driving but as it went, it carried away her sense of unease.

Kate frowned, who could have been hiding outside Josie's house and what was going on here? She glanced again at the picture before closing the curtains then turning towards Tim, she wanted answers.

Tim was standing in the kitchen with Josie wrapped up in his arms, and as Kate listened to her brother talking softly she realised the depth of his affection for Josie, it did not seem right to intrude so she turned away.

This was the first time she had been to Josie's house so seizing the opportunity to look around her first impressions were encouraging. She liked what she saw but more importantly, she liked the way the house felt. The place seemed comfortable and homely, the furniture carefully laid out for the best results. Magazines were scattered about and she studied the framed photographs of family and friends that were arranged on the little side tables. Personal effects that made a house a home laid scattered about and she smiled appreciatively. Moving towards a door, she pushed it open and her fingers searched for a light switch. The moment she entered the room she was surprised, it was in total contrast to the living room here chaos reigned. She had discovered Josie's studio. How many artists keep their work places neat and tidy, she asked herself.

The air was thick with an assortment of scents; paint, cleaning fluids and oils with colours splashed onto every surface. Canvasses of all shapes and sizes filled every available space, paintings and sketches were hanging on the walls but many more were simply piled up on the floor. Most of the pictures seemed to be finished but a few were obviously still in progress.

The state of the studio suggested that Josie was in possession of a cluttered mind but Kate did not believe that, turning off the light she returned to the living room and went to Josie.

Josie looked washed out, her eyes red and swollen Kate felt sorry for her. Her evening had been a great success but now it was ruined, it did not seem fair that it should end this way.

Reaching out Kate held her in her arms and something unsaid passed between them. Tim could feel the sisterly bond that they shared and, hanging back, allowed them some time together. Behind Josie's back, Kate passed him the paper that she was holding and the colour drained from his face. He recognised Lindsay Murray at once, he had met her on a couple of occasions and he liked her very much. Her warm personality was infectious but his overall impression was that she could be a little awkward at times.

There was no doubt in his mind that she was dead, the wound to her head was evidence enough but he found it hard to take in. Shaking his head, he dropped the paper face down on the table before moving away into the kitchen. He was confused and needed time to think so he occupied himself with the task of making a pot of coffee.

"Why is this happening?" Josie sobbed.

The sadness in her voice almost broke his heart and glancing over his shoulder, he could see them. They were sitting on the sofa with their heads together. Kate sensed him looking and glanced up, her expression questioning. She knew nothing of the events of the past few days.

When the coffee was done he joined them and placing their mugs on the little table, perched on the edge of a chair and told his sister everything. Where his version of Josie's visit to Scotland faltered she managed to fill in the gaps.

"He's obviously a very sick and devious individual who's playing a dangerous psychological game by destroying people's lives." Kate glanced at them both and reached for her coffee.

"There have been other pictures," Tim told her. "The police have them now."

"Copies?"

"No." He shook his head.

"So we must assume that all of your friends are potential victims." Kate said looking up at Josie.

Standing up she went to the table where Tim had left the picture then picking it up she studied it carefully.

"What am I going to do, it's all my fault." Josie said miserably her eyes welling up again.

"You mustn't think like that," Kate told her firmly. "It's not your fault at all; he's the one with the problem."

"We must find a way to stop him." Tim moved closer to Josie and slipped his arm around her shoulders. "If only we could anticipate his next move."

Kate ran her finger lightly over the picture then closing her eyes she relaxed and reached out into the darkness. She began to search beyond the room, projecting her mind out into space and time, and it was not long before she could sense danger. It was centred on Josie, she was surrounded by a negative energy and Kate did not care for what she saw.

Dropping the picture onto the table she shuddered, convinced that Josie's friends were no longer in London. Banishing these images from her mind, she returned to where they were sitting.

"What are your friend's names apart from Lindsay of course?"

"Sarah Hamilton and Lizzie Baines," Josie whispered.

Focussing on the names Kate turned them over in her mind. She called out to them in turn but it was not enough, she had to have something more tangible.

"Do you have anything that belongs to Sarah or Lizzie?"

Josie stared blankly at Kate.

"Kate is convinced that she has special psychic powers." Tim explained his voice full of scorn.

She stared coldly at her brother before going on. "If I could touch or hold some personal item then I might be able to pick up something."

Josie thought for a moment then putting her coffee cup down on the table got to her feet. "I have a hairbrush that Sarah left here a couple of weeks ago."

"That would be perfect," Kate smiled. "What about Lizzie?"

Josie chewed at her bottom lip. "I can't think of anything. I've got some photos," she added helpfully.

"That might be enough but I need something more physical a personal item would be better."

Josie left the room and they heard her footsteps as she hurried on the stairs.

"Why did you have to do that?" Tim growled.

"I'm sorry Tim but if I'm going to help I'll use any means possible." She could see he was angry. "I know you think I'm loopy but I happen to have a lot of faith in my abilities."

"Here," Josie re-appeared holding out a hairbrush. "I managed to find this too, it belongs to Lizzie." She held up a navy blue cardigan.

"Good," Kate smiled, "that's perfect."

Sitting down, she made herself comfortable and Josie watched her every move. Tim groaned inwardly, he was annoyed, Josie was full of expectation but he was under no illusion that she was going to be bitterly disappointed.

Kate focussed her energies on the brush. Long blonde hairs caught up in the bristles were good physical links to Sarah and holding onto it, she cleared her mind and began to feel the vibrations running through her fingers. Her heart was racing, and closing her eyes her brow creased with concentration then after a few moments her breathing became deep and even.

Suddenly she caught a glimpse of Sarah and a powerful force swept over her. Caught up in an emotional tide of confusion and pain Kate experienced feelings of fear and humiliation. She did not like what she saw but at least Sarah was alive.

Easing her mind carefully away from the deluge of sensations that threatened to engulf her Kate forced her eyes open, and dropping the brush into her lap, severed any further connection with Sarah.

Both Josie and Tim were staring at her in anticipation.

"She's alive and safe for the moment."

"Can you tell where they are? Did you see them?" Josie's questions were a torrent laced with impatience and concern.

"It doesn't work that way," Kate explained. "All I can hope for is a spiritual connection. I usually pick up on people's emotions, I can tell what they are feeling physically but I can't make contact with them or see them clearly."

Josie stared at her for a moment. "What about Lizzie?" She cried, holding out the cardigan.

As soon as Kate touched it, she experienced powerful emotions. It was as if she were physically assaulted and falling back into the chair her eyes rolled alarmingly up into her head.

Throwing himself down beside his sister Tim grasped her by the shoulders and held her steady but she did not respond to his touch. He had never seen her like this before and he was alarmed, he tried to snatch the cardigan away but her grip was too strong.

Kate rode the force as it ran unchecked throughout her body. It was a powerful current and as her muscles tensed, it was all she could do remain in control. Then she could feel Lizzie Baines.

Lizzie was in pain, her emotions were all over the place and her suffering was immense. The indignity of her situation was almost too much for her to bear but there was something else. Kate, standing firm in the face of the emotional onslaught was determined to use all of her powers. She had to discover what was going on, only then would she be able to understand. It took all of her resolve to regain some form of control but after a while, she learnt to become selective and sorting through the emotional deluge began to build up a picture.

Suddenly she jerked upright and crying out in alarm the cardigan slipped from her grip. She hugged herself tightly her body trembling and it was several moments before she became coherent. She knew Lizzie's secret.

"What is it?" Josie could stand it no more. Throwing herself down beside Kate, she gripped her arm and shook her gently.

Kate opened her eyes. "I need a moment," she murmured.

Gradually her heart rate returned to normal and she began to breathe more easily. Lizzie's emotions were still there inside her head and it was difficult to concentrate.

"Are you okay?" Josie cried, frantic with worry.

Kate knew that she could not tell Josie what she had seen. She owed it to the woman she had never met. She would not reveal Lizzie's secret.

"Yes I'm fine really, just give me a moment."

"What about Lizzie, what happened, is she okay?"

"She's okay," Kate nodded.

"I don't believe you, tell me the truth, you were thrashing about all over the place. Tell me what's happening."

Kate took Josie's hand and squeezed it reassuringly. She was deathly cold and her fingers were trembling.

"She is okay honestly, they both are."

"Then why were you so agitated?"

Taking a deep breath, she tried to explain. She told them that something very unpleasant was about to happen and unfortunately, there was nothing they could do to stop it.

"Enough of this mumbo jumbo," Tim was angry with his sister. He was annoyed by what she had just said and Josie was becoming even more upset.

Helping Josie to her feet, he took her in his arms. "Look, we must all calm down. We need to get this thing into perspective and work out what to do next." He glared at his sister.

"I suggest we let Josie get some rest. It's been a very long and tiring day for us all." Kate said looking up at Tim. "It's probably best that you stay here tonight."

Tim nodded and fumbled in his pocket. "Here," he said holding out his car keys.

"How can I possibly drive, I've had far too much to drink."

She telephoned for a taxi and promised Josie that she would be in touch soon. Then she left.

Chapter
NINETEEN

The following day they were introduced to Detective Chief Inspector Matthew Jordan. Inspector Lacey had passed the case onto his superior and he had briefed Jordan fully just moments before Josie arrived. Jordan listened very carefully to what she had to say, given this latest piece of evidence he was convinced they were dealing with a murder and he insisted that Josie tell him everything. He had already checked with his colleagues in Elgin but for the time being he shared Inspector Lacey's opinion. He could find no evidence to suggest that what happened to her in Scotland and the abduction of her friends were linked.

"But what about the Scottish postmark?" Josie said pointing to the envelope.

"Whoever is doing this must know about what happened to you in Scotland. It would not be impossible for him to get hold of a copy of the newspaper that ran the story; he may well have found it on the internet."

She was not convinced, no one could link her with the newspaper story but she kept her thoughts to herself.

"Besides," he went on. "Whoever is doing this is probably hoping to throw us off the scent. It's much more likely to be a local person, someone who knows the area." He paused, waiting for Josie to respond but she remained silent.

"Forensics will want to have a look at that." He said indicating to the latest picture that was lying on his desk.

DCI Jordan wanted to be sure of the facts before contacting Lindsay

Murray's mother. He hated delivering bad news even after all his years on the force.

Kate was waiting for them outside the police station. She had spoken to Tim earlier insisting that they get together, she wanted to discuss the designs for Josie's new website and was determined to do it right away. She felt that it would be a positive distraction for Josie, besides she wanted to spend some time with her, get to know her better.

Tim had to go to the gallery; there was a lot of clearing up to do from the night before so he left them to it.

"Promise you'll phone me later." He hugged Josie before glancing at his sister.

"Don't worry brother she'll be safe with me, no funny business I promise."

He watched them go. With their heads together, they were soon deep in conversation and he was happy in the knowledge that Kate approved of Josie.

"I don't need to ask how well you slept last night." Kate said as they settled at a table in a nearby café.

It was obvious to her that Josie had used make-up in an attempt to cover the dark rings around her eyes.

"As you see not very well," Josie made a face.

They ordered coffee. The lunchtime rush was yet to begin so they did not have to wait long.

"What did you make of the man with the wild hair?" Kate asked.

"The Scotsman?"

Kate nodded and reached for her cup.

"He startled me at first, I must admit. I thought him a bit odd but he was entertaining enough I suppose."

"Gregory MacLaren, do you think that was his real name?"

Josie paused holding her cup motionless over its saucer. "Why wouldn't it be?" She wondered where Kate was going with this.

"I just got the impression that he was being a little shy with the truth."

"Well isn't that what men tend to do when trying to impress?"

"Yes but not him, this was different."

Josie shrugged her shoulders and asked bluntly. "Is that why you gave him such a hard time or are you always like that with men?"

"Not with all men, just the ones I don't like." Kate did her best to hide her annoyance.

"I thought he was just making conversation that's all." Josie continued.

"I hardly had time to form an opinion besides, everything was happening so quickly my mind was in such a whirl."

Kate nodded and her expression softened.

"Something did occur to me though come to think of it." Josie said slowly and sipping her coffee made Kate wait before going on. "What I don't understand is how he knew about the incident in Scotland. I know it was reported in the local paper but there was no reference to me at all. The article didn't mention my name and there wasn't a picture either, so how did he know it was me?"

"Perhaps after reading about it he made further enquiries," Kate suggested, "besides, someone must have known it was you, the police, the men who rescued you, the fishermen."

Raising her eyebrows Josie thought for a moment. "Perhaps you're right." Sitting back in her chair, she sighed and crossed her legs under the table.

"So, have you got any thoughts about your website?" Kate changed the subject. "I've drafted up some ideas for you to look at." She dug around in her bag and producing a folder pushed it across the table.

They chatted for a while longer bouncing ideas off each other before finally reaching an agreement.

Kate walked Josie back to her house and as they turned into her road, she could feel the same irritating sensation that she had encountered the night before. A malignant force seemed to be reaching out towards them; it made her feel uneasy but Josie, unaware of Kate's discomfort, slipped her key into the lock and pushed open the door.

Mr Mac was watching from across the street. He had left his car earlier to go in search of a shop where he picked up some supplies but now he was back in his hiding place. He saw the small dark haired girl hesitate, she glanced over her shoulder before entering the house but he was satisfied that she had not seen him. He was content to remain where he was; he wanted to see what would happen next, besides he had to decide what to do about Josie MacDonald.

Some time later, a roadster screeched to a halt outside the house and he watched with interest as the driver forced it into a parking space.

A tall, well-dressed man got out and rushing to the door rang the bell for longer than was necessary. The curtains next door twitched, he would have to be careful, he thought, nosey neighbours might prove to be a problem.

Josie appeared and the man pushed past her. It was obvious that his intrusion was unwanted because her body language was less than welcoming.

Once inside Mike made his way into the living room. "So how was it at Timothy bloody Granger's yesterday then?" He began loudly. "I suppose he couldn't keep his grubby little hands to himself."

Throwing himself down onto the sofa, he glared up at her.

"Look Mike I'm in no mood for a fight."

"Did you sell any paintings?" He asked, the tone of his voice softening.

"It was a very successful evening."

Kate appeared at the studio door.

"Mike," Josie moved towards him, "I'd like you to meet Kate." She paused. "Kate is Tim's sister."

Jumping to his feet, he muttered something under his breath.

"Hello," he managed before thrusting his hand out towards her.

"Hiya Mike. So you're a friend of my brother's then." She eyed him like a predator its prey and his discomfort amused her enormously.

"Er, yes." He stuttered pathetically. He was caught off guard and he did not like it one bit. "Tim and I go back a long time as a matter of fact."

Glancing sideways at Josie, he could see that she was grinning.

"Funny," Kate frowned dramatically. "He's never mentioned you before."

Reaching out she took his hand and could read him like a book, in an instant she had summed him up. He was spoilt, selfish and shallow and had no respect at all for Josie. Although he was pleasing to look at, she despised him and Mike withered under her gaze.

"I've sorted out your website so I'll be off now." Kate said turning to Josie. "It was nice to meet you Mike," she smiled smugly before continuing. "Oh and by the way, you've forgotten your mother's birthday again."

"How could you possibly...?"

"Women's intuition," she winked.

At the door, Kate squeezed Josie's arm affectionately then kissed her cheeks. "Let's meet up again soon," she said smiling warmly.

Kate walked briskly along the street passing the roadster parked against the kerb and instinctively she knew it belonged to Mike. Her sense of unease was still there lingering menacingly at the back of her mind, so lengthening her stride she walked on.

Mr Mac slouched lower in his seat as she hurried past his car then he studied her in his rear view mirror. He had an almost overwhelming urge to go after her, he could pick her up, torment her and have some fun before killing her but he decided against the idea. There was something about her that he didn't like, he had experienced these feelings at the exhibition, she would make a very dangerous adversary and the thought unnerved him.

Thirty minutes later the man emerged from her house and Mr Mac watched as he kissed Josie's cheek. It was obvious from the way she held herself that she was not comfortable. Were they once lovers? He asked himself.

On impulse, he followed the roadster.

Mike was annoyed and driving his car aggressively barged his way rudely through the traffic. He could not help thinking about Josie's success, her attitude towards him had changed and it bothered him. She was more confident now and he did not like it one bit. He would prefer her to be submissive, quiet and emotionally dependant on him, he hated losing his hold over her. Gradually his authority was being undermined, the distance between them becoming an ever-widening chasm and he was sure Tim Granger was engineering this. Tim was an unwelcome adversary and meeting his loathsome sister had unsettled him more than he cared to admit. He knew that Josie and Tim were close, but he had no idea how cosy the situation had recently become.

Braking hard he just missed a cyclist, and cursing under his breath, swung his car sharply to the left the tyres screeching as it slid into the underground car park. The cyclist raised his fist and swerved just in time to miss the rear of the car.

Mr Mac braked and gave the angry cyclist more room than was necessary. He was unaccustomed to driving in such heavy traffic and following the speeding roadster had unnerved him.

Crawling past the opening to the underground car park he saw the brake lights glowing as the roadster came to a stop, then driving past went around the block and approached from the opposite direction.

He studied the building; it seemed to be home to a multitude of businesses, some occupying a single office whilst others took up a whole floor. Pulling into the underground car park, he stopped his car close behind the roadster.

The parking area served the whole building and leaving his car blocking the roadway he walked slowly towards the lift. He made a mental note of where the security cameras were situated then arriving at the lift door, rode up to the ground floor where he found the reception area.

A team of women were busy fronting the various businesses and offices in the building and as he approached the desk, he prepared to act out his part.

"Good morning Sir, how may I help?" A woman, smiling pleasantly at him, went through her well-rehearsed lines.

"I'm afraid I've had a wee bit of an accident in your car park."

"Oh dear," she made a face, doing her best to sound concerned.

"Yes I'm afraid I've damaged a car." He gave her the details and she tapped the keys on her keyboard.

"Mr Cowper-Smith," she frowned. "Would you like to take a seat while I telephone him for you?" She indicated to a waiting area.

"If you don't mind I'll wait by my car."

"Of course but can I take your name please Sir?"

"Mr Mac," he called over his shoulder as he walked away.

Pressing a series of keys on her keyboard, she spoke into a tiny microphone.

Mike swore under his breath as his personal assistant passed on the message, his day had started out badly and it continued to deteriorate.

Leaving his office, he raced down to the car park. The parking spaces had been made smaller in an attempt to accommodate more vehicles. This annoyed him because the cost of parking in the city was becoming exorbitant. He considered it just another tax and this was on top of paying a premium rent for his office space.

His footsteps echoed off the concrete surface as he walked swiftly towards the entrance ramp. He could make out a car parked close behind his then he saw a funny little man with wild hair and his anger began to rise.

"Sorry about this." The man called out and Mike registered an accent. He couldn't be sure if it was Irish or Scottish, he was not a keen observer of accents.

"I'm afraid I've run into the side of your car."

Pushing past him Mike ran his hand along the flank of his car but found no damage at all. He frowned and given no opportunity to face the man, felt a sharp scratch against his upper arm.

"What the hell," he growled as he stumbled against his car.

The ground began to tilt alarmingly beneath his feet and clutching desperately at the door mirror he collapsed against the bonnet. Darkness greeted him as he fell to the floor then Mr Mac moved in.

Grasping him by the shoulder, he lifted Mike up and guiding him towards his own car pushed him onto the back seat. Mike was semi-conscious, he was aware of a seat belt being fastened then his head slumped forward and darkness overwhelmed him.

Mr Mac was aware of only one wide angled security camera trained on the area and this was some distance away. Having inspected it earlier, he concluded that it was part of an old and very inadequate surveillance system. The lenses were cheap and dirty so the camera was unlikely to pick up much detail. Climbing into the driving seat, he eased his car out into the traffic confident in the knowledge that his number plate would not be identified.

Crawling through the crowded city streets Mr Mac wondered how long it would be before the man was missed and as if thought-activated a mobile phone began to ring.

Eventually the traffic became easier and following the signs north Mr Mac was pleased with himself, he had never abducted a man before and was amazed at how easy it had been. He had expected a fight or at least some form of token resistance but his victim was as docile as a friendly puppy.

He hoped the drug would be effective at least until he made a stop. He would give him another shot then, enough at least to keep him quiet for the rest of the journey.

Josie sat alone in her kitchen with her elbows resting on the table and her hands clasped beneath her chin. She was thinking of Kate Granger, she thought her nice enough, a little odd maybe but it was obvious that she did not always meet with Tim's approval. The thought of Tim filled her with warmth. He had never mentioned his sister before, it was true she had known him for only a few months but still she found it strange. Josie had been attracted to Tim from moment they had met. She liked him because he was quite unlike Mike. Tim was kind and understanding and never failed to make her smile. He had supported her immeasurably over the last few days and with him it felt right. Smiling again, she remembered the first time they had made love; it had been a wonderful experience.

With Mike it had been different, their relationship had been stormy, their romance doomed from the start. She soon discovered that he was a bully and he dominated her until she felt as if she were drowning. She had done her best to please him but recently he had become even more demanding and their relationship had hit an all time low. As far as she was concerned, it was over but he was finding this difficult to accept.

Her thoughts turned to the previous evening. It was obvious that Tim had taken a dim view of the things Kate had told them and she had overheard them arguing. Kate was definitely an individual and quite unlike her brother. She could be very blunt and scathing at times especially towards people whom she disliked. Josie was fascinated by her strange ways and if Kate had genuinely experienced the things that she said then why couldn't she tell them where her friends were being held? Perhaps she was holding something back, maybe the facts were too painful for her to reveal. Lindsay was dead, that was the horrifying truth, but what about Sarah and Lizzie? Kate had admitted that they were suffering and their situation was becoming worse.

Josie sighed it was all becoming too much, her thoughts were beginning to distress her and she must stop thinking about such things. If she continued torturing herself like this, she would make herself ill.

Rising from her chair, she made her way into the living room. She needed company, someone to talk too. She wanted more than anything to chat with Sarah, she missed the sound of her voice, her wit and her friendly laughter but she knew that was not possible. She craved a friendly ear, someone who would understand and help guide her through this dark period of her life. Reaching for the phone, she called her Auntie Molly.

Fifteen hours later Mr Mac nosed his car onto the driveway and gravel crunched as he drove around the carriage sweep. Finally, bringing the car to a stop, he switched off the engine and let out a sigh of relief. He was exhausted having driven through the night, his head was throbbing and his eyes were as dry as sandpaper and taking a few moments to gather himself, he listened to the silence that settled heavily around him. The sun was not yet fully up but there was sufficient light for him to take in the view and gazing out over the treetops, he could see all the way down into the valley below. A ghostlike mist lingered across the landscape but it would not be long before the sun burnt the milky shroud away.

From the top of the house, the view was magnificent. It was possible on a good day to see right across the bay and glimpse the distant mountains stretching away to the north. He remembered as a child spending many hours on the roof exploring the narrow lead lined service paths that wound their way between the chimneystacks.

He sighed and rolling the stiffness from his shoulders reflected on his journey. He had never been to England so often in such a short space of time; this was his third trip in just under two weeks. Shrugging off his thoughts, he studied the unconscious man through the rear view mirror. He had sedated him twice on the journey and was now facing the prospect of moving him. He would have to drag his dead weight to the cellar then secure him before he regained his senses.

He could not understand why he had taken him, what madness had driven him to do it. Perhaps it was to prove to Josie MacDonald that none of her friends were safe. Running a hand over his face he grinned, the thought pleased him and silently he congratulated himself on what he had achieved so far.

Hauling himself wearily from his car, he looked back along the drive and realised that it would be easier to bring the man in through the rear of the house. Jumping back into his car, he reversed into the courtyard between the house and the out buildings.

It was easier than he imagined dragging the unconscious man through the kitchen, and when he reached the top of the steps leading to the cellar, he stopped. Pushing him roughly against the wall, he held him there whilst searching in his pocket for the key to the cellar door and soon he was ready for the descent.

Both girls were lying on the concrete floor curled up beneath their thin blankets. Sarah raised her head as he appeared and her eyes widened with disbelief, she recognised Michael Cowper-Smith instantly.

Mr Mac dragged him to the spot where Lindsay had been just a few days earlier and grunting with the effort, heaved him against the wall. Beads of sweat from his brow stung his eyes and as he worked he fumbled with the chains, but soon had the unconscious man shackled into place. With his chest heaving, he stood back to admire his work.

"Get up," he growled as he moved towards Lizzie. Touching her with the toe of his boot, he watched with satisfaction as she flinched beneath the blanket, then reaching down he snatched it up and tossed it across the floor.

She was curled up with her knees folded up under her chin and her arms tightly wrapped around her long legs. Still she did not move and this annoyed him so reaching out he grabbed a handful of her blouse and hauled her to her feet. The flimsy material ripped and buttons bounced away across the floor.

Crying out she backed away and the chain attached to her ankle rasped noisily as it snaked across the floor.

"Don't hurt her." Sarah cried pitifully.

Mr Mac mimicked her sarcastically. "Then do as I say."

Turning back towards Lizzie, he was prepared for a struggle but she backed obligingly up against the wall. She was trembling and in no mood for a fight.

"Put the shackles on your wrists." He ordered and he watched as she fumbled nervously with the irons.

Mr Mac grabbed the ends of the chains and jerking them tighter, the sudden movement lifted her off her feet and she cried out in agony. Moving in he secured her ankles.

"No, no that won't do." His eyes narrowed as he stepped away. He shredded the remains of her blouse and Lizzie gasped with horror.

Mr Mac made a noise at the back of his throat as he watched her struggle. Her skin was clear and unblemished, it was as if she had been hewn from the finest stone and as she gasped her small breasts heaved uncontrollably. He was tempted to touch her but he had to deal with Sarah. Lizzie Baines was not going anywhere she would have to wait.

Turning away, he moved towards Sarah who was standing with her back pressed against the wall. Frozen with fear her eyes were huge, and clutching tightly at her blanket she looked exhausted.

As he ripped it away she cried out, then moving in he touched her. Holding her roughly against the wall he rubbed up against her, his hands rough against her skin. He grinned enjoying the moment and working efficiently he attached the chains to her wrists.

When he was finished, he stood back and with his head tilted to one side it was as if he was listening to something. Sarah watched as his expression changed and suddenly he lunged forward. With his face pressed up close to hers, she could feel him hot against her skin and holding her breath she resisted the urge to scream. Clamping her eyes shut in an attempt to hold back her terror she was convinced that he was about to rape her.

Growling like a wild animal as he pawed at her, his hands were all over her body and she could not stop herself from shaking. Inside she was screaming but she made no sound and after what seemed an eternity she opened her eyes.

He was gone.

Chapter
TWENTY

Swimming up from a darkened place where his senses were blissfully numb he slowly became aware of his surroundings. At first, he thought he was lying on a cold hard floor but it soon became clear that he was standing or rather slouching against a wall. His arms felt strange, the pressure on the small bones in his wrists sent pains shooting through his fingers and he was convinced that his hands were on fire.

The moment he opened his eyes light assaulted his senses and he groaned. Peering cautiously upwards his eyes began to focus as he squinted against the glare, it was then that he realised his arms were chained above his head. Shuffling his feet he managed to ease the pressure from his wrists and his fingers began to throb. Before he had time to work out what was going on he heard the sound, someone was sobbing and he realised that he wasn't alone in the room. Moving his legs, he searched for a more comfortable position before looking around.

He was in some kind of a dungeon, the light was dim but it seemed to intensify as it reflected from the whitewashed walls. His throat was dry and his head was pounding mercilessly. The muscles in his shoulders complained under the unaccustomed strain of supporting his weight, he had to find a way to get his arms free. He would not be able to stand the pain for much longer so moving his fingers he attempted to re-establish the blood flow in his hands but the muscles in his arms began to cramp. Groaning out loud he struggled to stand more comfortably.

The sobbing continued and it was beginning to annoy him so turning his head towards the sound he could make out a figure standing not far away. Blinking until he could see more clearly he gasped in disbelief. There was a woman chained to the wall beside him, her head was hanging forward so he could not see her face. The only discernable movement was the raising and lowering of her breasts as she breathed.

He looked again to confirm what he thought he had just seen. The sobbing was not coming from her so there must be someone else in the room.

Bracing himself, he took his full weight on his legs and as the chains above his head became slack, he was able to lean forward until he could see along the length of the wall.

There was another woman and unbelievably she was naked.

"What the hell!" he groaned, before leaning back. He had to relieve the burning sensation in his legs.

He closed his eyes in the hope of relieving the pain but it was no good. Images of the woman beside him flashed into his head, there was something familiar about her and it annoyed him that he could not recall instantly where he had seen her before. Bracing himself, he looked again and as she faced him, there was a glimmer of recognition in her eyes but she remained silent.

"Lizzie." he said suddenly. "I'm sorry but I can't remember your surname."

Lizzie almost laughed at the absurdity of it, she didn't care that he could not remember her name although he should have because it was only a few weeks ago that they were out socialising. Josie had introduced them and she could remember him clearly.

She had disliked him from the start, she hated the way he treated Josie and she knew very well the type of man that he was.

She did not bother to reply.

"Josie," he said as if reading her thoughts. "You're one of Josie's friends."

Resting his head back against the wall, the effort of thinking made him feel even worse and then he realised who the other woman was.

"Sarah Hamilton."

She raised her head to look at him as he leaned forward.

"What is this, some kind of a joke?"

"Joke, in what kind of sick world would this be a joke?" Lizzie barked.

"Oh my God." he muttered as realisation struck him.

Images of the man with the wild hair flashed through his head and he wanted to ask what had been going on but he thought better of it. He was feeling so unwell it was as if a metal band was tightening around his head and he began to feel dizzy. Saliva dribbled from his chin so closing his eyes he waited for the sensation to pass.

Slowly his memory began to return and the events leading up to this moment became clearer. He realised that the man with the wild hair had fooled him, lured him into the car park below the building where he worked but he had no idea why. What had any of this have to do with him?

He could hardly believe what was happening, it was absurd, chained to a wall like a prisoner in a medieval dungeon with two women.

"Where are we?" He asked no one in particular but before they could answer, Mr Mac returned.

Mike watched as he strode boldly in. He was dressed in a kilt and his body was covered in strange markings. Sarah groaned, she had seen him like this before and the consequences had been terrible.

"One of you will run free," he began. "Who will it be?"

He moved towards Sarah.

"Who the hell are you?" Mike demanded.

Reaching out with his hand Mr Mac was tempted to touch her, the voices in his head were insisting on it but he held himself back.

"I'm talking to you," Mike shouted even louder. "What's going on here?"

Lizzie held her breath, Lindsay had antagonised him and her punishment had outstripped the crime.

Mr Mac turned his head towards Mike; his eyes glowing like hot coals the expression on his face was a mask of pure evil. Drawing back his lips, he opened his mouth and let out a bloodcurdling scream.

Lizzie closed her eyes tightly and refused to be a witness to the violence that was about to erupt.

"Unshackle me you bastard!" Mike shouted, wrestling with his chains. "Let's meet on equal terms."

Mr Mac launched himself at Mike and when the onslaught began, it was merciless. Mike, crying out in frustration, was unable to defend himself as blow after blow rained down. After a while, he no longer felt the pain and on the verge of unconsciousness, he heard one of the women scream.

Lizzie could bear it no longer, she could hear every blow as it landed and when finally she opened her eyes she saw Mike's face covered in blood.

Mr Mac stepped back his chest heaving, he was breathless and it took him a few moments to control his rage. Turning towards Lizzie, he was a wild man possessed and reaching out he touched her. His knuckles were bloody, the skin chaffed and his fingers were rough.

She was at breaking point and utterly terrified. She knew that she was going to die, this she could accept but she did not want to die horribly.

Mr Mac moved closer and thrusting his face up against hers, she twisted her head away.

"Who is it going to be?" he hissed.

She watched horrified as he drew a knife from his belt and lovingly caressed the blade. Holding herself rigid, she saw his eyes darting between her and Sarah then she saw it in his face. The moment had come, he had made his choice and her world was about to fall apart.

He began moving very slowly at first, drawing out the moment. The light playing against the razor edge of his knife promised death but she knew he had something worse in mind. In desperation, she tried to pull her arms free from the shackles but it was useless and she cried out helplessly. The waiting was over the end had come.

Using his knife skilfully, he slashed through the fabric of her clothing, it was a miracle that her skin was not cut because within seconds she was naked, her secret places revealed.

His chest was heaving as he stood back and his face was tight with anticipation, then his expression froze. He was outraged and only just managed to stop himself from plunging the knife deep into her flesh.

At that moment she would have welcomed it, a sudden death would have been a blessing. She almost blacked out, the humiliation was too much and she broke down and sobbed.

Mr Mac was shocked; it was as much as he could do to contain his anger then suddenly he began to shudder. Laughter rumbled up from deep within his chest and he doubled over as he roared. He was astonished by his discovery.

Lizzie Baines was a boy.

It was a long time before she managed to calm her shattered nerves; emotionally she was a wreck. He had remained there in front of her for ages insulting her with the most awful obscenities but now it was over and he was gone.

"Lizzie," Sarah called out to her softly.

Sarah had recovered from her initial shock. She had no idea, she had no cause to doubt her friend's integrity Lizzie had always been just Lizzie. She was a friend with whom she shared her secrets, someone to turn to in times of need and she was always such fun to be with. She ought to be angry, offended by the deceit but she was not.

"Lizzie, please say something."

Lizzie had nothing to say, her life was in ruins and she had nothing more to give. She could not even look at Sarah she would never be able to face her friends again.

Mike had not yet fully regained his senses, that was one small mercy at least, his knowing her secret was a further humiliation waiting to happen.

"Lizzie, please talk to me."

The sound of Sarah's voice unnerved her and she hated herself even more for ignoring her friend. She thought her heart would break, all she ever wanted was to be accepted for what she was. She wished that life could return to how it had been but that was impossible and she was devastated.

Mr Mac swaggered boldly into the cellar where he moved into the centre of the room. He was holding a small jar above his head and suddenly he announced.

"Petroleum jelly for chaps!"

Then he raped Lizzie Baines.

Chapter
TWENTY ONE

During the morning, Josie received a telephone call from Mike's office and she was able to confirm that the last time she had seen him was the previous day. She had no idea where he was besides, at that moment she cared little for him or his whereabouts. She was still reeling from the objectionable comments he had made about her work and his unpleasant remarks regarding her relationship with Tim. What business was it of his anyway?

Whilst she was talking, her mobile phone began to ring. Picking it up she went towards the window where she glanced out absentmindedly at the cars parked along the street, then ending her conversation with Mike's assistant she touched a button on her mobile and held it to her ear. It was Kate, they chatted for a few minutes, Kate answering all her questions about the new website and when they had finished, Josie moved back into the studio. Turning on her computer, she wanted to add some pictures to her website. Kate had warned her that it would take a while to set it up to her liking.

An hour later, she had finished and satisfied with the results, leaned back in her chair, stretching her arms luxuriously above her head she groaned with relief.

She was happy to be making progress, the website was not yet ready to go on-line but as soon as it was complete Kate had promised to help her launch it. Josie smiled and coming out of the program clicked on the e-mail icon on the screen and went into her account. Scanning down the list of unread messages, she clicked on the most recent. It was a request for a commission. Skipping through it, she got the gist of the message and then she frowned. Moving the cursor over the attachment, she double clicked the mouse and a picture filled the screen. It was of a fine looking house built from bleached, weathered stone. Light reflecting off the walls made the flowerbeds nearest to the house appear too bright, the colours washed out, it was as if the photograph was over exposed.

The windows on the ground floor were covered with heavy wooden shutters and in the centre of the facade rose a magnificent stone staircase. It was an impressive feature that swept pleasingly up to a heavy wooden door.

The accompanying message requested that she re-produce the house on canvas. The size of the painting had been carefully detailed and she could visit the house before work began. There was even an invitation to stay if she felt that living on site would be more convenient.

Leaning back in her chair she chewed at her bottom lip. Whoever had sent the message had thought of everything and she liked the idea.

The building looked interesting enough; she could see it in her mind, a delicate watercolour reproduced not on canvas but perhaps handmade paper. It had potential especially with the shutters open and the sky reflecting against the windows. There were no other details, she had no idea where the property was situated so printing off a copy she typed a short message requesting more information before pressing the send button.

Mr Mac returned to the cellar carrying a small digital camera. He had washed the coloured dye from his face and was no longer wearing his kilt.

"Watch the wee birdie!" he said.

Pointing the lens at Lizzie, he began taking his pictures.

"This will give your friend Josie MacDonald something to think about."

Lizzie hung her head and was hardly aware that he was there. He had stolen her dignity and destroyed her life. The pain he had inflicted went far deeper than he could ever imagine, there was nothing more that he could do to hurt her.

Returning to his study, he loaded the pictures onto his computer and was tempted to e-mail them to Josie MacDonald immediately but resisting the urge, he hit the print button.

He thought about the message he had sent earlier and he grinned, the audacity of his plan appealed to him very much it was truly outrageous.

The idea of inviting her to paint a picture of his house had been a stroke of genius, including an invitation for her to stay whilst carrying out the work was just too much to ignore. How ironic it would be to have her staying as a guest whilst her friends were prisoners in the cellar. Shaking his head in wonder, he considered how he would make it happen.

Eventually he turned his mind to more pressing matters. Standing up he moved across the room towards an old chest where he began selecting items of clothing from his collection. It was almost time for Lizzie Baines to make her run.

Lizzie moved carefully pulling on the clothes, even the slightest movement left her crying out in agony. Pain searing through her abdomen and into the small of her back left her breathless and standing still for a moment she breathed in deeply waiting for the sensation to pass. She knew that something was wrong, a rupture had occurred deep within her and she had no idea how long she would be able to endure the pain. With deep breathing and will power, she would just have to manage.

Sarah looked on helplessly. Watching Lizzie struggle was almost too much to bear, all she wanted to do was to go to her and give her a reassuring hug. She wanted to say so much but there was little time. She was desperately worried because Lizzie had not spoken a word since the attack. She had retreated so far into herself that words of sympathy and encouragement were not sufficient to reach her. Sarah wanted her to know that nothing had changed between them, she would always be her friend no matter what.

She hated not being able to communicate with Lizzie, they needed each other more than ever but now it was too late. Blaming herself for Lizzie's desperate situation Sarah wished that she had been stronger. She would never forgive herself for giving him Lizzie's name.

An overpowering sense of dread settled around her and Sarah knew that she would never see her friend again.

Mr Mac appeared. Lizzie, resigned to her fate offered no resistance. She was exhausted and in far too much pain to care. She allowed him to drag her away and broken-hearted, Sarah called after her sobbing uncontrollably, her sense of loss was unbearable.

Mike glanced up, his face ugly with wounds. "Freak!" he muttered through swollen and split lips.

Sarah was devastated, his hateful comment sickened her but she was relieved in the knowledge that Lizzie would not have heard.

Lizzie was standing on the lawn in front of the house the cool breeze playing against her face. Closing her eyes tears squeezed out from beneath her lashes and she took in a deep breath. The sweet air was heavenly it was a beautiful morning. The sun had not long risen and was yet to warm the countryside, birdsong drifting on the breeze made Lizzie smile, the innocence of the tune stirred a childhood memory but there was no time for sentiment.

Staring into the distance, she watched as soft light played against the treetops the scene appeared magical like something out of a fairytale, then shaking herself out of her reverie she had only fifteen minutes in which to escape. Where would she run, there was nowhere to go. Time was ticking away, precious seconds, but strangely she remained indifferent, whatever happened it was going to be a lovely day.

White-hot pain tore through her body, it took her breath away leaving her doubled over and she retched before holding onto herself tightly. For a moment she dared not move, and waiting patiently for the pain to recede, she took deep breaths and prayed for the strength to carry on. When at last she could bear it, she turned away from the boundary fence and slowly made her way back towards the house.

Climbing the stone steps was an effort, each one a mountain of discomfort that made her light headed but at the top, she gathered her strength and pushing open the heavy wooden door stepped into the great hall. Glancing around she paused to catch her breath. She would have loved to admire the paintings and tapestries but her situation would not allow it.

Another wave of discomfort arrived and this time she began to pant, her breaths coming in short gasps. The pain was becoming unbearable and putting out her hand steadied herself against the wall until it passed.

Her strength was failing fast and it took a huge effort to get moving again but slowly she made her way towards the magnificent staircase. The house surrounding her was tranquil and calm, centuries of solid stability and family happiness had contributed to this atmosphere and it helped to steady her nerves. She thought how pleasant it would have been to stay here under different circumstances then, forcing herself to climb the stairs, she thought how wonderful it would be to live here when the house was full of sunshine and laughter. She imagined gliding magnificently down the staircase dressed in a beautiful evening gown and could almost hear music coming from the ballroom below.

Smiling sadly, she worked her way higher passing landings and corridors leading to bedrooms and dressing rooms. When finally she reached the top, her surroundings had changed. Here the decor was far less elaborate, all the trappings of wealth enjoyed by those below had disappeared and the beautifully carved handrail became plain and utilitarian. It was here that the servants had once lived perched high up under the eaves at the top of the house. Looking around at her gloomy surroundings Lizzie found what she was looking for. There was a small door at the end of the darkened corridor and guided by the hand of fate she went towards it. Thankfully, it opened easily and climbing out onto the roof she found a narrow lead lined pathway winding its way around magnificent chimneystacks. Glancing wearily up at the brickwork she admired each section in turn, it was as if they had been individually sculpted into works of art. The quality of the work was stunning, a credit to the men who had built the house so many years ago.

She appreciated the beauty of the architecture and strangely from here could see more of the house than was possible at ground level. Magnificent but ugly gargoyles stood guard over lead lined rain sluices that fed into exquisite cast iron water boxes. There were even small classical carvings set into niches all along the edge of the roof, these could hardly be seen from the garden below. Her surroundings were surreal and like a phantom, she moved slowly across the rooftop making for the low parapet that ran around the edge of the house. Like the battlements of a castle it was a barrier that held the roof tiles in place it also offered protection to the lead lined walkways from the worst of the weather.

Stepping carefully up onto the valiant ramparts, she had a magnificent view across the parkland. A multitude of colours spread out beneath her. It reminded her of a crochet quilt neatly tucked in around the gardens and beyond that, the forest extended out towards the horizon.

The breeze was much stronger here, it played with her hair and worried her eyes until they were moist and unable to hold back, huge teardrops rolled over her porcelain-like skin.

She spotted him the moment he left the house. He stopped on the lawn below in the same place where she had been standing earlier and she watched as he looked around. From this distance, she could not see the grin on his face or his look of anticipation.

Overcome by a great sadness Lizzie's heart ached as she thought of her parents. Her mother's face filled her vision and she could smell the sweetness of her perfume. Love filled her with warmth and at last her soul was filled with peace and contentment.

These were her final thoughts and spreading her arms as if to embrace the day she leaned forward, and launching herself from the roof made no sound she fell.

Mr Mac was startled; a sudden noise came from behind him. Turning around his grin froze on his face and it took him a moment to realise what had happened.

"What the feck." He muttered under his breath, then glancing up at the rooftop he moved towards the pathetic bundle to stare in disbelief at the shattered remains of Lizzie Baines.

The moment he entered the room Sarah knew that something was very wrong. He stopped in the middle of the floor his face black with rage and his body shaking.

"What have you done?" Mike lisped through broken lips.

Suddenly Mr Mac turned and struck him full in the face the force snapping Mike's head back until it cracked against the wall.

"No please," Sarah begged. "Not again."

It seemed an age before the violence stopped then all she could hear was the sound of heavy breathing. She opened her eyes as Mr Mac moved towards her, his cold black shadow seemed to engulf her and she felt a chill as he closed in.

He lashed out, his hands groping at her flesh and she screamed. She was terrified and could take no more of his shocking violence, she could do nothing to protect herself and had to wait for him to stop.

Standing back, he lifted his kilt. He was aroused and taking himself in hand, he moved in again.

"No," she screamed.

He froze, the expression on his face shocking, and for a fleeting moment there was confusion in his eyes. He seemed unsure, it was as if he knew that what he was doing was very wrong and slowly he backed away.

She was trembling so violently that it made her chains rattle. Sarah was at breaking point he had taken her to the limit and now on the verge of insanity, her heart was pounding madly and she was sobbing uncontrollably.

After a moment, he turned away and stormed of out of the room slamming the door behind him as he went.

It was a long while before she managed to regain control of her emotions.

"Mike," she whispered but he did not respond. She called out again louder this time and as he turned his face slowly towards her he grinned.

Her stomach lurched at the sight of him she was appalled by his injuries.

"I'm okay." He reassured her when he saw the frightened expression on her face. "Pretended to pass out."

"Don't provoke him," she pleaded.

Shaking his head, droplets of blood and sweat sprayed against the wall and he moaned quietly.

Slipping his arms under Lizzie Baines, Mr Mac carried her twisted and broken body to his secret place where he left her with his other trophies. He had taken pictures as she lay crumpled on the driveway and was now making his way back towards the house.

He was angry and stunned by her death he had not expected events to turn out this way. She had robbed him of the pleasure of hunting her down and now he felt cheated, the opportunity to look into her eyes at the moment of death had been lost. He loved to be up close and watch as their life light faded, it thrilled him to witness the soul departing from the body.

As a child, he loved to torture small defenceless creatures but as he grew older animals failed to satisfy his desires and now he needed more.

The first girl had been satisfying but he had not been smart enough to conceal his actions. Although her body was never found, he had been sent away for a very long time. Now he was in control, he played the game to his own set of rules but today he had been outsmarted. Lizzie Baines had left him angry and embittered.

He arrived once again at the cellar and going in took more pictures with his camera. This time he did not touch them, he did not even speak and as soon as he had what he wanted he went to his study and loaded them onto his computer. This time he didn't hesitate, he e-mailed them directly to Josie MacDonald.

Chapter

TWENTY TWO

DCI Jordan was passed a note informing him that another person had been reported missing. Sighing loudly he sat back in his chair before allowing his thoughts to focus on the events of his busy morning.

He could not stop thinking about Josie MacDonald, he thought her a nice enough young woman and he admired her honesty. She appeared genuine and he felt compelled to do everything in his power to help. It was his job after all but there were so many deserving cases and he found it increasingly difficult these days to give each one his undivided attention.

He eyed the paperwork that she had given him it was still there on his desk. Something was troubling him, he had not worked it out yet but he had an overriding feeling that he was missing something. He could not make up his mind about her allegations. The pictures she had presented to him were distressing enough, not the kind of thing a young woman would give to the police unless they were genuine.

He thought for a moment tapping the blotter on his desk with the end of his pen. Was there something more going on here, could she know more than she was letting on? His suspicious mind began to get the better of him and he sighed. He would go over her story once again; he owed her that much but that would have to wait because another job needed his immediate attention.

Running his hand wearily over his face he reached for the report. The victim this time was a man called Michael Cowper-Smith, an investment guru who worked in the city. Jordan despised men like him; his father had lost a substantial amount of money on the stock market a few years earlier having been advised by a man just like Cowper-Smith. With a grunt he sat up straighter he must remain professional his personal feelings were not welcome and he would not allow them to influence his work.

Going over the file again he made a decision, he would carry out the initial investigation himself. The mountain of paperwork he was facing was becoming impossible, he should delegate this job to one of his Inspectors but he needed to get out of the office.

Sighing heavily he ran his fingers through his hair then dropping the file on his desk got to his feet and made his way along the narrow corridor. Deliberately ignoring the confectionary dispensers that lined the walls he went towards the water machine and wrenching a plastic cup from the holder held it under the stream of iced water. As soon as the cup was full he drank it much too quickly and a band like iron tightened around his head. The sensation of pressure building up behind his eyes was almost unbearable but gritting his teeth, he ignored the pain and forced himself to drain the cup. When he was finished, he gasped and holding his hand out against the wall, he waited for the sensation to pass. He needed to feel the shock as the iced water hit his stomach it was gratifying and helped to chase away his demons. This was his way of reminding himself that he was still alive.

Returning to his office, he snatched his jacket from the hook behind the door then checking the details once more, committed them to memory.

The heart of the city could be a formidable place, but DCI Jordan had no problems locating the huge office block from where Cowper-Smith operated his business. Turning in under the building, he let his car roll down the ramp and took advantage of the underground parking. He ignored the unauthorised parking signs and left his car in the first available space, then walking past the lift that would take him directly up to reception made his way back to street level. He wanted to enter the building through the main entrance.

The building was impressive enough and looked as if it was made entirely from glass. Craning his neck he glanced up at the reflection of the sun; it splashed like liquid gold against the huge windows and he could only imagine the view from the top. The smell of money and success was everywhere and he wondered what it was like to compete against the entrepreneurs at the top. He knew how manic it could be, everyone trying to outdo each other in the commercial sector. His cousin had once worked for a company like this but had to retire early due to ill health brought on by the incredible stress of dealing with huge investments.

Jordan checked his reflection in the glass as he approached the rotary doors, then entering the building, went towards the huge desk where a group of receptionists were working. They were expecting him and he was shown into a waiting room that would not have looked out of place on a 1930's film set. He was amazed at the art deco designs and the pleasing curves of the furniture. The colour scheme had been cleverly thought out and the use of mirrors deceived the eye making the space seem much larger than it really was, then he noticed the modernistic paintings hanging on the walls. Moving towards one, he glanced at it briefly before settling back into a deep armchair. The picture was supposed to be of a racehorse but he failed to appreciate the style in which it was painted.

He did not have to wait long before a smartly dressed woman strode boldly into the room. Greeting him with a pleasant smile, she introduced herself as Ellie.

"Mr Cowper-Smith's Personal Assistant," she told him arrogantly.

Lucky Cowper-Smith he thought as he took hold of her cool, carefully manicured hand. First impressions were always very important and Jordan was definitely impressed.

Ellie moved fluidly across the room almost drifting on a cloud of expensive perfume then she settled on the edge of a chair. Jordan took the chair opposite, there was a small glass topped table between them but he had an uninterrupted view as she crossed her legs.

He guessed that she was in her early thirties but she possessed the poise and confidence of a woman twice her age. Her hair was dark and cut stylishly in what he would have described as chic and French but he knew nothing of fashion.

She was scrutinising him as intently as he was her and as soon as he realised that she was waiting for him to continue he shifted nervously in his seat.

Taking a deep breath, he began. "So Ellie, how long have you worked here?" He cringed thinking that it sounded like some cheesy chat up line.

Sensing his discomfort, she smiled. "I've been working with Mr Cowper-Smith for nearly two years now."

She raised her eyebrows and waited expectantly for his next question. Ellie was accustomed to having this effect on men and she was enjoying every minute of it. She was not about to make life easy for him.

166

"What is Mr Cowper-Smith's status here?"

"He's a senior partner; he runs the day to day business. You might say he's the managing director."

"Does he manage well?" Jordan grinned, recovering his composure.

"Oh yes," her eyes narrowed slightly. "He manages very well indeed."

She went on to explain a little about the business and the part her boss played within it.

"When he arrived yesterday morning was there anything different about him, for example, did he seem pre-occupied or worried in any way?"

"Not that I noticed," she hesitated. "He can be a little difficult at times but yesterday he was his usual self."

"Was he under any kind of pressure, from a client perhaps?"

She smiled anticipating where his questions were leading. "I don't think he'd upset anyone."

"I will of course need a list of his clients."

She made a mental note.

"Can I see his office?"

"Yes of course, would you like to do that now?"

He nodded and they rose together.

Ellie was attracted to him. DCI Jordan was a good-looking man and she was definitely interested, the opportunity to flirt with him excited her.

She liked the way he held her gaze and brushing against him deliberately she led the way along the corridor.

Cowper-Smith's workspace was huge it contained every modern appliance.

"My office is just through there," she indicated towards an interconnecting door.

Jordan smiled but remained silent, he wanted to get a feel for the place, try to get a mental picture of the man he was investigating.

Ellie watched him closely as he trailed his finger across the surface of the desk. She remained unobtrusive, leaning against the wall and when finally he completed his tour around the room, he arrived back to where he had started. It was then she told him about the funny little man who had reported damaging Cowper-Smith's car.

"Is his car still here?"

"Yes it is and it wasn't damaged at all. It was soon after he went down to the car park that we realised he'd disappeared."

"Did you take the message from the man?"

"No one of the receptionists did and she passed it on to me."

"I will need to speak to her."

"Do you think the events are connected?"

"Do you?" Moving away from the desk, he eyed her from across the room.

"I'm not sure, it was such a busy day yesterday, the last time I saw Mr Cowper-Smith was when I gave him the message."

"How did he take it?"

"He was angry at the thought of someone damaging his car."

Jordan nodded then something on the desk caught his attention. Leaning forward he reached for a small silver photo frame that had been tucked out of the way on the desktop. Ellie noticed his reaction and was sure that he recognised the face in the photograph.

"Do you know this woman?" he asked holding the photo frame out towards her.

"Of course, that's Josie MacDonald." Her frosty reply was lost on him.

Jordan was not a believer in coincidences and he was not a great fan of divine intervention but he was surprised to see a picture of Josie MacDonald on the man's desk. This changed everything.

"What's the relationship between Mr Cowper-Smith and Miss MacDonald?"

"Platonic," Ellie grinned with satisfaction.

"Have they known each other for long?"

"Eighteen months or so," she gave him the impression that theirs had been a stormy relationship.

He studied the photograph for a few moments longer then he replaced it precisely in the position that he had found it.

"I've got the CCTV tapes from the cameras in the car park. You can watch them in here if you like." She was desperate to move his attention away from Josie MacDonald, she would rather he focus on her so wriggling towards him treated him to one of her brightest smiles.

His thoughts were still on the photograph when he asked, "have you looked at the tapes from the car park?"

"No, why would I? I only collected them from Security this morning, just before you arrived."

"I see," he nodded before moving away.

Ellie sensed his change of mood. Suddenly he had become more serious and focussed, reminding her of a bloodhound who had just picked up the scent.

"Would you like some refreshments, tea or coffee perhaps?" she asked before disappearing into her office. She re-appeared almost immediately with the video tapes.

"Here," she smiled, holding them out to him.

Their eyes met and as their fingertips touched, a pleasant sensation ran through her.

The recordings were disappointing; in fact, they were next to useless. The camera nearest to where Cowper-Smith had parked his car was not in service so Jordan had to rely on a grainy long distance shot from across the car park. It was unlikely that even with computer enhancement he would be able to see a clear image. Jordan concealed his annoyance, he could not even make out the registration number of the car but the film did confirm that Cowper-Smith was assaulted and taken away against his will.

"Mr Cowper-Smith has been going on for ages about improving the security system," Ellie told him. "None of us girls use the underground car park you just don't know who might be lurking down there."

Jordan did not hear what she was saying. Going over events in his mind, the pictures that Josie MacDonald had given him set him thinking. There were just too many coincidences there must be a link somewhere. Cowper-Smith was a friend of Josie MacDonald's and if the man in the film had abducted him then he may well have kidnapped her friends. Jordan frowned and he made a decision. The moment he returned to his office, he was going to contact his colleagues in Elgin again.

Ellie accompanied him down to the car park and on the way they stopped to see the receptionist who had spoken to the man.

"He called himself Mr Mac," she told him. "He spoke with a Scottish accent."

Josie MacDonald had used that name when she told him about the journalist, slowly all the pieces were coming together. Cursing under his breath he realised that Josie was in grave danger, he should have listened to her.

Ellie watched him carefully as the colour drained from his face and she realised that he had made some kind of breakthrough. She had no idea what he was thinking but as his mood changed she could see him drifting away. She was not prepared to let that happen, there was no wedding ring on his finger and he didn't look like a man who was in a relationship, besides she did not much care if he was, as far as she was concerned he was fair game. She was going to make sure that he had her personal telephone number before he left.

Tim arrived at her house just after seven, he had intended to get there earlier but customers prevented him from closing his gallery any sooner. Since Josie's exhibition his business had taken an upturn, her work was suddenly very popular and people were still coming in to see her paintings. Other young artists under his patronage were benefitting from this influx of custom.

"Hiya," she greeted him with a kiss as she opened the door.

"Wow you look terrific."

"Don't be so surprised."

Earlier that day she had tried to paint but the events of the last few weeks haunted her mercilessly and her artistic flow was at its lowest ebb. She was so worried about Sarah and the picture of Lindsay was shocking but still there were doubts in her mind as to its authenticity. She refused to believe that someone would harm her friends.

Tim's advice had been sound, he had told her to relax, take care of herself for once and stop thinking about others. She had done as he suggested and was now feeling much better. She was determined to make their evening a success.

"So, where are we going?" he asked as he stepped in off the street.

"Nowhere, we're staying in."

"But you're all dressed up and you look gorgeous."

"Don't be silly," she made a face and leaned into him. "Do you like?" She whispered provocatively into his ear.

"Oh yes, I like very much."

He kissed her hard on the mouth and she responded by folding her arms around his neck. Breathing in the coconut freshness of her hair, he became aware of the seductive scent of her skin and it sent him wild with desire, but with an effort he managed to unwrap himself from her embrace then she led him into the kitchen.

The table was already set, scented candles gave off a pleasantly sweet fragrance and soft music was coming from the living room.

"Don't worry." She saw him glance towards the oven. "I haven't gone completely bonkers. The food will be arriving shortly," she giggled before going on, "I've ordered green chicken curry. I know you like Thai."

"Wow, you are organised." For the second time in just a few minutes he was amazed. "I needn't have worried so much, you seemed pretty upset on the phone earlier."

"Were you really worried?" she hugged him tightly. "Well that was this morning and as you can see I've put all that behind me now."

He was not entirely convinced but she was doing a great job, the transformation was miraculous.

Pulling away from him, she opened the fridge door.

"Would you like a drink?"

Glancing hesitantly up at the clock, he thought it a little early to be drinking.

"You can because you're staying here with me tonight." She looked at him seductively from across the kitchen.

"Well in that case I think I will."

Handing him a glass she filled it with wine then took him into the living room.

"I want this evening to be special."

They settled on the sofa.

"Don't even think about trying to escape."

"I wouldn't dare," he grinned.

Raising their glasses in a toast to each other he kissed her again and she snuggled into him. She was overjoyed at the way their relationship was developing.

Later when their food arrived, Tim busied himself in the kitchen. He opened the hot containers and in no time at all the room had filled with exotic aromas. Josie selected some music from a pile of CDs and Tim glanced in her direction, she had her back towards him. He realised how lucky he was to have found her, life without her would be impossible.

The music began to play and she turned to face him, it was as if she knew he was looking.

"I know you like this because I saw this album at your gallery the other evening."

"It appears that we share the same taste in music," he nodded approvingly, thankful that she could not read his thoughts. "So tell me, just when did you start going through my music collection?"

"One can tell so much about a person from the books they have on their book shelves. I happen to apply that same theory to music."

"Is that so?" He set the food-laden plates in their places at the table. "So what have you discovered about me then?"

"Oh you're far from perfect," she teased, "but there's nothing that a little female influence won't put right."

He grinned. "There's nothing wrong with me or my music collection."

"Oh I agree in principle but a girl can't be too careful especially with you arty types," she giggled again.

"Eat up before your food gets cold."

After their meal, he opened another bottle of wine and carried it into the living room. He loved the way they bantered, she was quick witted and amusing and every moment they shared was a joy. Their relationship had the promise of permanence about it and he was delighted. He had been attracted to her from the start but it had taken him a while to realise how she felt about him. He had no idea just how precarious her relationship was with Cowper-Smith.

"Penny for them," she whispered in his ear.

"I'm listening to the music."

"Liar," she dug him in the ribs.

"How do you know?"

"Woman's intuition."

"That's what my sister always says," he frowned.

"Of course she does, we are superior. You men are mere play things."

"Sexist." He kissed the top of her head and became serious. "I really should go and clean myself up."

Running her finger lightly over his stubble, she wrinkled her nose.

"I really do need a shower."

"I want you just the way you are warts and all."

Their lovemaking was intense; it started right there on the sofa and they pleased each other repeatedly before ending up in a tangle of limbs, breathless on the floor.

Her head was resting on his chest and she could hear the rhythm of his heart. She felt marvellous, her spirit glowing with satisfaction.

"I wish this moment would last forever," she said wistfully.

Tim was dozing contentedly on the edge of slumber. Their lovemaking had left him exhausted and he could easily have been in heaven listening to the voice of an angel.

"Come on," she urged running her finger lightly over his chest. "Take me to bed."

The following morning Josie was up before him. She was busy gathering up items of clothing that were strewn over the living room floor and could not stop grinning. Holding his shirt up to her face, she breathed in his scent and longed to be in his arms again. Her thoughts were never far from their lovemaking and she imagined what it would be like to have him there with her all of the time. She thought it a wonderful idea and fiddled absentmindedly with the third finger on her left hand.

She could hear movement coming from upstairs. The sound of running water from the shower drew her attention and making her way to the bathroom, she slipped out of her robe and stepped in beside him.

After breakfast, Tim was feeling a little better. The effects of too much wine the previous evening was beginning to wear off but still he decided to leave his car where it was and walk to work. The exercise would refresh him, besides it would do him good to walk off all the calories he had consumed the previous evening.

"But it's miles," Josie exclaimed when he told her his plan and then she looked away her face flushing with colour.

"What?" he grinned, he was aware of her embarrassment so reaching out he took her by the shoulders and gently turned her to face him.

"I would have thought you'd have used up all of last night's calories you naughty man," she whispered.

Pulling her into his arms, he squeezed her gently. She was soft and warm against him as he nuzzled her damp hair.

She could feel his excitement burning against her. "Timothy Granger!" She exclaimed in mock horror then whispered, "I love you Tim."

He responded with a kiss. "Do you know, apart from my mother I think you are the only person to have ever said that to me."

She thought her heart was going to break and a lump formed at the back of her throat.

"You make me feel so good," she murmured.

"I sort of feel the same way."

"Sort of!" she exclaimed pulling away so he could see the expression on her face.

He frowned then his expression softened. "Josie MacDonald I love you very much."

"You have no idea how much that means to me," she whispered.

Then the moment passed.

"You had better go but you have to make me a promise first."

"Your wish is my command my love."

"Hurry back to me this evening."

Josie was trying to paint but her mind was all over the place and she could not focus on her work. Mostly she thought about Tim but as the morning went on, she became increasingly guilt ridden. How could she be so happy when her friends were out there somewhere suffering at the hands of a lunatic?

Throwing down her brush, she went to her computer. She wanted to load some more pictures onto her new website but as soon as she logged on a message popped up on the screen. It alerted her to an unread e-mail and as she clicked on the icon, a picture of Mike appeared.

Jumping backwards in astonishment the chair she was sitting on flew across the room.

At first, she thought he had been involved in an accident, his face was covered in blood and he looked dreadful. Working the mouse, other pictures began to appear and she gasped in disbelief. Mike was chained to a wall just like Sarah and the others but it was the next picture that shocked her even more.

Lizzie was sprawled on a gravel pathway her red hair thick with blood, her limbs broken and at odd angles. Covering her face with her hands Josie gasped in disbelief and hardly able to hold back her tears she forced herself to look.

Lizzie was staring back at her from the screen, her eyes lifeless and as cold as glass marbles. Josie sobbed uncontrollably her tears coming in torrents and her chest heaved as she struggled for breath. She had been holding back for so long but now this latest shock was just too much. Reaching for the telephone with hands that were shaking violently she was unable to dial the numbers, tears blurred her vision and throwing it down, she lurched blindly across the room. Somehow, she managed to reach the small lavatory where she collapsed to her knees and began to vomit.

Sometime later, she came to her senses. Wedged into a tiny space between the wall and lavatory bowl she was cold and shivering with shock. Her legs, twisted beneath her were beginning to cramp and she groaned as she heaved herself to her feet. She had been unable to dislodge the terrible images from her mind and it was then that she made an important decision. She simply had to do something to help them.

Leaning against the small hand basin, she steadied herself before splashing cold water over her face then looking at herself in the wall mirror she gasped. Her eyes were red and swollen and her face was pale, she looked a mess.

Finally she moved into the kitchen then taking a bottle of chilled water from the fridge unscrewed the top and drank deeply. She could not face returning to the computer, she knew the screen saver would have blocked out the images but she needed time to regain her nerve.

After a while she summoned up the courage to face the screen, and picking up the chair from where it had fallen, sat down heavily before searching for the telephone. It was not in its cradle, it must have fallen to the floor but she could not locate it, she would have to use her mobile phone. Easing it from her pocket, she dialled DCI Jordan's number but he was not there. A voice at the other end of the line asked if she would care to leave a message but she declined the offer and ended the call. She thought about trying his mobile number but then decided against the idea. What she really wanted was to speak to Tim but he was busy and it would be unfair to worry him, besides there was little he could do.

Running her hand over her face, she thought about Mike. She had no idea how he had become mixed up in all this and the more she thought about it the more depressed she became. Riddled with guilt, thoughts of Tim worked their way back into her head. What right did she have to be so happy when her friends were clearly suffering, if she had stayed away from Scotland in the first place then none of this would be happening.

Sometime later, she had finished packing and was now stuffing items of make-up into a vanity case. Her mind was still in a whirl as she dropped her bags by the front door, then turning to face the mirror on the wall she asked herself what she thought she was doing. The police had told her to stay out of the investigation and she didn't need to be told just how dangerous it would be to go after this mad man, she could see from the pictures what to expect if he was to catch her. She tried DCI Jordan again but he was still not at his desk and she could not bring herself to explain what was happening to one of his colleagues. Regardless of the dangers she had made up her mind, doing nothing was no longer an option things had gone too far. She was going to Scotland but had no idea what she would do once she arrived. Her friends must be somewhere near Spey Bay that was where this whole thing had begun and she felt sure that was where it would end.

Her immediate worries were about the journey, it was such a long way and she had never driven that far before. She had not been near her car for weeks and had no idea how much fuel was in it or if it would even start. She had some idea that that Mike had filled it up with petrol then biting her bottom lip, she considered travelling up by train, but that was no good she would still need a car, perhaps she could hire one or even borrow her aunt's. The thought of driving something that she was unaccustomed to was out of the question, driving her own little car would be bad enough.

Pushing these thoughts aside, she began to focus on more practical things. Opening the fridge door, she lifted out an unopened bottle of milk and placed it on the table. She would give it to Mrs Robinson, the woman who lived next door. Next, she transferred a few items to the freezer then satisfied that nothing had been left to go stale, closed the fridge door.

Moving into the living room, she glanced around. The atmosphere had changed, not long ago this room had been full of love and joy but now it stood empty and cold, a stark reminder of how precarious life could be. She shuddered, it wouldn't take much to destroy everything that she held dear.

Going to the sofa, she rearranged the cushions and it was then she discovered Tim's mobile phone. It must have slipped out of his pocket the previous evening and picking it up she wondered how long it would be before he missed it. Taking it into the kitchen, she placed it on the table beside the milk then gathering up his car keys dropped them next to his phone. Next she scribbled a note and slipped it into an envelope along with a spare key. These she would leave with her neighbour, Mrs Robinson never missed a trick, she would spot him the moment he arrived.

In her studio, she packed a leather satchel and glanced longingly at her paints and brushes, she had no idea how long she would be gone but would have to make do with a camera, a small sketchbook and some pencils.

At last, she was ready. Snatching up the bottle of milk and the envelope, she went out to find Mrs Robinson.

Chapter
TWENTY THREE

The drive out of London was uneventful, it was well after the rush hour and the morning madness had calmed significantly. At first it seemed strange to be driving again, she could hardly remember the last time she had been behind the wheel of a car. Josie disliked driving and avoided it if she could. She felt intimidated by other drivers; Mike always insisted that she be aggressive when behind the wheel but it was not in her nature besides, the notion only frightened her even more.

She glanced at the fuel gauge, it was registering half full but she had no idea how far that would take her so she decided to fill up before leaving London.

The thought of driving on the motorway frightened her enormously and she hated the idea. Even as a passenger she felt uneasy surrounded by fast moving traffic. She had never driven on one by herself before and she began to wish that Tim were there beside her.

Following the route planner printed from her computer, she was now heading towards the M1. There was a seventy-mile stretch of motorway ahead, plenty of time to become accustomed to the motorway traffic, she reassured herself.

Glancing at her watch, she wondered what Tim was doing right now. The thought of him lifted her spirit but it was not long before images of her friends returned and she began to think more clearly about her situation. She still had no clear plan, all she could do was wait and see what turns up in Scotland. Turning her thoughts to Mike, their relationship might be over but she wished him no harm. Sarah had not liked him from the start and voiced her opinion without much prompting. She was acutely perceptive and predicted that he would be trouble; annoyingly she had been right. Josie realised of course that she should have listened to her friend but at the time had put Sarah's comments down to jealousy. How wrong she had been, she should never have doubted her friend's good judgment. Things were so different with Tim, making love with him felt so right, he was such a special man.

Her mind skipped back to Sarah, someone had once said that she had an old head on young shoulders. Sarah was the sister that Josie never had and she realised how lucky she was lucky to know her. Tears stung at the back of her eyes, she missed her terribly and gripping the steering wheel held onto it even tighter.

Josie was convinced that she was doing the right thing, she had to find her friends. Images of Lindsay and Lizzie haunted her relentlessly and she couldn't bear to dwell on what they were going through. If the pictures were real, then Lizzie and Lindsay were already dead but refusing to believe it Josie was determined to find them before it was too late.

Tim telephoned Josie's home number but there was no answer. Fortunately, his morning had been quiet, the only drama had been to parcel up some paintings for a courier who had turned up earlier than planned. He found it amusing that her paintings of Scottish landscapes were going back to Scotland. Someone had ordered them on-line from his website. He was selling more paintings that way and he wondered how long it would be before internet shopping took over completely, all he would need then would be a warehouse and a virtual gallery.

He tried her mobile phone but was put through to voice mail, she must have it switched off, he thought, and chose not to leave a message. He found it quite impossible to think about anything else, thoughts of Josie filled his mind and everywhere he looked there seemed to be reminders of her.

He made himself a cup of coffee and carried it into the gallery where he studied the paintings arranged around the walls. Josie meant so much to him so he made up his mind; he was going to tell her how much he loved her. It was against his nature to be so verbally intimate but he was determined she should know how he felt. He grinned and wondered what she was doing at that moment.

Just before the stretch of M6 toll road near Lichfield she stopped to re-fuel and grab a cup of coffee. Her journey had been straightforward so far and with every mile her confidence for fast motorway driving was improving.

Before leaving the services, Josie turned on her mobile phone and reported in to her Aunt Molly. She was expecting to arrive just after midnight providing there were no hold ups and of course, she did not lose her way. She had kept her aunt updated with events even though DCI Jordan had warned her against giving away any details. Josie and her aunt were in agreement, events in Spey Bay and the abduction of her friends had to be connected.

Tim arrived at her house just after six, he rang the bell and as if by magic, the neighbour's door opened. A huge black woman dressed in bright flowing robes filled the entrance.

"Mr Granger," she said with a wide grin.

"Yes," he nodded and drawn towards her he smiled. "Mrs Robinson I presume."

Her vast body shook with mirth and when she had recovered, she handed him a package. "Josie left this for you,"

Tearing it open, he shook out a key and Mrs Robinson told him that Josie was not at home.

"She isn't expected back anytime soon."

"Thank you." Tim frowned. "When did she go out?"

"Earlier this morning, an hour and a half after you," she smiled at him widely.

Tim got the impression there was nothing she didn't know about her neighbours.

"Did she say where she was going?"

"Don't you know Mr Granger?" her face becoming serious she eyed him suspiciously.. "She told me she would be away for a few days and would I be good enough to look out for you."

He was confused, she had not said anything about going away besides, she was expecting him to call round. Something must have happened so thanking her he slipped the key into the lock and pushed open the door.

The house was silent and frowning he made his way towards the kitchen, what could have happened once he had left that morning, he wondered, and why did she not telephone?

On the kitchen table, he found his mobile phone and he cursed loudly. The moment he switched it on the red light began to flash and an alarm sounded. He watched the LED screen as it went through a series of changes and strange icons began to appear. Selecting the GPS mode as soon as it became available, he followed his sister's instructions waiting for a few seconds as his phone converted into a tracking device.

A tiny map appeared on the screen but it was a few moments before he realised that the little red light was fast approaching Glasgow.

"What the hell was she doing in Scotland?" he cried out, refusing to believe the evidence in front of him.

This must be some kind of joke, he thought as he glanced around him. The house was empty, Josie was not at home and he was devastated. He stared at the screen again, and hating himself wondered how could he have been such a fool?

He should have realised that she would go off in search of her friends. She had been happy this morning when he left the house but something must have happened to make her disappear so suddenly. His sister had warned him that this might happen and as usual he was too pig headed to listen, he had failed to look out for Josie even after Kate had set up the tracking device. He cursed himself again, how could he have gone all day without his mobile phone?

Tim paced the floor in an attempt to put his thoughts in order, Josie had given him no indication that she was capable of doing anything like this. Flinging his mobile phone aside he went into the living room in search of the telephone. He found the handset on the floor under the computer table and snatching it up began to dial her number but it was no use, her mobile phone was either turned off or she was in an area of poor reception. Slamming the handset down into its cradle, he stormed into the kitchen, and reaching for his mobile phone confirmed her position.

He was amazed that she would do something like this and inhaling deeply he struggled with his spiralling emotions. His nerves were taught and his body trembling but he had to remain calm. It would do no good jumping to conclusions or running off after her, he would have to think this through very carefully and plan his next steps.

Moving back into the living room he searched for her telephone directory, it was on the table beside the sofa. Picking it up he flicked through the pages until he found the number he was looking for.

A woman answered his call and told him politely that she was not expecting her niece to visit any time soon so she must be at home in London. He was confused, he wanted to warn her that Josie was in grave danger and he was very worried for her safety but maybe Josie had not confided in her aunt. If she knew nothing about this whole affair then it would probably be wise to say nothing.

He glanced at the screen on his mobile phone for the hundredth time willing it to be wrong. He loathed the little red light that was flashing so ominously, it represented danger to everything that he held dear.

Suddenly he remembered the note, snatching it up from the table he stared at her small neat handwriting. It urged him not to worry and there was confirmation of her love, she promised to see him soon and had sealed the message with a kiss.

Her reassurances were meaningless and he was beside himself with worry. Josie was in grave danger, he didn't want her to end up like Sarah chained naked against a wall.

"You idiot," Kate shouted down the phone. "How on earth did you manage to leave your phone at her place?"

The last thing he would admit to was being hung over that morning and unable to think straight. He knew his sister well enough and braced himself for further verbal onslaught.

"If she's near Glasgow then she's been gone for hours," Kate was furious. "So what are you going to do about it?"

"Go after her of course," he told her. "I'm sure she's going to her aunt's in the Highlands."

"But she's got an eight hour head start, how do you imagine you're going to catch up with her?"

He had not thought about that but then he came up with an idea. "I could fly to Inverness, hire a car and be there by...," he glanced at his watch, "midnight I guess."

Her mind was working too but she let him continue.

"I have to organise things here first, I can't just up and leave," he paused for breath. "Will you take care of things whilst I'm away?"

"You don't think I'm hanging around here do you?"

"I need you to look after the gallery."

"What you need brother is me by your side besides, you have no idea what you are getting yourself into."

"And you do I suppose," he snapped angrily and could feel himself losing control.

"Listen to me," Kate began to outline her plan. "Forget flying it would be impossible for you to organise a flight at such short notice. We will go to Scotland together, share the driving through the night. If you're right about Josie going to her aunt's then that's where we'll find her in the morning besides, we have the tracking device."

Her plan was simple and he wished he had thought of it first. Kate was right, Josie would be exhausted after her long drive, she would have to rest and that is when the distance between them would be closed.

"I still think I should go alone."

"Look Tim I'm not arguing with you."

He could hear the determination in her voice.

"You're wasting time. Pick me up as soon as you're ready, I'll be waiting." She slammed the phone down before he could object.

He hated the way she always took control but he had to admit, his sister had the ability to see things objectively and it infuriated him. Heading towards the door, he began to focus on the decisions that he would have to make.

The final part of her journey took her up into the Scottish highlands. This was a place Josie knew well, she adored the mountains and the valleys the dramatic countryside never ceased to inspire her.

The gentle slopes became gradually steeper and she marvelled at the rocks that lay strewn across the landscape. The last ice age was responsible for that, huge glaciers had formed these valleys and the boulders she could see had been uprooted and ground smooth beneath the ice. The valley had probably not changed since then and it sent a thrill through her.

Heather growing at the roadside took on a darkened hue as the light began to fade and rabbits frolicked along the deer tracks. Josie knew that other animals would appear as soon as the light faded and she would have to be careful.

The last rays of light vanished behind the mountain and her car was swallowed up by shadows. There were no street lamps here and it would be some time before the moon would have the strength to illuminate the mountain roads. Flicking the headlights onto main beam Josie could not remember the last time she had driven in the dark. The streets of London were never in complete darkness, all night long they were bathed in incandescent light and there was seldom an opportunity to use headlights on full beam. Peering through the windscreen she had no regrets about leaving the city, her mood had even lifted a little and for a while she was able to forget the circumstances that had brought her here.

By the time she reached Elgin, the streets were deserted but she did not mind. Having the place to herself was magical, many of her childhood memories were associated with this ancient city and she liked to think of it as a second home. At just eight years old, her parents had brought her here for the first time and she had returned every year since, now the streets were as familiar as those in London where she lived. She questioned what it was that anchored her in the great city and could think of nothing to prevent her from settling here. She would of course miss her friends but they could come and stay from time to time. Leaving the streets of Elgin, she headed out towards the village of Garmouth situated just a short distance away.

When she arrived, most of the houses were in darkness, the village snuggled up and asleep in the landscape. A stranger could easily have missed it if it had not been for the occasional road sign.

A reassuring sense of familiarity greeted her and she began to recognise cottages and smallholdings on the outskirts of the village. Josie recalled the names of some of the families who lived here and her childhood memories came flooding back.

Urging her car along the narrow streets she came upon the hotel with its popular public bar and negotiating a corner she saw the little store and post office. There was still no signs of life, the village remained deserted. Slowing to walking pace, she passed the community centre and forgotten memories of a wedding reception suddenly came back to her. She wondered whose wedding it had been and searching her memory was a little girl again running wild around the hall playing with all the other children.

Finally, she arrived outside her Aunt Molly's cottage. A light was showing in the window, a welcome beacon for the weary traveller. The moment she turned off the engine the front door flew open flooding the tiny garden with light and Molly charged out like a defender of a castle ready to do battle. Howling with delight her voice disturbed the still night air.

"Darling child how was your journey?"

"Auntie Molly." Throwing her arms round her, she somehow managed to halt the charge. "It's so good to see you I've missed you so much. I can't believe I've driven all this way."

Molly, fussing around her niece, was overjoyed to see her again.

"You must be exhausted, hungry too I expect. Come on inside, put your bags down there, the kettle hasn't long been boiled."

Josie hardly had time to grab her things before she was hustled into the house. She did as she was told and Molly took great pleasure in making a fuss of her.

"Sit yourself down."

In no time at all Josie was given a mug of steaming green tea.

"Mince an tatties for you my girl." Molly said, loading up a plate with food that oozed delicious aromas. "Eat, you must be half starved."

"Not as much as you might think," Josie admitted, sipping at her tea.

"As soon as you're finished you can pop straight into bed. We'll have a nice little chat in the morning and you can tell me all about your plans."

Molly was overjoyed to see Josie but underneath her smiles was desperately worried. She knew why her niece had driven all the way up from London but did not want to break the spell that filled her little kitchen with happiness. There would be time enough to discuss the terrible things that were haunting her.

Fatigue soon caught up with Josie and her eyelids became heavy as her head started to nod. Surprisingly she had managed to clear the mountain of food from her plate and the comforting weight in her stomach was sending her to sleep. She had snacked on the journey but it had been hours since her last proper meal. She smiled and trying not to think of Tim listened as Molly chatted away in the background.

"Young women today are far too thin," she was saying. "What you need my girl is a dose of good Scottish fare and some fresh highland air."

Her little rhyme pleased her. "Rosy cheeks and curves in your breeks!"

They laughed together.

Josie slept soundly for a few hours but woke early. The air outside was crisp and fresh and the sky was as clear as a mountain spring. Nowhere in London would she find silence as loud as this.

Today she had some unpleasant business to attend to; she was going to re-visit the scene of crime in the hope of laying some ghosts to rest. Her most frightening memories were centred on the chase along the riverbank and the absolute terror of the North Sea. In her dreams he was always there, a dark evil figure, a presence from hell and typically, no matter what she did to get away he was just an arm's length behind. It always ended the same way, the freezing grey water dragging her down and stealing the breath from her lungs. She would wake up sobbing with her heart hammering against her ribs. The worst of it was the sense of hopelessness and the black clouds of despair that never seemed far away. Sometimes her depression was so deep that it would last for days, it affected her work and ultimately her health.

It was often said that criminals returned to the scene of the crime so why not the witness. She wondered if he had been back to gloat over his wickedness, would she encounter him as she wandered along the riverbank, would history repeat itself?

Her eyes danced nervously around the garden and she hugged herself tightly. Suddenly she smiled, she would probably find everything perfectly normal, a scene of tranquil beauty that was always there, a place where heinous crimes never happened.

She knew the police had found nothing, there were no clues to substantiate her claims and with the passage of time, it would be foolish to expect that something overlooked would still be there. She hardly needed convincing, she had to go, it was something she simply must do for her own piece of mind if for nothing else.

The journey north was very different for Kate and Tim. A lorry had shed its load over both carriageways of the motorway and although diversions were in place, Kate insisted that they stop. Tim was exhausted so they booked into a motel where he could rest. It would also give the authorities time to clear the road.

A few hours later Tim still looked tired, the rest had done him no good at all, shadows and worry lines were etched deeply into his face.

"We'll leave just as soon as you have eaten." Kate said, sounding like their mother.

He frowned miserably. Left to himself he would have charged off with no thought to his own wellbeing. Although he found her annoying, he had to admit, it was a comfort to have her along.

They might not always get on but his sister was an extremely clever woman. She was also a very private person who was misunderstood most of the time. He was quick to accuse her of being aloof and this he realised was part of their problem. Her work was regulated by government policy, bound by the official secrets act so even if she wanted to she could not tell him about it. He understood that she was often wound up in matters that were best left alone but unfortunately, this did nothing to make their relationship any easier.

Kate flipped open his mobile phone and checked the tracking device; Josie was still in the village of Garmouth. Tim started the car and they continued on their way.

Chapter
TWENTY FOUR

Mr Mac was losing interest in his captives, things had changed and it all seemed different somehow. Pacing the floor, he rubbed his forehead with the palm of his hand before stopping to think about Sarah Hamilton. This was usually sufficient to excite him but now even that was beginning to wear thin. Again, he wondered what it was that stopped him from having his fun with her. He had barely touched her and for some reason could not bring himself to do it. He frowned then turned his thoughts to Lizzie Baines. Her unusual death had unsettled him, he had never experienced that kind of behaviour before and he found it hard to accept. He wondered why she had chosen to end her own life, cheat him out of the chase and rob him of the experience. It left him frustrated and the voices in his head accused him of losing control. The death of Lizzie Baines had deprived them too, they had not had their fun either and were determined to apportion blame. He grimaced as the voices became sharp and intimidating. They quizzed him mercilessly asking why he had allowed it to happen. He was questioned about his decision to bring a man into their little game. He had never abducted a man before, what use was he to them, what was he thinking. Doing his best to ignore them, Mr Mac wondered what Josie MacDonald must be feeling. This man was close to her and he revelled in the knowledge that she would be very upset and worried about him. He thought about the pictures he had e-mailed her recently and wondered what kind of a reaction they had evoked.

He could not remember the man's name and screwing up his face he thought for a moment. Michael Cowper-Smith, that was it and repeating the name out loud he savoured the sound as it rolled off his tongue. Perhaps he should go and ask him what it was like screwing Josie MacDonald. He should at least tell this Cowper-Smith what he had in mind for his woman, it would be fun tormenting his mind with images of shameless suffering. Going into the kitchen, Mr Mac pulled a bottle of water from the fridge then made his way back towards the cellar.

Sarah heard him approaching and braced herself in anticipation of the mental torture that always accompanied his visits. Mike sensing her sudden apprehension began to stir. Though unable to sleep, he managed to keep himself in a state of semi-consciousness. He had the ability to switch off completely and Sarah could not understand how he was able to do this; she was far too anxious to relax.

Suddenly the monster was there leering at her in his usual way. She would never grow accustomed to this and her heart began to race. She would be next in his sordid little game and having seen what he had done to both Lindsay and Lizzie, she knew that he was capable of anything.

Moving towards her, he was careful not to make physical contact and slowly raising the bottle he was carrying, encouraged her to drink.

The water was cool and heavenly as she gulped it down. It quenched her thirst and ran in tiny rivulets over her chin.

He paused, allowing her to catch her breath then he surprised her by asking politely if she would like some more. When she had finished she watched suspiciously as he did the same for Mike.

Gasping for breath, Mike spat droplets of water between his broken teeth and Sarah prayed that he would remain silent, not provoke further violence. She would not be able to stand it, their situation was bad enough and she could feel herself losing grip of reality.

Sarah missed Lizzie terribly, now it was just her and Mike she felt isolated, he was no company at all and she was finding it difficult to remain optimistic. She and Lizzie had agreed that however bad things became they would find something positive to cling on to but now with her friend gone, she found this impossible and could not rid herself of her misery. It was bad enough having Mr Mac leer at her but with Mike there too it was just too much.

She had tried talking to him but he was so different, they seemed to have nothing in common, he was so angry all of the time. His aggression was a danger to them both and he had no idea how vulnerable she felt, his attitude was just making things worse.

"What did you say?" the sound of his voice startled her. "What did you say?" Mr Mac moved quickly towards her.

"Nothing," she replied backing up against the wall.

"I heard you say something," he insisted, pushing his face up close to hers.

Turning her head away made him angry and grasping her chin roughly, he forced her to look at him.

Crying out, she had no time to think and searching his face looked into his vacant eyes. They reminded her of pools of stagnant water.

"Leave her alone you bastard!"

Mr Mac focussed on Mike, "then it must have been you."

He lingered beside her for a moment longer then was gone.

Sarah could not stop shaking, her heart was hammering uncomfortably again and she had to take deep breaths in order to calm her nerves.

"What was that all about?" Mike lisped through swollen lips.

Glancing fearfully at him she was unable to answer.

Mr Mac wandered blindly through the house, the voices in his head were clearer now and all the chanting and whispering was beginning to make sense. Suddenly he stopped and throwing back his head howled like a wild animal, he could see a face that he recognised immediately. Her thick dark hair and clear piercing eyes seemed to grow in front of him as if she was a goddess appearing from another world.

It was the bitch who had challenged him at the gallery, he could feel her trying to get inside his head and the power of it was shocking. Reaching out towards him, she sought to strip away his mask but he was too strong and holding her back, he closed off his mind forging a formidable barrier to prevent her from getting in.

Her voice echoed inside his head chanting the same words over and over again. At first, he could not make out what it was that she was saying but as he listened, the words became clearer.

'We're coming to get you.' The voice continued relentlessly beating a tattoo inside his head and threatening to drive him mad.

Eventually it faded away leaving his heart racing. Miss bloody Granger he thought, what had it to do with her anyway? Hatred for this woman festered inside him until he was full of murderous images and he realised that he wanted to kill her. He would torture her first, make her wish that she had never been born and when he was finished, it would be as if she had never existed.

Suddenly the voices stopped and he staggered against the wall. Putting his hand out to steady himself, he dropped the water bottle as he lurched along the corridor. He had to get out and pushing open the door almost fell over the step in his haste to escape. Filling his lungs greedily, he drank in the cool air and immediately began to feel better. His head was clearer now and with each breath, he began to realise what he must do.

Josie MacDonald was close by, he could feel her presence and now he was calmer the voices in his head became clear. He was able to make sense of what was happening. The dark haired woman had unsettled him but he had managed to keep her out. It worried him that she could appear so vividly inside his mind, he had no idea what it was she was planning but he got the impression that she was just biding her time. Suddenly the whispering started again stronger this time and he listened, he needed to hear what she had to say. The message was unmistakable, she was coming to get him.

Somewhere along the road bordering Scotland and England, Tim Granger was driving as if his life depended on it. He had no idea where this madness was taking him. At first it had seemed simple, drive up to Scotland and rescue Josie, but now he was beginning to realise that it probably wouldn't be quite so easy. What right had he to presume that Josie would be pleased to see him? She had come all this way on her own and had not included him in her plans. He made a face and cursed under his breath. What would it look like him turning up unexpectedly with his sister in tow?

Glancing sideways at Kate, he could see that her eyes were closed and her brow was furrowed, it was as if she was concentrating on some task. Very slowly, the corners of her mouth began to curve upwards and a shadow of satisfaction passed over her face.

Josie walked along the footpath that took her away from the village and on towards Spey Bay. She passed quickly across the old iron bridge, her footsteps hollow against the ancient timbers and marvelling at her peaceful surroundings, she had to remind herself that just a hundred years ago this whole area had been alive with industry. She could almost hear the noise of the trains clattering towards the salmon stores that were situated further along the bay. At the same time there was the ship building industry operating on the other side of the estuary, the trains bringing materials and supplies to the men who worked there.

The natural beauty of the bay and the sound of birdsong kept the ghosts away and she could hardly believe that this was the scene of such a brutal murder. The level of the river had dropped considerably since her last visit. It was not so long ago that the springtime melt running off the mountains had filled the river, spilling floodwater onto the surrounding meadows. Now the balance of things had been restored and she could hardly imagine it being any different. The pasture beside the river was lush and the air was pleasantly warm, birds and bees went about their business and Josie could feel the joy of nature all around her. Suddenly, shaken from her trance she was startled by a jogger who mumbled a greeting as he passed and pressing her hand against her pounding heart she smiled nervously. At least this time she was not alone with a homicidal maniac.

Following the riverbank, she arrived at the spot where the murder had taken place. There was nothing there to see, nothing seemed out of place, the only movement coming from long grasses swaying gently in the breeze. Birds were darting amongst the reeds and her surroundings were as peaceful as the day she had discovered them.

Hesitantly she moved towards the spot where the woman had died. Nothing remained of the life that had once been, so opening her mind, she searched for the soul that had walked here but it was no use, she failed to pick anything up and was left disappointed.

Slowly she turned away and moved back along the track, she had no idea what it was that she had hoped to find, a distant or fragile echo of the murdered woman would have been some consolation but it was not to be. Taking a deep breath, she straightened her shoulders and began to focus on what she was going to do next.

Mr Mac wandered back into the kitchen his head heavy with thoughts. The voices had left him confused and he was still thinking about the black haired woman from the gallery. He tried to figure out how she had managed to get inside his head, nothing like this had happened before. The voices that haunted him were, he realised, of his own making but this one was different. Absentmindedly he began to fill a bucket with cold water. Her message had been clear enough however much he argued with himself.

He filled a second bucket and tossing in a sponge, it sat on top of the water. Searching for a towel, he pulled one from a cupboard before picking up the buckets and making his way towards the cellar. He had made up his mind he would drive into the village, if Josie MacDonald were in Scotland he felt sure that is where he would find her.

Stepping up to Sarah, he released the chains that secured her wrists. He paid no attention when she cried out and collapsed to the floor, he simply stepped over her and turned his attentions towards Mike.

The force of the water hitting him drove the breath from his body and threw him back against the wall. Mr Mac laughed as he watched Mike gasp then, going towards Sarah, he pulled her roughly to her feet and she staggered against him. Holding her tight, their faces were just inches apart and lust began to course through him but fighting temptation he pushed her up against Mike.

This was another act of humiliation; another method of torture that she had to endure. Sarah attempted to pull away but his grip was too strong and Mr Mac laughed cruelly as she struggled.

Mike, holding himself rigid was helpless and he could feel her distress washing over him in waves, all he could do was turn his bloodied face away.

Her heart skipping wildly, she was held up against him. Heat began to rise up along her neck and as it flushed into her face, she looked away.

He released his grip and she staggered backwards almost losing her footing in a puddle of water that had formed at her feet.

"Clean him up." Mr Mac growled then he was gone.

The door banging loudly, they heard the sound of a key rattling in the lock. This was the first time he had locked the door since Mike's arrival.

The drive into Garmouth took twenty minutes and Mr Mac made his way directly to the old woman's cottage. A small car that he had not seen before had been left on the road outside the gate; he guessed that it belonged to Josie MacDonald.

Driving by slowly he stopped behind the cottage next to the playing field where he waited. Peering through the windscreen he studied the lane, it was quiet and there was no one about but he did not have to wait for long. Josie appeared with her head down and her hands thrust deeply into her pockets. She looked troubled and from the way she was walking, he could tell that she was tired. Ignoring the urge to duck down behind the wheel, he remained motionless. He knew that any sudden movement would attract her attention and he wanted to avoid that.

She walked past his car unaware of his scrutiny and continued along the path. Squirming in his seat, he observed her in his rear view mirror and his breathing became ragged. He had not expected to see her up close, this was an unexpected bonus and as his thoughts ran away with him, he imagined her chained and helpless beside her friends in his cellar.

191

Miles away in a car that was speeding north Kate Granger stirred from her sleep. She opened her eyes and murmured something that was incoherent, then swallowing loudly her eyes adjusted to the light and she sat upright in the seat.

"He's found her."

"What?" Tim did not hear her clearly over the noise of the car.

"Oh nothing just dreaming," leaning forward she fumbled for her bag on the floor between her feet. Pulling Tim's mobile phone out, she studied the small screen checking the GPS signal.

"Anything new?" Tim asked as he glanced sideways at his sister.

"No, she's still at her aunt's house."

"We should be there by late morning I would think."

"What do you intend doing once we arrive?" she asked.

"I'm going to have it out with her, find out why she isn't willing to include me in this little excursion of hers."

"Is that wise?" she turned to face him.

"What do you mean?"

"Well it's quite obvious that she's on a mission. She seems determined to find the killer and rescue her friends."

He laughed bitterly. "And end up dead in the process, you've seen the pictures. Can you imagine what he does to them first?"

She didn't need to exercise her imagination, she knew exactly what he did to them. She had felt the horror and humiliation when looking at the picture of Lizzie Baines.

Kate remained silent for a moment brooding on her thoughts. "Look Tim we have to think this through. What good will it do if we are all captured and killed?"

He ignored her.

"Surely it would be wise to hold back, wait a bit and see what develops. We'll be in reserve ready to help Josie when she needs us most."

Taking his eyes off the road, he looked at her. She was right of course, what she said made sense but he could not ignore his instincts, he had to get to her before the killer did.

"Besides, where can she go without us knowing?" She continued, waving the mobile phone in front of his face.

It was clear that his emotions were in turmoil but they had to remain sensible. What they decided to do next could either save them or get them all killed. Tim remained tight-lipped and turned his attention back to the road.

"I know it's hard for you Tim but we are her only hope. She's going to get herself into some very serious trouble but we'll be there to help her." She sounded annoyingly sure of herself and he resented her for it.

Mr Mac was playing the waiting game. He checked the equipment in his car, carefully measuring an amount of clear liquid into a syringe before securing the plastic safety cap over the fine needle and placing it on the seat beside him. He looked to see that his pistol was fully loaded and that his long bladed knife was in the glove compartment. Satisfied that everything was in place he settled down to survey the cottage.

Chapter
TWENTY FIVE

"Did you find what you were looking for dear?" Molly asked the moment Josie appeared.

"It was a spiritually uplifting experience." She replied distantly as she settled at the breakfast table.

"You should have been a poet dear."

"I'm sorry," Josie made a face. "I was miles away."

"This will help you to wake up." Molly pushed a mug of strong coffee across the table and Josie breathed in the fresh aroma. She smiled, comforted by her aunt's presence.

"I found absolutely nothing," she paused and took a sip from her mug. "The police were right you know it's as if I imagined the whole thing."

"That's not true and you know it." Molly shot her a sympathetic glance and frowned as Josie began to massage the stiffness from her shoulder. "Are you alright?" she asked full of concern.

The pains from her injuries had mostly gone but the memories remained.

"I'll be fine, there's no need to worry I just ache a little sometimes."

"What happened to you dear was not your fault. You shouldn't go blaming yourself for everything else that's happened either."

Josie remained silent, there was so much that she wanted to say but her emotions wouldn't allow it.

Molly was amazed at how much Josie resembled her mother. The expression on her face as she sat with her elbows on the table was a picture of indecision and just like her mother; she was chewing at her bottom lip.

A lump formed at the back of Josie's throat as self-pity threatened, but in an attempt to shrug off her melancholia she buried her face in her coffee mug and fought back.

Molly busied herself at the stove, she could see that Josie was in a state of turmoil so remained silent but as soon as she thought her niece had recovered sufficiently she asked, "what do you intend doing today?"

"I'm at a complete loss to be honest. Coming up here seemed such a good idea. I naively thought that being close to where it all began would start a chain reaction of some kind that would lead me to the killer, but now I think I might have made bit of an error," looking up she sighed. "Now I'm here I don't know where to start."

Molly eyed her thoughtfully as she ran the dishcloth that she was holding through her fingers. She was truly concerned; Josie seemed so vulnerable sitting there in her kitchen. She was hardly the type to go tracking down mad killers and it was obvious that the strain of the ordeal had already left its mark. Dark smudges had appeared beneath her eyes and her face was the colour of ivory. The journey up from London on top of the pressure of the last few days had taken more out of her than either of them had realised.

Pulling up a chair she sat down and cradling her own mug of coffee between her hands she considered their options.

"Well," Molly began suddenly, "have you got any clues? Did this man give anything away in his correspondence?"

Morning sunshine filled the kitchen with a cheerful glow and suddenly Josie began to feel a little better. Just being there with her aunt was an antidote to all her troubles and she felt certain that together they would get to the bottom of it. She told her aunt about the awful pictures she had received through the post and by e-mail but she found it difficult to describe them in any detail.

"What was in the background of these pictures?" Molly asked in an attempt to disguise her shock.

Josie took a deep breath and searching for courage closed her eyes and forced herself to re-examine the pictures.

"Lizzie was lying on what could have been a gravel path or maybe a driveway."

"Could it be leading towards a house?" Molly asked, encouraging her to remember. "It must be somewhere remote."

Josie remained silent for a moment her face lined with concentration.

"It could be. I got the impression of space lots of space, it could be a large park or garden," reaching nervously for her mug she gulped down a mouthful of coffee before going on. "The other pictures were taken from inside a room with white washed walls."

"Why do you say white washed and not painted?"

"Well," Josie made a face before going on. "The walls were not smooth they were white bricks."

"A garage, washhouse or cellar perhaps?"

"Yes I suppose so." Josie nodded.

"Then it could be a house with a gravel driveway and large garden. A property of that size is likely to have a cellar," Molly made suggestions based on the information Josie had given her.

"During my exhibition at Tim's gallery we met a man, a Scotsman. Kate, that's Tim's sister thinks he might have something to do with it."

"Oh, and what made her think that?"

Molly, leaning forward placed her elbows on the table and studied Josie intently.

"It's all rather strange actually," Josie began, "I had just met Kate and she knew nothing about this dreadful business but she seemed aware that something was going on."

"Are you sure Tim didn't say anything to her? After all she is his sister."

"True," Josie nodded, "he may have done."

Molly could see that she was not convinced. "Tell me about this man, describe him, what did you talk about?"

Josie told her about the strange conversation they had about Elgin and its history and Molly raised her eyebrows as she listened.

"He does sound like a strange character. He's a Scotsman you say?"

"Oh yes his accent was a soft deep burr, he wore a fine kilt and smart tweed jacket and he was quite an eccentric. He reminded me of Einstein." Josie smiled. "I guess it must have been his wild hair."

"What's his name?"

"Greg MacLaren or so he said."

"And why do you say that?"

"Well, Kate didn't think that was his real name, I don't know why she thought that."

Molly shook her head she was not familiar with anyone by that name. "Why did your friend dislike him so much?"

"Kate is a little strange, well that was my first impression and Tim did warn me." She paused searching for the right words not wanting to be disloyal towards her new friend. "He told me not to take her too seriously."

"That's a strange thing to say about one's sister," Molly frowned.

Josie chose not to elaborate on Kate's 'special powers', she did not want to give her aunt the wrong impression, she liked and respected Kate too much.

"She simply took a disliking to him from the start. It was all a bit embarrassing really the way she went on at the poor man. It was I suppose a clash of personalities."

Molly studied Josie thoughtfully before making her decision, "I'll telephone my dear friend Rufus. If this character is genuine then someone must know him."

"We could always check the telephone directories." Josie said.

"Good idea and we could widen our search by visiting the library in Elgin. They hold copies of every directory in the country."

"Is there a computer at the library?"

"Yes of course dear." Molly glanced up expectantly.

Rummaging in her bag Josie pulled out one of her smart new business cards and pushed it across the table.

"Kate designed me a website and here's my web address," she tapped the card with her fingertip and Molly, staring at her blankly wondered where her train of thought was going.

"I have a message in my e-mail box." Josie explained. "Someone wants me to do a painting of their house. They sent me a photograph along with an invitation to stay whilst I work."

"How interesting," Molly picked up the card and studied it. "Maybe it's all coming together, this could be the house with the cellar."

"I've been so distracted lately that I completely forgot all about it. If Kate is right and Greg MacLaren is involved then I suppose he could have sent the message."

"It was anonymous then?"

"Well yes but I have the sender's e-mail address."

"Can you get onto your website from the computer in the library?" Molly asked.

"Yes of course and I could print off a picture of the house too."

"Brilliant," Molly laughed, "so now it looks as if we have a busy morning ahead of us." Pushing back her chair, she stood up. "We'd better prepare for action with a hearty breakfast."

Josie grinned, she was amazed by her aunt's enthusiasm for food and wondered how she managed to remain so trim.

Mr Mac followed at a safe distance. He guessed from the direction they had taken they were heading for Elgin. He was right and twenty minutes later they parked in the small market square. Driving past slowly

197

he parked his car in a convenient spot from where he could continue his surveillance.

The library was much smaller than she remembered and Josie found herself comparing it with the bustling centres of literature that she was accustomed to in London. Most of the other buildings in the square were from the same period but she thought the library in particular a very fine example indeed. She loved the high ceilings and intricate architectural details that were missing from modern buildings. These were substantial edifices to the elegance of times past, they possessed a character and charm that other buildings lacked. Inside, the juxtaposition was complete. The interior was bright, modern and practical, with shelves of books lining the walls. Josie was amazed to discover that the computer suite consisted of one rather outdated machine tucked away unobtrusively in a corner.

Moving towards it she discovered that it was not even turned on and wondered when it had last been accessed. Perhaps this was typical of the generation that used the library she mused. In London there was a campaign aimed at young people encouraging them to use these wonderful public buildings. Obviously the message had not yet reached this part of the country.

Settling herself in front of the screen she soon had the machine up and running and in no time at all the printer was churning out a colour picture of the large house. Josie sighed with relief when she discovered that there were no more new messages in her e-mail account and reaching for the print, she handed it to her aunt. Molly studied it for a few moments before admitting defeat, she did not recognise the building.

Once they had finished with the computer, they began the task of checking through the telephone directories.

"Surely if this Greg MacLaren is wealthy enough to own a large property he would be ex-directory." Josie remarked and tucking her hair behind her ear, fingered the scar running across her forehead.

Molly noticed how drawn she looked and decided they had done enough. "It's time we paid a visit to my friend Rufus," she said. "He lives a little way from here near Lossiemouth."

Half way to the door Molly grabbed Josie's arm. "Now you won't laugh if I tell you his full name will you dear?" Molly looked mischievous, her eyes gleaming with mirth.

Josie was eager to hear more.

"His name is Rufus Stone," she said trying to keep a straight face.

Josie, unable to hold back burst out laughing.

"You promised." Molly grinned.

"I did no such thing!"

They continued towards the exit.

"Well," Josie said as they left the building, "are you going to tell me?"

"Contrary to popular belief," Molly began, "he didn't change his name on some eccentric whim. His parents are to blame they could not resist calling their eldest son Rufus. He has brothers of course Robert and Henry, also named after the sons of King William, Duke of Normandy but the names Robert and Henry Stone don't quite have the same impact."

"So they named the poor man after an ancient monument in the south of England."

"It seems their father was an historian with a dry sense of humour, besides it's not any old stone, Rufus was named after a prince."

Molly inserted the key into the car door and turned the lock. "He's an extraordinary character is Rufus, a font of all knowledge. You'll soon see."

Mr Mac followed as they left the market square.

Rufus Stone lived comfortably in an old converted mill that had once ground oatmeal. The building was as quirky as its occupant, they both belonged to a different age.

Josie expected to meet a Scotsman but Rufus was as English as her aunt. He kissed them both affectionately and as he studied them, the light of his long lost youth glowed in his eyes. Wrapping his long arms around their waists, he welcomed them into his house as a loud roar from overhead shook the rafters.

"Oh don't worry about them," he nodded skyward. "One gets used to their comings and goings living so close to a military air base." He winked at Josie as she made herself comfortable in an ancient armchair.

Glancing around the spacious cottage style living room she found it most comforting. This was not what she had expected to find. The room was filled with the scent of wood smoke and stale pipe tobacco but it was not in the least bit offensive. She could see that the place was loved, it felt comfortable and lived in rather like a favourite pair of comfortable brogues. This was a special home, a man's domain and she wondered if it had ever been under a female's influence.

The moment they were settled Rufus disappeared into the small kitchen and it was not long before she heard the sound of boiling water being poured into a pot. When he appeared he was carrying a silver tray that contained all the ingredients for making tea and Josie smiled.

She noticed that the large silver teapot matched the tray but that was where the similarity ended. The rest of the service was made up of an odd assortment of bone china cups, saucers and jugs. The sugar bowl was huge, dominating the silver tray, it looked totally out of place but Rufus did not seem to mind. He poured their tea with a steady hand not spilling a drop and as he chatted away Molly beamed, amused by the sound of his voice.

"Right you old dog!" Molly began, "we've come to pick your brains."

"So not a social visit then," he winked at Josie again. "It's not every day I get the opportunity to entertain a couple of fine young women." He sat down heavily in his chair and grinned at them both.

"You old fool," Molly struggled to keep a straight face as she sipped her tea.

Rufus looked pleased, his eyes glowing with merriment it was obvious to Josie that he adored her aunt and she wondered just how long they had known each other.

"Well go on Josie dear show him your picture."

Josie rummaged in her bag and pulling out a folded piece of paper passed it to Rufus.

Rising stiffly from his chair, Rufus reached for a pair of pince-nez spectacles that he kept on a shelf above the fireplace and Josie watched as he clipped them carefully onto the bridge of his nose. He reminded her of a Dickensian character as he peered through the small round lenses and she was amazed to see even more lines appear on his heavily latticed face.

"Well, what do you think?" Molly was unable to endure the silence for a moment longer.

"Yes," he said nodding his head and calmly placing the picture on the table next to the tea tray he sat down in his chair.

"What do you mean by that?" she snapped.

"Buy, definitely buy that's my advice. It's a bit on the large side though but I'm sure you'll manage." He shot Josie a sideways glance and she could see that his eyes were full of humour.

"What are you talking about you old fool, we don't want to buy the place."

"Well you asked for my opinion and now you have it."

"No, no, no," Molly shook her head in mock frustration. "Where do you think it is?"

"Why ask me?" he shrugged, his face concealing a wicked grin. "Why buy a house if you don't know where it is?"

Josie buried her face in her teacup and hardly able to hold back any longer, giggled.

"I don't know why we bothered." Molly shook her head, going along with the charade.

Josie realised that they were as bad as each other and were enjoying every minute of it.

"Okay, okay," he held up his hands in surrender. "Calm down you old witch. I don't want you expiring here on my carpet and haunting me for the rest of my days."

Josie laughed and almost spilled her tea. Molly was overjoyed, it had been quite a while since she had heard that sound but then another jet roared overhead drowning out their mirth.

Rufus ran his fingertips over the print as if he was reading Braille then he grunted. Hauling himself to his feet he turned towards a well-stocked bookshelf and reaching up took down a volume of ordinance survey maps.

Placing it carefully on the table, he fanned the pages until he found what he was looking for.

"This house," he began, "is I believe called 'Montague Villa' and it's located," he paused as his gnarled finger traced a line over the map, "just about here."

They peered eagerly to where he was indicating. It was in the middle of a remote area in Speymouth forest near to the village of Fochabers.

"Can you tell us anything about the place or about a Greg MacLaren?" Molly asked.

"Greg MacLaren eh," Rufus sat down heavily and picking up his teacup his brow wrinkled as he thought for a moment.

"No, I'm afraid not. I used to know a Greg MacLaren but that was a long time ago, he's not your man."

"And why do you say that?" she asked.

"Because the good die young and Greg was a good man, he's been gone these past twenty years. No, the family who lived in Montague Villa are long gone too. They were landowners, gentry, wealthy people," he paused.

Josie watched him carefully as he poured tea from his cup into his saucer then he slurped it up noisily.

"Randolph was their name," he continued, "William and Eleanor Randolph. He was Laird of all he surveyed and much more beyond.

They had a son, young William, but they had no other children. Poor Eleanor almost died giving life to the boy and William did not see much point in putting his wife through childbirth again. Would probably have been very different had young William turned out to be a girl." He sipped from his saucer again. "William was a problem child you see, it was said that he was 'touched', he was a very disturbed lad indeed."

"What happened to him?" Josie asked.

"Well young lady," he eyed her seriously. "He spent most of his childhood locked away safely at Montague Villa. They had everything bought in for him you see, he was educated there of course but the world hardly knew of his existence. Unfortunately, he grew up to be a thoroughly nasty piece of work. It's said that he killed a girl, an English girl who was on holiday with her parents." He paused for a moment and Josie sensed a sudden change in his mood.

"Of course nothing was proven," he continued. "The Randolphs were a powerful family. They would have got away with it even if their son had been convicted of the crime. They didn't find the body you see so how could there have been a murder, that's what the authorities said at the time. Of course, the locals knew the truth. Those poor people, her parents had to return to England without their daughter. They came back year after year to search for her and that went on long after the case was closed, but then that's another story."

The atmosphere in the room changed and a heavy silence settled in around them.

"How did the authorities explain her disappearance?" Josie asked after a while.

"They simply said that the girl must have run off, probably found a young man," he shrugged. "Young William Randolph got away with it. Eventually he became so wild that one night the authorities came and took him away. His long-suffering parents could stand it no more, so they called in the men in white coats. He spent years in an institution but that was all thirty years ago," he smiled and sipped the last of his tea from his saucer.

"What became of William and Eleanor?"

He looked at Josie for a long time before replying and she could see from the expression on his face that he was far away, lost somewhere in the past.

"They died," he said eventually, "Eleanor of a broken heart and William a few months later. Hunting accident they said but it's generally thought that he took his own life," he paused again before going on. "He couldn't bear the disappointment you see having lost his only son and in such incriminating circumstances. There was no-one left to take over from him, carry on the family name, he knew he'd failed in his ancestral duty and he just couldn't face up to it." 202

"And the house?"

Rufus studied the picture for a moment. "Well, it looks as though someone is maintaining the place, the exterior at least. Of course the locals say it's haunted, they usually stay well clear."

He glanced at Molly who had remained silent throughout and she nodded encouragingly.

"Of course that's a load of bunkum, more likely William Randolph has returned to live there. He's probably a bit of a recluse, besides he wouldn't be very welcome in the village."

"Has anyone seen him?" Josie asked.

"I should think so, someone must have seen lights at the windows, smoke from the chimneys that kind of thing. He would have to go out to buy provisions. He's probably been seen in the villages around but he would keep himself to himself if he's got any sense."

"When did he return? You said he was institutionalised."

"Oh yes he was cooped up in the 'funny farm' for many years. I expect as those places were shut down he was re-introduced into society. You know the modern way of thinking, care in the community or whatever it's called."

Josie was amazed at his knowledge, he knew so much about these people. It was clear that Molly and Rufus were very close but when she quizzed her aunt about him all she would say was they had known each other for years. They had both lived and worked in London and when he moved away from the city they lost touch, it was pure coincidence that when she retired some years later and moved to Scotland they ran into each other again. That was all she would say on the subject.

Mr Mac waited patiently, he watched as they went into the old mill and after an hour, their car was still parked out front. He amused himself by counting the RAF jets as they took off then he counted them back in again.

After a while, he began to run through what he would do next and wrestling with his thoughts, struggled to make up his mind. He knew which road they would take back to Garmouth, he also knew where along that road he could make his strike he just had to work on the finer details of his plan. Starting his car, he drove back towards the town.

Kate and Tim arrived in Elgin at the same time as Mr Mac but he drove straight through whilst they parked in the old market square.

"We'd better find a place to stay," Kate said as practical as ever.

Left to Tim they would probably end up sleeping in his car.

Tim climbed out and stretched his muscles. His bones were stiff and his eyes tired, he would not be able to function properly until the stress in his body was relieved, he also needed some food. Searching the square, he spotted a pub.

Kate checked the GPS tracking system once again. Josie was still at a location just a few miles north of their position. She had been there for just over an hour and satisfied, Kate dropped the device into her pocket and hurried off after her brother.

Tim was hunched over a deeply polished bar with his nose stuck into a menu. The place was almost deserted apart from a couple of men who were sitting at a table huddled over their drinks. Neither of them looked up as she walked in.

"Any good?" she asked cheerfully, perching on the edge of a barstool.

"Yes. I'm having the Aberdeen Angus steak and ale pie." Passing her the menu, he ordered two cups of coffee before going off to find a table.

Their food arrived surprisingly quickly and as they picked up their cutlery Kate said, "We should find the local police station we may need their help in a hurry."

Tim nodded in agreement but made no comment, he was busy shovelling food into his mouth.

"Anyone would think you haven't eaten for days," Kate grinned as she watched him but he ignored her.

He had been in a black mood ever since she insisted on accompanying him but she could hardly blame him. Not only was he worried about Josie but also his business, he could not be away for too long as there was so much going on at the gallery. She knew that he resented her company, he would rather she remained in London to take care of things.

Kate had made all the arrangements for his gallery as soon as they were on the road, she would also have to make most of the decisions over the next few days. She would do nothing without planning it carefully first, he on the other hand was a man of action responding to situations as they arose. Kate abhorred recklessness she would ensure that this operation was well thought out from the start, she would also have to keep him in check and find ways to lift his mood.

Her priority now was to find them some accommodation, so enquiring at the bar, she discovered that there were no rooms available at the Inn but the Landlord told her of a place on the outskirts of town.

She telephoned the guesthouse and discovered that all they had available was one twin room and would she mind sharing with her brother. She would rather not but on this occasion would make an exception, she would have to endure his habits, so made the reservation.

"I've found us a room." She told him as she slipped back into her seat.

"A room?" he raised his eyebrows and stared at her.

"Unfortunately the woman could only offer me a twin room so against my better judgement I took it."

Tim looked at her questioningly.

"Well I'm not sure that I can put up with your snoring."

"I don't snore." He looked hurt.

"How do you know?"

"I've never had any complaints." He grinned innocently.

Settling back in her chair she folded her hands in her lap and looked pleased with herself. The air between them was a little lighter now and at last she had seen him smile. As soon as they had established their base, they could begin to make plans for the days ahead.

Chapter
TWENTY SIX

Kate used the shower first and relaxing under the hot stream of water washed away the stress of travel. When finally she emerged, she was ready for a barrage of accusations and references to the amount of time she had spent in the bathroom but to her surprise, the room was silent.

Tim was asleep on one of the beds. Smiling to herself, Kate slipped silently to where he lay and carefully removed his shoes then standing back, she studied him closely. The worry lines that haunted his face were gone and his skin was smooth, his expression boyish.

Suddenly the years melted away and she was a little girl again. At three years old, her mother had presented her with a baby brother and from that moment, her life changed. No longer was she at the centre of her mother's world. The arrival of that tiny bundle of joy meant the monopoly she enjoyed was swept aside and something from her childhood was lost. All at once, she had grown up and her mother began to refer to her as a 'big girl'. It was not long before she realised that big girls were expected to help with baby brothers, and worst of all there were times when big girls were required to entertain themselves especially when her mother lavished attention the new arrival. Of course, there were moments when she had her mother all to herself but her life was never the same.

The three years that separated them was like an infinite gulf that could never be bridged, so she became an independent and resourceful little girl who preferred her own company. Tim however was nothing like his sister, he remained reliant on those around him.

They were seldom referred to as 'the children' it was always Kate and the baby, so at the tender age of three she became an individual. Now of course the age gap between them was no longer an issue and she had long ago disposed of the label 'big sister'.

Moving away from the bed she attempted to shrug off these thoughts and sitting down at the dressing table, studied herself in the mirror. Remembering her childhood had stirred up some unwelcome emotions. There was no denying that it had been idyllic but from the outset something had come between her and Tim and it remained with them into adulthood. She loved her brother dearly but there were times when she found him quite infuriating. He was not a natural choice of friend but there was no denying him, after all, he was her only sibling.

Her grandmother had been her childhood ally and, as she grew up, they became inseparable spending many hours in each other's company. 'Chalk and cheese', grandma used to say, 'little girls are from Venus and boys are from Mars,' was another of her favourite idioms.

Picking up her hairbrush it hovered close to her head as she remembered the sound of her voice. The bond between them had been strong, she had worshipped her grandma and rarely a day would go by without Kate thinking of her. Staring at her reflection through half closed eyes if she looked hard enough she could see traces of her grandma smiling back.

Tim stirred and mumbling something incoherent, his eyes opened and he blinked against the bright light.

"Bugger," he grumbled, "did I fall asleep?"

Sliding his legs over the edge of the bed, he pulled himself upright and glared at his sister.

"Snoring like a little piggy," she smiled and rolled her eyes playfully.

Ignoring her, he yawned. "You were taking so long in the shower." He sniffed as he stood up and wandered across the room a little unsteady on his feet.

Kate smiled, she had expected him to come out with that one and pitied the woman brave enough to take him on for better or for worse.

"A woman's prerogative little brother, now are you going in there whilst I get dressed or are you just going to turn your back?"

He disappeared into the bathroom and shouldered the door shut.

Quickly she dressed before turning her attention back to her hair. Brushing it out until it shone it was not long before thoughts of grandma Jane crept back into her head. Her grandma had understood all of her moods, she always made time for her and with a guiding hand helped to steer a course through the minefield of adolescence. As she developed, Kate began to realise that she had some strange and sometimes rather disturbing powers. At first, she thought she was going mad but with grandma Jane's love and support was able to deal with her confusing and often disturbing feelings.

Of course, her grandma had seen the potential. Missing a generation, it had never fully developed in her daughter but her granddaughter had inherited powers that seemed even more remarkable than before.

Such unnatural abilities were almost impossible for a young girl to come to terms with, but gradually as Kate developed, she accepted the responsibility of such a powerful gift and began to use it to her advantage.

As Kate grew up, she realised that she would never have coped without grandma Jane. She became a discerning mentor offering wisdom and support and was careful to point out that generations of women had inherited these same unusual skills. Some of her ancestors had thought this a curse, often misunderstood and persecuted by the ignorant they were accused of all kinds of atrocities. In some cases, they were condemned as witches but in spite of this used their powers to heal the people around them. Bringing comfort to women in labour, they made soothing potions from herbs, healing the sick and divining water from the land. Others could see into the future predicting events before they happened and were often responsible for advising Monarchs in times of trouble.

Kate felt privileged to come by this knowledge and with grandma Jane's guidance had emerged with the strength of character to use her special gift. In her work it guided her hand, the power of her mind overcoming many complex problems and in her private life, her friends would benefit in times of need.

She sighed and moved away from the dressing table. Tim had never been able to accept her complex ways, her childhood had been so very different from his own.

Putting the finishing touches to her hair and make-up she made an effort to shrug off these thoughts. She had to focus her mind on Josie, she could sense danger ahead but this was hardly surprising given the circumstances, they would have to be very careful.

Reaching for Tim's mobile phone, she flipped it open and studied the LCD screen. Selecting the Global Positioning System the small red light began to flash in the centre of the screen. Josie was on the move, she was very close, passing within just a few miles of their current location. Kate was able to identify the names of the roads along which Josie was travelling and it soon became clear that she was heading out of town.

She touched a series of numbers on the keypad and the screen scrolled back then using the memory she was able to reveal Josie's previous location. From her bag, she pulled out a thin black box that was slightly larger than the mobile phone and using an infrared system linked the two devices together. The screen glowed green as the box, a mini hand held computer, came to life and using the keys on the phone she began to type in commands. Her eyes darting quickly between the keypad and LCD screen she watched as the program initiated itself and she smiled with satisfaction.

From the GPS system activated on Tim's mobile phone, she managed to lift a reference and feeding this information into the tiny computer began a search of the electoral role. Within seconds, it revealed a full name and address and Kate had to check the screen twice as the name Rufus Stone blinked back at her.

When Tim emerged from the bathroom, he was clean-shaven and wearing a towel wrapped around his hips.

"What's so funny?" he asked with a frown.

"I've just discovered where Josie spent the afternoon."

She began to explain how she had achieved this by showing him the electronic equipment that she had developed.

"Are you sure that's legal, whatever happened to the Data Protection Act?"

"You worry too much," she frowned. "Besides it's not as if we are going to pass this information onto anyone else. Look at the name, can you believe it?"

"Must be an alias," he grinned.

"Nothing has come up so there can't be anything else on the system."

"So you're saying he couldn't have changed his name to Rufus Stone."

"Not as far as the records show."

"His parents must have had a great sense of humour."

She nodded and wondered if she should share with him her growing anxiety but he turned away and the moment was lost.

Mr Mac saw them coming from his lookout. He had abandoned his car and clutching a small bag, made his way towards a narrow cutting where the road slipped between two steep banks in the landscape. He remained uncertain, usually his plans were carefully thought out and he was able to execute them with military precision but on this occasion his strategy was haphazard, it felt wrong and he was uneasy.

The voices in his head were gone, it was as if they were testing him, observing him as he worked and offering no encouragement or advice. Pulling a pistol from his bag he weighed it in his hand, it felt reassuringly heavy, it gave him a sense of power and lifted his mood. In order for his shot to be effective he would have to wait until the car was very close, this was not a long distance weapon.

From his position he had a perfect view and scanning both sides of the road was satisfied that there would be no witnesses.

His original plan was to hold them up just like a highway robber, shoot the old woman, subdue Josie MacDonald and return with them both to his house. He would use their car and dispose of it along with the old woman's body. His own vehicle was hidden amongst the bushes, it could not be seen from the road but if someone was to discover it abandoned so far out in the countryside they might become suspicious. This part of the plan disturbed him the most and he frowned, there were too many loose ends, it didn't feel right.

Eventually the car he was waiting for came into view and he tightened his grip around the pistol. His heart rate increased when he saw Josie MacDonald. She was talking to the old woman who was driving and her face was in profile. Her brown hair danced with the movement of the vehicle and as he watched, everything seemed to slow down. The car was moving steadily towards him and he could feel a sense of calm wash over him. Suddenly Josie turned her head and looked straight at him but he was high up on the bank overlooking the road.

Adrenalin surged through his body, the rush made him feel invincible but his hands would not stop shaking. He had to concentrate on the task, his shot must be perfect, it would not do to put a bullet through Josie MacDonald by mistake.

Raising the weapon he peered along the short barrel and his finger took up the slack in the trigger as he waited for the vehicle to come closer.

The old woman's face filled his sights and his finger twitched but suddenly the car hit a bump in the road and swerved out of his line of vision. Correcting his aim he let out his breath and his hand became steady again but it was too late, the car swept past. Cursing, he released the pressure on the trigger and all he could do was watch as they accelerated away.

When he returned to his car, he flung open the door and threw himself into the driving seat. Annoyingly a voice reminded him that his plan was flawed, there were too many variables and something was bound to go wrong. It continued arrogantly, telling him to bide his time.

Images of Sarah Harrington cut through his disappointment, thoughts of her filled his mind and soothed his overwrought nerves. Slumping down in the seat, he laid his head back against the rest. She was a constant in the chaos of his life, she had little choice in the matter. Perhaps that is why she remained untouched and alive.

At the guesthouse Kate was unexpectedly overwhelmed by a sense of relief, the tension that had been building up within her was suddenly gone and she realised that Josie must have survived an impending disaster. Closing her eyes, she let out her breath and attempted to focus her mind but Josie was no longer there.

Josie and her aunt drove on completely unaware of the catastrophe that had almost overtaken them. They were happy in the knowledge that their first day of sleuthing had provided them with answers and tomorrow they planned to visit Montague Villa.

Some miles away in a beautifully converted oatmeal mill Rufus Stone sat stiffly in his chair, he was staring at the colour print that his very good friend and her lovely young niece had left with him. The house in the picture disturbed him and as he studied it, his rheumy old eyes narrowed.

The following morning Josie was standing at the kitchen window but saw nothing of the view, her head was full of distressing thoughts that would not go away. Sighing loudly in an attempt to shake off her depressing mood she looked out at the garden. The early morning mist was gone and the clouds had drifted away leaving a clear sky. Soon the village would awaken to the sound of birdsong and the working day would begin.

She sighed again, heavier this time, and with the back of her hand brushed away a tear that had escaped from the corner of her eye. She could not stop thinking about her friends and the pictures inside her head were a constant reminder of their terrible situation. All her efforts to force them aside failed and even thinking about the good times they shared only made things worse. She felt responsible for their situation, Lindsay and Lizzie were almost certainly dead and as for Sarah and Mike, she had no idea. If only she had stayed away, not come to Scotland in the first place, then everything would be fine. She realised that self-pity would not help her friends so pulling a handful of tissues from a box tidied her face.

"Good morning, did you sleep well?" Molly breezed into the kitchen.

"Fine," Josie sniffed, her aunt's sudden appearance startling her.

Molly could see that she was upset so decided not to make an issue out of it.

"Time for a spot of breakfast don't you think."

Josie moved towards her aunt and hugged her tightly. Words were not necessary, the love that flowed between them was enough and as Molly gently rubbed her back Josie's sadness began to ease. With her aunt's love and support, anything was possible.

"Thank you," she whispered.

Chapter

TWENTY SEVEN

Detective Chief Inspector Jordan went to Josie's home later that day.

Mrs Robinson saw him the moment he arrived but chose to remain in the shadows of her living room where she could observe him. Josie had asked her to look out for Tim, she had said nothing about other gentlemen callers.

Jordan cursed, he was too late he should have called earlier or at least telephoned first. He had already been on the phone to Elgin informing them of his missing people and their connection with Josie MacDonald. He had also mentioned the name Mr Mac but there had been no response. The officer on the end of the phone took notes and promised to act on the information. Jordan also asked them to keep a lookout for Josie because he felt sure she would return to Scotland.

After his call, the officers in Scotland held a meeting to discuss what they had just learnt. One of the men had been involved in the MacDonald case, he was the officer sent out to collect her personal effects from the riverbank in Spey Bay but it was the senior officer, who initially had played down Josie's exploits, now remembered an old case. A woman had disappeared from the area many years ago and he felt sure that she was the daughter of an English family. The more he thought about it the clearer it became. The Laird of the Montague estate was implicated and it had developed into a very awkward case, some very high-ranking people had been drawn in and the whole thing had been covered up. He would have to pull files from the archive to confirm his suspicions but in the meantime he would dispatch a car to the estate, it wouldn't do any harm to check it out.

When they arrived at Montague villa, the officers found it deserted. There were no indications to suggest that William Randolph was at home. It was true that someone was taking care of the grand old house, the gardens had been tidied but there was no law against that, so climbing back into their car they drove away. Turning out of the lane, they went higher into the mountains just moments before Josie and her aunt arrived.

Molly swung the car off the narrow road and drove onto the wide sweeping driveway. Gravel crunched noisily under the tyres and Josie watched eagerly as the house came into view. Light was shining brilliantly from its white-stone walls and it looked stately as it occupied the landscape. It was even more imposing in real life; the picture she had printed from the computer had not done it justice.

Josie became aware of an odd atmosphere that surrounded the property. Although there was an air of opulence that houses of status seem to exude, this one left her feeling uneasy. The estate seemed well maintained but there were areas of the driveway where undergrowth was sprouting up through the gravel.

Molly brought the car to a standstill in front of a grand stone staircase and switching off the engine they sat in silence admiring their surroundings.

Josie made an effort to shrug off her negative thoughts and breathing deeply got out of the car. The scent from freshly cut grass and flowers in the borders sweetened the air but still she found nothing pleasant about this place. She thought the silence oppressive, and staring up at the house had to shield her eyes against the sunlight that glanced off the white washed walls. There was a low parapet running around the top of the house, and following it with her eyes, she could see little stone sculptures perched at the corners. Ugly gargoyles and garish mythical creatures stared back at her and she shuddered.

"Lovely architecture," Molly said wryly. She had also spotted them, and stepping from the car, gravel crunched underfoot.

"I wonder if there's anyone in." Josie started towards the steps.

"Nothing stirs the beast that slumbers here," Molly mumbled under her breath as she made her way along the path that ran beside the lawn.

Josie watched as her aunt turned the corner of the house and her skin began to crawl. 'What's the matter with me?' she asked herself as she climbed the stone steps.

At the top, she found a formidable looking door, an impenetrable barrier from the past, and reaching out towards it, ran her fingertips lightly over its intricately carved surface. History seemed to flow through the dark wood like an electrical charge.

"What have you witnessed in your time?" she whispered.

With both hands flat against the steel rivets holding the wood in place, she pushed but it remained a solid and immovable object. There was a bell pull to one side of a stone mullion and as her hand hovered over the chain, she decided against pulling it. Turning away, she hurried back down the steps and went in search of her aunt.

Mr Mac knew they were there; he had seen them from a first floor window and could hardly believe his luck. Josie MacDonald was standing at the front door of his house and his excitement was almost unbearable. The chains that would secure her against the wall of his cellar rattled inside his head. He grinned and licked his lips.

He would have to get rid of the old woman first; there was no point in involving her besides she was definitely not part of his plan. He glanced out of the window again but there was no sign of them so moving quickly to another part of the house, he managed to locate them in the courtyard below. He watched as Josie peered in through a stable window. She would find nothing there he had covered his tracks thoroughly.

He considered opening the door and simply inviting her in but he remained unsure. The voices in his head were silent, he would get no guidance from them.

Once she was inside the house, he could overcome her but shaking his head he realised that would not work. He began to pace the floor, he had to think of something fast because once they discovered there was nothing here they would be on their way.

Leaving the room he raced along the corridor and bounding down the staircase, taking the steps three at a time, he made his way to where he kept his shotguns.

Snatching a weapon from the wall bracket, he filled his pockets with cartridges and after loading the gun let himself out of the house by a small side door. He knew they were on the other side of the house but this did not prevent him from moving silently across the gravel and pushing his way into the thick undergrowth, he crept slowly towards the front of the house.

His heart was racing as he picked up her scent, it drifted sweetly towards him carried on the breeze from across the lawn and he could hardly contain himself. The sound of her voice as she called out to her aunt thrilled him and holding his breath he eased forward cautiously. Lifting his shotgun he fitted the butt against his shoulder and sighting along the barrel could see them clearly, they were no more than a dozen paces away. The old woman had her back to him and his finger strayed to the trigger, he paused as she looked up at the house. Her hands were resting on her hips and her legs were slightly apart, her weight evenly distributed. She was talking but he could not hear what she was saying.

He was just seconds away from squeezing the trigger when Josie moved into view. His stomach lurched and he almost discharged the weapon.

Lowering the barrel and cursing under his breath, he had almost taken out the wrong target.

Josie and her aunt walked across the driveway and as he watched she brushed a strand of hair from her face with the back of her hand. He remained motionless until they had passed then moving into a more comfortable position, he realised that he would have to do something soon because at any moment they could climb back into their car and the opportunity would be lost.

Suddenly turning her head, Josie looked straight at him and he froze. Time stood still as he waited for whatever it was that had caught her attention to pass. From the expression on her face and her body language, it was clear that she had not spotted him then she looked away. Breathing a sigh of relief, he watched as the old woman climbed the steps leading up to his front door.

"Shall we ring the bell?"

"There's probably no-one in." Josie called out as her aunt tugged at the ancient bell pull.

The force of the explosion lifted her off her feet and slammed her against the wall as splinters of wood and stone powdered the air around her head.

Instinctively Josie threw herself down behind the car, her senses reeling as panic surged through her. Her ears were ringing as the noise echoed back from the walls and slowly she lifted her head to peer toward the spot where her aunt had been standing.

Even from this distance, Josie could see where blood had stained the stone and her stomach tightened as she realised that someone must have taken a shot at them. Calming her nerves as best she could she summoned up the courage to move away from the car. She had to get to her aunt so keeping low to the ground, she covered the distance separating them and launching herself up the steps threw herself down beside her prone companion.

Molly's head was resting against the foot of the door and her face was deathly pale. At first, Josie could not tell if she was breathing or not and clutching at her hand held onto it tightly. The shock of seeing her aunt like this stunned her and she had no idea what to do next, cursing her indecision she reached into her pocket searching for her mobile phone but it was not there.

Crying out in frustration, she inhaled deeply in an attempt to steady her tattered nerves. She had to remain calm for her aunt's sake and forcing herself to think clearly she realised that her phone must be on the shelf in the car, she had put it there earlier.

Turning on her knees, she pushed her face up against the balustrade and searched the area below. Their car was standing just a short distance away, it was parked beside the bushes and as she waited, nothing stirred. She didn't want to move, it was not safe to leave the protection of the stone balustrade but what choice did she have? Josie glanced at her aunt and her chest tightened, she had to do something and quickly. Molly was in desperate need of help so making up her mind, she launched herself down the steps and stumbled towards the car. Tearing at the door, she dived into the driver's seat and reaching for her phone flipped it open but her fingers refused to work, they were shaking violently then suddenly lights flashed inside her head and her world went black.

Mr Mac could hardly contain himself, at last he had Josie MacDonald. Reaching into the car, he wrenched her upright and as her head lolled against the back of the seat her hair fell across her face. Eyeing her greedily he congratulated himself, it had been so easy and he had done it all by himself. Grabbing her roughly, he lifted her from the car. She was light and warm in his arms and the sensation that swept over him was one of victory. He had anticipated this moment for such a long time and now he was on the verge of realising his ambition.

Once inside the house he hurried along the corridor and shouldering his way into a room laid her down carefully on a sofa. She groaned softly and her eyes fluttered open, soon she would regain her senses, he must hurry. Leaving her, he dashed back the way he had come only to return moments later carrying a syringe. His hands were shaking as he pulled back her sleeve then he injected the clear liquid into her arm. Standing back, he admired his work and running his hand nervously over his face he could hardly believe it, Josie MacDonald was there in his own house.

Fighting the urge to strip her naked he could not wait to have his fun, but first he had work to do. He had to attend to the mess that was lying against his front door.

Shrugging on a pair of worker's overalls, he went to find the old woman and snapping on a pair of latex gloves he gathered her up in his arms and carried her to the car but the doors locked. Propping her up, he searched her pockets for the key then dumping her into the cargo space he slammed the door shut. With that part of his task done, he returned to the house to collect the things he would need to clean the step.

When he was satisfied, he stripped off his overalls and stuffing them into a plastic bag, peeled off the latex gloves. He checked the area once again for anything that he might have missed but the only evidence that anything untoward had taken place was the freshly chipped masonry and a few score marks in the door.

At last, he was happy and slamming the door shut, turned the key in the lock before picking up the plastic bag. He almost skipped down the steps as he made his way towards the car and squeezing into the driving seat, moved it back on its runners before swinging his feet onto the pedals. He altered the position of the rear view mirror and turning the ignition key started the engine. Letting it rev he waited for it to settle down and scanning the instruments he selected first gear. Throwing gravel up onto the grass, he spun the wheels before steering along the drive, then gunning the engine he raced towards the distant mountains.

He took the right hand fork where the road split and drove on for ten minutes before bringing the car to a halt. Looking over his shoulder, he found what he was looking for then releasing the pressure on the foot brake allowed the car to roll backwards. Swinging it off the road, it bumped over a low bank before ploughing into the thick undergrowth. Branches scraping along the side of the car scored the paintwork and tore away the plastic trim before finally it came to rest with its bumper hard up against a tree. Turning off the engine, he had to force his way out of the car by ramming the door against the undergrowth and once he was free, he locked the doors and threw the keys into the forest. He made his way back to the road, and stepping from the cover of the bushes, glanced in the direction of the car before he was satisfied that it would never be found.

Tim peered nervously towards his sister. "What's going on now?" he asked.

Kate studied the tracking device cross-referencing the information with a map that she had spread out on the floor, and with a frown, ran her finger along a thin coloured line. She knew that Josie had already located the house near Focabers but now as she looked at the flashing light on the tracking device, she did not understand what was going on.

"I wonder what she's doing there."

Tim, moving across the room, stared down at the map as Kate indicated to the spot.

"Admiring the view," he said dryly.

She looked up at him and massaged the side of her head with her fingertips. The throbbing was becoming more intense and she was afraid that it would develop into a migraine.

"Something tells me that we really should find out."

From the tone of her voice, he was not going to argue.

"Are you feeling up to it you look awfully pale?"

Ignoring him, she gathered up her things.

"Strange she should stop there," he continued. "According to the map there's nothing to see. It's in the middle of nowhere."

She glanced sideways at him and from the expression on her face, he could see that she was not happy.

"You shouldn't need that." She snapped as he folded the map.

"I feel happier having it along as a back up," he confessed eyeing her electrical equipment with suspicion.

Mr Mac returned to the room where he had left Josie, he was eager to be near her again. From the moment he discovered that she had not drowned, he had longed for this moment, capture her, possess her and take his little game to a satisfactory conclusion. He realised that without her he would not have had so much fun over the last couple of weeks.

Reaching out he gently touched her cheek, her skin was soft and warm and just being there beside her excited him. Moving closer he breathed in her fragrance. She looked as innocent as a child laying there on the sofa and his heart missed a beat. Stooping forward he lifted her up into his arms and her head bumped against his shoulder. An ugly bruise was beginning to appear along the side of her face where he had struck her and he began to feel guilty, pushing this thought from his head he made his way along the corridor and down the steps leading to the cellar, at the bottom he shouldered open the door.

"Josie!" Mike exclaimed the moment he saw her. "What have you done to her you bastard?"

Ignoring his outburst, Mr Mac propped Josie up against the wall and holding her steady fumbled with the shackles. First he secured her wrists before adjusting the slack in the chains. With her arms suspended above her head, he leaned forward and locked the iron bands around her ankles, once that was done, he pulled the chains tight until she was secure and stepping back he admired his work.

"Josie MacDonald," he said, his voice echoing around the room. For him this was a special moment, at last he had his trophy.

"I won't ask you again you animal," Mike shouted and unable to contain his anger any longer he fought against his chains.

Mr Mac turned swiftly and moved in. The first blow drove the air from Mike's lungs leaving him stunned then blow after blow rained down until deep inside Mike felt something break, soon after that he passed out, his legs no longer able to support him.

Satisfied that he would remain silent Mr Mac turned towards Sarah. His manic gaze filled her with dread and as she backed away the chains restraining her rattled, a cruel reminder that she was powerless to react.

Closing her eyes tightly she wished herself invisible, her heart was racing uncomfortably inside her chest and she wanted to vomit. He had not touched her yet but the stress of knowing it was inevitable weighed heavily on her mind, nothing could have prepared her for an experience like this. The grin on his face was one of pure evil, now that he had Josie, Sarah realised that he would no longer need her, she had outstayed her welcome.

The voices in his head were taunting him, leading him on they willed him to have his fun with her. He could not understand what it was that kept her safe and questions to which he had no answers filled his head. Reaching out he touched her face and as she turned away sharply her head made contact with the wall. He laughed and moving closer ran his fingertips over her skin. It pleased him to watch her squirm, knowing that she was terrified gave him an overwhelming sense of power. Pushing his face into her hair, he breathed in deeply and closing his eyes savoured her scent. He grinned and licked his lips.

He wanted her, it was now her turn, but still he hesitated. Something held him back, a voice was telling him that it was wrong and tilting his head to one side, he listened. It could not possibly be wrong, he argued with himself, she belonged to him, she was his to do with as he pleased.

Sarah cried out, she had reached her limit and her self-control was impossible to maintain. He was about to do unspeakable things to her but she would rather die, death would be preferable to that kind of torment.

Pulling back suddenly as if stunned, the misery that welled up from deep within her washed over him, and never before had he heard a cry so pitiful.

"I can't," he said, then throwing his head back he began to shout and reeling drunkenly across the room he argued with his conscience.

"How can I, it's not right."

The look on her face as Sarah opened her eyes stopped him short and he became silent. He was lost and confused and all he could do was stare back at her.

She dared not look away and was resolved to remain defiant, she must stand firm. If it were now time for her to endure the ultimate humiliation, she would remain strong and true to herself. He might have her body but she was determined that he would never have her soul.

He could not do it so he cursed, whatever it was that kept her safe was working. The invisible force surrounding her was much too strong and backing away, he was lost and had no idea what to do. Glancing round he looked at Josie MacDonald but all he could see was Lizzie Baines. She appeared to him like an avenging angel, a vision of light that danced radiantly before his eyes, and shaking his head in an attempt to clear away the spectre, he cried out but it was hopeless, her gentle soul was overwhelming and he could do little to stop it. She spoke of her suffering and he realised now that she had been special. She had given him a new experience, a perspective on life that he would never understand. She was not the same as all the others, he could see that now, she had lived her life differently and he should never have allowed her to end it the way she did. He had no concept of the agonies that he had inflicted upon her or the torment that had twisted her mind. She had been innocent and had done nothing to deserve him. Her end was more dramatic that he could ever have thought possible.

Gradually thoughts of Lizzie began to fade until finally she was gone and he could breathe more easily. Suddenly, nothing seemed to matter, he had his prize. It was all about Josie MacDonald and now she was chained securely against the wall.

Sarah collapsed when he left the room. She was exhausted, the effort of facing up to him had left her drained and it was a long while before her mind began to function again. All she could do was look at her friend and wonder at the circumstances that had brought them to this terrible place.

Chapter
TWENTY EIGHT

Tim steered the car urgently along the narrow road that skirted the foot of the mountain and where it forked swerved to the right. Here the trees grew thickly along both sides of the road, their uppermost branches forming a tunnel that effectively blocked out most of the light.

"We're very close," Kate told him, "drive slowly." Glancing down at the tracking device, her eyes focussed on the screen. "She still hasn't moved."

Tim grunted and slowed the car to walking pace.

"There," she said, pointing suddenly to the right, "in there."

Bringing the car to a stop, Tim peered at the barrier of trees. He could see nothing out of place the foliage was as impenetrable as a brick wall. Jumping from the car, he walked back along the road to where the branches appeared damaged, and crouching down, he inspected surface of the road. Tracing his finger over the marks left in the dust it soon became obvious that a car had left the road.

"Here," he called out to Kate.

She looked up just in time to mark the spot where he disappeared into the undergrowth, and a few moments later was pushing her way through the branches. As soon as her eyes grew accustomed to the gloom, she saw it. Josie must have driven off the road but she realised that something was wrong, things were not what they seemed. From the way the car was facing it must have been travelling in reverse when it crashed into the trees. Kate looked closer and frowned, there was insufficient damage to either the car or the surrounding undergrowth for it to be the scene of a high-speed accident.

222

"It must have been dumped deliberately," Kate said confirming Tim's thoughts.

"What's going on here?" Tim pressed his face up against a side window.

The car was empty but he could see a mobile phone in the passenger foot well.

"Try Josie's mobile phone." He told Kate and as she dialled the number a muffled ring tone sounded from the car, she glanced at her brother.

"Where the hell is she?" Tim looked around before pulling at a door. It was locked, so climbing over the foliage, he stumbled around the car checking the other doors as he went.

"Look." Tim heard the urgency in his sister's voice. "Is that blood?"

Bending forward he studied the door seal and found what appeared to be traces of blood. Kate was horrified and as she stared at her brother the colour drained from her face, suddenly her knees buckled and she cried out.

"Are you okay?" Tim caught her in his arms and held onto her.

"We had better get that open," she said stepping away from him.

Tim nodded and grabbing at the door handle, put all his strength into tearing it open. It would have to swing upwards but that was impossible as the corner of the car was wedged up against a tree.

"We need to clear this away," he grunted.

His chest heaving with the effort, he tore at the thick branches and the sudden movement showered them in fine needles and small pinecones. He tried the door again but it was still no good, it would not budge, glancing around he searched for something to use as a lever.

"Wait here," he told Kate.

Stumbling through the undergrowth, he returned to their car and after a few moments reappeared carrying a wheel brace.

"Stand back and look away, you don't want a face full of glass."

She did as he advised and the noise of the window breaking in the confined space was deafening.

"Oh no!" he exclaimed as he pushed his head into the car.

"What is it?"

At first, Tim thought he had found Josie but after squeezing into the back of the car, he discovered that it was a much older woman. Pulling back, he straightened up his hands covered in blood.

"We have to get that door open."

Shoving past his sister he grabbed at the door with slippery fingers and working feverishly at the locking system managed to break it open.

Kate, standing back, gave him room to work and pulling the mobile phone from her pocket checked the signal strength before dialling the emergency services.

"We haven't got time for that," he hissed through clenched teeth.

The effort of tearing at the metal was making him sweat and as she watched, the sight of blood made Kate feel nauseous.

"Get back to the car," he told her. "Turn it around and don't drop it in the ditch."

He continued forcing the door until finally it swung open and wedged against the tree. Squeezing into the cargo space, he slipped his arms under the woman and lifted her from the wreckage. He was appalled at the amount of blood, they would have to get her to a hospital immediately.

Pushing his way back to the road, he grunted with the effort and as he emerged Kate had the car facing the way they had come. Carefully he slipped the unconscious woman onto the back seat before wiping his hands down the front of his shirt. Without wasting a moment, he dashed around the car and throwing himself into the driver's seat gunned the engine.

"Where's the nearest hospital?"

"Elgin." Kate told him.

The car shot away and Kate breathed deeply. In an attempt to calm her tattered nerves she closed her eyes and began to wonder what had become of Josie. They had been up at the house she was certain of that and now Josie was in grave danger. Opening her eyes, she glanced sideways at Tim who was hunched over the wheel and driving as fast as he dared. He must be out of his mind with worry, she thought, and gripped the door handle tightly as the car flew along the narrow roads leading back towards Elgin.

The hospital was a collection of unremarkable nineteenth century buildings clustered tightly together on the outskirts of the old city. A decade earlier most of the buildings had been refurbished but their dated walls were merely shells housing modern state of the art equipment.

As soon as they arrived, Molly was taken to an emergency treatment room where a team of medical staff assessed her injuries. Kate and Tim were shown to a room where they could wait until the police arrived and Kate spoke to the woman at the reception desk, giving her their details. Although she knew the injured woman was Josie's aunt, they had never met before so she could not positively identify her. She decided to keep this information to herself, telling the receptionist that they were visitors exploring the area and had come upon the road accident quite by chance.

When they were finished, she turned towards Tim who was huddled in a chair. He was beside himself with worry, his imagination running wild with images of horror and torture. He looked up expectantly when she appeared.

"Any news?"

"Not yet, they must still be assessing her injuries. She's in a pretty bad way." Her voice trailed off not wanting to state the obvious, besides, Tim was well aware of the situation.

"I still can't believe Josie would get herself involved in a stunt like this." He said.

"I'm sure she didn't intend to, she obviously underestimated the man who's doing this. Anyway who in their right mind would expect to be attacked in such a way?"

Tim stared at her his eyes as cold as steel. "Who would have thought he'd chain people to a wall and torture them, it's the twenty first century for goodness sake."

She knew he was right.

"She should have told us where she was going. Lucky we had the tracking device in place."

Kate wanted to remind him that things would have been very different if only he had taken his mobile phone to work with him instead of leaving it at Josie's house. Tactfully she remained silent, besides he was sure to be aware of his error.

"So what do we do now?" Hauling himself out of the chair, he began to pace the room. Stopping in front of the window, he studied the view across the car park and couldn't shrug off the vision of Josie in the hands of this mad man. He thought about the house, he should be there now looking for her.

"She might not be a prisoner." Kate could read his thoughts.

The atmosphere surrounding him was oppressive and she could sense him becoming even more frustrated.

"Then why do we think she's still there, what state do you think she's in? You saw her aunt."

"Let's not jump to conclusions you know that won't do any good, besides, we haven't got any evidence to suggest that she's been injured."

"Yes I agree," he nodded. "But we don't know for sure that she hasn't. What we do have is her aunt covered in blood, her body apparently ripped open by gunshot wounds."

Kate clenched her jaw, she was upset by his remark and was unwilling to take this argument any further.

Tim sighed loudly and returned to his seat. He had never experienced anything like this before and his nerves were in shreds. Josie was very special to him and it would be impossible to go on without her. Running his hand over his jaw he made himself a promise, as soon as this was over he would never let her out of his sight again, for better or for worse their lives would be as one. He had never been so sure of anything in his life.

Kate watched him closely with growing anxiety and gently probed the side of her head with her fingertips. She could feel a headache beginning to form and her mouth was dry.

"I'm going to find a cup of tea or something," she said before going off towards the reception area.

Rufus Stone received a telephone call just fifteen minutes after Molly was admitted, and now some thirty minutes later he was hurrying through the main doors.

Kate glanced up as he appeared and could not help overhear his conversation with the receptionist, moving closer she listened carefully when a doctor arrived.

"Your friend has lost a lot of blood Mr. Stone." He began. "We've taken her into theatre, the next few hours will be critical."

Rufus frowned, he had more questions than there were answers and finally the doctor hurried away leaving him in the capable hands of the duty social worker.

Kate watched as they moved from the reception desk, her thoughts drifting with their conversation. She knew he was the man Josie and her aunt had been to see the day before and she was hoping that he would prove be a valuable source of information. Perhaps he could tell them more about the house where Josie was being held. She wanted to know all about the man who lived there, she needed to discover as much as she could before going there herself.

Suddenly pain exploded inside her head and she cried out as a kaleidoscope of colours flashed across her vision. Gasping loudly, she fell to her knees and dropping the cups that she was holding, hot tea spilled across the floor. Pain ripped through her abdomen and a choir of voices filled her head, there was so much noise that it was almost unbearable. A man's voice rose above the rest and then she heard a woman scream.

Gripped by the hand of fear, her blood ran cold as strange emotions flashed into her head. Suddenly it became clear, Josie was in pain, she was defenceless against the monster. She could see him clearly and she cried out. He was staring at her, he was very close and suddenly his hands were all over her body, his hot breath stale against her cheek.

Kate cried out and scampered away across the floor. Taking her head in her hands she tried desperately to make the vision go away, she was terrified and completely overwhelmed by the emotional torrent that held her firmly in its grip.

Suddenly a doctor was there beside her, his hand resting on her arm he did his best to calm her. The sound of his voice was distant but through her turmoil she found it soothing and focusing her energy on him, he became a psychological lifeline.

Reaching up she held onto him tightly and unable to hold back she began to weep, but before she had chance to regain her senses something flashed before her eyes. It was hard and cold against her skin and as she fell back into the pit of despair, a sharp stabbing pain nibbled at her skin.

The vision increased in intensity but all she could see was a whirling storm of angry lights. Suddenly it became clear, he was holding a knife and her body went rigid. Unable to defend herself against his onslaught she was convinced that he was about to plunge it into her body.

Gradually the scene faded away leaving her breathless but still she was lost in the depths of her unconscious mind, the nightmare was not over yet.

Coming at her again, he forced her up against a cold uneven wall and there was nowhere for her to go. Through her panic, she could hear a rattling sound, an ugly noise that burned deeply into her mind and its companion was physical pain. Strangely, this is what she focussed on in the darkest moment of her terror.

The image began to fade again leaving Kate trembling.

"Call Mr Granger."

Garbled words filled her head but she was unable to make sense of them. Frantically she tried to harness her powers, return to some form of reality and focus her mind on anything that would give her the strength to fight back. She was confused and distraught, the appalling experience had arrived so unexpectedly leaving her no time to prepare but now she was beginning to rally.

Helping hands and soothing words coaxed her gently back from the abyss but a distant scream snatched her away again. This time she slumped into unconsciousness, tea and coffee from the cups she had dropped soaking into her clothes.

On the edge of a village not far away, in the cellar of a large white house, Josie MacDonald hung helplessly in chains. Her body was bruised and her throat was raw from screaming, she had almost lost her mind.

A mad man with wild hair had cut away her clothes then violated her with total disregard for her feelings. Her mind was numb but she felt no fear, she was hollow and empty, devoid of all emotions.

Kate opened her eyes and tears spilled over her cheeks and soaked into the blanket draped around her shoulders. Miserably she pulled it tighter; she was devastated.

Her mind was still not entirely her own and she felt like a spectator inside her own body. She did not like the sensation one bit and using a technique that had worked many times before, anchored herself to her surroundings, only then was she able to analyse some of her thoughts.

It was an effort to separate reality from delusion. Something dreadful had happened but she was not yet ready to probe her memory and analyse it. She needed time to gather her strength, steel herself and reinforce the protective barriers that she would need to keep him out.

"What's going on?" Tim's voice filled the little sterile cubical.

She was resting on a trolley and had not realised that he was there.

"I'm afraid your wife collapsed Mr. Granger." The doctor looked up from where he was fussing over Kate.

"She's not my wife, she's my sister."

"Oh I beg your pardon." The doctor looked uncomfortable.

After a moment, he asked. "Does your sister have a history of this kind of thing?"

"No," Tim looked at him, "no, of course not."

"Is she diabetic?" he continued. "Does she suffer from any allergies?"

Questions came in quick succession. "Is she pregnant?"

Tim stared at him opened mouthed, then he shrugged his shoulders. "No, I don't think so." Taking a step backwards, he needed time to take it all in. "No of course not, she would have told me if she was."

His concern turned to anger, he was infuriated with himself and annoyed with Kate. He was tired with the whole situation but above all, he was mystified. He could do without this sudden twist, he had enough to cope with and thrusting his hands deeply into his pockets, he frowned.

The doctor nodded and mumbled something before he left them alone.

"How are you feeling?" Tim asked once he had taken a deep breath.

Lowering himself into the chair beside the trolley, he reached for her hand then attempted to smile.

"I'm not sure." She said, focusing on his face.

"Do you know what happened?"

"No," she replied a little too quickly.

"The doctor wants to carry out a few tests. He asked me if you were pregnant."

She looked up at him sourly. "I've got the mother of all headaches but I can assure you, you're not about to become an uncle, not for a long time yet."

"You feel so cold," he said touching her arm.

Behind his smile, she could see his concern but Kate was determined that her emotions would not give her away. She may feel cold but it was her mind that was frozen and in a state of shock.

Tentatively she began to analyse what had happened. Unconsciously she had been processing everything that had taken place and had now begun to work it out. The appalling experience left her feeling vulnerable and she was not yet strong enough to evaluate the results, but of one thing she was certain, Tim must not find out, not yet anyway. Sneaking a look at him, she could see the strain pinching at the corners of his eyes and his mouth was a fine line stretched across his face. He was obviously finding it increasingly difficult to cope and her heart went out to him.

Tears welled up in her eyes again. "Can you pass me a tissue please, I really don't know why I'm so emotional," she lied.

It will be bad enough when he discovers the truth, she thought. How could she begin to explain that the woman he loved had been attacked so viciously then raped by Greg Maclaren.

Chapter
TWENTY NINE

Mr Mac haunted the corridors of his house like a demented spirit. He was still dressed in his kilt and his body was painted with the symbols of a Celtic warrior. With his hair greased into spikes that resembled devils horns, he appeared even more fearsome.

His mood was dangerous, fuelled by the excitement that normally follows a battle or moments of extreme stress, fire coursed through his veins. He had achieved all of his goals and now after gorging on the spoils he was satisfied, Josie MacDonald was safely installed in his cellar. He grinned and licked his lips.

The uncertainty that had accompanied the last few weeks was now over and his little game was coming to the end. Nothing stood in his way and not a thing could go wrong, he was in total control and he felt euphoric. The voices in his head were howling their approval, they congratulated him and urged him on, he had their full support. This was a new experience for him, at times there had been nothing but arguments, they were usually at loggerheads but now it was all over and together they were invincible.

Letting himself into his study he poured himself a large measure of single malt before collapsing into his favourite chair. Savouring the burning sensation, he held the scotch in his mouth, allowing it to trickle slowly down his throat and as the sweet, smoky fumes rose into his nasal cavities, his eyes watered and he let out a satisfying sigh.

Glancing up he studied her paintings. They had arrived a few days earlier and were now hanging on his wall. The irony was not lost on him and in mock salute raised his glass to Josie MacDonald.

He let his thoughts wander allowing images of the evening he had spent at Timothy Granger's gallery into his head. It seemed such a long time ago now so much had taken place since then but in reality, barely a week had passed.

He enjoyed her paintings a great deal, she was such an accomplished artist. He loved the way she blended fine brush strokes using colour to create an illusion of light and shade. It was such a clever technique her ability to make the most of the textured paper that she liked to use was unique. He could hardly believe that not only did he have some of her paintings but the artist was also a guest in his house.

He smiled and as his mind raged on, he began to appreciate how much he had enjoyed himself recently. His first ever trip to London had been an adventure that filled him with extraordinary excitement. He hated everything about the English but being there in the principle city had given him an opportunity to study its people up close. Josie's friends had interested him the most and immediately his plan had emerged. It seemed strange now that just a few weeks ago he had never even heard of Josie MacDonald. That thought stayed with him for a while then rising from his chair, he went to refresh his glass.

He would now have to dispatch Cowper-Smith, he could no longer stand the man's whining, he had served his purpose and was of no further use. An idea flashed into his head and his eyes narrowed, perhaps he could perform one last task, again he grinned and licked his lips.

Lifting his glass to the light he studied and admired the clear amber liquid. Fire danced in the lead crystal and it fascinated him, following it with his eyes, it reminded him of diamonds in the sky and the weight of the tumbler in his hands was reassuring.

Tim was leaning against the wall in the reception area. He was aware of people milling about but paid little attention to them, his mind dwelt on other issues. He was worried about Kate; she had never collapsed like this before and must have had some kind of reaction brought on by the strain of the past few days. He would never be able to understand her ways and he wondered at their relationship. How could they be so closely related when their lives and even their ethos was so very different?

He considered sending her back to London but instantly dismissed the idea, she would never agree to that. The more he thought about it the more he believed that the shock of discovering Josie's aunt had tipped her over the edge. Perhaps she did not possess the emotional strength that she gave herself credit for.

Pushing himself away from the wall, he wandered dejectedly across the foyer towards a chair. Another wave of anger surged through him as he thought about the danger that Josie was in and he struggled with his feelings. A sense of guilt washed over him and he felt hopeless just sitting there waiting, he sighed heavily again and rubbed his hand over his face.

The police were involved now so he must wait until they turned up. They were sure to want to talk to him and he had a feeling that he would need their help before long. He wondered how much he should tell them, more to the point what would sound credible. He suspected that all they would be interested in was Josie's aunt and how they came to find her.

He went over the events in his mind again, it was clear that her car had been deliberately hidden in the undergrowth and it didn't take a detective to see that she had suffered shotgun wounds. Perhaps Josie was in the same condition, dumped in a ditch somewhere. If that were true, she would probably have bled to death by now, shuddering at the thought he descended deeper into despair.

They had searched the area where the car had been abandoned but found nothing. Kate was convinced that Josie was still at the house and he was inclined to agree with her. Struggling with his doubts, Tim thought about Josie's aunt, would she survive her injuries, had they found her in time?

His mind raced on twisting and turning until he found it impossible to relax.

"How's your sister?"

Tim failed to see the man walking towards him and was startled.

"I hope you don't mind my asking."

The voice was soothing to his ear, a friendly sound that was reassuring and cultured.

"Not at all," hauling himself up Tim turned to face the man. "It's kind of you to ask."

The old man's grasp was surprisingly firm as they shook hands.

"Rufus Stone," he said with a grin before indicating towards a quiet corner.

"You and your sister found my friend I understand."

232

They settled into comfortable chairs facing each other before he continued.

"They are saying it was a road traffic accident." His eyes narrowed as he noticed the dark patches on Tim's jacket.

Tim realised that he knew more than he was letting on.

"What's your connection with Josie MacDonald?"

"Why do you ask?" The question took him completely by surprise and Tim countered with a question, giving himself time to consider his answer.

Rufus' expression softened, he was impressed by the young man's guile. "I overheard your sister call out her name when she was down on the ground so naturally I assumed you are connected in some way."

"We are good friends," Tim replied. "And you're a friend of Josie's aunt?"

Rufus nodded calmly but made no comment and seconds passed before Tim realised that he was waiting for him to continue.

"We followed Josie up from London," he said cautiously. "She's unaware of that of course."

"And why would you do that?"

Tim ignored the question. "There are a number of others involved," he hesitated, struggling for the right words. "All friends of Josie's."

They were silent again as Rufus considered what Tim had just said. He sighed deeply and his eyes grew dark.

"So it's much worse than I realised." He said running a hand wearily over his face.

Tim looked uncomfortable and shuffled in his seat. "It has something to do with that house," he said his mouth going dry. "Montague Villa."

"Yes indeed I'm afraid it has." Rufus studied him carefully and wondered how it was he knew the name of the house.

"Are you related to Josie?" Tim asked suddenly.

"Why do you ask?"

"Just curious," he smiled. He wanted to know more about Rufus, discover what part he had to play in all this.

"I know Josie has an aunt living up here but she has never mentioned any other relatives."

"No, she wouldn't would she."

Tim struggled under the weight of the old man's scrutiny.

"She has no idea who I am, we met for the first time yesterday. Like you I'm just a good friend."

An awkward silence followed.

There was so much that Tim wanted to know but he was unsure how to proceed with his questioning.

"You want to know don't you young man?" It was as if he could see into his mind and read his thoughts.

"It's a long and tragic story that began many years ago," he began and the light in his eyes suddenly burned brightly. "Much water has passed under the bridge since then," he whispered, "but not so much as to wash away the pain."

His mouth became a thin line drawn across his face and Tim had to shuffle closer in order to hear him.

"They paid me a visit yesterday," Rufus admitted. "Full of questions they were. They asked me about the house, your friend even had a picture of it. She said someone had sent it to her." He smiled and the muscles in his face relaxed. "Her wounds were caused by a shotgun," he continued, his words totally out of context with their conversation.

"Yes," Tim nodded grimly.

"Then you have cause to worry young man." Rufus eyed him sternly. "He's back."

"Who?" Tim looked up.

"Randolph, William Randolph the younger."

"Mr Mac." Tim said softly remembering something that Josie had said and Rufus stared at him. "Greg MacLaren lives there."

"Who's to say? Maybe they are one and the same."

"But Greg MacLaren's harmless, he's an eccentric art collector."

He began to describe the man he had met at his gallery and Rufus listened very carefully.

"It could be him," he nodded. "It was so many years ago."

"I don't understand."

"Randolph is back and it's happening all over again." Rufus fixed him with a penetrating stare, "History repeating itself."

Tim had no idea what he was talking about.

"Your sister is almost ready to go Mr. Granger." A nurse appeared at his side, the sound of her voice startling them both.

"She's asking for you." The nurse smiled.

Tim stood up ready to follow.

"Be very careful young man." Reaching out, Rufus grabbed hold of Tim's arm and hauled himself up out of his chair. "Don't let your sister out of your sight when you go up to that house, not for a moment."

A shiver ran through Tim as he reached for his outstretched hand.

"It may already be too late for the others."

Tim walked away, hoping desperately that the old man was wrong.

Kate was sitting up in bed her back supported by a cloud of soft pillows. She looked infinitely better, her face was flushed with colour and her eyes were glowing brightly.

"Before we go," she began as soon as he appeared. "I want to speak with Rufus Stone."

"There's no need." He told her all about their conversation but kept Rufus' warning to himself.

Kate also kept a tight rein on her thoughts, much of what Tim said meant more to her than he could ever know.

"So how are you feeling?" he asked guilt ridden for not asking sooner.

"Oh I'm okay," she smiled, "diagnosis a virus, prognosis good if I take it easy. Oh and by the way I'm not pregnant," she grinned wickedly, her small white teeth flashing in the bright artificial light. "Pass me my trousers will you. Are they dry yet?"

Mr Mac paused and pressed his hand flat against the door. The wood was cool against his skin and he grinned in anticipation as a rush of adrenalin coursed through his veins. Rolling his shoulders in order to ease the tension from his muscles, he listened but the voices in his head remained silent. They were reluctant to offer him guidance and he knew they were waiting patiently, watching his every move. Taking a deep breath, he pushed the door open.

As soon as she saw him, Sarah whimpered like a lost puppy and wished that she had remained silent. He was the monster in her worst nightmare and now it was creeping across the floor towards her.

Pushing backwards against the cold wall in a fruitless effort to get away the unforgiving barrier that was always there pressed against her back. Closing her eyes, she prayed silently that he would lose interest and move away but as soon as the thought entered her head, she hated herself.

Suddenly he was there beside her his breath hot against her cheek, and every sinew in her body tightened as stale whisky fumes washed over her. The hateful chains at her wrists and ankles rattled, the hard, cold sound only adding to the tension in the room, it made her skin crawl and clamping her jaws tightly together she managed to stifle a scream. If she could remain silent then perhaps he would leave her alone.

Unexpectedly his teeth nipped at the side of her neck and she cried out in shock. His breath became ragged as his hands played over the curve of her hips and her stomach lurched.

He laughed softly, a strange sound that rattled at the back of his throat and she knew that if she opened her eyes she would be facing some hideous creature from hell. She wanted to scream and keep on screaming until someone came to rescue her from this madness.

He moved his hands slowly up over her shoulders and along her arms and she could feel the tension in his fingers as he began working at her wrists. The shackles that were holding her suddenly became loose and her arms were free. Her legs, unable to support her gave out and she slumped forward against him. She had no feeling in her limbs, they were lifeless and uncontrollable, but slowly the feeling in her fingers began to return, her hands throbbing painfully.

Pushing her roughly against the wall, he held her there until she regained her balance and she cried out as cramp threatened her tortured muscles. Bracing herself as best she could, Sarah used the wall for support as Mr Mac bent forward to loosen the chains at her ankles.

As he worked, she struggled desperately to remain in control, the urge to vomit as her stomach tightened with shock and hunger was too much and finally her legs gave way and she collapsed.

She had no idea how long she had been there on the cold concrete floor, it was as if her body belonged to someone else, her muscles twitching as the feeling returned to her tortured limbs.

Mike strained valiantly against the chains that were holding him but it was a futile gesture, they would never break. He no longer felt the sting of the cruel metal shackles as they gnawed at his bones, all he wanted to do was to break free and protect his companions against further attacks, but there was nothing he could do he would never break free. Reeling from shock and exhaustion, images of what he had seen remained inside his head and he knew that the sound of Josie screaming would stay with him for the rest of his life. He stared coldly at Mr Mac, his eyes burning with hatred. If he could, he would kill the man with his bare hands and feel no regret, but all he could do was to look on helplessly.

Sarah was at the end of her endurance and his heart went out to her, she did not deserve any of this, none of them did. Although he had suffered numerous beatings this was nothing compared to the humiliation and brutality that the girls had to bear. Turning his head Mike looked at Josie, she appeared to be unconscious. He should not have to see her like this, never in his wildest dreams could he conjure up a situation like this, they were helpless and completely at the mercy of this crazed lunatic. She was battered and bruised and he could not even begin to imagine what was going on in her head. An overwhelming sense of sadness washed over him and his chest tightened as he realised that she may never recover from this.

She had been such fun to be with and he enjoyed her company, but they never seemed to be completely at ease with each other. He had no idea when their relationship had started to go wrong, or what it was that had come between them but he would take the blame, none of it was her fault. As these thoughts went through his head, he began to realise that he had been such a fool. Not once did he appreciate how wonderful she was and now it was too late. He become conscious of the fact that he had never respected her, she had been just another plaything, a pretty girl to parade in front of his friends and he was ashamed to admit it. The realisation of it shocked him and he began to scrutinise his life. He may have lost Josie but he made a promise to himself. In future, he would be more understanding where women were concerned he would respect their opinions. He groaned and was not certain if the sound had been real or inside his head, he was torturing himself with self-pity and it had to stop.

Sarah cried out as Mr Mac hauled her roughly across the floor and Mike, shocked back to reality, opened his eyes as she was dumped at his feet. He was sickened, up close he could see what she had become. Her ribs stood out against her pale skin and her chest was heaving like bellows, she was terrified, no longer the pillar of strength that she had been. Mewing pathetically like a creature in agony, she clawed at the cold concrete floor and one by one, her brittle nails began to break.

Reaching down Mr Mac grabbed her roughly and pulled her to her knees, as Mike looked on in silence, fearful at what was to come next.

Mr Mac moved into the centre of the room. He was an abomination sent from the depths of hell to run amok among the innocent. His mission was to rape, torture and murder without conscience and he was as dangerous as a cobra that was ready to strike. This time however when he moved he did not strike, he simply left the room.

The atmosphere changed the moment he had gone, Mike could feel it and he realised that he was still holding his breath.

"It's okay Sarah, he's gone." He said in a whisper and slowly she raised her head.

 Josie opened her eyes, they were swollen and sore but she had no more tears left with which to wash the horrors away. As her mind began to work, she thought about her aunt and the shock of seeing her unconscious on the step covered in blood came rushing back to her.

Sarah moved slowly towards her friend. "Josie," she whispered. "Oh Josie, look what he's done to you."

Mike swallowed hard as a lump began to form in his throat and for the first time since he was a child he wanted to cry. He watched as Sarah, climbing stiffly to her feet, reached out and touched Josie's face with her fingertips. Mike could feel the tenderness that flowed between them and was heartened when Josie began to respond.

He felt like an intruder, he should not have to witness this. Josie and Sarah were sharing a private almost intimate moment, and it was impossible for him to understand how they could take solace in each other at a time like this. He was relieved that Sarah was there, he would never have been able to cope with Josie alone, Sarah knew instinctively what to do and was able to break through Josie's defences.

Emotions stirred from deep within him and he remembered something from his childhood. Memories of his mother that had lain dormant for years came bubbling to the surface and he smiled. Suddenly he could feel her presence and he remembered a period of his life that had been pure and simple, an innocent time filled with unconditional love. As a child, he had taken his mother for granted, never questioning her motives. He shuddered and looking away became angry with himself, he was shocked and ashamed at feeling such emotions.

Mr Mac came back carrying a sponge and a bucket filled with water but something else also caught Mike's eye and his muscles tightened. Mr Mac was holding a knife.

He dumped the bucket in the middle of the floor, then coming up behind Sarah, wound his arm around her waist and lifted her off the floor. Turning her away from Josie, he swung her around until she faced Mike then giving her a push she staggered into him. Her elbow raked against his broken ribs and he buckled as pain ripped through his chest.

Mr Mac held her against him and forced her face up close to his.

"How does it feel?" Mr Mac grinned and licked his lips. "How does it feel to have a naked woman rubbing herself up against you?"

Mike was appalled and simply stared at Mr Mac, his eyes burning with rage.

Sarah could do nothing but hold herself rigid, she dared not move.

"Do you want her?" Mr Mac whispered.

Suddenly he pulled her back and in a single movement shoved the blade he was holding up against her throat. The razor edge stung her skin and she felt faint as her head whirled in a mass of confusion.

"Strip him," he hissed into her ear. "Why shouldn't he be naked too?"

Mike couldn't hear what he was saying, but from the horrified expression on Sarah's face, it was obviously nothing pleasant.

Mr Mac released his grip and Sarah collapsed at Mike's feet.

"Go on," he commanded. "Get on with it."

Slowly she struggled upright and began moving her fingers over the remaining buttons of his shirt. It was impossible to remove the garment as his arms were chained above his head.

"Rip it off," Mr Mac ordered.

It was already torn and the fabric parted easily then she gasped. Sarah was horrified at the extent of bruises that covered his body. Uneven lumps pushed out from under his skin where his ribs were broken and carefully she avoided these tender places.

"Now his trousers."

She fumbled with the buckle of his belt. She could use it as a weapon, she thought, pull it through the loops and swing it like a sling. If she aimed the hard edge of the buckle towards his head maybe she could knock him out.

Moving up behind her, he slapped her hand away. It was as if he could read her thoughts and taking hold of the buckle, tore the belt free. Mike gasped as the loops holding it around his waist gave way.

"Get on with it," Mr Mac hissed.

Her fingers were stiff and would hardly work but she managed to unfasten his trousers and ease the waistband down over his hips but she could go no further, his legs were splayed wide apart held by shackles. Mr Mac shoved her aside and the blade of his knife flashed as it parted the fabric easily.

Sarah felt sick, Mike was standing there in front of her wearing nothing but his underpants and now she was expected to rip them from him too.

Looking into his face she searched for some kind of reaction but his expression was stony, his gaze fixed on the mad man who was standing behind her.

"Go on do it."

She could feel the tip of his knife nipping at the skin between her shoulder blades so she did as she was told.

Mike hung against the wall and Mr Mac stood back to observe him, he grinned and licked his lips.

"Now wash him." He indicated to the bucket of water and sponge.

With no choice but to obey, she carefully sponged dried blood from his face and working the water over his chest, discovered that his body was as hard as iron. His muscles were solid knots and he hardly flinched as the icy cold water ran over his broken ribs.

Mike tore his mind away from what she was doing, under different circumstances, he would have been aroused but he focussed his hatred on the man who was pulling her strings.

When she was finished, Mr Mac grasped her by the neck and forced her face close to Mike's. She was terrified and he could feel her quivering against him.

"Make him hard."

She could hardly believe what he had just said but with the point of the knife resting against her spine, she had little choice but do as he said.

"What's the matter with you man?" Mr Mac bellowed. "Do you prefer the touch of a man?"

Shoving Sarah aside, he stroked the point of his knife against him.

"What do you expect?" Mike lisped through swollen lips.

"I expect you to ride this young lass."

He forced her up against Mike again, but appalled by what Mr Mac expected, she could not do as he asked. Mike remained unmoved, he was not going to rape her for this mad man's entertainment.

Mr Mac, roaring with frustration, moved quickly across the room and Sarah's eyes widened as he pressed his knife hard up against Josie's throat.

"Do it," he hissed.

Josie cried out and the sound of her friend's distress cut deeply into her. Sarah looked into Mike's eyes but saw nothing, it was as if he had shut down completely. Josie screamed again and Sarah's head whipped round, her friend was in mortal danger and suddenly she snapped.

"Get off her you animal," she screamed.

Flinging herself across the room she crashed into him, the momentum drove the knife from his grip and sent it skittering across the floor. Leaping up onto his back, she drove her fingertips into his eyes and Mr Mac bellowed out a curse. Caught completely off guard he twisted and turned, bucking wildly until he threw her off. She landed heavily on the concrete floor then he moved in. Kicking out, the force of his boot drove the air from her lungs and lights flashed inside her skull. Desperately she rolled into a defensive ball in an attempt to avoid further injury, but this enraged him even more so he kicked and punched until she lay still.

Curled up at his feet she no longer presented a threat so standing back he caught his breath before turning towards Josie. She stared at him her eyes wide with shock and revulsion.

Suddenly he had an idea, pushing his hand into his pocket he fumbled for a moment before kneeling down beside Sarah. Josie could not see what it was that he squeezed into her hand but when he was finished, he stood up and moved away. Glancing back at Josie he grinned and licked his lips.

Chapter
THIRTY

They left the hospital and drove back to the guesthouse in silence and when they arrived, the place was deserted. Tim was happy with that, he was in no mood for explanations. Going straight to their room he stripped off his bloodstained clothes and showered for the second time that day and whilst he was washing away the stress of their ordeal, Kate kept herself busy by making tea from the little complimentary tray. She had built a dam inside her mind to hold back the horror of her ordeal but unfortunately, the wall was fragile and could be breached at any moment.

Tim emerged from the shower some time later wearing nothing but a towel and it was immediately clear to Kate that the therapeutic effect of warm water against his skin had done nothing to improve his mood. She smiled wearily and offered him a mug of tea.

"I know you want to get up to that house but then what?" she glanced at him. "We must have a plan."

Tim studied her thoughtfully. Dark smudges had formed under her eyes and she looked drained. She was putting on a brave face and it would be unwise for him to tell her how awful she looked so, turning away, he took a mouthful of tea and kept his thoughts to himself.

"Whilst you think about your plan it's my turn to freshen up." She said fingering the ends of her hair. "I won't be long I promise."

As soon as she stood up her world tilted on its axis and a stab of pain shot through her head. Screwing up her face, she gasped and almost collapsed.

"Are you alright?" Tim shot across the room and held onto her tightly.

Images filled her head and she heard Josie scream, she could feel her pain and frustration. Leaning against her brother she clutched at his arm for support then closing her eyes she tried to chase away the demons. It was happening all over again.

Tim was full of concern, he could feel his sister trembling, the blood had drained from her face and a haunted look had replaced the light in her eyes.

"I'm okay really," she told him. "I must have got up too quickly."

Tim did not believe a word of it.

Gently she prized herself away from his grasp and probing at her temples with her fingertips did her best to ignore the terrifying images that were playing out inside her head. Taking a deep breath, she straightened her back and disappeared into the bathroom closing the door behind her. Reaching for the shower tap she turned it on and used the sound of water falling into the tray to drown out her groan. Tim must not know the extent of her distress, so propping herself up against the sink, she studied herself in the mirror.

She knew what was happening to Josie, she had felt his hands on her body, had seen the look in his eyes and experienced the terrible things that Josie was going through. Like her friend, all Kate wanted to do was to curl up in a corner and be by herself.

Kate was powerless there was nothing she could do. She had to keep reminding herself that it was not happening to her. It was imperative that she quarantine her feelings, keep them locked away in a place where she could analyse them subjectively without danger of being overwhelmed.

Tim sat down on his bed and sighed, he knew Kate was keeping something from him. He wished she would open up, not be so guarded all of the time. Clearly she was exhausted and the stress of the last few days was catching up with her but he could not afford the emotional effort or the time to worry about her. Josie must remain his primary concern and he had to get inside that house.

Shaking his head, he sighed again as he thought about his sister. The scene at the hospital kept running through his mind but he had no answers, reaching for his clothes he pulled them on. He was not going to hang around here for much longer.

"Kate," he called out loudly as he knocked on the bathroom door. "I'm going out for a walk."

The door opened and she appeared shrouded in a cloud of perfumed steam and wrapped in huge towel.

"Okay Tim I won't be long." She promised.

Once outside he could breathe more easily and glancing along the street, he went towards his car that was parked just a few yards away. Fingering the door handle he was tempted to take off on his own but thought better of it, so moving away, hunched his shoulders and thrust his hands deeply into his pockets.

Rufus Stone's words rang persistently in his ears and like a mischievous child refused to go away. He had warned him that Kate was in danger and it was up to him to look out for her. The old man had been insistent and it unnerved Tim to think that he was putting his sister in danger.

He had no idea what it was they had become involved in or what bound them all together. Maybe the police in London had been right and there was no link with what happened to Josie in Scotland, it could simply be people in the wrong place at the wrong time but he refused to believe that, deep down he knew there was something more sinister going on.

He sighed loudly, and pulling his hand from his pocket, glanced at his watch and swore under his breath. He was letting his mind get the better of him and time was slipping away. What he needed was a plan, Kate was right she was always telling him. Their next objective was to get inside that house, he had to find out if Josie was still there. Kate was convinced that she was and, on this occasion, he was inclined to agree with her. He looked up at the sky, the sun had disappeared behind a cloud and suddenly the afternoon became as miserable as his mood.

When he returned Kate was dressed. She was sitting at the dressing table putting the finishing touches to her hair and he couldn't help but notice how much better she looked.

"I think we should consult with the internet," she began, glancing at her laptop. "We need to find out as much as we can about the Randolphs and Montague Villa."

He nodded in agreement but made no comment. Why hadn't he thought of that?

Putting her hairbrush down, she moved away from the mirror and settled on the bed beside him then, reaching for her laptop, she lifted the screen. Her long, elegant fingers danced over the keys as she logged on and Tim watched as she concentrated on the screen.

"Rufus told me that something like this has happened before," Tim told her. "Like history repeating itself." He filled her in with the details.

"We should start by checking back issues of the local newspaper," she suggested. "Did he tell you when these events took place?"

"No he didn't mention a specific date."

"Never mind, we'll do a general search and see what we can find."

Words filled the screen and she sifted through various articles but after a while, she realised that it was a hopeless task. There was just too much information, she would have to refine her search.

Typing in the name William Randolph the screen came alive with references about the local landowner.

"It seems that William Randolph was a highly respected man, a Laird I suppose one would call him. He had his fingers into many things, local politics, businesses and farms. He seemed to enjoy the local hunt meetings, he was quite the country gent." Scrolling down the page, she discovered more. "Ah, he was also a Justice of the Peace."

"What about his son?" Tim asked.

There was very little information about William Randolph the younger.

"He was born in the early sixties, was an only child and enjoyed a privileged upbringing, everything that one would expect from the local gentry. Okay," she said scanning the words on the screen, "let's try this."

She typed in the words Montague Villa and a picture of a house appeared.

"The same picture that Josie had been sent." Tim recognised it immediately.

"Look at this," Kate said, pointing to the headlines further down the page. "Young woman disappears in Elgin." She checked the date; it was the summer of 1978. "It says she was an English girl on holiday with her parents. The police searched Montague Villa and the estate. It seems to have caused an outcry at the time. William Randolph, respected JP, pillar of the community was suspected of being involved."

Reading through the article quickly the story began to unfold.

"William Randolph and his wife Eleanor were questioned about their son whilst he was being held at the police station in Elgin. He was under suspicion of abducting the girl but the case was dropped due to the lack of evidence. The girl was never seen again."

"Hang on a minute," Tim said. "Go back a bit, what was the girl's name?"

Scrolling back, she discovered the name of the victim.

"Helen Stone." She looked up at Tim. "Bit of a coincidence don't you think?"

"I knew it," he nodded, "there had to be a connection with Rufus Stone. Helen must have been his daughter. He kept that one close to his chest." Tim frowned. "He was very careful with what he said but I got the impression that his story was personal and not just some local historical facts."

Standing up he paced the room.

"So Josie's aunt must have known too, after all she's an old friend of Rufus."

"Not necessarily, she might not have known him then, it was a long time ago."

"I can't believe they would never have discussed it, what are friends for?"

Kate harboured doubts but kept them to herself. "Well I'm certain Josie didn't know anything about this or she would have told me."

She continued reading through the remaining articles but learned nothing more.

"Let's assume that Greg MacLaren is in fact William Randolph the younger," she began. "I wonder if he knew about the connection between Josie's aunt and Rufus Stone. That would have given him cause to kill her especially if he thought she had discovered his real identity."

"But why would he think that?" Tim continued to pace the room whilst listening.

"If he kidnapped Helen then maybe he targeted Josie because of her connection with Rufus Stone through her aunt."

"No I can't accept that." Tim said shaking his head. "This is all conjecture. You know what Josie told us, she was simply in the wrong place at the wrong time."

Kate was silent for a moment. "I suppose you're right, Josie was already in Spey Bay when she saw him murder that woman. He couldn't possibly have known her then or engineered a meeting like that."

"What does it matter anyway?" Tim asked. He stopped pacing and looked out of the window. "Josie has to be up at that house."

Turning towards his sister, he caught sight of her expression moments before she managed to compose herself.

"We had better get up there then," she said shutting down the computer.

Chapter
THIRTY ONE

The sound of blood rushing through her ears was like water crashing against rocks, and her heart was beating uncomfortably against her ribs. Sarah was lying face down on the cold concrete floor and she felt dreadful. She attempted to roll over onto her back but the effort was too much and a wave of nausea washed over her. Groaning loudly she managed to ease herself into a more comfortable position and after a few moments her senses began to return.

Unpleasant memories came flooding back and she groaned again. Someone was crying softly and as she listened, she realised that it was Josie. Steeling herself, she flexed her muscles and working through her discomfort arranged her limbs before stretching out tentatively on the concrete floor.

Her body was a mass of bruises, she must have been mad to attack him, something as insane as that could only have had one outcome.

Hauling herself up into the sitting position, she looked up at Josie. Her friend was distraught and she looked awful but Sarah was relieved when Josie smiled through her distress.

"Sarah, are you okay?"

Josie had not spoken since her ordeal had begun and the sound of her voice filled Sarah with hope.

"Yes I think so." She nodded.

"You're crazy, you could have been killed."

Sarah shrugged her shoulders, Josie was right of course and she began to wonder how he would react towards her when he returned, pushing these unwelcome thoughts aside, she chose not to dwell on the matter.

"Sarah." Mike's voice sounded reassuringly strong. "Come over here and unlock my chains."

"Sarah," Josie spoke softly, "did he give you a key?"

She frowned, she had no idea what they were talking about.

"A key Sarah, did he give you a key?" The desperation in Mike's voice was obvious. "There on the floor by your feet."

He was right, a small key lay on the concrete floor where it had fallen from her hand.

"Why is he doing this to us?" She muttered miserably.

"Because he's mad and we are innocent victims."

"No," she shook her head, "there must be more to it than that, what about Lindsay and Lizzie?"

"Come over here Sarah." The sound of his voice invaded her thoughts and she wanted to cover her ears with her hands.

"Unlock these chains."

"No." She drew back, her eyes wide with fear. "It's not safe, you know what he did to Lindsay and Lizzie, he took them outside and he murdered them."

"No Sarah you don't know that, don't believe what he told you." Mike continued. "Don't think about that now just help me out of these chains. I'll get you out of here I promise."

"But it's hopeless don't you see?"

Sarah picked up the key and held onto it, it was cold against the palm of her hand and she hated it vehemently.

Mike, looking on anxiously began to doubt her strength to use it.

"It's not hopeless Sarah," Josie began. "You have to believe him. Mike is going to get away from here and he's going to find someone to help us."

Gradually they managed to convince her and Sarah found the courage to carry out the task that she had been set. She hated herself and knew that he would never get away. How was she going to deal with knowing that she had sent him to his death?

Standing up on tiptoe, she reached for the shackles that were holding his wrists. His fingers were blue, cold and lifeless and the moment he was released, his legs gave way and they collapsed in a tangle of limbs onto the concrete floor.

Mike almost passed out with the pain and groaned loudly as his fractured bones ground together. They remained still until his agony had passed then Sarah freed herself and gently began to massage the life back into his muscles. He was not in good shape and she began to wonder if he would make it out of the cellar at all.

Slowly he began to recover his strength and as the warmth flowed back into his arms, he flexed his fingers and moved his hands. Cautiously he stood up and looked across at Josie; she was shocked by his injuries but managed an encouraging smile.

Reaching out, he helped Sarah to her feet before placing his arm around her shoulders and leaning against her, he limped a few paces across the floor. His progress was slow at first but as the life returned to his tortured limbs he began to feel stronger and after a little while was able to walk unaided. Grinning like a child at his newfound freedom, he was eager to get going.

"Don't worry," he said, and reaching out he touched Josie's cheek with his fingertips.

There was so much that he wanted to say but he could not find the words. He realised now that he had treated her so badly, he had said some terrible things and he wanted to beg for her forgiveness.

"Thank you." Seemed inadequate but it would have to do.

A lump formed at the back of her throat and she was unable to tell him to be careful. She had seen the way he had looked at her and it broke her heart. They had been close once, that much was true but although their relationship was over, she hoped they could remain friends. Tears streamed over her face as he turned away and she watched him as he limped towards the door.

When he was gone, she remained sobbing hopelessly for some time. Overcome by a terrible sense of loss she knew that she would never see him again. Sarah could feel it too, and going to Josie embraced her friend and together they wept.

Mr Mac was waiting, his plan unfolding perfectly he could hardly contain his excitement as Mike emerged cautiously from the cellar.

When he reached the top of the steps Mike stopped to listen. His heart was hammering against his fractured ribs, each beat sending a flutter of discomfort through his chest. His body was still numb from the injuries that he had sustained but as he moved, his tortured flesh was beginning to recover and doing his best to ignore the increasing pain he relied on adrenalin to see him through. He had managed to remain positive in front of the girls but now he was alone he began to wonder how long it would be before his strength failed.

In front of him stretched a gloomy corridor that seemed to run the length of the house and as he stood there, considering what to do next, the whole situation reminded him of something out of a horror movie. Moving forward cautiously, he used the shadows for cover. The thick carpet underfoot felt good, especially after standing for so long on the cold concrete floor and the air here was a few degrees warmer.

He had to find some clothes and a weapon, he was certain that it would not be long before he had to face the mad man.

Up ahead he could see a door standing slightly open and pausing, he pressed his ear up against the wood. The room beyond appeared to be empty so he went in.

The atmosphere inside was stale as if it had been closed up for a long time and as he glanced around his eyes become accustomed to the gloom. Crossing the room, he inspected the heavy wooden shutters covering the windows. Built from solid wood and as effective as steel bars, there would be no escaping that way so turning around he spotted a pair of leather trousers draped over the back of a chair. There was also a pair of riding boots standing beside a small table, the coincidence was too much, they must have been left for him to find.

The trousers were a perfect fit, the soft, warm leather reassuring against his skin. The boots on the other hand were a little tight but it was good to have something on his feet. With renewed confidence, he was now ready to face whatever was waiting.

He made his way to the hall and stood facing the huge fireplace that dominated one wall. The scale of it was impressive and in the grate, he found a heavy iron log basket blackened by time. This was resting on the most ornate dog irons he had ever seen and he wondered how many generations a roaring fire had greeted on a freezing cold day.

Hanging from the wall above the fireplace was a number of ancestral paintings, each one staring down at him dispassionately. In some of the faces, he thought he could see a trace of the man who had treated him so badly and looking around he marvelled at the opulence of the place. The house was well appointed and here everything seemed normal, even the air in this part of the building was light and faintly perfumed by wood polish and time.

Turning his back on the fireplace he searched for a weapon, he did not have to look far. An assortment of small round shields and ancient swords had been arranged in a pattern on the wall, some of them so old they would not look out of place in a museum. Reaching up he winced as pain shot through his chest but ignoring the discomfort, he drew a blade from its bracket.

The weapon felt good in his hand and childhood memories of super heroes came flooding back to him. Swinging it through the air, he tested the balance and it felt good in his grip. The edge was sharp, certainly sufficient to cause serious injury, this thought made him feel invincible and he grinned. Hefting the sword, he lunged at an invisible target and practiced for a few minutes. At first, it was an effort but once his muscles began to respond, he felt more comfortable and dancing across the hall his confidence increased with every step.

Now that he was suitably clothed and armed, he had to get out of the house so turning towards the heavy wooden door he pulled it open and stepped out into bright sunlight. The brightness of the day blinded him at first but after a few moments, his eyes adjusted and he began to see clearly. Peering over the ornate stone balcony, he had to decide which way to go. The park stretched away towards the tree line at the edge of the forest and continued down into the valley beyond. Looking the other way Mike studied the sweeping gravel pathway until it disappeared around the corner of the house, then cautiously like an animal on the edge of a meadow, he began to make his way down the steps. At the bottom, he found the gravel driveway flanked by thick rhododendron bushes and other shrubs, the foliage could provide him with the cover he needed to make good his escape.

Walking quickly across the gravel he stopped at the edge of the lawn and feeling the warmth of the sun against his shoulders it was good to be alive. During his darkest moments when chained like an animal to the cellar wall, he thought that he would never feel the sun on his back again.

Gripping the hilt of his sword, he swung it like a walking stick and using it for support, made his way towards the gate. He was intending to go down the lane where he believed he would find a village and some help. That was the only plan he had but suddenly he began to lose momentum and becoming unsure of himself, he had no idea where he was. He had never been here before and the last thing he could remember was being at work in London. Glancing around, it soon became obvious that he was a long way from the city, for all he knew the nearest town could be miles away. He would have to find some kind of transport.

Turning the corner, he limped into the little courtyard that separated the outbuildings from the house, and heading for the nearest structure, pressed his face up against the glass window. This was some kind of storage building, originally it had been a tack room when horses were in use on the estate but now it stood empty. He checked the stable block next door, then the coach house, pulling at the doors and peering in through the windows as he went but they were all deserted and secure. Moving away, he glanced around the yard looking for signs of recent movement. The gravel was smooth, either the yard was unused or it had recently been swept level. There had to be a car somewhere, he just had to find it.

Suddenly he saw movement and turning his head could see Mr Mac standing a short distance away. He was dressed in his kilt, his upper body bare and his skin decorated with swirls of blue. His hair was stiff with red dye and formed into spikes that stood up on top of his head. Mike had seen him dressed like this before and thought he looked ridiculous. Squaring up to him, he felt the hairs on the back of his neck stand up.

Mr Mac sneered menacingly and raised the heavy sword that he was holding; the vicious looking edge catching the light did nothing to ease Mike's apprehension. His own weapon seemed inadequate now against the superior blade but left with no choice he had to adopt an aggressive stance. He had heard somewhere that attack was the best form of defence but this hardly filled him with confidence. They eyed each other like boxers before a bout and Mike shuddered involuntarily as Mr Mac grinned and licked his lips. His stomach lurched, he had no idea how to fight with a sword and realised now that he had probably made a huge mistake thinking he could use it effectively.

At first, Mr Mac simply stared at him. He seemed relaxed and confident and slowly with deliberate movements began to move forward. As dangerous as a snake he swayed from side to side, stepping lightly on the balls of his feet. Mike swallowed loudly, his throat suddenly going dry as he waited for Mr Mac to strike.

When the attack finally came, the impact of the blades coming together sent a shock wave along his arm and he staggered backwards. Mike stumbled on the loose gravel underfoot but adrenalin surging through his system gave him the courage to stand his ground and fight. Moving forward he leaned into the attack and lifting his arm managed to block another lunge. Hacking away with his blade, he was able to gain some ground and each time their blades came together sparks and metal splinters shot into the air but it was not long before the muscles in his arms began to complain. The sword was becoming heavier and the force rippling through his muscles jarred his teeth with every impact.

It was not long before Mike began to tire, his strength fading fast in his injured state, his ribs burning as his breathing became ever more ragged. Sweat stung his eyes and every sinew in his body complained as he stumbled backwards. Mike sobbed with frustration as dread began to tug at him and fear rising up from the pit of his stomach confirmed that he was doomed. He knew that he could never win, he was lacking both the strength and skill to fight with a blade but desperately he fought back. For a time he seemed to have the upper hand and although Mr Mac was an excellent swordsman, he was taking small wounds. Cuts began to appear on his upper arms and chest where Mike's efforts had drawn blood and this gave him a glimmer of hope.

Mr Mac allowed him to think that he was in control. Cleverly playing Mike, he drew out the last of his energy before moving in for the kill.

Suddenly Mike missed his footing and stumbling on the loose gravel he lunged forward in a bid to maintain his balance, the tip of his blade finding nothing he was no longer in a position to defend himself.

When it came the blow took him by surprise, the razor edge of Mr Mac's sword slashed through muscle in his upper arm and Mike swore between clenched teeth. A burning sensation ripped through his shoulder as he staggered backwards but somehow he managed to remain on his feet. Bringing his sword up he fought back with renewed energy but he was giving ground fast, beaten backwards by superior swordsmanship.

Blow after blow rained down in an attack that was relentless and each time their blades clashed Mike lost a little more of his strength. The effort of sustaining such a dance in his depleted condition was beginning to tell, his arm was numb with the shock and the pain in his chest was sickening. He would have to finish this soon before his body gave up completely.

Desperately he searched for a weakness but Mr Mac was in prime condition, he was a powerful man and drawing deeply on his reserve Mike moved forward catching his opponent off guard. Jabbing with his sword, he managed to regain a few steps but his efforts were frustrated as Mr Mac simply sidestepped and fought back.

Mike's heart was hammering against his fractured ribs and he began to panic. His head was pounding with the effort and his eyesight was fading as wave upon wave of dizziness threatened to overcome him.

Mr Mac, suddenly twisting his wrist moved in fast swinging his blade in a wide, flat arc. Mike felt no pain, time simply stood still as the sword in his hand became incredibly heavy. He could no longer hold onto it and letting it drop he fell to his knees as exhaustion and shock finally overcame him.

Slowly a burning sensation spread through his abdomen and his face twisted as the pain grew in intensity. He realised that he had received a mortal blow and pushing his hands up against his stomach, he could feel hot blood pumping through his fingers and looking down his eyes widened in disbelief.

Mr Mac stood over him his chest rising and falling rapidly, and leaning against his sword he was the victor enjoying every moment of his triumph.

There was no one left to save the girls from this monster and tears of frustration ran freely over Mike's cheeks. His face screwed up as a fresh wave of pain spread throughout his body, he had failed and he hated himself.

Mr Mac, moving forward pulled a dagger from his belt and began to laugh, he seemed to know what Mike was thinking and stepping up behind him grabbed a handful of hair and wrenched his head backwards. Looking into his eyes, he moved closer savouring the moment and pushing his face up close began to whisper in Mike's ear.

At first, the words were meaningless, just another muddled noise whirling around inside his head but with an effort he forced himself to listen and suddenly they began to make sense.

Mr Mac told him how much he had enjoyed having Josie, he laughed and jeered, taunting him with the details and then he told him exactly what he was going to do to her next.

Mike, struggling with anger and shock wanted to kill the man who was filling his head with such filth but then he felt the sting of a blade being drawn across his throat. For a few seconds everything remained clear but as his life drained away, the last thing he saw was a monster staring down at him.

Mr Mac grinned and licked his lips.

Chapter
THIRTY TWO

Tim drove the car quickly along country lanes leading towards Montague Villa and Kate sat nervously beside him. Outwardly she appeared calm but was worried about how he would react once he discovered what was going on up at the house.

Unwelcome thoughts regarding Josie's emotional state nagged at her constantly but Kate had to remain strong, she was reluctant to experience any more of the torment that her friend was suffering. She was even more unwilling to share her feelings with Tim and, staring out of the window, kept herself busy by watching the passing scenery.

The house looked innocent enough nestling on the hillside its white stonework shining brilliantly. Kate knew it was just an illusion and glancing nervously at Tim she could not tell what he was thinking. He appeared composed but she knew him better than that, inside he must be in turmoil. They had not discussed the details or speculated on the horrors that they might encounter but he had seen the pictures that Josie had been sent.

"Are you ready for this?" The sound of his voice startled her and she wondered if he had been reading her thoughts.

"Yes I think so, let's get it over with."

They left the car at the front of the house where the staircase curved its way up to the front door and, following the gravel driveway on foot, made their way towards the courtyard behind the house. They went in silence, both lost in their own thoughts.

There was no evidence of occupation but it seemed wise to check out the grounds before attempting to enter the building. Kate shuddered as she observed the heavy the wooden shutters that covered the ground floor windows, she thought the building cheerless and it left her cold. Glancing at the widows higher up, she could see the clear blue sky reflecting in the glass.   She would rather be anywhere else but here, going into the house was the last thing she wanted to do.

Steering her mind back to the task in hand she assumed that the principle bedrooms would be found on the first floor, the smaller attic windows that she could see at the top of the house must once have been occupied by the servants. Looking up at the roof, she could see the low parapet running around the edge just above the gutter and wondered if the roof was accessible. She knew that in other large houses like this there were narrow access pathways running all over the rooftops. She studied the grey slate roof for a moment longer before returning to the front of the house where she found Tim.

He was at the top of the stone steps scrutinising the huge wooden door.

"This must be where Josie's aunt was shot." He said grimly, pointing to the marks made by lead shot scoring the stonework. There were fresh grooves in the door from where splinters had been torn, the lighter coloured wood beneath the darkened surface now revealed.

"Do you think we should go in through here?" Tim looked at his sister.

"I thought we'd decided not to use the front door, you know what happened to Josie's aunt."

"Well apart from smashing in a shuttered window I can't see any other way in," he snapped. "Just look at the place it's like a medieval fortress."

She knew that he was right and placing her hand against the door, traced her fingers over the wood, the ancient graining was as hard as steel.

"He might have set a trap," Tim said his voice softer this time.

"No he wouldn't be expecting an assault through here."

Reaching above his head Tim felt around the top of the doorframe searching for any weak points but the door was as secure as the shuttered windows.

"How do you think we are going to open it?" Tim asked, taking a step back.

"I can." She sounded confident. "It's only as secure as its locks."

Tim grunted and turning away moved towards the top step.

"Wait." The tone of her voice stopped him.

"What about an alarm system?" He said turning to face her.

"We'll worry about that once we're in besides, he won't be expecting us to have a key." She pulled something from her pocket.

In her hand was a small flat silver object and twisting its base she pressed it up against the brass escution plate.

"There are two locks on this door," she told him.

"How do you know that?"

Glancing up at him, she grinned before pointing to the key hole lower down.

"What's that thing?" he asked nodding at the little box that she was holding against the lock.

"It's a light amplification by stimulated emission radiation unit."

"A laser!" he raised his eyebrows.

"Oh it's just something I knocked up, thought it might come in handy one day."

Suddenly the huge mortise lock clicked and she grinned with satisfaction then turning her attention to the second lock, it was not long before the door swung open.

"How did you manage that?" Tim was amazed.

"By stimulating matter," she shrugged her shoulders.

With a shake of his head, he wondered if the thing could be used as a weapon.

Once inside they spent little time admiring the grand staircase or the family paintings.

"Maybe he has her in a room upstairs." Tim started across the hall towards the staircase.

"No."

He stopped suddenly and turned back towards her.

"She's in the cellar."

"How do you know that?" he frowned.

"Women's intuition," she wanted to tell him what else she knew but she couldn't.

Leading the way it was as if she was a regular visitor to the house. She took him along the darkened corridor where she could feel Josie's presence; it was all around her and seemed to intensify with every step she took.

Suddenly there was a noise from up ahead and they froze. Kate almost cried out when a firm hand grasped her by the shoulder and pulled her roughly from the passageway into a side room. Standing close behind her Tim whispered encouragement into her ear and resting his hand lightly against the door listened as the figure in the corridor passed close by.

Kate's breathing was ragged, she was afraid the noise would give them away so holding her breath, she watched wide eyed as Tim edged open the door. They could hear the man muttering to himself as he made his way along the corridor.

"Greg MacLaren," she whispered recognising his voice.

"He's talking to himself," Tim said holding his face close to hers.

"Probably responding to the voices in his head."

Tim threw her a questioning glance then easing the door open grabbed her by the hand and led her from the room. It took every ounce of her nerve to stop from fleeing the house.

She was painfully aware of what would happen if Greg MacLaren got his hands on her. She also knew that she would not be able to cope with the punishment that Josie had endured. The possibility of that happening did not bear thinking about so she focussed her mind on sending Josie a message of hope.

Tim stopped suddenly and indicated towards a narrow flight of steps.

"The cellar," he whispered.

She nodded and following him closely, they made their way down into the darkness.

Filled with dread she held back and began to imagine all kinds of horrors ahead. She wondered how Tim would react, in a few moments she would know.

Tim found the door and pushing his ear up against it could hear faint noises coming from the room beyond. As it swung open, the full extent of the horrors was revealed.

Josie, chained against a wall like a victim from a horror story was naked, her body covered in bites and bruises.

"Josie," Tim cried, he could hardly believe his eyes.

Her red-rimmed eyes widened with shock the moment she saw him and she gasped, he was the last person she expected to see.

Moving reluctantly into the cellar Kate could see another girl curled up on the ground. She was also naked and her thin shoulders twitched as she sobbed. In an instant Kate was at her side and crouching down did her best to comfort her.

Tim glanced at his sister his mind reeling.

"What the hell!" he growled his initial shock turning to anger.

He looked again at Josie who remained silent, from the expression on her face and her physical condition he could see that she had been through hell. Words seemed inadequate as he laid his hand gently against her cheek.

"Take over from me here." His sister's voice cut through his despair. "Comfort her if you can but find something to cover her with first. I need to work on these chains."

Moving quickly, Kate wanted to get out of there as soon as possible, the thought of being caught in the cellar filled her with dread. Already the walls were beginning to close in around her but she managed to hold back her fear.

Glancing at the rags that were scattered over the floor, Tim could hardly believe that these were the remains of their clothing. Picking up a blanket that he found discarded in a corner he wrapped it carefully around the girl's shoulders and the moment she looked up he saw a glimmer of recognition in her eyes. Supporting her gently he helped her to her feet.

"Tim Granger," she whispered and for the first time since her abduction, Sarah smiled.

Kate had already used her laser on the chain that secured Sarah's left leg and was now working on the shackles holding Josie. As soon as she was free, Josie slumped forward, her legs no longer able to support her. Kate, staggering under the weight of her friend, grunted as she lowered her carefully to the ground. She was appalled by Josie's injuries and began to rub life back into her frozen hands, careful to avoid the places chafed raw by the shackles.

"Come on," Tim urged. "We'd better get out of here." Shrugging off his jacket, he pulled it round Josie's shoulders guiding her arms carefully into the sleeves.

She was aware of his presence but avoided making eye contact with him she was still in too much shock.

Kate struggled to support Josie who found the first few steps excruciating. Her legs refused to work properly and there was a dull ache niggling at the small of her back.

Tim helped Sarah who seemed stronger. "Do you need me to take over with Josie?" he said glancing back towards his sister.

Kate didn't need to answer, the look on her face told him all he needed to know. Josie required the comfort of another woman so it was Sarah who dropped back to help them leaving Tim to scout the way ahead.

He realised that if they were discovered in the house there would be little chance of defending themselves and it seemed to be taking forever as they made their way slowly along the long corridor.

As soon as they arrived in the hallway Tim grabbed at the brass handle and hauled open the door, between them Kate and Sarah hurried Josie out onto the stone steps and down onto the driveway. Resting for a moment, they re-grouped on the lawn in front of the house.

Josie seemed stronger now and her sprit lifted the moment she saw sunlight. Moving away from Kate she reached out for Tim and slipping her hand into his, they made their way towards the car.

Glancing at her sideways Tim held her gaze before she looked away. She did not want him to see her like this but he looked so distressed and she couldn't just ignore him. Until then she believed that rescue was impossible, she had resigned herself to the worst but now it was as if she had suddenly woken from a terrible nightmare. Tim and Kate had appeared from out of nowhere and still she had no idea how they had achieved it.

The car was standing on the driveway just a few yards away and to Josie it was such a beautiful thing. It represented the rest of her life, an image of salvation, her chariot back to the real world.

Kate arrived at the car first and wrenched open the door as Josie and Sarah threw themselves onto the back seat. Tim fumbled in his pockets searching for the ignition key before slipping in behind the wheel and with unsteady hands engaged the key.

Kate looked back over her shoulder fearful that MacLaren would be somewhere close behind them. It would not be long before he discovered that the girls were missing and scanning the windows she sighed with relief, he was nowhere to be seen.

Tim turned the key, desperate for the engine to start but it took a while for him to realise that something was wrong, the engine refused to turn over.

Leaping from the car he tore open the bonnet and peered into the engine bay. The cables connecting the battery had been cut effectively disabling the car and his stomach lurched. Not only did MacLaren know they were there but he was also playing games with them.

Dropping the bonnet back into place he glanced fearfully around before turning to face his sister. With Rufus Stone's warning echoing clearly through his head, he moved quickly. Going to the rear of the car, he pulled open the boot lid, Kate appeared beside him and he told her what had happened.

Efficiently they organised themselves gathering up a raincoat and two pairs of wellington boots. Tim realised that one pair would be too big but the girls needed something to protect their bare feet.

Kate felt uneasy, the hairs stood up on the back of her neck and she could feel her skin begin to crawl. She knew they were being watched, she could feel his eyes boring into her but she could not tell from where he was likely to come. Pulling her cell phone from her pocket her fingers danced clumsily over the keys then flicking back her hair she held it to her ear.

Suddenly an explosion split the air and she was thrown forward onto the gravel. Tim, knocked off his feet, landed heavily on his face beside the car as the side window shattered.

"Tim," Kate screamed, "are you alright?"

Heaving herself up she went to where he had fallen and throwing herself down beside him placed her hand on his shoulder.

"I'm okay," he groaned.

The noise of the explosion left him reeling, it was as if bells were ringing loudly inside his head.

Grabbing a handful of his shirt, Kate helped him to his feet and they crouched low behind the car. She was certain that the shot had come from the bushes to their left, and glancing over her shoulder was satisfied that both Josie and Sarah were safe. They were using the car as a shield.

"He obviously doesn't want us to leave the party," Tim grinned.

The immediate danger had passed but he felt sure MacLaren was biding his time, waiting for them to make their next move.

Tim checked to see that the girls were unhurt. They were going to have to make a run for it, they could hardly remain huddled behind the car indefinitely.

Popping his head up, he studied the way ahead and did not like what he saw. Whichever way they went they would have to cross open ground, they would be vulnerable, exposed to the dangers of further gunshots before they could hope to reach cover. He estimated the distance to the boundary fence, it would take a while for them to reach the other side of the lawn but it was their only realistic option. If they keep going down into the valley, he guessed they would eventually end up somewhere near Spey Bay and once there it should be possible to find some help. He considered his strategy before outlining his plan to Kate.

"If we make a run for it as a group and he shoots with both barrels it's likely we'll all be hit."

"We should go one at a time that way we'll offer him smaller targets and if we run quickly..." She didn't need to complete her sentence.

Tim didn't like it one bit, the odds were stacked against them and he felt certain that at least one of them would be hit whilst attempting to cross the open ground.

"Head for a different spot along the boundary fence," he began. "Once in the cover of the trees we'll re-group." Doing his best to sound confident, he glanced at each one of them in turn.

They nodded in agreement then Sarah went first. She covered ground at a surprising pace weaving as she ran and with knees bent, kept low to the ground.

Five seconds later Tim watched as Josie limped away at a much slower pace. Holding his breath, he fully expected the shotgun to go off and bring her down but she made it safely across the lawn, only then could he breathe easily.

He touched Kate's shoulder and she leapt away like a sprinter out of blocks. She reached the fence in record time and throwing herself over landed heavily before disappearing into the long grass.

Now it was his turn. The moment he left the cover of the car Tim felt his panic begin to rise, he knew that he was the prime target. MacLaren was sure to think him more of a threat than the girls, he was expendable, he had no use for him.

In no time at all he arrived at the boundary fence and flinging himself over began to crawl face down until he reached the cover of the long grass. His breath was ragged as he searched for the girls and he groaned with relief when he found them huddled together at the base of a huge tree. He was amazed that they had all made it; now all he had to do was get them away from this place.

The bay was at least five miles away and they were ill equipped for a cross-country trek, both Josie and Sarah were exhausted they were also carrying injuries but there was nothing he could do about that. Pushing these unwelcome thoughts from his mind, he crawled from the cover of the bushes and discovered a pathway running through the trees.

"I lost my mobile phone by the car." Kate told him as she came up on his shoulder.

"I know and I left mine in the car," he chewed at his bottom lip. "Look, if I can make it back to the house maybe I could telephone for help."

Glancing at him, she shook her head. "I've been thinking the same thing. I'll go, besides they need you."

Tim was appalled by her suggestion. "You know what he'll do to you." The moment the words left his mouth, he regretted saying them.

Fixing him with a determined stare Kate did her best to hide her fear.

"Then I must find a phone quickly or you'll have to come back to fetch me," she swallowed noisily. "Besides, he'll keep me alive for a while at least, that's more than he'll do with you."

He thought about what she had just said and knew that she was right. They were being hunted, both Josie and Sarah would slow them up but by drawing MacLaren away, their chances of escape would improve significantly.

"Be careful." Reaching out, he touched her arm affectionately and hated himself for letting her go. He knew it was wrong, Rufus Stone had given him a clear warning and he could not help feeling that he was failing his sister. Kate in exchange for Josie and Sarah, it did not seem fair.

"Right," he said, banishing these thoughts from his mind. "Once you've called for help lock yourself somewhere in the house or in one of the outbuildings. When Josie and Sarah are safe I'll come back for you." His words flowed smoothly and his positive tone filled her with courage.

Squeezing his shoulder Kate smiled at him and her small white teeth flashed.

As she moved away, she glanced back over her shoulder just before the others disappeared from view. At the same moment, Josie looked up and their eyes met. Kate had never seen Josie like this before, her expression was haunting, she was pale and drawn and she had been through hell. Even from this distance, Kate could feel the emotional torment that surrounded her friend and it was then she realised that Josie had not yet uttered a word. In the next instant, she was gone, and Kate, left alone shook her head and sighed. She would have to remain alert if she were to avoid capture.

The undergrowth surrounding her was thick and unnervingly silent, there were no birds singing and no small animals rustling in the under-growth, she was utterly alone. Suddenly a branch snapped close by, it sounded like a small explosion in the stillness and she froze, peering around nervously. Holding her breath, she searched for the source of the noise and at the same time focussing her mind, she reached out. Cautiously testing the air she begged the spirits of the trees for their help and drawing on their strength, cast her mind outwards in ever widening circles. It was not long before she could feel him, wave upon wave of dark emotions poured into her head and she was shocked. His mind had deteriorated since their first encounter and now he seemed to be on the verge of madness, she shuddered, he was a very dangerous man.

He was somewhere close but she could not see him, hopefully that would mean that he could not see her either, so crouching down even lower she pressed herself into the undergrowth. She would have to be more careful, his poisonous thoughts were powerful, far stronger than she had imagined and she would have to protect herself from becoming overwhelmed. It was imperative that she have contact with him on an unconscious level, this was one of the tools in her arsenal, she had to know what he was thinking in order to outwit him, so taking a deep breath she tried again. This time she was more cautious and emptying her mind of negative thoughts, surrounded herself with purifying light before setting up barriers that he would find difficult to penetrate. Only then did she begin casting around, she wanted to open up a channel between them and almost immediately she could feel him. He seemed to understand what she was doing and it excited him. Kate was appalled to discover that he was so receptive; this was not a good sign. His powers were more developed than she had imagined, he could use them against her, get inside her head and anticipate her moves. This was a very daunting thought, one that she had not bargained for.

Drawing back quickly she reinforced the protective barriers surrounding her. She knew he planned to kill Tim she also knew that he wanted to play. He was intending to halt their progress, turn them back towards the house and haunt them all the way.

It was his hatred towards her that she found most disturbing, she had no idea that he loathed her so much. Shaking her head in disbelief, she had to get moving so cautiously she made her way back towards the fence and found the spot where they had crossed earlier. She was certain that he was unaware that they had split up and she smiled, for now at least she had a small advantage.

Glancing over her shoulder, Kate studied the trees, he could be hiding behind any one of them and she could feel his energy, he was much closer than she had realised. Suddenly he was there inside her mind and she was appalled. She could feel him breaching her defences and filling her head with obscenities. It was just a game to him, a game that she was unwilling to play, so rallying her strength, she managed to push him out.

Her heart was thumping wildly and she was breathless, she had never known anyone with such mental strength before, the only thing in her favour was that his psychological powers were underdeveloped. It would be like dealing with a child but she would have to remain cautious, he might be child-like but he could prove to be a very dangerous adversary.

Moving cautiously like a cat stalking a mouse, she knew that as soon as he realised she was alone she would become the hunted. She had to put some distance between them, entering the house would not pose a problem, there were no physical barriers to overcome this time but going back in there was not something that she was keen to dwell on. Tim was right of course, the house was full of places to hide but she would be much happier once she had contacted the police. Until then she would just have to outwit him.

When the blast came, it split the air around them and knocked Sarah off her feet. Burying her face into the damp leaf mould, she clawed at the earth with her fingertips wishing that it would swallow her up. The moment her initial shock had eased, she realised that if he were going to kill her then he would have done it by now. Turning her head to one side, she could see Tim; he was lying on the edge of the clearing with his back towards her.

"Tim," she called out, and crawling to where he lay, reached out and touched him.

She was stunned, his shirt was soaking up blood from several ugly wounds in his back and looking around nervously, she swallowed down her panic. They were on their own in a small clearing between the trees and she would have to deal with the situation herself. Touching his neck, she felt for a pulse and not once did she stop whispering words of encouragement.

"Sarah," he groaned softly.

She could hardly hear him at first but as he opened his eyes, she watched as they focused on her face.

"Where's Josie?"

Sarah glanced around the clearing, there was no sign of her and with guilt tugging at her heart, she had not spared a thought for her friend.

"Go," he told her, his voice gaining in strength. "Head towards the river, you should be able to find someone in the bay." Swallowing noisily as a wave of pain swept over him, he almost lost consciousness.

"Leave me," he insisted. "You must get away from here, find help."

She could hardly find the courage to do as he said but she knew he was right and rising reluctantly to her feet she glanced around once more, fixing the location in her head. She must remember where she had left him, only then did she begin to run.

All she could think of was Tim, she had never seen such wounds before and was afraid that he might die. These thoughts spurred her on, the last thing she wanted was the death of another friend on her conscience. Tears gushed over her cheeks as she realised that Mr Mac could return at any time to finish him off.

Kate heard the second shot as she emerged from the woods but she did not allow it to distract her. The house was in sight with only the

265

lawn separating her from the telephone. The urge to head back into the woods was almost overpowering because she knew instinctively that Tim was hurt. His pain and frustration swept over her in waves and all she wanted to do was go to him. Pushing these urges aside she launched herself from cover and sprinted across the lawn.

The front door was open just as they had left it, and passing the car, she glanced at the spot where she had dropped her mobile phone but it was gone. Sliding to a stop and kicking up gravel, she ducked inside the car to look for Tim's phone but that was missing too. Abandoning her search she bounded up the stone steps and bursting into the hall slipped on the polished tiled floor. Picking herself up, she glanced around quickly before deciding which way to go. There were several doors leading off the hallway and starting with the nearest she began throwing them open checking each room in turn.

Pausing for breath, she tucked a loose strand of hair behind her ear, this was taking too much time so she began to scan her surroundings logically. The corridor ran the length of the house going in both directions and hesitating, she had no idea which way to go. Taking a deep breath, she attempted to slow her racing heart, and searching for a clue found nothing to help her find her way. It crossed her mind that there might not be a telephone in the house at all, perhaps he relied on mobile phones.

Lifting her chin, she focussed her senses and realised that something had changed. She could feel him, he knew where she was and he was coming for her. Like a bloodhound, he had located her scent and was now sniffing her out. She did not have much time, he must not be allowed to catch her, she knew what to expect if he did and she shuddered. She would rather die than let him get his hands on her.

Hurling herself along the corridor she relied on her instincts, there must be an office or a study located somewhere in the house and as she went she tried all the doors until at last she found one that was unlocked. It led into a large workspace, it was an ancient kitchen that resembled some kind of time capsule, it looked as if it had not been used for years.

Rushing forward she danced around a heavy wooden table that stood in the middle of the floor and on the far side of the kitchen she could see a door. The word 'Office' was stencilled in black lettering on a white panel and racing towards it, she discovered that it was locked. Reaching into her pocket, she pulled out her laser and with shaking fingers made some adjustments to the settings before holding it against the locking mechanism. A few moments later, there was an audible click and the door swung open.

Standing on a desk in the middle of the office was what she was looking for. With no time to lose, she rushed in and snatched up the receiver, there was a ring tone and hurriedly she began to dial a number.

Speaking rapidly into the phone she begged for help. The man on the other end of the line was reassuringly efficient but it was not until she mentioned the name William Randolph that she was taken seriously. His attitude changed immediately and with a sigh of relief, she knew that at last she was getting somewhere, this however was short lived because suddenly the line went dead.

Kate froze, her whole body trembling with nerves she took a deep breath and exhaled slowly in an effort to calm herself but it had no effect. Mr Mac had arrived and he knew exactly where to find her. Dropping the receiver onto the table, she fled from the room. She had to get as far away as possible but as she went, it was with a feeling of doom. He was bound to find her wherever she went, it was only a matter of time. She would have to keep moving, try to stay one step ahead, that was the only way to survive.

Rufus Stone heard both shots and stony faced he glared at the trees at the edge of the meadow. No one would be hunting in the woods today, he thought and poaching with a gun was most unlikely.

His Land Rover was parked on the bank beside the river, he had driven as far as the path would allow and was now preparing to strike out on foot.

His movements were sure and swift as he lifted his hunting rifle over the tailgate, and running his hand over the mechanism, he smiled as if acknowledging an old friend.

He began loading rounds into the weapon and grunting with grim satisfaction checked the sight against some distant target before slinging the rifle over his shoulder. Pulling a hat from his pocket, he rammed it on his head and last of all secured his vehicle before setting off with the vigour of a man half his age.

Earlier he had been at the hospital waiting for news of Molly, and only when he was satisfied that he could do no more did he return home to collect his things. He made a telephone call to an old friend stationed at the RAF base at Lossiemouth, if he was going to have to pay a visit to Montague Villa, he wanted to have someone he could trust covering his back.

His conversation with Tim Granger left him in no doubt that he was going to take his sister to the house and Rufus could not let these young people go in alone. There was going to be trouble, he was certain of that.

This was the moment he had been waiting for, William Randolph had to be stopped, he had been allowed to get away with it for too long.

Rufus made his decision based on years of experience, going in covertly through the forest would not only bring him to the rear of the Montague estate but the trees would offer him cover, besides anyone fleeing from the house on foot would most likely come this way.

The moment he entered the forest his senses sharpened and he experienced the thrill of the hunt. Suddenly he was a young man again and straining his ears, he listened for unusual noises amongst the trees, especially the sound of cries of distress. Further along the path a pheasant broke from cover and Rufus laughed as it rattled out a warning.

Hefting his rifle from his shoulder, he weighed it expertly, in his hands it was an effective weapon and despite advancing years he was still an expert shot. Thumbing off the safety catch, he continued along the narrow path that wound its way through the trees. Apart from a light breeze playing through the treetops there were no other sounds so he moved forward in silence.

The further he walked the darker his surroundings became and as the undergrowth thickened, light failed to reach the forest floor so dense was the canopy above his head. Broad leaves and cross-stitched branches formed a living shelter, a world where red squirrels and birds lived. Rarely did these creatures drop down to the forest floor, the earth surrounding the trees was covered in a carpet of moss and lichen, nothing else would grow in this twilight world.

Suddenly without warning, a figure stumbled onto the pathway ahead and he dropped into the prone position. Pulling the butt of his rifle into his shoulder, his finger brushed the trigger instinctively and his brain analysed the shape that filled his sights, he was prepared to use the weapon.

The moment she saw him Sarah cried out and collapsed, her world turned black and losing consciousness she lay still.

Rufus scanned right then left, the muzzle of his weapon tracking with his eyesight until he was satisfied that she was alone, only then did he relax and begin to move forward. As he approached the young woman, he could see that she was exhausted, her face was pale and there were dark shadows around her eyes. She was dressed in nothing more than a coarse woollen blanket and a pair of wellington boots.

"My word," he exclaimed and crouching down beside her, he shouldered his rifle and helped her up into the sitting position.

Startled by his touch she cried out as her eyes fluttered open.

"Don't be alarmed my dear I'm here to help you." It was obvious to Rufus that she was in considerable distress but as he spoke, her terror turned to relief.

"Are you with Mr Granger?"

Her eyes widened at the sound of Tim's name and she nodded in response.

Leaning back on his haunches Rufus smiled and pulled a water bottle from his pocket, holding it to her lips he encouraged her to drink.

"Tim has been injured." She whispered breathlessly as soon as she was finished drinking. She told him that they were being hunted and Tim had been shot.

"Right young lady, I think you'd better show me where he is. Do you think you can do that?"

He watched as she glanced over her shoulder and her eyes became wild with fear.

"Don't worry," he reassured her. "You'll be quite safe." He helped her to her feet.

They heard Tim before they saw him, the sound of his groaning reached out towards them. He was lying in a clearing between the trees and before Sarah had chance to rush to his side Rufus placed a restraining hand on her shoulder. Using simple hand signals, he told her that she must remain where she was and keep very quiet, he wanted to be sure the way ahead was clear and they were not walking into a trap. Silently he disappeared into the undergrowth and circled their position.

Sarah looked on helplessly as Tim writhed painfully on the forest floor. She was appalled and was desperate to go to him but she had to wait, do as the man said and remain hidden. It seemed an age before he reappeared, he was smiling and together they made their way towards Tim.

Throwing herself down beside him Sarah tended his wounds using the field dressings that Rufus produced from his pocket. He was satisfied that Tim was in no immediate danger, he might have lost a lot of blood but he was young and strong.

"Can you stand?" Rufus asked.

Tim nodded and gritting his teeth pushed through his pain. He managed to struggle to his feet but stumbled against Sarah, putting his arm around her shoulders, he leaned against her and slowly they made their way towards the forest path.

"Take your time and keep moving, go along the path towards the meadow. Someone will be waiting there to help you." Reaching out he touched them both and smiling with encouragement was gone.

Josie was bowled over by the blast as red-hot streaks filled the air around her. The sound of tearing leaves and the dull thud of lead shot stripping bark from the trees terrified her and as soon as she hit the floor she rolled into a ball and covered her head with her arms. She could do nothing more but wait for him to come.

Nothing happened and after a while her hearing returned to normal. Opening her eyes she wondered if it was safe to get up, time seemed to stand still and all around was silent so raising her head, she glanced up before climbing cautiously to her feet, it was then that she saw him.

He was standing to one side waiting patiently for her to move and as her eyes widened he grinned and licked his lips.

Kate was moving quickly through the house using her senses to help guide her way. She was terrified and her stomach cramped at the thought of being caught but pushing her fears aside she scanned her immediate surroundings. She was desperate to locate him only then could she avoid him. Suddenly there was movement from the corridor ahead, dodging sideways she slipped into a room and closing the door pushed up against it. Her heart missed a beat as she fought to control her breathing. Nervously grasping the brass handle her fist closed around it tightly and she pressed her ear to the wooden panel. There was movement coming from the corridor, Mr Mac was muttering to himself, he seemed to be struggling with something.

Josie was in no condition to resist as he dragged her back to the house, she knew how violent he could be and he also had a gun. She had little choice but to accept the fact that she was once again his prisoner. There was however a glimmer of hope, Tim's sister Kate had gone off to raise the alarm and Josie was left in no doubt that help would arrive soon. Kate was an extraordinary woman who would achieve her objective.

Kate could hear a voice and her eyes widened in shock, clearly it was a woman in distress and backing away from the door, she searched desperately for somewhere to hide. Gripped by fear she was convinced that at any moment he would come crashing into the room, she had to get out.

Crossing the room, she drew back the lock that held one of the window casements, the mechanism was stiff and it complained noisily as she pushed the sliding sash upwards. The outside shutters were closed and with trembling fingers, she fumbled with the catch. The moment it was released the shutters swung open and she slipped out over the window ledge. Lowering herself down into the flowerbed, she kept her back pressed up against the wall and made her way towards the corner of the house.

Peering gingerly round the cornerstone she had a clear view along the front of the house. To her left thick vegetation flanked the driveway and not far away, partially hidden by the bushes, their car stood disabled on the drive. This she observed in an instant and feeling her way along the length of the house she stumbled over small bushes and flowers that were growing in the border.

Glancing into the distance, she longed for the sound of sirens. By now the police should be speeding towards the house but all was disconcertingly silent. There was no one else around, she may as well have been alone, the only person on the estate.

Suddenly without warning a shutter crashed open and she screamed, leaping into the air she threw herself clear of the wall and ran.

"I can see you!" Mr Mac chanted in the voice of a child and leaning out of the open window, he laughed.

Fleeing across the flowerbed she dashed blindly across the lawn, the hairs on the back of neck bristling and her muscles tense. She was convinced that at any moment she would be shot, but nothing happened. Risking a glance over her shoulder, she could see that he was gone. The window where he had been moments before was empty, and stopping to catch her breath, she considered her next move. Without too much thought, she started back towards the house and with hardly a change of stride launched herself in through the open window.

Landing heavily she rolled to a stop on the carpet then scrambled to her feet. The door leading from the room was open and she froze. Holding her breath, she strained her ears but could hear nothing coming from the corridor so pressing her back up against the wall, she took a few moments to regain her breath.

Mr Mac grinned and licked his lips. Observing her from his hiding place, he silently congratulated himself for correctly anticipating her next move. He knew that she would not be able to resist the open

271

window and was impressed by her swift arrival; she was proving to be far more entertaining than he had expected. He was looking forward to teasing her for a little longer before killing them both.

Josie had been dumped in the cellar with her hands bound securely behind her back. He had not bothered to chain her to the wall so struggling to sit up, she took stock of her situation. Something was happening beyond the door, she could hear muffled sounds coming from the corridor, suddenly she heard a woman scream then the door crashed open and Kate fell to the floor. Before she had chance to recover he was upon her, wrenching her arms cruelly above her head, he lifted her easily off her feet and expertly shackled her wrists. He tightened the chains and Kate cried out as pain seared through her joints. She was suspended against the wall and her worst nightmare was about to begin.

Moving in he secured her ankles and managed to avoid her desperate efforts as she kicked out. When he was finished he played some slack into the chains, lowering her until her feet touched the ground and tying off the loose ends, he stood back to admire his work.

Kate was in agony as pain shot through her joints and it was all she could do to stop from crying out. Her eyes widened with shock as suddenly she felt him inside her head. He was using some kind of psychological technique to undermine the balance of her mind and in her weakened state found it impossible to block him out. Struggling desperately to close off the link, she resigned herself to the fact that he might have her physically but she was determined that he would never invade her mind.

Closing her eyes tightly she frowned with concentration and did not see the knife as it appeared in his hand. In one swift movement, he lunged forward pushing her up against the wall. Kate screamed out as the chains tightened pinching her skin cruelly between the links, and straining against him, she opened her eyes. The blade flashed menacingly as he began cutting away at her blouse and flinging the ruined fabric aside, he started on her trousers. Holding herself rigid she dared not move, the blade was cold against her skin and the thought of it slicing into her was terrifying.

Josie's head was pounding and reeling with shock she couldn't allow this to happen, she must do something to help Tim's sister. Although she was helpless with her hands tied behind her back, she rolled onto her back and kicked her legs into the air. Gasping with the effort she twisted her arms down under the small of her back and almost dislocated her shoulders then, slipping her wrists over her ankles the manoeuvre was complete, her arms were now in front of her.

Mr Mac was standing with his back to her admiring his work and Kate was beside herself with grief.

Josie scrambled awkwardly to her feet determined to stop him from having his way and as she looked at Kate their eyes met. Her face was distorted by revulsion but she was desperately trying to tell her something. At first Josie couldn't make it out, the message was unclear but following her gaze she saw a small silver object lying on the floor. Rushing towards it, she picked it up. It was heavier than she expected, about the size of a small mobile phone the screen was smaller and there were not as many buttons. Josie had no idea what it was, or what she was expected to do with it.

"Hold it against the rope, twist the knob then press the red button. Make sure it's pointing away from you."

The instructions were clear enough and as Josie did as she was told the rope binding her wrists fell away. The metallic object vibrating between her fingers became warm to touch and she could feel a concentration of energy running through it.

Amazingly, Mr Mac was oblivious to all of this, his attention was fixed on Kate. Suddenly his hands were all over her body tearing at the remains of her clothing and Kate screamed as he pressed himself up against her. It was then that Josie realised she could use the object as a weapon. The invisible beam of light had cut through the rope with ease so it would do the same to him. Without thinking, she stepped up behind him and pressed it against his back and when she pushed the button the effect was instantaneous. Like a wounded beast he reared up. Throwing his arms into the air, he knocked Josie off her feet and reaching backwards, his fingers probing at the wound, he fully expected to find the hilt of a knife sticking out of his flesh. The stench of burning flesh hung sharply on the air and with the echo of his screams bouncing off the walls he turned towards his attacker.

Josie was stunned, she just had time to protect her head with her arms before the onslaught began. Lashing out he punched her with his fists and the force of the blows drove her backwards against the wall. She was helpless, she could do nothing to protect herself and closing her eyes she waited for him to plunge his knife into her body but suddenly the attack ceased then he was gone.

She almost vomited and as her legs turned to jelly tears streamed endlessly over her face. Collapsing with shock and exhaustion onto the cold concrete floor it was a while before she was able to pull herself upright. She was in agony and all she wanted to do was lay there curled up in a ball. Her body was covered in ugly red wheals and bruises but she had to move, he could return at any moment.

Kate was horrified by his outburst of violence and could hardly believe that it had just happened. Never had she witnessed anything like this before and she felt sickened.

Josie dry retched and her stomach compressed deeply into her abdomen. When she was able, she regained her breath then began to tremble. She was clinging perilously close to the edge of sanity and strangely, if it were not for the physical pain she would have slipped over the precipice.

"Josie."

Above the noises that whirled around in her head, she heard a familiar voice.

"Pick up the laser and set me free."

The anxiety in her friend's voice stunned her and she struggled to make sense of the words. Rubbing the hurt from her limbs, she leaned back against the wall, every muscle in her body was complaining.

"Pick up the laser please Josie get me out of these damn chains."

Josie, doing as she was told, wrapped her fingers around the silver object and picking it up moved unsteadily towards Kate. With shaking hands, she held the laser against the shackles before pushing the red button but nothing happened, there were no vibrations this time and no sensation of flowing energy.

"Adjust the setting." Kate was desperate.

"It's no use it must have been damaged." Josie said as she stood back.

Kate sobbed and her face twisted with terror, she was devastated.

"Don't let him touch me please Josie I can't cope with that." She was trembling so violently that the chains rattled against the wall.

Kate was helpless and no longer in control, her immediate future was in the hands of others and she did not like it one bit. It took her a few moments to gather her senses, the effort was debilitating and she hated herself for her lack of composure.

Glancing at Josie, she wondered how she had managed to hold herself together.

"I'm sorry," her voice was a whisper. "I managed to telephone the police earlier they should be here at any moment."

"Look." Josie said. "I'll just have to distract him until help arrives."

Kate nodded, she could say no more. Words were as hopeless as the broken laser that lay on the ground at her feet.

Chapter

THIRTY THREE

Josie scrambled up the steps leading from the cellar and paused at the top to listen. The house was as silent as a church and all she could hear was the sound blood rushing through her ears. He was nowhere to be seen, she could not even sense his evil presence close by, so launching herself along the corridor she headed towards the hallway.

The front door had been thrown open and pressing herself flat against the wall she edged close enough to peer out. He was standing on the lawn below shouting and raving like a man possessed, he seemed even more frightening as his voice echoed around the park. She could not make out what he was saying but he appeared to be having an intense argument with someone. Glancing cautiously round the doorframe, she moved slowly out onto the top step but there was no one else in sight. He was alone and the moment he turned, she could see an ugly wound in the centre of his back his skin scorched and blackened by the heat of the laser.

She had to make her move before he decided to return to the cellar. Heading down the steps and onto the gravel, she had to decide which way to go. With his back towards her, he had not yet seen her. She needed to attract his attention, she must draw him away, so squealing loudly she began to run. He spun round the moment he heard the sound and roaring menacingly started after her.

Stumbling on the loose surface, she careered round the corner of the house. She had no clear direction or plan, all she wanted to do was draw him away from the cellar and keep Kate safe, she also prayed that the police would arrive soon.

It did not take him long to close the gap between them and as he moved in she could hear him breathing heavily. A little way ahead was an ornamental dry stone wall and beyond that a grass lawn neatly laid out around a pretty flowerbed. The ground sloped gently away towards distant parkland and cresting the rise, she leapt over the wall and the garden opened up in front of her. In the distance, she could see the boundary fence, her mind processed this information quickly and careering over the neatly manicured lawn, she gained the cover of a small collection of shrubs and bushes. Pausing for breath, she risked a glance over her shoulder.

He was standing on top of the wall observing her from a distance. Not yet following her down onto the lawn, he matched her progress on the higher ground. He knew that she could see him so he waved casually. In his hand, he carried a long bladed knife and holding it up so Josie could see he turned the blade until it caught the sunlight.

Panic bubbled up from within her and with a little scream; she turned and fled. The ground continued to slope downwards towards the edge of the lawn and it was then she saw a brick structure built into a bank. At first, it looked like the entrance to a tunnel going under the boundary fence, changing direction she headed towards it.

At the mouth of the tunnel, she found a solid oak door blocking her way, and grasping at the iron ring pulled with all her strength. Glancing frantically over her shoulder, she could see him making his way towards her and with renewed effort strained even more, heaving at the door with all her strength until finally it yielded. Forcing her fingers into the gap between the edge of the door and the frame she levered it open a little more. The rusty hinges complained but finally she managed to squeeze in through the gap.

Inside it was very dark and moving away from the entrance, she kept close to the wall feeling for the uneven brickwork with her fingertips. The air was cold and damp, clammy against her skin and slipping on the cobbled floor, she fell heavily trapping her arm beneath her. The pain in her elbow was excruciating and as she cried out the sound bounced eerily off the walls.

Picking herself up she held her breath and strained her ears, she thought that she could hear him and suddenly he was there standing beside the door.

Moving deeper into the dungeon-like gloom she realised that it was not a tunnel at all, there was no light ahead. The darkness frightened her and the damp musty air was becoming difficult to breathe. The prospect of going any further unnerved her but she had no choice, she had to find a place to hide. Feeling her way forward she went cautiously into the darkness.

Crouching down low she made herself as small as possible and wondered what he would do next, she did not have to wait long. Pulling back the door, he squeezed in through the gap and disappeared.

Josie stifled a scream, she was trapped and alone with a madman who wanted to kill her. She began to think that it had been a grave mistake coming into this wretched place.

Rufus emerged from the forest just in time to see William Randolph disappear round the corner of the house. It was obvious that he was up to no good so scaling the perimeter fence Rufus hurried across the lawn after him. He reached the corner of the house as Randolph was striding down the slope and looking past him, he could see where he was heading. Rufus could make out the faded red brickwork built into the grass bank and it reminded him of the entrance to the underworld.

Lifting his rifle, he peered down the telescopic sight for a closer look. The heavy wooden door was partially open and he guessed that someone had passed that way recently.

"An old icehouse," he muttered to himself.

Swinging the muzzle of his rifle round slightly he aligned the cross hairs on the centre of Randolph's back but before he could get off a clear shot, he disappeared from view.

Rufus frowned and wondered what the man was doing running towards the icehouse. He would have to find out so breaking into a trot, made his way down the slope reaching for his torch as he went.

Josie shivered, the cold damp air was soaking into her bones and she shuddered as the cloying scent of mould and decay stuck at the back of her throat. She watched the entrance as clouds of condensation from her rapid breathing gathered around her head. This was a grim place in which to die, she thought, if he were to kill her here no one would find her body. Pushing these unwelcome thoughts from her mind, she focussed on the thin shaft of light that was coming from the entrance. She had no idea where he was, he vanished the moment he entered and had not yet made a sound.

The musty air was oppressive and Josie began to tremble, the darkness intensified around her and she found it increasingly difficult to hold back her panic, she simply had to get out.

Listening carefully she tried to locate him in the shadows but it was impossible to penetrate the gloom. She had to remain calm and forcing herself to think logically she realised that he must be standing still. If she could not see him then he would not be able to see her.

She began to move slowly towards the thin shaft of light creeping silently with her arms outstretched and her fingers probing the air for obstacles. Suddenly there was a noise and she froze. He was close by, she could hear him breathing, she could even feel the warmth from his body and holding herself rigid, she hardly dared to breathe. Her senses were screaming inside her head but with an effort, she forced herself to remain silent.

The noise he made as he fell startled her and she almost cried out. Clamping a hand over her mouth, she darted away and collided with the damp brickwork. He must have heard that she thought, as she picked herself up from the floor.

The meagre shaft of light coming from the partially open door was a beacon that showed her the way, and from it she was able to get her bearings. Urging herself forward she realised that she was still holding her breath so letting it out silently, she heard him utter a single unpleasant word as he stumbled against an unseen object. His expletive, bouncing eerily around the walls, sounded much louder than it really was and as it resonated in the enclosed space, it filled her ears with confusing messages that disorientated her even more.

Suddenly she realised what he was doing, he seemed to be making a methodical search of the area following some kind of grid pattern and if she didn't move faster, he would catch her. The only way to avoid him was to move into the area that he had just checked, and forced to play a game of cat and mouse, she was steered further from the door and all she could do was hope that eventually she would end up close enough to make a run for it.

Keeping low to the ground, she probed the space ahead with outstretched arms, and creeping silently prayed that he would not double back and drive her further away from the light.

Suddenly he was there beside her, gripping her wrist tightly like a spider with a fly, he wrapped her up in his arms. Lifting her off her feet, he squeezed the air from her lungs until she thought her ribs were about to break and swinging her away from the light he threw her to the ground. Josie cried out as she felt his breath hot against her cheek but this time she fought back when he took hold of her.

Struggling and swinging her arms wildly she tried to fight him off but it was no good he was much too strong. He crushed her against his chest and she had no option but to remain still. Catching her breath, she tried to hold it in but the pressure from his grip was too much and she squealed.   Struggling desperately she did what she could to get away but it was in all vain, she felt the bite of a cold, sharp blade against her skin and she froze, her eyes bulging with terror.

Suddenly a bright light blinded her with its flash and thunder filled the air. The impact threw her towards the vaulted ceiling and she lost consciousness before hitting the floor.

A light was shining painfully into her eyes and she was half crazed with fear. Someone was calling out her name, a familiar voice that seemed to be coming from a great distance.

"Josie MacDonald."

Her ears were still buzzing from the echo of the blast and the pain in her head was sickening.

"Josie, its Rufus Stone. I'm here to help you, you're safe now, it's all over."

"Rufus," she whispered.

Forcing herself to her knees, she could feel the strength of his body close to hers and leaning into him, she was desperate for human contact. Rufus held her in his arms and he could feel her body trembling. "Steady on young lady," he chuckled.

After a while, he helped her to her feet and they stumbled into the sunlight.

"It's alright he's gone." His smile was reassuring and it filled her with hope.

She could hardly believe that it was over and the stress and horrors that she had endured came flooding to the surface. She thought about Lindsay and Lizzie and in floods of tears, she wept.

Holding on to her tenderly Rufus steered her away from the entrance of the icehouse, he knew there would be more than one gruesome corpse hiding in there. He had marked the spot where Randolph had fallen and now it hardly seemed possible that after all these years he had finally managed to rid this beautiful place of a monster. The relief that washed over him was absolute, it filled him with an overwhelming sense of justice but he pushed these thoughts from his mind, it was hardly the time to be thinking this way. First, he must ensure the safety of the young women who were caught up in this terrible crime, there would be time enough later to consider the consequences of what he had done.

They heard the sound of sirens in the distance.

"Here they come, the cavalry have arrived," he looked at her and smiled.

"Kate's still in the cellar." Josie sobbed.

"She is safe now," he said squeezing her shoulder affectionately.

With him beside her, she realised how lucky she was to have a guardian angel like Rufus.

"Your young man and his companion should be on their way to hospital by now." He told her about how he had found them in the forest. "I had them send a helicopter out from Lossiemouth." His eyes flashed mischievously and he appeared much younger.

Josie snuggled against him, and holding her tight, he began to think of his dear friend Molly.

Once the police arrived they released Kate from the cellar and she was made comfortable in the back of an ambulance. Josie joined her and they were both taken to the hospital in Elgin.

Rufus spoke with the police Inspector explaining how he had shot William Randolph and when they opened up the icehouse, they began to probe the darkness with powerful beams of light. None of them apart from Rufus was ready for the horrors that were about to be revealed. They recovered the body of William Randolph, then found ten other corpses, some of which had been there for years.

Michael Cowper-Smith lay on a trolley, he had been eviscerated and his throat cut. The broken body of Lizzie Baines was lying beside her friend Lindsay Murray and as they moved deeper into the icehouse, the full horror became apparent. Some of the bodies were too far decomposed to identify but others had been semi-mummified by the cool air.

Rufus took his time searching over the remains and eventually came upon the body of a young woman. Kneeling down beside her, he took a closer look.

She was dressed in what remained of a woollen cardigan and a short tartan skirt. Her face was set in a wide grin, the parchment skin drawn tightly over bone and teeth. Holding out his hand Rufus steadied himself against the wall and silently whispered a prayer then, composing himself, he took a closer look.

Still in place around the small bones of her once slender wrist, he found a tarnished silver charm bracelet and suddenly he could see her as she had once been. She was a beautiful and vibrant young woman and he smiled as his memories came flooding back. Standing beside her mother it had been a blustery day, the wind chasing her hair around her face. It was the day of her eighteenth birthday, he and his wife had given her the charm bracelet as a gift. Touching it gently with his fingertips he realised that was over thirty years ago. He could hardly believe that he had been searching for so long and all the while, she had been here. He was unaware of the tears that rolled over his cheeks or the soft sound of grief that poured out of him.

"Are you alright Sir?" The hand of a young police officer touched his shoulder.

"Yes son," Rufus smiled up at him. "I've just found my daughter."

EPILOGUE

Tim greeted Mrs Robinson with a cheery grin and a nod of his head. She was standing in the doorway of her home, her huge frame filling the space and her wide smile concealing most of her features. Her shockingly bright robes flowed easily around her as she moved and he was reminded of a phoenix rising up out of the flames. Mrs Robinson always made him smile and he was grateful to her for that.

Letting himself into Josie's house, he called out a greeting and she responded almost immediately. As usual, he found her working in her studio.

Josie was mending slowly but there were times when her nightmares were more than she could bear. Memories of Mr Mac tortured her mercilessly, depriving her of sleep and any kind of normality, it was then that she would spiral out of control and tumble backwards into a deep chasm of depression.

Tim remained her constant companion, he was her rock, he offered her stability and unending support and he nursed her through her darkest hours.

Their life together had just begun and he was amazed that after all she had been through, she had not rejected him out of hand, she could easily have hated men for the rest of her life. Her therapist had reminded Tim that it would be like this, it was going to take a long time for Josie to recover and these were early days, he would have to remain patient.

At times, Josie hated everything that was dear to her and she found it hard to forgive herself. Tormented by the deaths of her friends, guilt and depression were her constant enemies. Some days she would find herself teetering on the edge of sanity and she would feel isolated and alone. Talking to Sarah helped immensely, this was part of her recovery process and they had been encouraged to share their feelings, tell each other what they were thinking and confront their innermost demons together. By doing this, it was hoped they could support each other.

Sarah in many ways was the lucky one, she could not understand why she hadn't been raped and murdered like her friends. She had not escaped entirely though, psychologically she was deeply wounded. Her physical injuries might have healed but it would take a long time for her to come to terms with the terrible shock and torment of her ordeal. Unlike Josie, she would never again be able to trust a man completely.

The support their therapist gave helped enormously but sometimes the only person Josie could turn to was Sarah. At times like this Tim found it very difficult to accept but he was learning to deal with Josie's moods. Her therapist had equipped him with the strategies that he would need to help him come to terms with Josie's state of mind. It was tough for him too; he had his own demons to confront. The gunshot wounds to his back were healing and he had no lasting physical injuries. He was able to deal with his mental scars by keeping himself busy and looking after Josie but it broke his heart to see the woman he loved so traumatised.

Tim pushed the door to her studio open and leaning against the wall, was content to watch her work. Josie, stepping back from a huge canvas, tilted her head to one side. He loved this gesture; she did it often when concentrating. He could not see her face but he knew she would be frowning and screwing up her eyes, critically examining her work. She was holding a rag that she used to clean her brushes, and turning towards him she smiled and he knew that everything was alright. Tim was delighted to find her relaxed and in good humour, even though he thought she looked tired.

"Hi, how are you Tim?"

"Oh I'm okay."

"Did you have a good day?"

"Quiet thank goodness, we've sold most of your paintings though."

Glancing around the studio, he could see very little that he would be willing to display in his gallery. Her work had undergone a sad transformation. No longer was she painting the delicate landscapes that people had come to expect. Now much of her work consisted of daubes of colour that were applied in thick blocks painted in an abstract kind of way. He felt sure, however, that given time her work would recover.

"What do you want to do this evening, shall we go out or do you want something in?" He often asked this question, he was concerned that she was in danger of turning into a recluse.

Absentmindedly she wiped the last of the paint from her fingers then folding her arms protectively across her breasts she frowned.

"Chinese," she said, her face lighting up, "telephone for a take away."

"Okay," he nodded. "Shall I open a bottle of wine?"

"You do that whilst I jump in the shower."

Sweeping past him, she touched his arm affectionately but sadly, she avoided making eye contact. Tim smiled as he watched her go. There was a time when they used to shower together, making love took up most of their time but these days she showered alone.

Her choice of a food was hardly surprising, they rarely went out anymore. They did not even go to Scotland for the funeral, the price for Josie had been much too high but they planned to visit soon, maybe at Christmas time.

Her therapist had told him to expect this kind of behaviour and together they were working on a strategy that should one day soon release Josie from the safety of her house in London.

Josie was now the owner of her aunt's charming little cottage. Molly had survived her injuries but had spent four long weeks in hospital, now she was convalescing in the beautifully converted oatmeal mill that her dear friend Rufus had restored.

Sadly Rufus had passed away peacefully soon after the funeral of his dear daughter. He had overseen the recovery of her remains from the icehouse on the Montague estate and had organised a quiet but beautiful memorial service for his beloved only child. The final chapter of his heart-rending story had ended and now Rufus and his family were together again. United in death they were at peace, interred in a vault in the cemetery close to where he had lived.

Molly loved her new home; it meant so much to her knowing that her old friend was still there in so many ways. Wherever she turned, she saw his shadow and could feel his presence in the very fabric of the old mill. He had put so much into restoring his home, it had become an extension of himself and she was content to live there for the rest of her life. He had left it to her happy in the knowledge that she would love and care for the place as much as he had, besides one day it would belong to Josie.

Much later, when they had finished eating Tim left Josie relaxing on the sofa with her wine glass. Collecting up their dirty plates and empty food containers, he carried them into the kitchen. He loved this time of day the house was peaceful and the hour was late, time was their own and nothing else seemed to matter. Glancing back over his shoulder, he studied her and she was unaware of his scrutiny. He noticed her distant gaze and even though her face was partially hidden by the shadows he knew that she was weeping silently. He had grown accustomed to the way she absentmindedly brushed the tears away from her face with the back of her hand and although he wanted to go to her, hold her in his arms and comfort her, he knew she needed time to grieve alone.

Sighing deeply he dumped the plates into the sink. He would be spending the night in the spare room, it was his room now. He spent so little time at his flat these days, he thought perhaps he should put it on the market or at least rent it out.

Returning to the sofa, he eased himself down beside her careful not to invade her personal space.

"I'm stuffed," he said rubbing his swollen belly.

"We'll be thirsty later. Chinese food always makes me thirsty." She sounded distant.

"More wine?"

Holding out her glass, she smiled as he topped it up. Slowly she was coming home, day by day the fearful barriers that she had constructed around herself were beginning to crumble and the Josie that he loved so much was returning to him. With time and a lot of tender loving care he knew that all would be well, she deserved the best that he could give and he was determined that she would have whatever she needed.

"Penny for them!" she nudged him with her elbow. "You are looking far too serious."

"Now there's a phrase I haven't heard in a long time."

She smiled and this time it was genuine.

"I was just thinking about the gallery," he lied. "We'll soon have to re-stock with some more of your landscapes." Glancing sideways at her he hoped to have planted the idea. "Do you think you could do some more?"

Sipping at her wine slowly she frowned, taking time to consider her answer.

"I'm sure I could," she whispered. There was so much more that she wanted to say but sadly could not find the words.

Reaching out he touched her arm and Josie shuffled in her seat. Leaning forward she placed her glass carefully on the table then sitting back clasped both hands in her lap. Tim could see that something was troubling her, her eyes were huge and the corners of her mouth were turning down. A cold shadow seemed to engulf her and she shuddered, finally she turned her head towards him and said.

"I think I'm pregnant!"

Biography

Kevin Marsh has lived in Whitstable with his wife Maria for thirty years; they have two adult children who are now pursuing their own careers. Kevin has worked in Manufacturing Engineering since leaving school and for the last twelve years has taught the subject in FE colleges. His hobbies include painting using acrylics, he regularly exhibits his work. His interests include history, reading historical novels and he has recently discovered the wonders of e-books.

Acknowledgements

I would like to thank Mark Webb at Paragon Publishing for his help and guidance in getting The Witness into print. Also with the initial proof reading, Anna Christodoulou and Mark Garbutt, who did a sterling job ironing out the wrinkles, any remaining are purely down to me.

Thank you to Maria, my wife and harshest critic, who continues to put up with me as I spend most of my time typing away on my laptop in a spare bedroom which I like to call my study.

Lightning Source UK Ltd.
Milton Keynes UK
UKHW020245270121
377716UK00004B/334